This is a work of fiction. Any similarity to real persons or events is entirely coincidental.

Mabbs-Zeno, Carl C.
 No Hero Nor Heroine / Carl C. Mabbs-Zeno
 ISBN 978-1-7375868-1-4

No Hero Nor Heroine

a novel from
Carl Mabbs-Zeno

Peterborough, New Hampshire
2021

No Hero, Nor Heroine

Contents

Part I: NoVA Blues

1. Waterbed

Wesley dragged the bundle of long boards out of the garage, banging and scraping against whatever was nearby. It was too heavy to lift although he could have cut the duct tape that held the planks together and removed them one at a time if he cared at all about damaging anything. By the end of his first hour of cleaning up, he almost gave up on finding anything worthwhile in the garage and was concerned now only to get everything outside, into the piles forming on his driveway. The larger one he would pay to have hauled away and the smaller he would move to a storage unit a few miles away on Telegraph Road for $19.95 a month.

These boards had been the frame for his waterbed. He had bolted the frame from unfinished two-by-tens and thought it very clever back when he had few tools for making functional furniture. After several years of adequate service, they had lain against the back wall of the garage for the ensuing twenty years or so -- he avoided calculating their exact age.

It was a triumph of sorts for him to see the back wall of the garage, despite the heavy accumulation of cobwebs, dust and nameless rubble which had found its way there via slow silent forces involving, perhaps, rodents and insects, and the simple physics of material decline. The last time he had seen it, when he put the waterbed frame away as if he might get a new rubbery mattress for it someday and would need the rough frame again, he had worried the boards would get in the way of opening the passenger-side car door. He should not have worried, not about that. The car had never been parked in the garage after that day, with or without passengers. More things had soon been placed "temporarily" in the garage and the car was permanently crowded out to the driveway.

Mattie, my dearest, are you as ashamed as me by the wealth we have squandered in accumulating all this junk; things we saved because we believed they still had utility and then hid away and forgot until this grand day when I send them to the dump? Do you not feel outrage that we are too lazy to resell or recycle this stuff? Do you have sympathy for the people who will have to do without things that we have hidden for years and are now destroying? Do you remember when the Joads abandoned their home in The Grapes of Wrath and took everything but an unmatched, broken shoe and some remnants of baling wire because they needed everything they had? Mattie did not answer because she was not there.

Wesley had painted the garage interior (bright white walls, smooth gray floor) when they first moved in and was disappointed to see the apparent corrosion now that a portion of the walls and floor had become visible again. Thinking he might clean up the garage while clearing the floor, he went back inside the house for a broom to sweep the first small, fully cleared space and brush off the wall. He would get a bucket of soapy water and a sponge later, when it was empty, before moving back in anything going to storage, if seeing everything up close did not convince him to shove the whole shebang into the big pile.

Before Wesley was back in the garage to select the next treasures for sorting, Ken came out of his house across the street. Doubtless he had been watching all morning, looking for a chance to insert himself.

He stood on his side of the street, a cigarette hung from his lips while he spoke (and while he did not), dressed in his standard pajama pants, slippers, bathrobe and stiff, drooping cowboy hat.

"Cleaning up?"

The question was so stupid, Wesley could not imagine a comment sarcastic enough to use even in talking to himself.

"Just throwing away everything I haven't seen in a decade or two, Ken. Want to help?"

"So you're throwing all this away? I can have some of these things?"

"Not yet. Right now, I'm taking everything out. I might keep some of it. Come back tonight and take whatever you want off the lawn. The junk guys will be coming tomorrow."

"Sure you don't mind?"

"If I leave it, I will have to pay someone to take it away so you'd be doing me a favor."

"OK, if it helps you out."

Ken had not done anything to help anyone in the past 22 years. Wesley realized he could get back at his self-centered neighbor by saddling him with useless junk to cram into his garage. He knew Ken would take something, just because it was free. And whatever it was would be in his garage until his kids cleaned it out after he died, which to all appearances would not be far in the future. Ken had emphysema and carried an oxygen tank with him whenever he left the house. Inside he plugged himself into a larger oxygen system with a tube long enough to reach all his rooms. It was not the emphysema exactly that was likely to hasten the day when Ken's garage would be emptied, it was his casual disposal of his cigarette butts and matches in a house with oxygen tubes and an oxygen tent over his bed. There had been two house fires that Wesley knew about, two large enough to need the fire department, but he suspected there were other incidents. In Wesley's estimation, fire was the most likely end for Ken, although he did not entirely dismiss the possibility that the neighbor one house farther up the hill would beat him to death before any of his other potentially fatal dangers played out. Wesley was prepared to be entertained by a final fight between the two neighbors since he did not think the world would be any worse off without either of them, even if one or both of them became a ward of the state after their confrontation.

Despite Ken's despicable personal habits and self-destructive stupidity, Wesley had always gotten along well with him. Long before Ken's health was conspicuously compromised, Wesley had begun to do him small favors. The first one was mowing his lawn. Ken never mowed it and it had become a breeding ground for weeds. Wesley respected Ken's right to live *au natural* and he would never have complained but he did want his own lawn to look respectable by the standards of the Washington suburbs, although "respectable" to Wesley included a degree of rustication that proved he had enough environmental regard to limit his use of fertilizer, pesticide, herbicide, and water. In his second summer, Wesley realized Ken was never going to tend his lawn, so Wesley began to mow it whenever he mowed his own. He did not ask permission and did not mention it when he decided to lime Ken's yard to cut down on the violets and, maybe get some real grass going. Since Ken did not comment on that either, Wesley felt welcome to rake the leaves when fall came and shovel the walk when it snowed. The subject came up once, briefly, after a few years of this minor maintenance. Wesley happened to meet Ken at the mailbox. He was walking and Ken was in his pick-up, and Ken said, "Oh yeah, thanks for mowing the grass. I coulda paid someone to do that."

Wesley answered, "It's OK. We both have tiny lots. It's almost as easy to do two as to do one once you get the mower out and everything." The subject never came up again in the ensuing years. Wesley suspected it made himself feel better more than it helped Ken.

When Wesley emerged from the garage with another load of junk, Ken was still standing on his side of the street watching.

"Where're you movin' to?" he called out.

"New York," Wesley answered, "the state, not the city."

"How come you're goin'? You're not old enough to retire, unless you hit it big." Wesley was not surprised by the question since he already knew Ken never followed the news where his reasons for moving had become conspicuous. In contrast to Wesley's long-running compulsion to know all the news that was fit to print, hitting it big was a preoccupation of Ken's. Over the years, he had tried a new line of work every couple years unless following charlatans was a line and he was merely doing variations on it. He never had any money so it was only his labor that could be exploited, mainly selling on commission, door-to-door at first, then through the mail and, eventually on the internet. He was very proud to be tech-savvy although it never translated into much income.   His house had not been painted or repaired since Wesley moved in across the street although he regularly had his car "detailed."

"I worked for the government, the Feds. We don't hit it big."

"So why're you leaving?"

"Just time for a change, you know. "

This was an answer good enough for Ken. It was not that Ken understood from the minimal response that Wesley did not want to talk about it, which would not have been unusual since they had not talked much about anything in over twenty years except for their neighbor at the end of the street, but Ken was satisfied that feeling the time for change had arrived was sufficient. His only remaining question was why it had taken so long, but he was talked out and would savor that question from the comfort of his recliner while he watched the shopping channel in case a bargain turned up.

Wesley did not watch Ken retreat. He had hardly been aware Ken had come outside. Ken's presence had always been so unsubstantial, Wesley could wonder if his appearance had been real or just a mental artifact of minor indigestion. He dropped a roll of wire for fencing a vegetable garden he had never planted back when the trees were small enough to let light onto his back yard, and rested his hands for a few moments because the wire had bitten into his fingers, not enough to really harm them but enough to hurt. He rubbed his hands together to flatten out the creases and felt disgust that his hands were so soft.

§§§

"Let's get a waterbed. Have you ever tried one?"

"Never did, but I was always curious about them."

Wesley might have honestly said "mildly curious, curious enough to lie down on one if the occasion were presented, not curious enough to buy one; one should buy something one knows one likes, not merely tried," but that

7

level of honesty would have been counterproductive at this sensitive stage of preparing to move in with a girl. It bode well that she was thinking of pleasure in bed... unless she was thinking she was bored with him already, even before they were really started, and the water bed might make things more interesting for her. Wesley felt they had not had sex even once to the full potential of the act since the futon in her apartment was not comfortable for two people. If they were positioned so they took up no more surface than one person, there was too much weight on the thin cushioning and it hurt whatever bones were on the bottom of their personal pile. Thus, he was always partly on the floor and twisted by his focus of ensuring she had full advantage of whatever comfort the futon could contribute. Futons did not live up to their reputation as part of a groovy, youthful way of life. Its groove was, in Wesley's assessment, no more than a way to justify getting by without the expense of a real mattress, although he was well aware that cheap was good. And that is what bothered him about the waterbed idea. Didn't Mattie know waterbeds were expensive, part of a groovy way of life for established adults and apprentice drug dealers?

She either read his mind or independently shared its contents. "I guess they're too expensive for us at this point."

"We're not going to be students much longer. Let's look at them. Won't cost anything to check 'em out."

He suddenly felt false for saying this, for so transparently trying to accommodate her whim when he had no real interest in waterbeds.

"Oh, I don't think they'll let us try one out in the shop, not enough to see what it feels like when you get going."

Wesley laughed and leaned over to kiss her. Waterbeds were sensually indulgent and that was where both of them had their heads for the past week, ever since they realized they were going to live together.

Like the clever young law students they were, they found a way to make it work, buying the waterbed mattress without a frame and bolting four heavy boards from the lumberyard to keep the huge water balloon safely contained, assuming safety did not consider whether the aging joists underlying her bedroom could handle the weight.

Her rental contract had a clause saying waterbeds were not allowed -- it had clauses to say hardly anything was allowed. Wesley had calculated the weight of the water must not exceed the weight of the people he was planning to have at a party someday, maybe when he and Mattie finished school, and no one worried about too many people collapsing the floor.

Should law students have taken their contract more seriously than other people? They had been more serious, that is, they had read the thing. As for following every letter, Wesley was not intimidated by a piece of paper as long as they did not actually do any damage. Wesley said they should just take a small chance and deal with the consequences if there should ever be any. Mattie did not like the idea but she was willing to bend to Wesley's brash extra-legal approach. It was something she found attractive in him. He did not mention to her that the more likely disaster from a waterbed would be a leak that ran a hundred gallons of water into the space between their floor and the landlord's ceiling. His omission was consistent with the strategic information release lawyers sometimes employed but he knew it was inappropriate for a couple in love, so he paid for his dishonesty with a nagging worry that the bed would be punctured someday when they were about to leave for a long weekend and would return to an eviction notice. That day never came and they eventually moved to a house in the Washington suburbs after graduation without any disaster, leaving Wesley quietly smug about having accepted the risks that were now passed.

They set up the waterbed in the new house on the first floor but over the basement so it was again supported by floor joists. This time the risks were merely damage to the house, not compounded by violation of a contract. After a few years, the disaster finally happened -- risks add up over time. It was hardly the disaster they feared and they had to laugh at themselves for ever worrying. In the middle of the night, Wesley felt cold and he pulled up the blanket before noticing it was already covering him and before noticing it was wet. He jumped up and pulled Mattie out of bed as if it were on fire. A seam had rent over several inches, releasing water until they had both sunk slowly to the bottom of the bed, that is, to the floor. The water was warm and they did not notice immediately, not until it started to cool from evaporation. The plastic liner of the bed remained intact and the only water that fell outside the bed dripped from their pajamas as they stood in the dark wondering at their luck, both good and bad.

The next day, after sleeping on a temporary bed of couch cushions and pillows, they bought a real waterbed, raised from the floor by a frame with storage drawers, flanked by padded sides you could sit on while tying your shoes in the morning, and headed by a set of shelves too shallow for books but good enough for a clock radio and some memorabilia. The old frame, the four two-by-tens, were stored in the garage pending an unlikely need for a second waterbed or some alternative use.

2. Rocking Chair and Walking Sticks

Next, Wesley extracted the rocking chair he had intended to repair. He had not forgotten it but he had no use for a rocking chair so its broken rung never rose to a priority high enough for action and, Wesley now understood, never would. When he first found the chair at a yard sale, he thought it would be easy to fix and that the world would be a better place with one more functional object at virtually no cost. If he had a porch looking out on the foot traffic on Main Street in a town with a Main Street, and he were thirty years older, he might have cared more about the rocker.

He stepped back inside the garage and looked around for something else easy to remove. Everything had to come out but it would be better, he now thought, to take out the things to be hauled off as trash first and worry about the things to keep or give away later. This approach would entail a lot of stepping over and around, which could be hazardous when he was carrying something large enough to block his vision of the floor. It also entailed remembering what was in the boxes piled three or four high that he should have labeled when he put them out there. If he could just throw out a few things to create space in the back, he could push the boxes back there and maneuver more efficiently.

In the back corner on the right leaned a pile of sticks and poles and like objects. He wrapped his arms around them and lifted them over whatever was on the floor so he could sort them in his staging area on the lawn. A bamboo cane he had saved in case some use turned up someday rattled to the floor and a single shoe fell from the bundle. He recognized the shoe but could not recall why it was among the sticklike objects or why it was in the garage at all. He tripped over something and heard the clatter of more things falling but did not look at them because he was focused on where to put his feet next. In the light outside, he stood the load on end and looked through it, seeing nothing worthwhile, just leftover pieces from minor construction projects, metal corners from wall board he replaced in the living room, sections of PVC pipe from the bathroom renovation, more bamboo from his basketry ambitions during his undergrad years, leftover trim from when he replaced the window in the living room, a shower rod removed when he put the sliding glass door on the tub, and, falling from his grasp just as he got outside, a short stick cut from a thicket in the town park just up the hill from his home. He kicked the stick forward until it was on the lawn and then stepped over it to place his armload of narrow objects on the trash pile. The PVC pipe held his attention for an additional moment. He could still imagine some use for it someday, not a specific use, but a material with such strength and flexibility would certainly meet a need someday. He leaned forward and fished it out of the tangle and then, without hesitating, tossed it into the center of the pile as if that was why he had lingered over it. This move out of the Washington area would be, had to be, light.

The walking stick still lying on the lawn was not treated so hastily. It was not large enough to compromise the austere principles behind the move and it elicited so much nostalgia, Wesley wondered that he had ever let it disappear into the Sargasso Sea of his garage. It fit his hand well, being just the right length and having a smooth knob worn from a fork in the original branch. He took a couple steps across the lawn with it and then remembered why he had put it aside.

He could feel Ken's eyes on him, an image of pretentiousness prancing like a hipster of another era and class. He took a few more self-conscious strides, lifting the tip of his swagger stick to exaggerate the display of his imagined cool. From beside the street, he balanced the stick on one finger and flipped it onto the pile where it bounced off in a single glancing hop onto the grass, escaping the pile of doomed objects, where he left it on his way back into the garage. If it was clever enough to jump away like that, maybe it deserved to live.

Back in the garage, he worked through the history of his stick, a history he knew back as far as his first days at the house. One of the features of the neighborhood that had attracted Wesley and Mattie when they were house hunting was the town park a block and a half from the short cul-de-sac where they eventually bought their two-bedroom starter place across the street from Ken. Wesley had looked forward to exploring the park and learning what animal life and flowering plants survived in the neighborhood Eden. He imagined walking there in the mornings before going to work, disregarding the weather, and eventually showing Mattie on sunny, leisurely weekend days what he had worked out of the natural history of the place.

Moving in had required their first two weekends and every working day until that point had been so busy in the office that Wesley did not get out for a morning walk, but they finally got out to the park on a breezy day in mid-September. Mattie noticed the park designers had not provided any parking spaces, proving it was intended for use only by local residents. It made them feel like owners. A heavy signboard beside the opening in a decorative split-rail fence had been routed with the words "George Duncan Park." From there, a paved path wound downhill to a log bridge over a wide, shallow, stony creek which Wesley recognized as catchment for runoff that must have been increased well above natural levels by all the surrounding pavement and rooftops. Flash floods had scoured the creekbed of all plant life but as long as they did not look closely, they could see a reflection of the original Eden within walking reach of their humble first house together. There were flowers in the warm months and seed pods in the fall, birdsong in the spring and a bland Washington version of autumn foliage to remind them of, if not fully display, the natural cycle.

Duncan Park was not a disappointment, not initially. They loved its echo of the world beyond the beltway and the separation it offered from the artificial constructs enveloping the rest of their days. With its tranquility so out of character for the locality, they could focus their thoughts on each other when walking hand-in-hand and talking about the minor things that were hard to fit into the tight schedule of weekdays in a house used mainly for eating and sleeping. Over the years, however, it shrank in their view and Mattie soon wearied of its worn ways and its caricature of wilderness and, eventually, even of the block-and-a-half walk to reach it.

In their first year of living here, Mattie felt pressure to spend more time in the office, pressures she rejected until she saw working extra hours was the only way to do her job well and she desperately wanted to do her job well. She worked at home until late at night and always struggled to wake up fully in the morning to be ready for her carpool at 7:30. She was meticulous about hygiene and allowed that to take up the morning time she had used to be stylish when she was at school. Does a stylish look not also help in a career, at least for a woman? She thought not, or not necessarily. She was a background person, a lawyer in an office, not representing her Agency with the public. The persona she cultivated exhibited an intimidating expertise. She was not trying to be anyone's friend, but no one wanted her as an enemy. Walking in Duncan Park felt false to her, as if she were pretending for some reason that it was beautiful when her forthright view was that it was no better than a remnant of the natural world, sadder than the purely and honestly artificial urban environment that had given up on nature.

Wesley's relationship to the park had evolved differently... In his first year he became excited by his work and felt a pleasure in doing more of it so he caught the Metro train at 6:30 to get his work day started early, leaving ever less time for morning leisure but he went to the park most mornings anyway, leaving the house at 5 o'clock more as an exercise routine than as a nature walk. Most of the year, he was walking in the dark so the sad state of the woodland was hardly noticeable and the variation in light and weather fed him a superficial impression of exploration. The early hour made the place his, consistently lending a legitimate sense of privacy and space despite the surrounding congestion, steady noise, clamorous competition, and rapid pace during the rest of the day. Over the years, the repetition only added to his pleasure, strengthening his ownership of the hour. This small indulgence had a price in shortening his evenings. He aimed for hitting the sack at ten o'clock although he usually started for bed at ten and hit it fifteen minutes later. With the time pressures of his lifestyle, he had become very efficient in both his morning and evening toilet.

On his first few trips to the park, he explored every trail, whether made by man or animal, but soon developed a pattern of taking only the main route, the wide one, paved and relatively flat. It ran the full length of the park and connected to the parking lot of an apartment complex, allowing him to return via roads without retracing any steps. This was the least likely route to see animal life, but he knew the only animals were suburban ones and they only made him sad. He allowed no greater ambition than to take a good suburban walk, rather than a bad woodland walk.

He kept an eye out for a walking stick. Each of the first sticks he tried was flawed in its weight or balance or length or texture but he had been impatient to get one so he was free to think about other things and each for one walk. He held a superstition that the right one would turn up on its own so he had never taken any tools with him to the park to improve a stick or cut one from a larger branch. Usually he broke a dead limb from a tree and then broke it to length. The unintended consequence of these slap-dash constructs was learning what made a good stick for him: what length it should have, what weight was strong enough, what trees had clear wood so his hand did not blister, etc. And one day, as was inevitable, he came across a stick that was just right in every respect except that the two broken ends were rough and cracked. He brought that one home and rounded off the ends with a pocketknife.

It felt like progress in life to have the stick leaning by the back door, awaiting use, company when he was alone and, possibly, helpful in steadying the way around an obstacle or easing down a slope. Unfortunately, he was not in the habit of leaving by way of the back door and he tended to forget to take his stick. Then he would search out a temporary one, feeling a slight irritation with himself for his inefficiency. Somedays he remembered but those days were few since he operated mainly out of habit at five a.m.

Eventually, Mattie grew tired of seeing the stick by the back door and, being sensitive to the prospect of his using it again, she placed it by the garage door where it sat for a couple weeks untouched since Wesley did not know it was there and then Mattie then felt justified in relegating it to the garage interior where it lost any chance of being seen until the day when they would prepare to vacate the property. Meanwhile, Wesley understood Mattie had moved it and he did not want to be accusatory and question why she had done so; it was only a stick from the woods whose merits were invisible to anyone but Wesley. Furthermore, once he realized she had taken the stick, he stopped using one on his walks; it would only have been a reminder of the perfect one he had lost. When he came across it again while cleaning out the garage, he felt neither affection nor nostalgia for it. They had not been together long enough, had not shared travels or travails enough to bond. It was simply one more object he had once thought he wanted and now was pleased to remove forever from his inventory.

Wesley kicked at the broken rocking chair he had set beside the trash pile and tried to break it further so it would take up less space in the trash truck which charged according to the volume of his trash. The rocker skidded away from him. The shock to his leg was not matched by any apparent damage to the rocker and he then simply threw the sturdy but broken chair onto the pile. Better to admit defeat on a minor point than to expend a greater effort toward a tiny victory.

3. Old Shoes

The lonely shoe he had dropped came back to his mind. Its presence in the garage was illogical but he knew well what shoe it was. He went back to retrieve it, perhaps find its mate, and throw them into the trash pile. It would only take a second-- he could toss them out the door from where he picked them up, or picked *it* up if only one was apparent. The second one was likely not far away and would not long escape his vigorous clean-up.

It was a well-worn, blue, track spike. ...A right shoe, so he tried to remember if he had torn his right or his left ankle with his spikes while high jumping. This might have been the guilty implement of the tear that had cost him six stiches. He had never minded the scar on his ankle. He had not even missed one track competition since the injury occurred after the competition season-- junior year of high school. He had ambitions that summer to get really good in time for his final year. He had good reason to believe he could improve. He was still growing and his performance so far had been limited by feeble devotion to training. The scar was shown off as marking his level of effort although exceptional effort was not the reason he had kicked himself. He would not call it clumsiness either-- just an odd twist while going over the bar or, maybe, into the bar. Track stardom had not followed. He pursued several events throughout his senior year and scored points largely by checking which events were weakest in the upcoming opponent. Organized sports ended for him in high school without regret or glory.

Sports had begun in fifth grade with a taste of fame and acclaim that carried him through half a dozen years of ambition. Their roots lay for Wesley with baseball in the years of Mickey Mantle. He loved to play in the neighborhood games and held his own with kids his own age or even a little older. When he tried out for little league in fourth grade, however, he faced a level of pitching he could not hit from a kid he knew and always thought was too fat to be athletic. Then he was asked to catch some fly balls hit by the coach, balls higher than he had ever seen in the back yard and that he could not judge. He wanted to play second base rather than the outfield but he was intimidated by the boys from town who ran forward to grab grounders rather than waiting for them to roll up and who spouted baseball jargon like it was their first language.

He decided on the day of that try-out to abandon sports -- a single day in a boy well short of puberty and a resolution that ended up applying only to giving up organized baseball. He was not one to persevere. Attribute that to his mother. She had given him the idea that he was destined for greatness, although she had never specified what field held that destiny. Not baseball, he concluded at the age of ten. Real destiny needed no effort-- it would reveal itself eventually although at that age sports would have been a really great field to conquer.

His parents supported his exploration of opportunities. He took piano lessons for a year, more than enough to establish he was no prodigy. Just to be sure it was not a weakness specific to that instrument, he tried guitar on his own a couple years later and convinced himself his dearth of musical talent applied across a wide range of instruments. At school, he took Spanish, which he acknowledged was a relatively easy language for English-speakers, but his progress was agonizingly slow so he knew language skills were not to be his gift. Math was a possibility in that he was better than some and hated it less than most. Science was his favorite subject and he held open the prospect that some scientific discipline would turn out to hold a career for him once his classes were advanced enough to find a focus. That would be consistent with his mother's vision in contrast to the actual mediocrity of his early years.

He continued to like playing baseball and soccer and tag, at least among his underachieving, rural peers. At school, where he mixed with the town boys, he stuck to playing on slides and merry-go-rounds where his daredevil stunts were admired. His strength seem to lie in showmanship rather than inherent athleticism.

On the last day of fifth grade, Mrs. Straley, his teacher, organized a race among all the fifth graders to see who would be the champion for the year. They were to run up a small hill to the swings, go around them, through the basketball court (with its child-height hoops), and down the paved track back to the parking lot where Mrs. Straley held a rope to show the finishing line. Charlotte held the other end because she wore braces on her legs and could not run. It looked like fun. Wesley did not know where he had seen a race with a finishing line but he knew blasting through a rope was the official way to end it. The kids crowded by the edge of the pavement below the swings and waited for Mr. Reed, from the class across the hall, to call out "ready, set, go." Wesley had positioned himself well and stayed in the leading group up the hill. He looked ahead and wove his way to the left of the pack so he could cut close to the swings when he made the turn. When they headed toward the basketball court he was near the front and he began to notice his name being shouted from behind. "Get her, Wesley! Get her." Darlene Ruppert was in front, a girl. He always liked Darlene although he might never have actually spoken to her. She was tall and athletic but Wesley had never imagined a girl could win this race. It looked unfair, counter to male destiny. He could marvel at her and admire her success except that he was hearing the desperation of the town boys calling to him to save the honor of their gender. When he reached the pavement of the basketball court, Wesley thought he could feel his sneakers grasp the surface and drive him forward. He was not accustomed to trying very hard but he resolved to run himself to exhaustion this one time. Going down the slope to the parking lot, he passed into the front. When he ran through the rope, which Charlotte never dropped but Mrs. Straley, fortunately, did, neither Darlene nor anyone else was in his peripheral vision.

The boys noisily congratulated him, every one of them. None of them resented losing to him since they were all beaten by a girl anyway. Darlene was angry with him even though he had only done what he should. She never spoke to him in sixth grade or through the years of high school.

The thing he learned that day that stuck with him was not about Darlene. He never figured he had a chance with her socially. It was about making an effort, that it mattered, or might matter sometimes. This was a huge disappointment to learn that his mother's vision, as he understood it, was flawed. Greatness would not accrue to him automatically.

That day he thought he had found his super-power. In sixth grade there was no class race so he remained recognized as the fastest kid in school. In high school, however, he tried various sports and learned there were faster kids -- not many, so he might be the fastest on any day in a particular game and could hang onto his hope of rising to a grander calling built on footspeed.

He stayed away from the sprints where he could not compete with the natural talent of at least two boys his age. And he stayed away from the long races where the work required to excel was daunting. He ran the hurdles where a little practice in technique ensured he would beat anyone who had not worked on the event. His best event was high hurdles because technique was more important than sprint speed.

And he high jumped, in his junior year becoming the best in his school among those who did track. Usually the opposing school only had one high jumper better than him and sometimes that guy was missing on meet day with a cold or something. He hoped to grow with age into better performance, which he did, but never good enough to qualify for the state-wide meet.

No one paid much attention to track in his school although all sports were given some respect. He was known as successful because he did score points for the team although his points came to him only when he faced a weak field. He was not anxious to provide any details that could cast his superficial reputation into doubt. At least he did not deceive himself that earning a letter this way proved he was an athlete.

Why had he saved a pair of his spikes? (Certainly he had not intentionally saved one shoe -- the other had to be in the garage somewhere.) The shoe was new when he was a high school junior and had been large enough to last through senior year. He had saved the shoes on the hope of maturing in college enough to run and jump although the competition in college would be an order of magnitude more challenging. He once looked over the team in his freshman year and then searched for potential areas of fame and fortune outside sports.

4. Environmental Law

Wesley lifted a heavy cardboard box that he deduced must be filled with books and staggered to the lawn where he slid it down his legs to reduce the strain on his back as he bent over. The box began to tear. It had not been taped shut and was not strong enough for its load, especially since it had mildewed along the side where it had pressed against the wall. He folded the top back and suddenly became conscious of a car coming into the *cul de sac*. There was only one house past his on the street so it was either that neighbor or someone to see him.

He knelt down so his butt would not be displayed toward the car and wished he had lowered the box more gracefully. Nearly every encounter with his only neighbor other than Ken had been thoroughly unpleasant but he could not ignore that she was just as sexy as the day she moved in ten years earlier. The car stopped at his driveway and he realized it probably was not her so he turned around. Surprisingly, it was her car. The window slid down.

"I know why you are leaving. You cannot live here without your wife."

It was the sexy neighbor. She was initiating a conversation without a complaint or request though her tone was short of courteous. Maybe the celebrity, notoriety really, of his recent troubles made him more interesting for surely she was incapable of sympathy. Wesley wanted at first to thank her for her kind thought and it was a kind thought in the context of recent events yet he could not force himself to open up that much to his neighbor, and his face took on a wry smile at the irony that he himself lacked any sympathy of thought at this moment and he then blamed her for his malevolence. However, he needed to say something or she would pull away into her driveway with yet another instance of his rudeness to tell her sister so he said "Thank you" without any sincerity behind it.

"Where are you going?," she asked as if they had a normal relationship for the suburbs, the sort in which households without children treated each other with the formal civility due strangers regardless of the number of years they had lived within view of each other.

"California," he answered. New York was the first thought that came to mind. Neither was the truth and the truth would not have any place in any of his answers to her. The truth was he had not decided where to go. New York was too close to even pretend to himself as a destination; he wanted to choose a place he imagined to be safe from ever seeing this neighbor or anyone else he knew from northern Virginia although seeing her was not in itself unpleasant.

"What's in California?"

Wesley could hardly believe his ears. They were having a conversation, their first in a decade without obvious animosity, as he was in the process of moving out.

They had first met on the morning after she arrived. Neither Wesley nor Mattie had noticed anyone moving in until Mattie saw a shadow go by the living room window. They looked out and could not believe what they were seeing. A young man was building a pile of cut shrubs on the lawn, the shrubs Mattie had selected one by one and Wesley had put in five years earlier along the property line and which were now affording the privacy that had motivated their planting. He ran outside, not angry, just amazed at the error someone was making. His anger came along a few moments later as he surveyed the damage and realized he was too late to save the hedge.

"What are you doing?" he asked in a controlled voice.

"My sister needs me to take these down," he answered with a heavy accent. Wesley looked at him closely to guess his nationality. He was a stocky fellow, with short hair that revealed no clear cultural background. He wore rumpled khaki pants, a tight T-shirt and workboots, the same outfit he was to wear through the ensuing decade. "She is afraid of the snakes."

"But those bushes are five feet on our side of the property line. See the stake there with the ribbon it?" Wesley said it this way but he was thinking, "those bushes *were* five feet on our side of the property line."

At this point the neighbor's understanding of English deteriorated and he mumbled something in Spanish so Wesley asked to see his sister. The brother's English had deteriorated so quickly he could not even comprehend Wesley's request hence Wesley abandoned the man in front of him to knock on the door to the house. Wesley had not realized anyone had bought the place yet; he tried not to pay any attention to the activities in the houses around him which was easy since this was the time of year when he was never home in the daylight hours except Sunday.

The woman who answered his knock was a shock to Wesley. She was in her late twenties and by far the sexiest woman he had ever seen in the suburbs. She wore a clingy blouse, tight pants, and high heels as if she were going clubbing at ten am. Her hair was long and pulled back in a trendy fashion; her makeup went as far as lipstick and false eyelashes yet the effect was not cheap, probably because she was naturally attractive so all the refinements seemed fair, as if she deserved them. She shone a smile designed to disarm whomever was at her door and it had some effect on Wesley although he would have been courteous anyway.

Wesley introduced himself and welcomed her to the *cul de sac* before making his complaint. She did not give her name, merely nodded as he spoke until she understood he had come by to point out the damage her brother was doing. She then apologized in good English, lightly accented, for not knowing exactly where the property line was and went to mention that the bushes were not very attractive ones anyway. Wesley said he had planted for a reason and would plant new ones which he anticipated she might want to pay for. She agreed it was appropriate if he really wanted bushes although she would have to see the estimate before agreeing on how much was due. Wesley wanted to mention that the new bushes would be smaller than the ones the one they had cut down and that installing them would be laborious since her brother had cut them rather than dug them out. The strip would be a mass of roots. But he held his tongue on these issues and silently decided to install them himself to save her the cost of labor. He worried that his generosity was due in some degree to her physical charms and plotted how to avoid mentioning this cost to Mattie but his self-assessment, while he waited as she spoke with her brother, concluded that even though he could not help but notice how she met the standards of mainstream glamour, he did not really care. His tendency was to be harder on her than on a person of conventional appearance, just to prove to himself he treated everyone the same although the effort he expended to avoid caring would prove he cared about it in some way.

A couple weeks later he left an envelope at her door with three estimates from landscapers and made a notation that he would use the cheapest one and do the work himself to hold down the cost. He included his phone number. She never called and never responded in any other way so after a couple more weeks, Wesley put in new bushes. He left a copy of the invoice on her doorstep and never heard anything about that either.

Thus, it was clear from this opening that they would not be inviting each other to any holiday parties, but Wesley and Mattie were surprised at the number of negative interactions they accumulated over time. The next time they spoke was when the young beauty shouted at Wesley for allowing a tree branch to fall over the property line and damage her roof. Wesley apologized and pointed out that he was not liable for such damage, however, when he went over to look at the branch, he added that it had not come from a tree on his land. It belonged to the absentee landowner of the small adjoining woodlot. Mattie loved the whole encounter but Wesley's initial defensiveness had not served the relationship well. She came back to complain about the leaves that blew into her lawn in the fall and which could be proven to have come from his trees. Wesley blew the leaves off her lawn when he was cleaning his own and Ken's lawns but Mattie said he should never do it again, that the obnoxious woman could not be allowed to win. In the winter, the bill for plowing the street was split five ways, there being five homes on the street, as it had always been done but only four houses paid their share. Wesley had paid the contract and faced the choice of insisting on payment from someone he did not like or going back to the three other houses, or just eating the cost. He did the latter. Neither he nor Mattie was the sort of lawyer who insists on winning a small claims contest.

In the spring the brother was digging holes for a fence and cut the underground TV cable. The cable company wanted to charge Wesley and Mattie for the repair and Wesley said they would have to claim reimbursement from their neighbor. That incident ended as a victory for Wesley and Mattie and a loss for the cable company. As the seasons went by, the incidents continued, becoming entertaining in their pettiness, and giving Wesley and Mattie ample opportunity to be liberal to a peevish young woman.

The trials they endured were not objectively any more minor than the ones Ken endured but his fed a war between the two houses at the end of the street, a war that affirmed the wisdom of Wesley's policy to avoid as much as possible everyone living in view of his home. Ken and the woman fought over inconveniences they caused each other, and which became more common and purposeful over the years, leading to screaming insults and threats at each other or at each other's' houses. When they threw trash and leaves and branches across their property line, Wesley eventually cleaned up the mess because it was clear it would shift back and forth across the line forever, and Mattie did not like seeing it. She forbade Wesley from intervening, but he found chances when she was not looking to rake up leaves or pick up fallen branches or bag the papers blown across the line, and she knew he was doing it.

When the hard-working brother broke the water line into Ken's house, it was Mattie who went outside into the street to quiet the dispute which was about to become physically violent between the skinny old man and the firm young beauty. Wesley had not noticed the confrontation brewing but Mattie always seemed to be monitoring the street and she told Wesley to stay back while she handled things. He watched through the window without hearing what was being said. He saw Mattie run out to the pair as if she constituted emergency assistance. He knew she would take Ken's side regardless of whatever facts were on display. She did not like him any better than she liked the woman, but she knew Wesley got along only with Ken. The combatants were surprised to see a third party on the scene and each stepped back for a moment but soon were arguing as volubly as before, maybe even more so, now having an audience.

Wesley folded his arms on the window sill and rested his head to watch the show at the curb. Ken could not stand still for long, his hands gestured wildly even when he could not think of something to say, as if they were administered by a different brain than the one represented through his voice. His face was more strongly associated with his arm movements than his words, constantly forming and reforming expressions of incredulity or anger, or derision, as if he had studied at a school for acting, which he may in fact have done through a correspondence school.

Ken was entertaining to watch without sound, yet it required an effort for Wesley to turn his eyes away from the young woman. From his window, Wesley felt safe in staring at her so he could more fully appreciate not only the shapes of her hips and legs and ankles and waist and arms and breasts so clearly displayed, but also the vigorous and intricate movement of all those parts, movements that contrasted starkly with the awkwardness and illogic of Ken's spasms. She was as a dancer, a performer, who utilized her flexibility and her quickness and her coordination as if trained to it. Even her occasional "grand pause" was arresting to the observer.

Wesley felt jealous of her physicality but no desire for her. All his desire was ever directed toward Mattie whose personal strength in all its dimensions shone so brightly the other figures in the street were obviously doomed to her domination. There was no contest to watch, so he watched the beautiful neighbor as he might watch a beautiful sunset, a temporary pleasure, a gift from God.

He did not notice anyone listening to Mattie, nearly always Ken or the woman was yelling, and yet after a mere couple minutes, they all turned abruptly and walked back to their respective houses. Mattie came in muttering what Wesley knew were the strongest swears she could devise. She had learned all her swearing from him, not because he swore, but because he had been around more profanity and had paid attention to it, so he taught the words and phrases to her. The lessons served her well when cable television came along and she wanted to understand the late shows, or when she wanted to mutter to herself with passion.

She went into the kitchen to continue preparing dinner and Wesley jumped up, well aware it was mandatory for him to attend a debriefing. He knew she had resolved something since the pair had stopped fighting abruptly and he knew the resolution would only be temporary since the hostility between the neighbors had too much history to be ended by anything less than terminating residency on the street by one of the parties. Thus, Wesley had one question in mind when he glided into the kitchen, stepping quickly so Mattie would not have a chance to demand that he come in to hear her story. "Why did you bother to go out there? I would have thought you might have enjoyed ... no not enjoyed ...would have thought they deserved a punch and a scratch."

"California?" the Latin beauty asked through the window of her car, bringing Wesley back to the present.

"Yeah, I transferred to one of the National Parks ...buying stuff for the souvenir shops."

Wesley impressed himself with his quick inventiveness. He had not planned on what lie to tell her and yet this one had come out smoothly. In fact, he had no plan for what lies to tell anyone. He would not have remembered which ones were for which person anyway so it was best to go with whatever sounded good for the person in front of him. This pertained only to the folks in his neighborhood. If all went well, they would be the only ones to ask where he was going and none of them knew him so they were easily taken in. The people he knew and who knew him should have no idea he was going anywhere, but if someone from his office did hear he was moving, his stock answer would be that he was going to a condo in the suburbs to cut his living expenses.

Buying stuff for souvenir shops? He had no idea how to do that but the arrogant, sexy neighbor probably knew no more about his professional abilities than that he worked for the Federal government. As a recent immigrant working in the private sector, she knew nothing about how easily one might transfer from a job in Washington to one in a National Park. Actually Wesley did not know either despite having been in the Federal workforce ever since finishing college. He had no connection to the Park Service. He thought it ought to be obvious he was not a shopkeeper and he felt a little insulted that she accepted his lie so easily. He could see he had told a weak lie because his subconscious wanted to prolong the conversation. A flush ran up his neck as he watched his clumsy flirtation. It came not from guilt at betraying Mattie in the back of his mind — they were beyond that kind of guilt now. It came from the more serious sin of lowering his guard at a time when he needed to be rigorous. This woman he barely knew, who was as close to a personal enemy as he had in the world, had dropped her guard for a moment out of curiosity, and he had failed to place his privacy as the highest priority.

He could regain his leadership in enmity by turning his back on her before she sent him off so he tapped on the roof of car and said "I gotta get back to it." Doubtless she was unaccustomed to men turning away from her but Wesley did not see her reaction. After nearly ten seconds of silence, he heard her car pull away and then into her driveway, the car door open and a few steps on her walkway to her door. Then he could place her where she belonged and forget the whole encounter.

The tattered box of books sat apart from both the keep and reject piles. He remembered why the box had gone into the garage for storage-- it required sorting and he could not sort it without Mattie's guidance since most of the books had been hers and she never wanted to sort books. With her gone, he was empowered to make the choices.

Ever since elementary school when his third grade class was given new social studies texts and taught how to open a book for the first time by folding back a few pages to the left and a few pages to the right until the middle was reached and the binding thereby was prepared for use because books were valuable and fragile, like the wings of a luna moth or his ninety-five-year-old great grandmother. He had thus been taught that books ought to be respected, so he had always regarded them with due reverence and a conviction that they were never so old or worn their life deserved to end.

He pulled back the flaps on top of the box and quickly recognized Mattie's books from school. The law books were out-of-date and could be trashed without guilt over failing to donate them locally or send them to a needy library overseas. These he tossed onto the trash side. He thought only a few moments more about the literature text books. They displayed some timeless art in miniature halftones and commentary designed for students, thus nothing in a form anyone would ever use no matter where he placed them. No classic novels with hardback covers and insightful introductions appeared in the box. Wesley respected such books but planned to buy them and read them after he retired since his work sapped all the brain concentration he possessed at his current stage. There were a few paperbacks by authors Mattie had favored when she still read fiction. She had liked Tom Robbins who featured Sissy Hankshaw, a heroine Mattie could admire for her peculiarities and independence. The author's photograph on the back cover showed a youthful, broad smile and the long hair still extant in some parts of America in 1976. Wesley wondered if it would bring him closer to Mattie if he read one of these but as soon as the question formed in his mind he knew the answer was that this lost interest of hers offered no clue to preserving any part of their relationship and he was relieved to dump the paperbacks along with the other contents of the box into the trash heap.

One of the law books tumbled down to Wesley's feet as if it were begging for a reprieve. Wesley laughed at it to show his commitment to its irrelevance. He picked it up and looked at the spine to read its title: Environmental Law, a course he had enjoyed and that had some use in his eventual work although the topic was not central to his job. A surge of respect ran through the fingers holding the book and was blocked from traveling to his core by a counter-surge of logic from his brain, reminding him that electronic repositories, with their advanced search algorithms and continuous updating, were far more accessible than textbooks, no matter what relevance the contents retained. Newly minted lawyers would be familiar with more recent and more relevant precedents than the ones catalogued in published matter. What he and Mattie knew as the classic cases were no more than historic context now. He felt the firm binding and suspected it was too strong to tear apart. Slowly he opened the front cover and grasped the first ten pages and tore them from the volume. Then he separated the last ten or so pages and tore them out. *You want a reprieve?* he asked silently. *This world is merciless. I am merely its agent with no capacity to alter its inclinations.* He tore a few more pages from the front, a few from the back, a few from the front... He watched the pages scatter, rarely falling into the trash pile, making a mess on the nearby portion of the lawn. He imagined Ken watching from behind the curtains over his picture window, possibly thinking, "It's OK, I don't want an old book anyway," and the sexy neighbor looking out over her kitchen sink thinking "What is wrong with that man now?" and he would be equally agnostic about the impression he left on each of them. The pleasant nostalgia of his environmental law class had turned quickly to a burning anger that Mattie was not beside him sorting through their shared past.

In the first day of Environmental Law, he had been full of confidence. This was a topic he wanted to know, one in which he would excel, perhaps the only one where he would excel. His confidence came not from his interest in the legal topic exactly but from his broad experience in the workings of nature that would, logic dictated, give him an edge in this class, from biology courses where he had loved dissection, to tramping in the woods where he loved to get lost, to reading John Muir which took him to an earlier time when preserving beauty was the challenge rather than preserving the planet itself. Brimming with anticipation at entering a course where he would be the impassioned class leader, he looked up just as the lesson was starting and saw the late-arriving woman. She was a pleasurable sight that added to the prospects for the course. He suspected she was a year or two older than himself; she looked mature though still young, of course. She seemed smart and sexy. She would be the star in any course so she was to be his competition in this class, his class. It was the competition that motivated his next move, not the ambition of getting a girlfriend. She was beyond his reach as a girlfriend but he did not intend to make that obvious from the start. He pulled out the chair next to himself and motioned toward it as if he already knew her. The class had already quieted with the entry of the professor a moment earlier. Everyone looked at the last student to enter. She nodded toward the professor as a light apology and climbed past several open seats to move next to Wesley as if she already knew him. She barely acknowledged his gesture other than by accepting his invitation and yet Wesley thought she turned a glance toward him as she settled in, and he was not sure whether it was to see if he were worth her interest or if she was thanking him for making her welcome in a slightly awkward situation.

That first lecture had not disappointed Wesley although there had been no room for discussion from the students so he had no chance to demonstrate his supposed underlying expertise. As it came to a close, he began to plan the gesture he would make to the exciting creature seated beside him. He was not experienced in meeting girls but he saw this as a command performance, his having made the first move already. He stood along with everyone else when the professor closed up his bundle of notes, partly to show the woman that he was relatively tall, which might make up for his boyish face and chunky physique. He looked to her to say something friendly about the class. He had not chosen any words to use; he knew he was too poor an actor to make them convincing; he had heard pick-up lines and they always sounded sleazy. He had decided he would not mention the weather or immediately give his name or reference her late arrival or complement her or indicate pleasure in her anonymous company during class. He decided to say how he liked the direction the professor was taking by opening with a review of cases on "nuisance" and move toward more recent cases addressing issues that had never been pursued until science was available to demonstrate environmental harm more broadly. He had half formed a sentence toward this purpose when she looked up from piling her books together and looked him straight in the eyes. She was physically direct with everyone like that. It was disarming but that is not why she did it. She was not calculating in a way to promote herself; she was not competitive. There was an innocence in her comportment like a child who has no idea of the effect of her presence. Wesley thought it was possible only because she was beautiful, not like an actress who was obviously seeking to impress, just a native attractiveness direct from her maker. His sentence stopped before he completed it and he forgot where it was headed for a moment. His mind recovered quickly, but not quickly enough to continue before she spoke.

"Do you want to walk over to the museum?" She was referring to a small art museum on campus, an institution Wesley had not noticed. He answered casually that he would like a walk just now. He did not mention that he had another class to attend in less than ten minutes and he had resolved not to miss any more classes, not this week or any week, no matter how intriguing the company might be, but this was an historic opening and could not be missed. He had no capacity to suggest rescheduling. He gave his name and she said "I'm Mattie."

5. Box of Hats

The next box to be removed was originally the same size as the book box but had been crushed over the years by the weight of the books on top of it. Wesley saw that it should have been placed on top of the stack. It probably had been there at some point and then was shifted to the bottom one day when he was looking for something and moved things around. The box was so light, he could not think what might be inside and hoped it was not something precious that was now destroyed. He peeled back the lid and saw it was full of old hats from the days, years actually, when he was trying to establish himself as an interesting person. Mostly he had the flat ones variously called "newsboy" or "eight-quarter hat." He had a Mao cap in Army OD with a red plastic star on the front and a ship captain's cap consciously lacking the "scrambled eggs" on the brim which would have nominally denoted an Admiral or some other high naval official.

There was a felt cowboy hat left over from the high school summer he went camping in New Mexico. He had tried to keep it sharp as new while the hats his buddies had bought became soiled and bent. Sometime in the second week they were caught in a hailstorm and he sheltered under a rocky ledge, mainly to protect his hat. The other boys either thought he was being a sissy or they were jealous of his pristine hat. They tore off his hat and threw it into a muddy stream. It was swept away before he could reach it. He bushwhacked along the stream for thirty minutes until it reached a beaver pond where the flow slowed and he found the hat again. He took off his boots and waded into the pond to recover the now broken-in chapeau. His best friend had followed along, out of sight, feeling guilty for participating in the vandalism, unsure of his own motive for that participation. Wesley was not as upset as he had expected to be and he was pleased when his buddy turned up. There was the triumph of finding it again to salve his ego too. After that trip he did not wear the hat. It never fit in back east, regardless of its condition.

For a while his favorite hat was a stiff Panama. He bought it at a department store when he got his first credit card. It was too expensive for his circumstances but he gave into the temptation to make his first impulse purchase. He once overheard some girls in his contract law class, where he only spoke when questioned directly by the professor, saying they liked the hat. Of course he was very proud of it after hearing them. Some years later, he was wearing it on the Washington Metro and a young man mentioned as they were leaving the train that he liked the hat. Wesley smiled and nodded in response. Then the man asked if Wesley was driving toward the Cheshire Apartments. Wesley agreed to give him a ride. They were not on the route to his house but were not far out of his way. When they got there the man asked if Wesley would like to come in for a cup of coffee. Wesley declined and he felt self-conscious wearing the hat anymore but it was soon to be retired anyway as it was getting dirty on the brim where he handled it most and the inside was getting dark from sweat.

He went through the newsboy hats he had formerly enjoyed wearing. They were more appropriate to his college days. Nonetheless, he wore them for a few years after college while he slowly developed and adopted a personal style appropriate to his professional position. He was surprised to realize that the classic, bland attire and language of Washington would become attractive to him. He had never imagined himself wearing the gray flannel suit, had never desired to "fit in." Like so many youths of his generation, he had tried to overcome what he saw as his inherent mediocrity by displaying his unique personality through the symbols of rebelliousness or creativity or entertainment or self-conscious humor and none of it had fit comfortably and none of it had made others admire him. Success in forms he had not anticipated eventually changed him, mostly in the form of Mattie who, to his amazement, loved him despite having no appreciation of his hats.

Finally, after these years away from his hipster pretentions, he could see how silly he must have appeared. His mustache had been excessive. He thought it made him look fierce, an appearance he needed since he was, in fact, pathologically mellow. It was embarrassing to recall how shallow he had been, like the songs from that era he had thought were so sophisticated and were actually bubblegum. The only reason he was not depressed by the image of his own youth was that he somehow got beyond it. Mattie had seen beyond his awkward lingering adolescence and he had risen to fulfill her vision of the adult he could become. He had always preferred to be a contributor to society. It took him longer than some to see how to do that.

With no more need to attract a woman, he had ceased to care about appearing distinctive and dressed to be effective in his job so he could help Mattie live the life they wanted. Hats had no place in his Federal worker office and imitating personal flair through haberdashery would have been a burden to his career. They had occupied a place in his garage out of nostalgia for the days when his identity was fluid. The crushed and mildewed fedoras, panamas, boaters, berets, and other passé symbols of rank and occupation were sad reminders of the money he had spent in search of himself but he felt no remorse as he tossed them onto the junk pile. He had worked out who he was and was satisfied enough with that. He was certain enough the troubles that led to his lonely spring cleaning had not originated within him.

Wesley lifted up the last box against the wall, the one under the box of crushed hats. It was full of typed or printed paper. As he lifted it, he heard a clatter. A baseball bat, softball bat actually, had been sitting on the box where it was wider than the carton with hats. He had hung the glove on the bat to keep it off the floor. He had intended for it to sit there for a season, and not for so many years. They belonged to Mattie and had only been used one time.

The softball bat had been purchased when they were finishing law school and could not afford to buy toys. But the graduating class was having a picnic and she heard someone saying there would be softball. She had never played softball although she remembered wanting to play when she was too young to have the requisite skills. The older kids in her neighborhood would not put her on their backyard teams. She had tossed the ball back and forth with a few other tomboys but never played in a legitimate game, one with bases and scores. Thus, when she wanted to buy a bat, ball and glove for the department softball game that might take place, Wesley dared not argue as he had heard the story of her baseball career many times and knew of the psychic scars it had left.

On the day before the picnic, she wanted to learn how to play. Wesley knew that would be a futile effort but again was in no position to argue. He had no glove and did not anticipate needing one with her pitching. From 15 feet away, he tossed her a gentle underhand softball which she caught, thrilled at her apparent natural talent and already angry once again with the neighborhood boys who had wasted its best years. She threw it back toward him, overhand and wild. It hit the ground halfway between them although she had put enough energy in it to reach him, she had released it too late to achieve the appropriate arc. Wesley chased it down and then stepped back a little and tossed her another. It was just slightly short of reaching her. She leaned forward but did not take a step. With her arms outstretched, she made a basket of her hands and screamed in pain when the ball hit the tip of her bare hand. She ran inside to do something to fix it. Her first guess was that running it under cold water would somehow help but that made it hurt more. At the college clinic, the X-ray showed the catch had caused a small crack in one phalange, not something that could be splinted and not something she could ignore to get into a game at the picnic. The people at the picnic played volleyball rather than softball anyway.

Soon after they took their professional jobs in Washington, Mattie signed up for the office team to play on weekends in the spring somewhere on the mall downtown.

She had still never played in a real game but she regarded herself as an adult and able to assert her right to play. Her office welcomed anyone without regard for their level of sporting experience anyway. She missed the first and only practice because something came up and then she missed the first game for the same reason and soon the whole idea of joining in office games on the weekend was forgotten.

The box on the bottom held the reports he had written in his first five years in Washington: legal briefs on topics his bosses identified, research on topics he judged to be important to pending legislative proposals, a few longer articles intended for publishing in a professional journal although only one a year typically made it to publication and no one found them relevant anyway. After five years in his job, he accepted that the shelf life of his work was limited to a few months at most so he ceased saving things outside the official office files and, more importantly, he ceased working on anything to be used more than a couple months in the future. This change in behavior led to his first major promotion.

6. Becoming Bureaucrats

Wesley and Mattie finished school on the same day and negotiated jobs separately but simultaneously. Washington had thousands of positions lawyers might fill and tens of thousands of lawyers applying but it still remained the best place to find careers for both of them. Neither was much concerned about riches or fame, preferring the idea of public service and the job security associated with Washington. Mattie had the better grades and probably the better recommendations and she was more concerned about getting a position with room for growth. Her higher standards for a position she would accept exactly offset her stronger record and they started work within a month of each other.

Wesley was assigned to a desk facing and abutting his officemate's desk, like a partner's desk of a hundred years before. His officemate had been working there two years yet he offered Wesley no advice and hardly any conversation. He did not even take his books off Wesley's desk until the secretary came in and scolded him like a mother with a teenager. Wesley thought him peculiar but did not judge him as rude or surly or stupid or self-centered or inconsiderate, although it might have been fair to apply any of those terms. Wesley was too excited to have his first professional job and to have a respectable job title inside the door of the Federal Government. He expected to rise quickly when his capacity was recognized rather than his modest academic performance. He was, however, not unrealistic and had no plan to rise very far, just far enough to have a good salary with work that was respectable in Mattie's eyes.

On that first day, he did not know what his work was. His boss introduced him to a few people and dropped him off at his desk, leaving the impression the secretary would answer any remaining questions. It seemed wrong to ask her what he was supposed to be doing. He should get guidance from the boss. Wesley figured it was a busy day for the boss or that he was being tested for his initiative or for his grasp of subtle hints he had, in fact, missed. After his officemate refused to give more than single word answers to any inquiry, Wesley decided to be creative and knocked on a couple nearby office doors to introduce himself and, more importantly, to see what the office did. Mattie would have figured out such details during her interview or would not have accepted the position. Wesley saw it was time on this very day to grow up, to take charge of his future and to stop assuming it would be sufficient to merely meet the qualifications set before him.

During that first week, the few people who were willing to have a conversation, did not ask for his help with their work and volunteered no specifics. He was not experienced enough to be much help to them so, probably to their credit, they would not spend time suggesting what he should do. As a group, they left the impression their work was confidential, even from him. Later he realized the most important task the staff faced was identifying an issue to research. They were leery of bringing in anyone who might dilute their control of their issue.

He was in the Department of Agriculture's Legal Research Agency's Land Branch's Rights Division's Northeast Issues Section. There was every reason to believe he would soon have business cards embossed with the seal of USDA and focused on his full name followed by a comma and "LLD." He might need a large card or a small font to list all the levels of the bureaucracy above him. His niche in the bureaucracy could be justified by his interest and attention to environmental law. He had not studied anything about agricultural land rights in the Northeast so he decided to do some reading in the Agency's law library. He soon learned USDA had an excellent library and he learned where the relevant case files for his topics were located. He could never absorb the meaning of those cases on his own but he brought some books back to his desk to get a feel for his new field and to remain available for whatever office activities came up.

On his first Monday, his boss came in and, ignoring the officemate, asked Wesley if he was settling in and whether he had any questions. Wesley had questions, embarrassing questions for someone who was drawing a salary, yet he managed without very much awkwardness to convey his interest in getting a concrete assignment.

"You figure out how to contribute as you go forward seeing what issues are driving the office," the boss answered unhelpfully. "For now, you can work on a response to this letter," and he dropped a letter on the desk. "Begin by saying it had been forwarded to you as an expert on the subject. Shouldn't be hard for you so try to get back to me today with a draft."

The letter was exciting. It was addressed to the President of the United States. Wesley was writing an answer on the President's behalf!

The letter was either a question or a complaint, depending on how generous the reader was. A farmer was questioning Federal policy regarding payments on land set aside for conservation. Wesley was no expert but he vowed to be one within twenty-four hours and he happily piled up texts in the library to fulfill that pledge. It was easier than he expected because there were several very clear descriptions of the policies and the justifications for them. He even found arguments like the one in the letter and rebuttals from actual experts. Although there were certainly controversial aspects of the policies, they were not relevant for this letter. Wesley could honestly reply with positive statements. He prepared a draft by the end of the day he had received the letter and turned it in to the boss in time to catch his carpool.

He went back to his office for his briefcase and coat, feeling as if he had finally become a contributing member of society. As he headed down the hall, the secretary called him back. The boss wanted to see him. Wesley did not think his letter had left her desk so quickly so he was surprised it turned out to be the reason for calling him back.

"Good response," the boss began and Wesley thought it was very courteous to complement him so soon. He prepared to say "thanks, and I need to catch my carpool" but fortunately he did not get the words out. "Have a seat. This won't take long." Wesley put his briefcase on the floor and sat in the chair beside the boss's desk. He did not want to hold up his carpool or miss it in his second week. He knew carpoolers hated unreliable members. "You have covered the issue accurately, I would say. I'm not as familiar as you are with the policy details but they seem right. However, you see, the purpose of writing a response to a citizen's letter is to prevent any more letters from the citizen. Don't piss him off so he gets mad, of course. And don't give him a basis for arguing a point any further. Around here we are not in a position to affect policy so there is no point in arguing with us. Make him as happy as you can. Tell him he has a good question and the government takes note of this issue and may address it in a future Farm Bill although there are citizens on the other side of it too. Something like that. One paragraph if you can-- a short paragraph."

Wesley had elected to go to law school partly because all his life people had told him he should be a lawyer. What they meant was that he liked to argue. He understood why they said this and he disagreed with them. He did not *like* to argue, he just disliked to hear poorly supported statements. Now, on his first task as a lawyer, he felt his neck flush and his brain began to outline a verbal response to this insult to logic. Surely government workers at this level of professionalism would not acknowledge their job was to give empty replies to serious citizens. If that was the way in this office, if that was his job, he would leave now and refuse to accept the paycheck for his first and only fortnight.

Fortunately, Wesley's words were a few seconds slower than his thoughts and he hesitated, looking at the desk. He was a little intimidated by this man who knew how to make a career in Federal service, who probably had a nice house in the suburbs and went to the Kennedy Center for concerts and raised some children and compromised as needed with the shifting Administrations that took power in Washington. He had risen to a supervisory level over an office of professionals. He knew what the office was supposed to do and it must, at times be more than to pacify citizens with the gumption to write the President.

Wesley stammered out "You think a good answer can be done in a paragraph?" His voice felt weak and he struggled to avoid clearing his throat which would have only emphasized his discomfort. He resolved to speak more firmly next time.

"Maybe not a short paragraph. Be generous, but don't make it an essay for publication in the law review. Look at the language he uses—not academic. He is a farmer, a profession essential to our survival, but not a job you or I would seek. What he needs to know is that letters like his don't move Washington. He is free to give his opinion and we will listen and, well, maybe he needs to notice his voice is one of thousands on this topic. Truthfully, we do record the subject of his concern and if we get a groundswell of related letters and calls, we would report it up the line to the Under-Secretary."

"We record the subject of each letter somewhere? Should I be doing that for this one?"

"Verla does that before it goes to staff like yourself. It's called 'controlled correspondence'. She will record your response as well. It is important stuff. We take it seriously but do not invest as much as we would in a Congressional inquiry or a briefing paper for a court case, you know. Anyway, guess you need to be going home. Maybe you can knock out a revision before you take off?"

His voice went up like a question but it was not really a question. Wesley answered that he would be pleased to give it another shot. He called the leader of his carpool as soon as he was back in his office. They had waited the required ten minutes for him and called a substitute. They needed four in the car to use the carpool lanes. They were already on the road so his call did not help. They needed to know he would not be coming before they wasted ten minutes plus the time to bring in one of the subs. No threat was made. None was needed as the message was clear enough.

§§§

With two professionals in the house, it was hard for either Wesley or Mattie to play the role of supportive spouse in the standard manner of sympathizing with the news of the day rather than carrying on the habit of the workday and examining each other's reports, making recommendations on how to address their deficiencies. Neither knew the other's job well enough to be recommending what to do and neither could avoid it entirely, yet over the first few years of married life, their love had been strong enough to teach them to take turns at being the central character in a Washington drama, uniquely qualified to tell the tale and to take or leave the advice of the other without further explanation. Thus when Mattie came in on a rainy night in November and began to tell her story even before she had taken off her coat, Wesley knew his place was to listen, to capture the details and to say only enough to prove he was paying attention and appreciating her plight or her wisdom or her courage or her luck or whatever was the key element in the story.

"I am ready to file something on that creep Raleigh. I have the goods on him this time. It feels good, more than merely 'good', to finally have a case. He won't be ready for me. It's not the case I was trying to find or the one he would be trying to hide from me."

"What do you mean, 'not the case' you've been working on?"

"Right." She stopped for a moment which Wesley suspected was a test of how engaged he was in the conversation.

"You were getting together a list of his victims. Did you find some that were especially clearly linked to him?"

"No, nothing like that. That *is* what I had in mind for the past few weeks. There are so many people, Muslims of course, that he screwed with his program, the statistics made it obvious to analysts, but a jury or a politician needs an innocent face to give a crime emotional content. He was careful to stick it to relatively devout or fanatical men, the sort that sound and look otherly, knowing that would protect him from legal action from people like me."

"So what did you find today?"

"Not today, exactly... I didn't just find it but I finally pulled a different tack together into a single brief and it is solid. I got him on abuse of authority, you know, corruption. It is not as important as his years of discrimination but it is so blatantly illegal and apolitical, he won't have a defense once I pop it on him."

“You’re not a prosecutor, you know.”

“Not in a formal sense but in a practical one, I am for this one. Oh, I’ll go to the Justice Department. He may never know I had anything to do with it. Justice’ll want the credit for themselves so they won’t say anything about their source. I will even keep up my civil rights attack so he thinks I am still focused there.”

“I like that way of thinking. Keep him looking away from you. He can be really nasty. I wouldn’t want to threaten him.”

“He already knows I threaten him. He just doesn’t take my threat seriously. I imagine he has someone watching what I come up with... I doubt I have scared them so far.”

“If they knew you, they’d be scared.”

“Nice of you to think so.”

“Is there someone in Justice you trust to take this?”

“Don’t worry. I can handle it.” Wesley had stepped beyond his appointed role.

“Are you going to pass it in on one piece or will you have to work on it with Justice?”

“Probably I’ll have to stay with it for a few months, to ensure it’s done right.”

“What’s the corruption?”

“Better you don’t know the details, Honey. They could lean on you if it comes to something.”

“I’d rather they lean on me if they start to lean on you.”

“It’ll never get back to me anyway. It’s funny how it came to me. I didn’t notice for a long time a pattern in the interview responses. I was so into the civil rights thing, I wasn’t tracking the money. You would have noticed.”

“That’s my role at work, watching the money.”

"Most of us think that's boring but I have to admit, it is a good thing to do. Anyway, these guys I was interviewing tended to complain about how much their lobbyists cost them and one day I started to take that concern seriously. I guess my own prejudice was holding me back, thinking they complain about money because they don't have much. I started asking how much they were spending on these independent agents and the figures were much too consistent. I could not easily believe the market for these shadowy services to get through the bureaucracy was so efficient that the agents competed themselves into a firm market price. In fact, none of these guys had been able to talk their agent into a discount. It was more like the crystal clear price of branded soft drinks than the foggy price of a used car. Conclusion: there was one seller of these services. Who better than the bureaucrat supposedly being lobbied?"

"That's a clever rhetorical flourish. And now you have evidence that will stand up to legal scrutiny?"

"I am not presenting the case today, you know. I know I need more evidence. The good thing is I have started looking for a different kind of thing. He's not the true believer in bigotry I thought he was. His bigotry, and this is a common thing, is just a way to direct attention from his scam. He does not mind being hated apparently. Maybe he finds consolation in being hated for a purposeful façade."

"You think he is artful with bias? Oh, his chauvinism is real enough. It does not matter why you do it. His bigotry is certainly present in his actions. You may not have built a case the courts will accept fully but you convinced me months ago."

"Doesn't matter to me what's in his heart. It is enough that I have learned he is not the clumsy oaf he projects himself to be. This is a Washington hoax, a capital classic. It has been done before so many times, there must be some precedents to follow in getting to him."

"Maybe not so easy to tie him to it. It's a successful model. Hardly anyone remembers the last time it was done so we are ripe to repeat it. Should we teach history? Promote a more responsible media?"

"It's always done a little differently. They make it so easy to hate the racism, we stick with the emotional connection and forget the less interesting, more enforceable corruption. Their fellow bigots feel our hate and are thereby vindicated in theirs. What we do now? I don't know about the big 'we' but the little we, meaning me and my agency, we take on this bastard."

"And specifically where do your well founded, historically aware suspicions take you next?"

"And that gets us to the end of this conversation. None of your business, Dear." She finally began to take off her coat, having stood with one hand on the doorknob since she stepped inside.

"OK, I can see that. Let's put it aside for the evening. Anyway, I am excited for you, for making progress, even if I do not know exactly what the progress was."

There were parts of Wesley's work that could not be discussed as well. Forthcoming contracts could not be mentioned outside the office, although there was never any risk that Mattie or her friends would gain some competitive advantage in applying for a USDA contract. The debates over who should be awarded a contract were also confidential. It was a courtesy to Mattie that he never told her anything she could not repeat to anyone. There were many things she would not want to repeat or that might be awkward to repeat, but nothing illegal to repeat. There was little temptation to talk with Mattie about the contracts on his desk. He did find his work to be valuable and interesting but he knew it would not be either to someone who was not wrapped up in the long range purposes and endless details. You had to know the people involved in the decisions, the applicants and the politicians and the technical experts and the lawyers and the accountants, in order to appreciate the humor in an incident, the pathos in an outcome, the irony in a decision.

Wesley took the wet overcoat from her. "I'll hang this up over the tub until it dries. You want some tea to celebrate whatever the hell your progress was today? The water's already hot."

"Yes, let's celebrate. I'll take some of those cookies with the chocolate on one side. I know they're not good for me but we have them in the house and they ought not to be wasted."

"I know. One ought not to waste food while there are children starving in China."

"Not today so much."

"Starving somewhere."

"We must save the children, Honey. Break out the cookies."

Mattie had not always been so aggressive. The case concerning Raleigh was the first she had tried to direct into a prosecution. Her usual role had been to guide the clients assigned to her on how to stay within the law, and to protect them from law suits or prosecution or other legal hazards. Her advice was carefully constrained to legal compliance and was normally accepted. The staff appreciated that she kept her distance from policy matters and confined herself strictly to areas of her expertise. Some of the lawyers took their positions as authority to advise every time they had an opinion, as if their position had been earned by their personal general brilliance rather than by a specific, often narrow, form of training. When she first arrived, she was often questioned when she advised against something one of the senior people wanted to do, but she was always backed by the General Council and everyone soon accepted that if she spoke up, she knew what she was doing. In fact, she had a lot to learn when she first arrived but she was humble enough to ask her supervisor or other more experienced colleagues for guidance. Her greatest strength in those early days was in recognizing where legal issues might arise - it took some years to understand how to resolve the common ones while the solutions to the uncommon ones remained always dubious, even long after they had been moved to the inactive files in the Beltsville archives. Dealing with Raleigh was exceptional in every way.

Mattie had not given him a thought when he joined the bureau; it was not the bureau she supported directly, merely the one she backed up when things got busy. He had been there about a month and she had not yet met him when an interaction alerted her to his character. On a day when the lawyer assigned to his branch, Sarah, was away at a conference on the West Coast, his secretary sent a message asking Mattie when she could see him. It felt a little officious, Mattie thought, for him to set up an appointment when he could have called her himself and introduced himself amiably.

His office was noticeably cooler than the standard in the rest of the building. She understood that keeping a cool office was a strategy for some people to keep them alert, like an alternative to coffee. It was in her nature to think well of this new person, someone she had not met. Most of the higher level bureaucrats were smart and dedicated even if they might have awkward personal characteristics, like officiousness. When he came in, her impression shifted immediately, not to a negative one but mainly to an impression that he was extremely good looking with an effortless perfection in his features and his manners. His skin was a brilliant white, not unhealthy, almost otherworldly. His jaw and chin were carefully shaded with a dense black beard of hairs exactly the same length, three sixteenth inch she estimated, not as long as the hairs of his eyebrows. His sleeves were rolled up twice but that did not lend any informality to his crisp white shirt because the sleeves were so neatly folded back, they looked more a matter of high style than comfort.

She was not attracted to him but could not help noticing his beauty. It was not effeminate, but not especially masculine either. He was too slender and fine boned to be, to be what? She was judging him on his genotype and ashamed for it. Was she thinking he must be gay? There was no basis for an opinion on his orientation and there was no reason to take note of it except that it would be interesting and might turn out to be relevant in the office politics at some point. All information was potentially relevant, wasn't it?

He did not shake her hand or introduce himself and hardly looked at her. Gay or straight, he was not showing any sign of sexual tension. And she was wondering why she was observing this.

"Are you familiar with the regs on green card application?" he asked without any introduction, as if they had worked together for years.

It was a vague question. She had not worked on those regulations but she could look them up easily enough. Since he was new to his position, he might not know any details. She decided to be less cautious than usual. Was she trying to impress him and if so was it because of the stature his unusual appearance gave him or because they were both still new or because he had not shown her more respect?

"Yes, we all work with them," she answered in a confident tone without expanding on her level of expertise. *Let him ask what he wants to know rather than have me speculate on whether it is something I can handle off the top of my head*, she thought to herself.

"There is a press inquiry about us. Seems someone out there thinks or wants to claim that we are not fully compliant. I did not hear what exactly they are saying we are doing wrong."

"The regulation is regularly monitored. I would have to know what concern the press has in order to offer any explanation of our performance. Can you tell me where the inquiry came from?"

"Some out-of-town newspaper, from Tampa I think."

"Did you get the inquiry in a written form?" *Why do I have to beg you for information on a question you want answered?*

"Yes, OK. Ask my secretary for a copy of the e-mail ...came in yesterday." He looked down at some papers on his desk while Mattie sat in front of him. Ten seconds passed in silence before Mattie spoke.

"Is that all you need from me right now?"

"Yeah, that's all. Thanks. Let me know what you find out."

A couple of polite phrases came to Mattie's mind, empty words to close out the meeting, like "I'll get right on it" or "Happy to look into this," but she felt he was being rude to her, ignoring her as soon as he spit out his orders so she examined the phrases more than necessary for the occasion and then too much time had passed for anything she might add to sound casual. She knew it was best to be generous and say something anyway but he was not waiting for anything more and would not feel any consolation in an additional courtesy. She had been dismissed. His behavior had not been excessively rude or unusual, merely irritating which might have come from her mood as much as from his although she was not aware of feeling out of sorts before the meeting. The real issue was to check into the accusation.

His secretary did not know anything about the e-mail but she was anxious to please and did not want to go back to her new boss on this, so she searched through the messages from the previous day and asked Mattie if first one and then another was likely the right one. Eventually Mattie looked over her shoulder and scrolled though the return addresses rather than the subject entries until she spotted one sent from the Tampa Bay Times. Reputable journalists generally used their firm's address to help establish themselves as legitimate members of the press. She glanced at the message and then forwarded it to herself. "Thank you for your help," she said to the secretary without thinking of whether the secretary had been helpful. "I can take it from here."

Back in her office she read the reporter's e-mail which conveyed a complaint that the Bureau was discriminating illegally in its review of immigrant work permits in Florida. The assertion was not backed by any data or other evidence. It came from an Imam who heard stories from other American Imams at a conference, stories that showed a pattern, he thought. Mattie doubted it could be true since the program was closely monitored so she looked for the data that would show if the program was being done properly. She was not familiar with the monitoring data and it could not be found as easily as the regulations on how it should be done, so she needed to consult with Sarah and put off the issue until Sarah's return, figuring she could probably just turn it over to Sarah at that point. There was no reason to hurry but she did write a note to herself on a post-it to be sure to get back to Sarah as soon as practical. It might help her relationship with Raleigh if the issue did not linger. She preferred that he would not feel it necessary to call her back about it.

Sarah came back on the following Friday and Mattie followed up her e-mail with a late morning visit to mention that the only business she had covered in Sarah's absence was a complaint from a journalist. Sarah did not seem concerned since she too knew of the monitoring program and had confidence in it. On Tuesday Mattie checked again with her, trying not to nag at her colleague but wanting reassurance that Raleigh would not be asking about it. Sarah answered that Raleigh would not be saying anything—he probably did not even remember it.

§§§

Some moments pass by without notice but are called to mind later and found to have been stored away in an accessible place in the brain, leaving the brain to wonder if the moment had, in fact, been noticed by some subconscious element that should have spoken louder at the time. Yet every moment of potential importance cannot be fully examined. Life is too busy. Nothing would get done as time would be taken up in caution limited only by how much trouble an individual is capable of imagining. Mattie had a creative imagination and a cautious nature, but she also was terribly interested in getting things done. She was confident she ought to drop the complaint. It was Sarah's job to follow up if anything needed following up. Later, of course, the moment of this conversation came back with crystal clarity as if preserved in liquid nitrogen, and Mattie knew she had not listened to her own inner guardian.

7. T-Shirts on a Table

The next box bulged as if it held a water balloon and Wesley had no memory of its contents. On the top it was marked only with his own name. He bent his legs carefully to avoid putting too much stress on his back when lifting it but it was not as heavy as it appeared. On the back he read an upside-down but revealing description: commemorative t-shirts. *Oh good,* he thought, *there will not be anything in here I want to keep.* In this case he did not mind having stored the box for some years. Most of its contents had probably seemed significant at some point in the past but after their years out here with the spiders and mildew, their true value was apparent. Nonetheless, he thought it would be fun to look through them one by one.

The first few came from the Cleveland Indians. Mattie had grown up near Cleveland and thought the Indians were her team. When the Expos moved to Washington and became the Nationals, she decided to switch her allegiance but by then she was not much of a baseball fan so her switch had not meant much more than getting a new t-shirt and a cap. The Nats shirts, including a couple he had gotten when the Nats appeared destined for the playoffs in 2012, were somewhere deeper in the box. The Nats had the best record in baseball that year and won their division by six games. Then they lost to the Cards in the first round and never made the playoffs again. He knew the shirts had never been worn and for a moment wondered if he could give them to someone and then he remembered no one wanted anything from him.

There was a t-shirt near the top from the Earth Day 2000 celebration on the Washington mall. Doubtless shirts from other Earth Days were also in the box. He and Mattie used to wear them when they went down to the mall to hear the music and listen to the EPA Administrator make a speech. He had a vision of somehow contributing to the planet's stability but it was obvious that buying the shirt or wearing it or hearing the speech was not helping anything. The last time they went, it was raining and they never put on the shirt. He had thought the shirts might make an interesting historical collection which he could hang out on some future Earth Day but it was not interesting enough that he had ever looked at them himself much less put them on display for anyone else. Some of them were getting old. Would anyone regard them with nostalgia? Mementos of the EPA when it was under the administrator of the party no longer in power were not likely to be popular. It would be an act of political resistance to put them out? Neither the current ins or the career staff was looking backward. The collection was folded into a topical bundle which he threw onto the trash pile as if he were shooting a very soft basketball.

His next decision concerned a t-shirt left over from law school. It bore a now obscure slogan of its day, a slogan from Nixon supporters: The silent majority is neither. Not as extreme as his undergraduate slogans although he could not afford to buy single-issue shirts back then. He did not mind the slogan but he would not wear it on his chest. Who would care? Besides, the t-shirt was cheaply made and would not hang well on him.

A few t-shirts with even less to recommend them emerged next from the box, birthday presents from a sister who did not keep up with him but thought he liked to wear bold political statements, something that was never true but which was almost true for a few years before he had a career. He liked the one with a Star Wars twist: Let the forest be with you. And he thought it was clever to say "I would live in a world where a chicken can cross the road without having his motives questioned," but not enough to say it aloud or to wear it on his clothing. He laughed a little at one he had bought for himself because it was perfect for him although he had not actually worn it. He had not expected to show it to anyone, but to wear it as an undershirt to remind himself of himself. It said "Top ten reasons to procrastinate: #1." He had learned procrastination from his mother who was very good at it. At the bottom of the box, the last one to come out was his favorite. He had worn it until the fabric was thin and the letters were faded. It bore only the word "peace." In 1968, that was radical. It had fit him too snugly back when he wore it although he liked that, the feeling that he was bulging through it, not from bulky muscles but not as softly as he would now. It would be absurd to put it on again.

The melancholy memories from the mildewed t-shirts should be no surprise for someone cleaning out a garage, but Wesley also suddenly realized he was finding almost nothing from the most recent six or seven years. Maybe they had learned to stop accumulating useless paraphernalia; maybe it took more than six years for things to be demoted to the garage; maybe they had developed better taste with their rising income and did not buy junk anymore; and maybe, and this option had a loud ring of truth, they had replaced sloganeering, pleasure reading, educational reading, handicrafts, vacation travel, family birthdays and holidays, sport fanship, and all other rubbish-accumulating pastimes in favor of work.

Wesley and Maggie had extended their weekday hours in the office to a daily average of twelve hours each in addition to an hour commute each way. The house had declined into a place to recharge for the next day or week, not a place to live. The change was gradual and, while unplanned, it was acknowledged and accepted. They did not speak of it, but both regarded it as a temporary condition and as a worthwhile stage in their careers. In Federal work, one does not expect to become rich. In fact, one ought not to become rich from Federal employment. The motivation for clocking extra hours, for which there was no prospect of overtime pay, was influence. They went in early and left late to be sure they never missed a meeting, formal or informal, and still fulfilled their solitary duties. They sought influence, like most of their colleagues, not for power and glory, there being little of that to go around once the political people had taken their portion. The purpose of influence is to have effect, to serve.

Wesley had learned in his first year of work that it was terribly easy to work in the Federal bureaucracy without having any effect for an entire career. Remembering his passivity before meeting Maggie, he feared slipping into the available ease of irrelevance, like an addict who reminds himself every day for years and years that he is capable of returning to his habit..

Creative researchers and innovative policy advisors must spend a large part of their effort in understanding what has already happened. Changing the future in competition with all the others in Washington who wish to move the government in some way, and whose direction is not based on an understanding of science and history and legal precedent, is exceptional. But when a lawyer, who has carefully done the background labor and been inspired with a unique vision of what could be done better on some point within his or her expertise, and has maintained the relationships with decision-makers to move the idea forward, effectively sees the influence expressed in Federal policy affecting millions of people, there is more reward than fame or money could provide, for it carries no taint of petty selfishness. Personal self-respect and the silent regard of one's peers was all that drove Wesley and Mattie during this period after they had learned their way around their own niche in their professions.

§§§

The t-shirt box had been sitting on a small table which was itself an especially frustrating find. It had never been used apart from holding t-shirts off the floor in the garage. Wesley lifted it over his head as he clambered over whatever remained near the front of the garage and criticized himself for starting to clear the garage from the back, which he realized he had done because he was most curious about the things in back where he had not looked for years. When he got outside, he walked down the driveway to the street and put the table on the curb. Later he would put a sign on it with just the word "free" unless it was gone by the time he got around to making the sign. Things usually disappeared pretty fast from the curb even though traffic was not heavy on his street.

The table helped date when the t-shirts had been retired and vice versa. He remembered buying the table. It would have been late in the third summer after they moved into the house. The t-shirt box had to be more recent than that, and some of the shirts were probably much more recent, perhaps by several years after he put the table there.

During the first summer after he and Mattie moved in, Wesley routinely had jogged in the morning, under the railroad bridge and then along the river. It was a quiet route where he seldom saw anyone, allowing him the illusion that he was in a rural area. There were ducks on the river most mornings and sometimes a flock of Canada geese. In the spring of the year of the table, the town or some other entity began to build a new bridge for the railroad track and his route was blocked, so he devised a run through the neighborhood. If he ran at 5 am, it was still very quiet. There is plenty of light for running in Washington's May and June at that hour but it is too dark to be sure of safe footing by October. It took a couple weeks to work out a route just the right length and with enough diversity to be amusing. There would be no wildlife or natural scenes but he could change streets a dozen times in thirty minutes, giving him something to think about. There were no milkmen doing their route of course, not for the past twenty years, and he was too early to see children at their school bus stops but a few people were usually about. There was a dog walker who was always on Timber Lane with her golden retriever as he went by, reflecting both his and her obsessive adherence to schedule. There was an older woman walking her two corgis in imitation of the Queen, the British one, he imagined, but she was not as precise and he saw her at an unpredictable location if he saw her at all. He tried to figure out if she was walking the same route but at varying times or if she varied her route as well. It took him most of the summer to be certain that it was the latter. And there was a woman who always sat on her porch, writing on her laptop. He did not notice her the first few times he included her street on his route but she must have been there because she was there every morning, rain or shine after that. Once a cat ran across the street in front of him and he watched it run up to the porch where it was greeted by the woman. In the fall, when it was cold outside, she was still there, bundled up in a hood or scarf and fingerless gloves. He peeked toward her as soon as he rounded the corner to be sure she was there, one more element of the environment to monitor to pass the time and keep himself moving.

He did not want to think when he ran. Morning was his most productive time but he could not save, that is, could not write down or memorize, his good thoughts while running, so he filled his brain with repetition and found that to be mentally relaxing, delaying real mental activity until he was on the Metro and could extract what his unconscious had processed since he had left the office in an exhausted fog the evening before.

The woman typing on the laptop never looked up when he came by, as far as he had noticed out of his peripheral vision. She seemed dedicated to her work. It was her dedication that intrigued him and he googled her based on her address and learned she was Nori Odoi, a writer of magazine stories. He wondered if she wrote of her life and had ever described sitting on her porch every morning. And he realized she might be sitting there all day doing her writing.

He never went down her street except when he was running. Maybe, he imagined, she even mentioned in a narrative that some guy ran past her house at precisely the same time, rain or shine, until the roads became slippery with icy patches in the winter.

Some of her articles were on-line. One contained a poem about a "climbing tree" that took him back to his childhood when he felt very close to trees. He liked that it had very little punctuation because as a child he would have liked English to work that way. It began:

how long
my friend
have you waited?
roots digging deeply into marshy soil
trunk thickening, splitting into two
limbs reaching upward into the sun

She always had a mug of tea sitting on the floor beside her and something small and snack-like on a plate, presumably something she had baked. Wesley thought he might have violated her privacy by looking her up and by noticing her every time he ran by even though she never glanced his way. In the next summer, he began to plot a way to speak to her, mainly to introduce himself so he would not feel guilty for knowing something about her. He did not devise a way to graciously meet her but that was all right with him as it gave him an exercise to occupy his mind for most of the summer devising a strategy with the right degree of both friendliness and social distance.

One morning as fall approached and the day was not yet fully lit, he watched her take a drink from her mug, and

lean down to set it next to her plate by her feet and he began
to wonder why she had only a single chair on her porch. It
was large enough for a table and there was plenty of room for
more furniture. That thought did not help him toward a plot
to meet her but it gave him an idea for something to do. He
bought a small table, plastic, like her chair, and decided to put
it on her porch anonymously one night and then to enjoy
seeing her use it as he went by. Somehow, illogically, that
would alleviate the guilt of his intrusion even as it was a greater
imposition on her anonymity.

He drove along her street at dusk on the evening after
he bought the table to see if she was still on her porch. The
porch was empty and the house was dark. He had not
brought the table with him but it would have been a perfect
opportunity to put it out. There would be others, he
assumed. ...But there were not. The next day, she was not at
her post and he never saw her again. She had moved away
on the day he got her the table. He did not google her again
to see where she had gone; it had no relevance to him. He
read another one of her articles, not sure why. He had no
time for magazine reading. He kept the table on his deck for
a few days until Mattie asked why he bought it, asking in a
disapproving way since she did not like the cheap plastic.
Soon after that the table was in the garage, late in their third
summer of living in Alexandria.

8. Trouble Arises

The table brought out a sad memory, not a disastrous
one like the ones he was forming closer to the day when he
cleared out the garage, but a negative one that he would have
preferred to never regain: a waste of money for the table, a

cool idea that went nowhere, a tale not to tell. He needed to find something positive to offset it.

A small box that had been stored under the table was pristine, apparently unopened. Wesley did not recognize it and figured it must be something Mattie had bought and never used. He stepped over a loose pile of heavy metal components that had once been part of utility shelving but had been rendered useless by the loss of a highly specialized piece that held them together. When he moved his second leg over the shelving, his toe caught on a piece sticking up from the pile, his weight fell forward, his knees buckled, and he staggered into the pile, noisily scattering the useless metal and banging his shin on something with a sharp edge. Under his breath, he cursed the pain shooting up his leg. He should have found a way to repair the shelves or given up on them long ago-- they had lain in wait to pay him back for his neglect, planned their revenge well and bitten him sharply. He rubbed his shin as he used to do when he was a child and hurt himself. He could sense a slight burning sensation in addition to the throb of the bruise so he pulled up his pant leg and saw he had skinned the shin so it was bleeding already. He gave a brief thought to bandaging it, to clean it and to protect his pant leg from the blood but he did not care enough about infection or soiling his pant cuff to bother.

In the moment of sharp pain, however, he had recognized the box. Inside was a funky teapot, a treasure he found on a day that was not scheduled to be special so he was especially pleased to have found a gift for Mattie, a gift for an ordinary day, a teapot that shone crisply in its glaze, a black-and-white pyramid with a handle and a short spout, not an item to be used but an ingenious item to see.

Mattie never saw it before it found its way to the back wall of the garage. Wesley remembered placing it under the table which had at that time already been in its place for a few years. He did not want to find the teapot again and yet, inevitably, here it was.

He had the box in his hand, wrapped in brown paper at the shop, when she greeted him at the door one dark evening a half year ago.

"Who is Sammie?" she said before he had even shut the door. It had been cold that day. He had been wearing his long coat. The months since then had dragged out painfully.

"You're going to have to give me more of a hint than that? I don't know any Sammy personally." He answered, still in a good mood but wondering where she was since he could not even see her. She was sitting on the couch and shouting out to him at the door.

"She seems to know you well enough."

"She? Sammy is a female that I am supposed to know?"

"Apparently. And know very well."

It was coming to Wesley. "There is an intern, no, I mean a fellow, a fellowship sort of fellow, in the office named Samantha. I never heard her called Sammie."

"Bingo."

"What did she want?"

"I think she wanted you but she got me and then she got awfully embarrassed and then she blathered on, and anyway, she told me more than she intended. More you would have wanted."

"What the hell are you talking about? What did she say?"

"She told me."

"Told you what? I don't know anything about her. She's a fellow in the office. She hardly has any business with me."

"Charlottesville. She told me about Charlottesville. The conference last fall."

Wesley's neck flushed. He hoped it did not show on his face. He had dinner with Samantha at the conference, just the two of them on the second night. It had not led to anything, not even any personal words, but he had been aware of her gender during the dinner and had felt a little guilty for enjoying her company. She had been easy to enjoy: bright, personable, well dressed and well formed. Before the conference he had hardly spoken to her. They had been in office meetings and he had offered her help in a generic way as he did to all fellows. She had sought him out at the conference, calling in the favor he had offered. She sat beside him and whispered questions about the presentations. It was off-putting to Wesley. She seemed to be trading her company for help although he was waiting to see exactly what "help" she was going ask-- a job recommendation even though he was not familiar with her work, editing a paper with substantive input to the results, a tip on what was coming up-- the sort of things a junior person might wheedle out of a senior person. He had dinner with her to see what she wanted. She had chosen a booth in back of the quiet restaurant in the conference hotel. She let him pay for her meal which was not quite the professional thing to do but he thought she was young enough not to know the protocol.

"Nothing happened in Charlottesville that I know of."

"Please. I'm not stupid."

"Of course you're not, but I still don't understand what you're talking about."

"About your affair. About sleeping with her."

"Well, that didn't happen. Nothing remotely like that. Is that what she said?"

"Not right away, but yes, that's what she said."

"I cannot imagine why she would say that." He really did not, but the truth did not insulate him entirely from feeling guilt. His mouth went dry and his voice came out weakly. "She has no reason to do me harm. I can hardly wait to see her in the office tomorrow."

"I bet."

"C'mon. I deserve the benefit of the doubt, don't I? Some stranger makes an off-the-wall accusation. Let me see what's going on."

"Be sure to let me know what you decide."

He could not shake the deep impression of shame although he knew he had not done anything inappropriate; he had merely enjoyed a dinner at a professional event with an attractive colleague. Even before that dinner, Wesley knew that Samantha was strange for a person in his sort of workplace, but she was too unimportant to attract much thought about it. Could she have wished for something from him and was now exacting revenge on him for not noticing? It was implausible that she wanted to sleep with him that night. She gave no sign of it and even if she had been too subtle or shy for Wesley to notice, it would never have happened. He did not want that -- he was more than content to be sitting nearby for a short time, as if he were in an alternative life. If Mattie did not exist, he might have been more flexible about what could be accomplished with the young beauty but in a world where Mattie did exist, and he could not and would not forget for an instant that she existed, his understanding of sexual attraction was defined by her and could not be performed beyond parody by another. He was hardly present at that dinner with Samantha, he like a spiritualist's ghost incapable of interacting with the person in front of him beyond some vague vibration of the table and a remote clanking of chains.

Inside was a funky teapot

9. Samantha Lost

Breakfast was frigid as a naked dawn on an iceberg raked by a fresh polar wind. Mattie silently made the coffee for both of them while Wesley chattered about anything that came to mind other than the household crisis. He hoped he had managed to plant some seeds of doubt in the story from Samantha, by being his familiar self rather than the stranger in a story whose content he did not really know. He had hardly slept, and leaned throughout the night against Mattie, not daring to move, to show her he remained close. Mostly

72

he was anxious to get to the office to confront Samantha and get an explanation of why she or someone using her name had called Mattie. A drunken prank was his best guess and yet a very unlikely scenario to have from the staid folks in his office who might know her name.

He was the first one in, as usual, and his anxiety continued to rise as the clock passed the time when others began to arrive but no one turned up in Samantha's cubicle. By 9:00, he decided to ask if she had called in. He had not noticed up to that point that anyone else was acting strangely, but when he asked the secretary if Samantha had called, she spoke most peculiarly. Wesley knew her well and rarely spoke with her without some teasing remark but she hardly looked up when she replied that she doubted they would be seeing Samantha this day and maybe not for the rest of the week. Wesley asked for her home phone number but the secretary answered that she could not give that out. It was an inappropriate response. Wesley had authority to know the home phone numbers of anyone in the office but he did not argue the point.

He walked around the office a little, saying "good morning" to a few co-workers and confirmed that everyone was acting unfriendly at best. Everyone seemed to have heard he had slept with the fellow. They looked at him strangely or not, depending on their concern for gossip, but they had all heard it. Worse, she was not there herself to explain what she had done. He had hoped the call to Mattie had come from someone else, that someone had made the call for some nefarious reason and that Mattie could call Samantha and know it was not her voice she had heard making the accusations. Many people at the conference might have seem them having dinner but he had no enemies there or anywhere. He was not worth hating or fearing. But with Samantha missing on the day after the call, she did seem to be involved. Meanwhile, the rest of the office could see her absence as validating the rumor of Wesley's involvement.

He went down the hall a few doors to see Lucas. Lucas would tell him straight. Lucas, an IT specialist who always spoke with the precision of a geometer, offered the only sympathetic ear. He was a friend, someone who always cared about what happened to Wesley over the weekend and was willing to share his own stories, but not an intimate friend. Just a friend at work; he was of a different age, with a different job and different commitment to his career, living a life defined largely by his devotion to his family.

"Yeah, I heard some bullshit about her and you. It was weird. She left in tears yesterday they said. She asked for a priest or something. She may be wacko but you might want to avoid talking about her right now. So she called to say she's not coming in today 'cause she's so upset. You know what else is weird? That I know all this. It's none of my business but everyone knows about it. At least they know there is something. They don't know actual facts. We don't do much scandal around here. This story is getting promoted way too much."

"Thanks for talking to me. I don't know what to say. I didn't know anything until I got home last night. I don't know what she is accusing me of doing but I didn't do it. ...I guess that's what they all say. I don't even want to know what she is saying. I just want her to stop saying it. No, I want more than that, I specifically want her to take it back somehow, in a way Mattie accepts."

"Anything I can do?"

"No, you shouldn't have anything to do with this. It'll get cleared up. I really appreciate you talking about it though. I hate hearing less than anybody else about it."

Lucas watched Wesley walking toward his office, and saw he still strode with the confidence of a senior member of the staff. He liked Wesley and could not imagine his being guilty of this or anything else. He wished he could help and worked through a few ideas, ways within his skills that he might help his friend. These thoughts kept him from his work until a brainstorm hit him. He sent an e-mail to Wesley.

SUBJECT: Another topic entirely
>Remember that writer who moved out of your neighborhood a couple years ago before you ever met her? What was her name? I'd like to see if I could get her address. She deserves to know about that table you nearly gave her.

Lucas hoped the idea would perk up Wesley, at least remind him he was a good guy. A half hour later, Wesley sent a note back:

SUBJECT: Re: Another topic entirely
>I tried to find her to say something about that table in case she found it amusing, but nothing came up in my search. I did not try very hard; messages from strangers are rarely welcomed these days. Doubtless you are better at using the internet, but please don't put a whole lot into it. Just if some easy way gets an address. She is Nori Odoi. She has published some magazine articles and poems, but does not have a website.

Lucas knew he should not spend any more time on such a personal task but he liked the challenge and justified his effort as adding to the office productivity if it helped put Wesley at ease. Within ten minutes, he set a follow-up to Wesley:

> SUBJECT: Re: Re: Another topic entirely
>> Ms Odoi moved to Paris. Her cat died in quarantine. She has an apartment on Rue de Rennes. It looks cheap for Paris. That's the "left bank." Her e-mail is noricat@gmail.com.

> SUBJECT: Re: Re Re: Another topic entirely
>
>> Thanks man! That's good news. I can send her my anecdote without worrying her that I want anything from her at this distance away in time and space.

And that, Lucas thought to himself, *is the magic of the internet,* but his real pleasure came from feeling he had done something kind for a guy down on his luck. He turned back to his job but felt a small glow of accomplishment from his quick investigation and from Wesley's apparent appreciation of it. While he manipulated the department's budget request tables to clarify their appearance, a simple task for him, his subconscious was free to examine the Samantha issue. What had he seen in her during the few weeks she had been around? Had he heard anything about her during that time? What work did she do? He knew almost nothing about her, but his quick success finding the poet gave him an idea. He should check into Samantha's on-line presence. Wesley could get her address himself from the secretary, Lucas figured, but Lucas' experience with internet research might find something more to help explain her odd behavior of the last day. That would be a real boost for Wesley.

An hour later, he reluctantly returned to the budget preparation. His research had revealed more by its gaps than by its substance. Although he gained access to the office personnel files, he could find nothing significant about her. Since she was a political appointee, she had not gone through the rigorous review he and the other civil service employees faced, and did not provide the same extensive documentation but even so, her file was surprisingly thin.

He had thrown the gauntlet at his own feet and would take it up with vigor when he got home. Something valuable to Wesley must lie behind this peculiarity.

10. Samantha Found

While pondering the unopened gift, Wesley decided the garage was becoming too dark to navigate safely through the remaining detritus. His leg had not been bruised by his clumsiness, but by the dark. He positioned his feet securely and risked proving he was inept and carefully threw the box out the door toward the garbage pile. It landed on one of its corners, about two feet short of the target and spun up and onto the half-full box of books, a successful, even if lucky, trick toss.

The garage light could be turned on by pulling a string hanging below a bare bulb and above a huge sack full of rags. Wesley knew there were only rags in that sack but the stuff inside had not always been rags. He did not doubt they held their own sad stories from the past but he would not look any closer. He went to the corner by the big door and turned on the outside light. Wesley felt a wet drip on his leg and knew his leg was still bleeding. Once he focused on it, he knew he had banged it hard enough to leave a mark for a week. He did not reach down or make any other motion that would acknowledge the pain. It was nothing beside all that was hurting him.

Suddenly he became aware of a small sound of gravel grinding under someone's footsteps. *Ken has been watching the evening approach and is impatient to rummage through my garbage,* Wesley suspected. He was irritated by Ken's unnecessary desperation. He knew Ken had a reverse mortgage that ensured his basic needs would be met. He just could not miss a chance at a jackpot, even with the low odds coming out of Wesley's cast-offs.

"Wes!" a voice called out, not Ken's, too friendly. Wesley whirled around and took a moment to recognize Lucas. Although Lucas was his friend, maybe his only current friend, neither had ever been to the other's house. It was not that kind of friendship. It was a friendship neither mentioned but both assumed was secure. They enjoyed the assumption. He had probably come, Wesley figured, just to reassure Wesley but it was embarrassing because Wesley had not told him he was leaving. He had not told him in order to protect him. It was not good to be considered close to Wesley.

"Lucas! How great to see you!"

"No names, please!" Lucas said looking over his shoulder guiltily, leaving Wesley to feel badly for embarrassing his friend. "Bet you're surprised, huh?" Wesley thought it would not be hard to figure out Lucas was the visitor if anyone really wanted to know. He was the only short Black man well known to be Wesley's friend.

"How come you're walking?"

"An abundance of caution. Let's go inside."

Wesley led the way. As soon as they stepped inside, Lucas asked "What are you doing? Movin' out?" The house was a split foyer style, revealing its construction date in the early Sixties. Anyone coming in the front door had to immediately go up or down half a flight of stairs. It was not a good arrangement for maintaining a conversation. At the top of the stairs, Wesley gestured toward the living room and turned toward the kitchen to find something to be hospitable with, but he tossed an answer back to Lucas before he left the room.

"Yeah. Very quietly, but legally. I'll do it legal to keep it quiet."

Lucas followed Wesley to the kitchen. He was not concerned with following any traditional standards of social grace.

"Good idea all around. I might have suggested something like it myself."

"You think I should move away?"

"I'm scared for you, man. The coverage of your alleged drama a few months back is nothing compared to what's online right up to today, the anti-social media."

"I'm not scared any more. I'm passive. Just starting over." Wesley's hand was resting on a cabinet door but he was not sure why. The cabinets had already been emptied. He had been living for a week out of a small cardboard box of kitchen utensils. "Let me make you some tea or would you rather beer?"

"Beer," Lucas answered succinctly. He followed Wesley to the refrigerator and hovered by his shoulder while Wesley fumbled through the drawer for an opener. "Can't I just twist it off?"

"I guess so. I don't know. I don't drink 'em. They're just here in case of visitors."

"You have many visitors out here in the 'burbs?"

"Hardly ever. None lately."

Wesley found some crackers in his box and spread them onto a paper napkin. They drifted back into the living room. Wesley took a cracker and sat on the sofa. He had nothing to drink.

"What do you know about the 'burbs? Have you ever been this far out of DC without boarding an airplane?" Lucas was from downtown Chicago and always made a point of how urbane it was even though it was neither New York nor LA.

"So I don't know NoVA. Am I missing anything?"

"I don't know anything about anything anymore." Wesley replied softly.

Lucas leaned forward. "I know something, something big enough to draw me outside the Beltway."

Wesley reached for another cracker. "Take one. I have plenty more," he offered. Lucas looked down at the napkin and took a cracker but did not eat it.

"Remember that woman you never met: Nori Odoi? The writer?" Lucas asked with a smile, remembering the woman he had traced to Paris a few months earlier. Neither had any intention back then of contacting her - they enjoyed, each for his own reasons, knowing where she had gone. They might have followed up to learn why she had moved, but they thought that was getting too personal. Wesley called it "creepy" when Lucas mentioned it would be possible and Lucas immediately agreed.

"I remember her," Wesley answered. "You come out here today to see her house?"

"I felt smart for finding her. Her going to Paris made it a little challenging. I figured maybe I was smart enough to find Samantha."

"Did you find her?"

"Actually, yes; in a way."

"So where is she?"

"Wait. You have to understand she was way hard to find. She did not want to be found for sure. First off, she is not real. Samantha is her stage name. Officially registered as such. She never used it for any stage but our office. She is a plant. A trap for you."

"Someone wanted to ruin my life and hired an actress to do it?"

"Apparently."

"That's too good to be possible. At least it would have been good if you had found this out while I still had Mattie.

"I've been working on this since that first day. There's nothing good about it now, my friend. Somebody wanted to hurt you really bad. I can only suppose you know who."

"Not after me, I think."

"Come on. That much hatred? At least you know someone crazy and rich enough to do this."

"I meant, not me, I was not the target. But how could **you** know this? Is this a good guess on your part or gospel truth?"

"I know you enough to know you don't want the technical details, not on a computer exercise and that's what this was. I had help from some friends in the business. I would not come to you in my state of panic if I were not sure.

I got her social' from her file in the office. It's not hard in our office to find something like that."

Lucas did not look to be in any panic, but Wesley realized what an oddity it was for Lucas to travel out to the suburbs and even to hide his car from view when he came. Only one person could have hired an actress like this and only one reason could have motivated him.

"And I know you, Lucas, well enough to understand you are not prone to panic. Look, I would not have asked you to get into this. Your tidbit is just not enough to tell me what this is about. What a champ you are for believing in me and doing what you did! Now I am agreeing with you that you should be scared and I want you to get out of it. I didn't know who I was running away from and now I do. That will make it a lot easier to hide." He took another cracker and the room was silent but for the sound of his chewing. "So can I speak to her, you think?"

"Sure, I have her cell and everything, but maybe you would be better sending the police. She must have broken some laws with what she did. Whatever made her do that, she is something nasty."

"Nasty? I guess so," Wesley answered sarcastically. "The police have not been helpful so far in finding Mattie. They are less and less helpful. They told me to stay in NoVA unless I report to them. Seems they've decided without any evidence that I have done away with Mattie out of embarrassment over some girl they can't find but you can. Maybe this information would motivate someone with police power to look beyond the idea of a domestic dispute but I think I need to know more before I can find which police to trust. Some of the higher level ones I met are especially unsympathetic. My lawyer said I should not trust them completely and run every query through them. And I am not sure I trust him, my lawyer, anymore either. At the least, I can try to find a way to know more without threatening someone who could harm Mattie further."

"You think someone is holding her? You think she has been harmed already?"

"Mattie did not disappear on the basis of that phony story. The story was just to hide that she was taken, kidnapped I mean. It sounds silly and paranoid to say it but that's what it is. There is no way she would just disappear on her own over that Samantha call. I have no idea where she is and only a small idea about why she is there but Samantha must know, or maybe she knows... maybe knows something. Actually, the ideas are popping in and out of my head right now. If you can get me to her, there is hope of a breakthrough. Maybe my life is not the waste I was starting to think it was turning into."

"So what's your idea for who's behind Samantha's act?"

For a moment Wesley imagined this partnership of two amateur sleuths tracking down Samantha and making a deal to trade silence on her role for getting Mattie back. Then he realized how far over his head he would be. Already he had walked into a trap in complete naivete and lost his wife and reputation. They would be two schoolyard hoopsters facing an NBA team in their game of corruption.

"No way, Lucas. I am not letting you get any deeper into this mess. What's next..."

"I'm already in it. Let's talk it out anyway."

"Really, this is more than nasty. You have a great wife and two kids. You have already stuck your neck out more than you should have. I'm going away and leaving no forwarding address. Mostly I planned to hide, but maybe now I can try to fight back, especially if Mattie is still out there.”

“’If’ she is?”

“Yeah, ‘if’. I don’t know the situation in detail but anything is possible. I think you already realized that. You, man, need to be smart about your family. You don’t want a call to your wife like the one Mattie got.”

“That’s true. And I don’t abandon my friends either.”

Wesley had to pause at this retort, and nodded slightly to himself to acknowledge what his friend was saying.

“I’ll stay in touch and if I need something you can do without risk, I’ll get back to you on it. Meanwhile, drink your beer. I got to finish cleaning out my garage ‘cause I’m pulling out of here in a couple days. And now you’re going to tell me where I’m going.”

Lucas was not happy with what Wesley was saying but he saw the logic in it and did not argue. He showed his concurrence by tilting back his head to take in the rest of the beer. Wesley stood up but did not return to the garage.

“You have Samantha’s contact info written down for me?”

Lucas nodded and took an envelope from inside his shirt. “I addressed it to you and put a stamp on the envelope in case I dropped it or something.”

Lucas led the way down the stairs and Wesley asked from behind, “You ever hear her called ‘Sammie?’”

“Doubt it. If someone had said something about ‘Sammy’, I would not have thought of Samantha.”

“That’s what she called herself on the phone to Mattie.”

“Makes her sound cute.”

"She was pretty cute."

"Exactly. She was a cute girl. She did not belong in a serious place like our office."

"I like your point, but our place is not any more serious than a lot of places that do just fine with cute girls, I imagine. But our place is not a place where anyone really cares what you look like, don't you think? And if you are that good looking in a superficial way, you know, cute, you tend to go where it does you some good."

"I never thought she belonged with us... not that she was acting, just that she would not last. Those low level political appointees, you know..."

Wesley looked at the information Lucas had handed him. She was in California. He did not know the West Coast. He had always dismissed it as a mirror image of what he knew in the east, except for having bigger surf, newer money, and relatively recent political power, the latter being the difference he cared about. Of course he had to admit Washington institutions were not old in relation to those in Europe or China or India or the Middle East or Japan or many other places whose roots he did not know well, but political within America was centered in DC and the forces that took Mattie were old school political.

Wesley noticed his head had been shaking. "Sorry, Lucas, my mind is wandering. It does not want to deal with the clues you've brought me. They're giving me a rush of ideas about what I can do after nearly giving up on doing anything meaningful; at least they seem to enable action."

"Take your time, Wes."

"San Francisco? This, this... I balk at using the words that describe what this is or who this is: a conspiracy, a mob, white-collar gang, kidnapping, murder, fraud or con. I want to get Mattie back but I think I am scared to do anything against ***them***. She was taken or convinced to go away by people with more power than I could ever assemble. With the effort they went to get control of her, I can see they're not about to let me get away with anything. So, if I try anyway, having damn little left to lose, I'll have to do it alone. Then whatever happens is my fault and no one is hurt by my desperate attempt at heroism."

"Or to your credit if it works out."

"I can't visualize this working out."

"Yeah, me neither, but I also can't visualize you dropping it."

"Yeah, me neither. What the hell should I do? You don't have to try to answer that. I'll do something. I'll act. I just gotta get focused."

"So do you already have a theory about what happened to her, to Mattie? All I did was track down an actress."

"I'll tell you this much; I know who's likely behind it. Mattie was closing in on an investigation. But she didn't give me any details and I didn't listen closely to what she did say. Of course her office won't help me. I doubt she kept them fully informed on every idea while doing her investigation. I may have an ace in my hand."

He did not tell Lucas any more than this hint but there was a basis for believing Mattie's investigation was the reason for the conspiracy. He had found a letter tucked in his back door a week after the disaster began. The letter was from a lawyer who said he had some sealed evidence Mattie had given him and that he would release it in ways she had instructed, including telling Wesley more, unless the lawyer heard from her every thirty days or less. The lawyer included some things only Mattie and Wesley would know. It also said Wesley should not pursue the case as long as the lawyer was hearing from her. Wesley did not find the letter completely convincing. It should have included a way to contact the lawyer. It probably, he thought, came from the kidnappers in order to keep him quiet. When he got the note, he had run out of ideas on what he could do to help her and he did not trust the police to find her lawyer so it hardly mattered. Now, however, Lucas had given him a lead, a lead the police should have been able to find in the first week. It seemed they were not trying very hard to help, maybe even protecting the conspiracy.

"And you haven't heard anything from her or about her in all this time, all these weeks, months it been now, I guess?"

"I hear you thinking I'm a fool to believe she's still alive if I think this person she was closing in on is so dangerous. Maybe she's not. Maybe she put some documentation someplace safe to protect herself. Maybe it protects me too." Wesley heard himself saying more than he wanted to say to Lucas. Let Lucas have reason to hope his help was not too late. "That's the thread on which I hang my hopes. Anyway, you gave me something I can do. ...Talk to this actress and see if she knows anything or if I can use her to get the FBI or somebody like that to follow up. At this point, the police in all its forms have given up on me, decided I am crazy to deny I ran her off with infidelity, an old story, a waste of their time unless a body turns up someday. I am surprised I could not find someone competent to take me seriously and I am trying not to see the conspiracy reaches into law enforcement, you know. All levels of law enforcement seem more threatening to me than sympathetic.

It feels as if there has been communication among them. I am in a perfect position to become paranoid. How can I tell if I am building fears from mere insecurity? I am not deluding myself that I am important, but it seems possible that Mattie is important to someone other than me. Seeking self-importance is a basis for paranoia, right? I get sent to social workers who are sympathetic but haven't anything to offer but sympathy. They won't confront the officers of the law. I might need a good lawyer, one way better than I could afford."

Lucas nodded but held his tongue. Wesley was talking himself out and Lucas saw his role as the ear in the room to legitimize Wesley's speaking aloud.

It would not be easy or cheap to chase her down. Wesley knew nothing of the techniques it would require. Still, there was nothing else to do once he got away from NoVA. He had not planned to look for a new job or to do anything more specific than feel some peace. ...Simply to get away from the memories, the illogical embarrassment, the glaring lack of sympathy from most of the people he had regarded as friends. What should he have expected from his own community, wholly dedicated to career advancement, believing their particular careers embodied a higher ethic than the quotidian traditions of chasing lucre in support of a core family, buying the shiniest innovations coming to market, and paying lip service to a religion when its holidays came along?

He had visualized his future as a transient. It was not suicide; he would be existing somewhere. Away from Washington, a career was not necessary -- it was enough to wash dishes or something else to eke out his daily bread. It was an appealing idea if he could stop thinking about Mattie.

Part II: On the Road

11. Starting Out

My paranoia seems well justified. Raleigh and whomever is working with him or whomever he is working for in whatever scheme underlies my ridiculous circumstance, and has won over my friends, my colleagues, the media and the justice system. It has been done but my paranoia does not contain the usual conclusion that I am worth the trouble. Could it have been so easy to take everything from me? It seems like a lot of effort on his part but perhaps it was easy for someone with immense power, someone higher up than Raleigh. And that top-level decisionmaker probably sees no threat from me. All I did to fight back was tell the truth in the face of a clever, well executed scheme to smear me. Every step I took had been obvious, anticipated in advance by my unknown enemy and discredited before I took it. Unknown! Raleigh was the only person I heard Mattie say she was targeting, but it could have been anyone. She wouldn't tell me what she was doing. That was proper but it left me naked.

Wesley did not know how to live without the securities of countless institutions that had always supported him. He did not think of himself as a person of privilege but that is because he could imagine privileges he never had: no inherited millions, no brilliant talent, no family connections directly to power and fame. At the same time he was aware that he had followed an easy path open to only a tiny fraction of a percent of the humans on earth. A young, healthy, educated, White American male lacking privilege? He'd had a bank account since he was ten, a social security card since fifteen, a driver's license since sixteen, a wife since twenty-three, a job with the Federal government since twenty-five, a diplomatic passport since he was thirty. He had never avoided the police nor had reason to. His wild youth was a fiction he had given himself because he thought he ought to have had one, lightly laced with behaviors his mother might not have approved: one drunken night to see what it felt like, a speeding ticket one morning when he had overslept, some indiscreet flirting with a young married woman when he was himself single, an angry outburst at a party when a drunk insulted Nelson Mandela. What else? His poverty in college had not been enough to cause him to drop out for lack of tuition or to take a job that would shame him in later years. The lowly, although adequate, jobs he took in his student years were soon a distant memory, no more relevant than the misfortunes of a character he had known from a book.

It perplexes me that Raleigh, I'll call my nemesis that for lack of anything more accurate, Raleigh, has stopped messing with me. He seems to have expected me to give up after all appeals to conventional legal remedy were frustrated. Is that what spoiled, privileged people do? Is that what I have done? Not sure, but I don't think so, not at this moment anyway...

If Raleigh had been willing to go so far as to kidnap Mattie or worse, he could have gotten me completely out of the way. I may not have shown much initiative in my first fifty years, but I am... well, maybe it is a fully rational decision to leave me alone, the unproven but widely accepted visible explanation for Mattie's disappearance.

It is also possible Mattie is protecting me by arranging to release some or all of the evidence she is holding with her lawyer to protect herself. She could not keep track of my health and welfare but the lawyer could be watching me. It would be a messy standoff. They could not hurt her too much or her lawyer would let out the evidence. They could not hurt me or the lawyer would let it out. Either way, she would lose her leverage and be finished. Maybe she was negotiating to destroy part of it in return for a guarantee of safety for me or herself.

Stop kidding yourself. You have no idea what Raleigh is thinking or doing or why he is thinking or doing it.

I did not give up on Mattie. I just had no idea of what to do. I was overmatched and knew it. Now Lucas, a man willing and able to reach beyond the proper assigned measures, has given me something, a knife I can carry to the gunfight. Not enough in itself but enough to prove I've not given up. I wonder if Raleigh realized that taking away my privileges might push me to change my tactics, to do something unexpected? You win another round, Raleigh, like all the rounds where I play you by the rules. I don't know how to do otherwise but here comes! You won't be looking for me in San Francisco.

Wesley did not know how to live off the grid, how to hide from someone with access to the instruments of official power. He had seen The Bourne Affair and Day of the Jackal and knew he lacked the heroic proficiencies those movies used to fascinate an audience of dreamy, adventure-starved boys. Nonetheless he would borrow whatever he had found doable in the dramatic fictions he had seen or read or imagined on his own. For starters, he would keep it simple, avoid electronics, stay away from all that had identified him in the past.

He took cash from an ATM, but not so much that it would cause suspicion. He sold their cars for cash. Altogether, he assembled fifteen thousand dollars in twenty-dollar bills. He would put the house on the market after he left and planned to move the money from the sale into cash as soon as he could. If someone was watching him, they would know by then that he had run.

When he took a load of things to the Goodwill store, he wandered through afterwards and bought a couple humble outfits, right down to the underwear and socks. He felt a little guilty for taking advantage of the low prices but figured he had good justification for using these clothes to help him hide. He was pleased to find he liked wearing them. He had dressed well for work so he was used to moderately expensive clothes with up-to-date styling. It was helpful to his professional reputation and, more than that, Mattie appreciated his effort. But it always felt like a costume, not true to his nature. Going better than his nature had been acceptable but not comfortable. The final touch to his appearance was a cheap haircut. He could not see the difference between cheap ones and expensive ones but since Mattie had always insisted on his going to her salon, he suspected there was a way to see a difference.

The last time he had ridden an intercity bus was to get to his sophomore year of college. If he dropped out of view unexpectedly, no one would be watching the buses for him. A ticket to San Francisco cost just over $200. The trip would take a little over three days. He bought cheaper glasses and cut his hair and changed into a used country-and-western outfit before going to the bus station. No cowboy hat-- that would be too obvious, but a style no one who knew him would expect. He bought some C&W music to carry in his duffle. On the bus he carried *People* magazine and stuck a well-reviewed, thin novel, *Prince of the Clouds,* between the pages. He did not recognize himself.

When he climbed on board the bus and headed for a seat near the front, as this felt right to him and then remembered he was not to be himself. He looked down the aisle and found an attractive woman and did what he would not normally do -- took the seat beside the most attractive woman with an open space beside her. He asked if the seat were taken already. It was not necessary, he thought, to be rude just to hide himself.

"Going all the way to St. Louis?" he asked. Up close he saw she was older than himself, perhaps significantly so. She had some wrinkles on her face and some gray in her hair. He could not tell much about her body but her face was nicely composed if a bit bony, suggesting she was slim. Her shoulders looked broad at the moment. She wore some make-up, even a little lipstick, an item not common back in his office. She looked good to him. In his new persona, he was able to think of her in that quick, superficial way, as if he did not have a wife he loved which may have been the situation in truth anyway. "Am I married," he wondered, "if Mattie no longer exists?"

"Jus' ta Midway Plaza," she answered, rolling her eyes up to see him without turning her head. "You know, middle of Pennsylvania."

It was too small a response to encourage him to say more, but he did not want to leave it hanging open so he closed it off saying, "I'm going to St. Louis." He pronounced it as "Looey," not "Lewis." He knew he could not effect an accent but he tried to insert a word when he thought of one he could say in an alternative way.

She nodded slightly to show she understood although that was unnecessary. Then she waited for his next remark. She was showy enough to expect a man who chose to sit beside her on the bus would want to talk. He took out his magazine. It hid his book inside, a book that might reveal more of who he was than the supermarket checkout aisle publication would show. She leaned back and waited. More passengers clambered aboard, not filling all the seats before the door was closed and the driver announced their departure. Without the commotion of their finding seats and putting away luggage, the fuselage settled into a static state. Wesley looked out the window as much as he could from his aisle seat without being obnoxious.

He did not feel much like reading, not right away. There would be plenty of time for that on this trip. On overseas flights, he delayed opening his book to absorb the commotion of the start-up and to look over the people. They were seldom interesting in themselves but they always comprised a complex set of peculiarities, always made the setting unique and by observing them, he could stave off boredom a while and shorten the feel of the flight. Then he would read fifty pages of a book or until his eyes tired enough for him to rest comfortably before the distraction of a meal. The bus clientele differed in details from the airline crowd but there was much overlap. Wesley did not want to turn the trip into a mental assignment so he did not try to list the differences and similarities, but he did try to be generous in his unconscious assessment of his current fellow travelers. He believed in the working class and presumed that was what surrounded him. Although he had never been a member of that class, menial jobs during his school years notwithstanding, he had an idea of what made it up and he was troubled to realize how little his contact had been. He had never felt like a powerful figure in Washington, but he could see that the standard critique that people like him were out of touch with the mass of America had truth in it from his example. He looked around himself to see what the folks nearby looked like. The light was not as good as on an international flight and he could only see a half dozen faces with any clarity. There was not much to entertain him other than the book he had brought along.

"You live there?" she asked Wesley. It had been five minutes since the bus had started moving.

"St. Louis? Nah. I live in Oregon, eastern Oregon where we don't keep the hippies." Wesley did not know what people living in Oregon sounded like but he doubted she did either. She laughed a moment at his joke. The ice had been broken. Neither said more immediately. Wesley closed the magazine to show he was not reading. He looked forward. She turned her head toward him and looked him hard.

After a further lag of thirty seconds she said "I live in Pittsburg but I'm seeing friends in Harrisburg first."

It was an invitation to engage more. It showed a confidence in her appeal although the confidence probably signaled that she had assessed Wesley as not so good looking as to be beyond her control and not so bad looking as to be avoided altogether.

"Never been there, not yet anyway. All I've seen of it is Three Rivers Stadium on TV when the Steelers are playing."

"They shoulda done better last year. They had the horses; just too many injuries."

Wesley had long before lost interest in watching football but paid some attention to it for occasions when it lubricated the conversation. He did not know anything about last year's Steelers.

"Rothesburger," he said.

Any quarterback's name sounds like a short version of a big story. She nodded as if he had said something appropriate and maybe even insightful.

Wesley thought the conversation was going well despite its glacial pace. It was certainly nice to be having it, an everyday sort of back and forth without any Washington issues at the center. *I ought to ask her name,* he thought. Then he realized the conversation was over since she was snoring. He looked over at her slouching into a deep sleep. She was collapsing into her seat like a deflating balloon. When she finally stabilized, her head was leaning on Wesley's upper arm, not quite as high as his shoulder. He stared at her face. It looked lovely in the dim light, not an angle he had ever seen in a fashion photo, but very relaxed, as if she knew him and trusted him, as if he were protecting her or, at least, comforting her, except that the posture was entirely unintended, the mere outcome of gravity and cramped seating. Her closeness felt good in place of the conversation, neither of which was substantive enough to be taken seriously but both of which helped Wesley get through the hour until his arm went numb and he had to change his position which woke her up whereupon she quickly leaned the opposite way.

Wesley turned on the light over his seat and read for a while. It was well past his usual bedtime and he was relaxed, glad to be doing something toward finding Mattie but he was not tired. He felt more confident than was justified by the clue Lucas had handed him. He did not know who was responsible ultimately for Mattie's disappearance, nor was he close to learning anything that would justify any legal action. Moreover, he even lacked any evidence that Mattie was still alive. The note from her maybe-lawyer felt certain to be just a ruse to keep him quiet although he often thought of it as an encouraging sign she might be out there plotting a comeback. He knew in his core that his confidence was excessive, so he avoided reviewing what he knew or guessed. He had gone over it all so many times there was nothing more to be drawn from it. He needed more information and he was determined to get some in San Francisco though it might not be the specific information he needed. When his mind drifted off the page of his book, he imagined impossible scenarios in which he gets his revenge with vigilante violence as in dozens of movies he had never watched but which he knew from involuntarily seeing their trailers.

Suddenly the words of his novel asserted themselves. The protagonist, a certain Colonel Carlo Terzo, was a military strategist, a professor, who had never seen a battle despite going through World War II in the Italian army. His researches assumed that military history should be analyzed for lessons in life. In the novel, Terzo was retired and lecturing his lone student when he remarked: "You never win, ...except in rare exceptions, by merely defending yourself. You must, sooner or later, resolve to attack."[i] It would have been an obvious comment in another context, but Wesley appreciated the erudition of the fictional Terzo, or the book's author, and this bit of advice seemed to speak to him directly.

He saw the advice applied in his own few months as a fencer in high school. He had a rival on the epee squad, a tall fellow who did not look athletic and therefore it bothered Wesley that he was so hard to beat. They were in the same class and were equivalent in talent but differed in their approach. Wesley followed the advice of their coach and was always on the attack. He felt it covered up certain shortcomings, his inability to parry the second and third moves of an attack from an opponent, and it forced him to fence intuitively rather than planning what he was doing. He was always pushing forward, probing for a weak response, not thinking ahead more than a fraction of a second, using the feel of the blade more than his eyes. His rival never, ever attacked. Wesley wondered what he was thinking because he was always reacting rather than acting. Maybe he anticipated what attack Wesley would bring. Perhaps he knew Wesley too well because he won most of the matches between them. And yet Wesley did far better in matches against other schools, not enough to win consistently but enough to be the best epee at his school. His aggressiveness seemed to help him more than made sense to him. In his coursework, he was cautious and systematic, but in fencing, he knew to attack.

He had confronted Mattie's presumed kidnappers with well-considered public statements and patient replies to the absurd legal charges threatened against him, mild and careful as his approach to a career, as he had adopted in law school and as served him well to that point in life, but it was not working anymore and he would look for a way to attack, listen to Terzo, maybe allow his intuition to help, to temper rather than to suppress it in favor of predictable response. He could not plan how to go forego planning, but, like a fencer, he could press forward and feel for an opportunity in the moment. Whoever it was who had done this did not fear him as much as they had feared Mattie. They thought they knew what he would do or could do. He would do something else, something out of character, something bold, a lunge, a *fleche* attack. No warning would be issued to be *en guarde*.

Around 4:00 a.m., less than a half hour short of the Midway Plaza stop, he caught himself dropping the book and he quickly packed it into his pocket, thinking it might blow his cover to expose the book title to someone. People such as he was claiming to be did not read Italian novels on the intercity bus. He still had the innocuous *People* covering the book but if he dropped it and someone picked it up helpfully, that person might notice from the small font and fine paper and lengthy paragraphs that this was not a familiar style, not pulp of the sort associated with a person as he appeared to be. And then questions could come up. He would not be invisible. It was an absurd fear, fueled by his imagined B movie scenarios, and he resolved to hide more consciously the side of his real self that was a book snob. Maybe, he considered, he could carry an actual pulp novel in a different pocket in case someone was nosey.

He was just reaching the land of Nod when he felt the bus sway into a sharp, slow turn and bright lights flooded the interior. They had arrived at Midway Plaza. Wesley squeezed his seatmate on the arm to wake her. He considered taking out his handkerchief to wipe the spittle from her lip. It was too grand a gesture for an invisible man but he remembered it for another day when he might be himself again with another woman who was not Mattie.

It less of a gesture than a practical thing that he stood in the aisle to let her out without climbing over him. He asked which bags were hers from the overhead rack but she had only a folded, light jacket up there. She also had a large handbag that had been under her feet and he wished it were large enough that he could legitimately offer to carry it out for her. As it was, that would have been suspiciously inappropriate, although it would not have been clear what inappropriate motive might have been behind it.

She turned around before going down the aisle and said, using full words, "It was nice talking to you."

Wesley had too many thoughts in his head at that moment to respond quickly-- he knew he should not act as felt natural, however, he was not sure what the person he was playing would have said -- and then she was gone and Wesley concluded his silence had been exactly the right response. He had smiled broadly in the instant when he was trying to formulate the right words. He doubted she could have noticed it in the poor lighting and, besides, while departing, she had hardly looked his way.

Wesley slid over beside the window and awaited a new traveling companion. A few people looked at his seat without making any motion to sit beside him. He tried to look safe but doubted a woman would choose to sit beside a middle-aged man of his unimpressive appearance. The bus door closed and he thought he was lucky to have space to lounge loosely for another nap. The bus backed up a few feet and then opened its door again. A young Black man with no luggage and no coat scooted up the stairs and went straight to the seat beside Wesley as if it were reserved for him.

"Hey!" he said as if they knew each other and Wesley nodded back to him, uttering his own "Hey," but it soon was obvious the conversation was over in that twice uttered word of no particular meaning. Anonymity was fine with Wesley for a middle-of-the-night ride.

Sometime before dawn but when some brightening was reaching the lower edge of the sky, Wesley sat up straight, conceding that the discomfort of his various postures exceeded his exhaustion and defeated further sleep. The young man pulled off his headphones and asked "You vote for Trump?"

Wesley could hear words coming from the earbuds on the man's lap, suggesting that he was listening to talk radio or, perhaps, a news program.

In his stupor, Wesley did not remember to play his role and quickly answered, "No, no, no, three times over. I voted for Hillary and it was not a close call." Then he realized he was playing himself and stopped before adding details about having worked for certain candidates or about being a Federal worker proud to have served under Obama.

The man in the seat beside Wesley did not notice anything odd in the reply. He pulled his ballcap over his eyes and said, "All right then. I can go to sleep here beside you."

Since Wesley was now awake, he took out his book and started to read. The fellow beside him lifted his head to peer under the brim of his cap and asked "Good book?"

Wesley closed the book on his finger to hide the title. "Good enough... You know, if the light bothers you, I can just put the book down. It's still nighttime, I'd say."

"The light don't trouble me. I'm only going to Pittsburgh anyway," he answered without opening his eyes. "'Good enough' don't sound too good to me. You should read a book you really like."

"Well, this is the one I have."

"Sounds like a lousy excuse for keepin' your woman. 'This is the one I have.' Keep lookin', man. Life's too short to waste on 'good enough'."

Whoa! Must be a teacher or a preacher. Wesley looked him over and could not see a preacher in him.   "I know you're right and this is still the only book I have."

The man lifted his cap to the top of his head but continued to slouch comfortably. "You married?"

Wesley was not used to lying and saw this as an opportunity to practice. He realized he should have worked out a complete backstory for the character he was playing and regretted he would not have a chance to do so before answering.

"I was," he answered, hoping he had put a recognizable tinge of sadness in his answer that would justify his delay in responding. "Divorced now. I don't see her or anything so we don't fight. No kids, anyway." He thought his neck might be reddening with the lie. It was too dark to be seen.

"She vote for Trump?"

"No. I mean I don't really know. I haven't seen her in a couple years, but she's smarter than me so I am pretty sure she would not go with him. So... are you married to the love of your life?"

"No, I never met her. Wish I had. 'Least I didn't settle for good enough."

"Still looking though?"

"Not really. Got to live my life. She's missed her chance."

"Come on, you're still young."

"Young for some things... not for marrying. Women want to find somebody by the time they're twenty. When you're past thirty, they figure there's something wrong with you. Sometimes I think they're right about that. If I had a family, I mean if I made a family, I'd really stick with 'em. I'm too old to be starting out now."

"Well, don't turn her down if she finds you."

"I have a girlfriend but nothing serious. Just for company somedays, not all the time. I can only take a woman who's not really in love with me for a few hours. We got nothing to talk about, you know."

Wesley decided to call the conversation a win and to end it there. It made sense to stop talking with that last point. If there was nothing to talk about with a woman, there must not be much to say to a stranger on a bus. He reopened his book and tilted himself in a way that hid the title, but he could not focus on Sartorelli and his "Prince of the Clouds." He felt like Peter in Gethsemene, having denied Mattie to save his own neck. She would understand, better than Jesus had if Wesley understood the undercurrent of that famous passage in Matthew.

The sudden silence felt rude to Wesley. He should have added a closing thought, but then, such courtesy came from his old persona. It was good that he was not acting like himself but not as liberating as he expected it would be to forgo the polite responses of his class. Habits die hard.

After a few moments, his eyes became heavy. He reminded himself it was the middle of the night and closed the book on his finger before remembering to put the bookmark on the page. By the time his hand had fallen into his lap, he was dreaming, aware that he was dreaming, arriving in San Francisco where Mattie was waiting for him at the bus terminal. "Who says," he dreamed to himself, "you can't control your dreams?" But if he could really control the dream, he would not have remembered inside the dream that he was dreaming this.

12. Rusty

The bus schedule gave Wesley an hour in Pittsburg, time enough for a good breakfast. A diner within view of the bus station was open and busy when he came in the door at six fifteen. This was just how he envisioned his trip would be in his new persona. He sat at the counter, remembering how he used to eat breakfast at a drug store with his grandfather during the summer he spent in Florida when he was twelve. He had not sat on a stool at a counter since then. Mattie had asked him to avoid eggs ever since a doctor had given him a moderately high reading on his cholesterol. Sausage was a treat reserved for holidays. He had not looked at the menu before ordering three eggs sunny side up and plenty of buttered white toast to sop up the yolk. A working man's fare was essential to maintaining a full disguise. He had the link sausage and black coffee. He only drank lattes in his former self. He measured a rounded teaspoon of sugar for the coffee. He thought it would make him look like a regular coffee guy rather than a meticulous one.

The breakfast came out of the kitchen so fast Wesley wondered if his order was so common, the cook had it on a plate before he walked in. He slid one of the eggs onto a triangle of toast, salted and peppered it liberally, and then sliced it into two oversized bites. He ducked his head toward the plate as he brought one dripping forkful to his lips and tasted an ancient memory of a time when a mouthful was really full and needed no apology. He washed it down with coffee before it had all been swallowed. At this moment, he was not himself and it felt very good.

After paying, fifteen minutes remained to get back on the bus. The clock in the diner matched his watch but Wesley did not want to cut it too close, so he did not linger when he passed a vendor with a wagon of beautiful looking fruit. The sun had cleared the horizon, not enough to provide any warmth, but enough to make it a new day; a bright, fresh start, insulated by one more step from Washington, if not from the troubles that had driven Wesley outside the beltway. After a few more steps, he turned back to the fruit seller. His subconscious claimed there were pomegranates on the wagon. It had to be his imagination, but he went back to confirm his sanity. There were pomegranates and he took the risk of a minute's delay to buy one for a snack after he woke up from the nap his breakfast would induce.

When he climbed back onto the bus, a boy was sitting in his seat, that is, the window seat Wesley had occupied. He asked the boy if the aisle seat was taken and the boy nodded "no" but climbed out anyway and motioned to Wesley to sit by the window. The boy was self-assured in his actions but did not utter a sound. He was twelve years old although Wesley could only guess his age roughly as something short of puberty. He wore denim jeans pressed into a crease along the legs, revealing to Wesley thereby something of the boy's maternal influence. He wore a western-cut shirt, also crisply laundered, revealing a hint of the boy's destination, since it would not be easy to find such a shirt in the Pittsburg area, or so Wesley imagined. Wesley offered the window position to the boy and received only a nodded "no" again, so Wesley clambered across to the window side. As he leaned past the boy he saw a scrap of paper had been pinned to the boy's shirt, including in large letters, a name, so he said, "Excuse me, Rusty."

"I can't talk to anyone who isn't in a uniform," the boy declared.

"OK," Wesley answered, and being unable to just ignore this well-behaved boy, he added, "If you decide you want to look out the window a while, just point to it and I'll move. I've seen it all before."

"I'm not supposed to sit where I am boxed in," the boy said in further violation of his rule of silence.

"OK, I guess I never thought of that. Still, if you change your mind, just point; then if you want to move back, we'll shift again. It can be a long ride."

Rusty sat upright, facing forward as if he were watching a movie screen toward the front of the bus.

"It's all right if you just listen, right?" Wesley asked. "You can just nod if it's allowed."

The boy knew he was being mocked but he nodded in the affirmative through his scowl and then looked at Wesley in anticipation of whatever was going to be said.

Wesley nodded back at him and settled silently into his seat. He studied his pomegranate, having not looked at one closely since he moved away from his parents long ago. With his finger he poked at the dried stamens but the tube was too small to reach inside. When he was a boy, he could have done it. Maybe his fingers were smaller; maybe his mother got larger pomegranates. After a few seconds the boy understood no conversation was forthcoming from Wesley and turned his attention back to the front of the bus as it pulled away from the station. Wesley watched the dim and dull streets go by, the bus changing direction several times, going through neighborhoods the residents would regard as distinctive but which blurred together for Wesley into a dismal urban landscape worth his attention at the moment only because the effortless movement of a passenger bus through the maze was diverting. He knew he could have and, perhaps should have, regarded more deeply the post-industrial scene and the circumstances of its inhabitants.

After all, he had not been to the rustbelt since it had earned its moniker, but he had lost any interest in learning anything that did not bear on his mission to find Mattie.

Wesley saw this excursion through the city and suburbs as a chance to hone his new identity. If he lived here, what would he be thinking, doing, wanting, earning, loving, hating, eating, reading? Why would he get on an intercity bus? The questions came easily enough but the only answer that thrust into his consciousness was how seeing the suburbs composed of single-family homes on neat, quarter-acre plots bordered by sidewalks and serving quotidian families unconcerned with the nasty dramas inside the beltway was that his highest priority on a beautiful spring day might be mowing the lawn. It was an arrogant put-down of middle-American stereotype but it was truer to his early years than a diner breakfast. He had loved the scent of cut grass when he was too young to use the mower and then, when he was older, mowing became one of the few chores around the house he did not resent doing when his father asked him to help out on the weekend. It was easy and sweaty and noisy and fragrant. He liked seeing the finished portion of the lawn accumulate like a graph of his labors.

Eventually the bus reached a highway and the movement outside the window became a fast, steady flow that irritated Wesley with its apparent attempt to hypnotize him. He turned his eyes to peer at Rusty and saw the boy still stared ahead. "I've been on this bus since Baltimore."

The boy turned his head a few degrees.

"I tried to sleep and did not get much but now I'm wide awake. I'll feel miserable tomorrow."

The boy turned his head all the way toward Wesley.

"Are you going far? I'll give you some options and you nod when I get the right one. OK, let's say 'far' is all day, at least until dark. Are you riding this bus far?"

The boy nodded cautiously and affirmatively.

"Are you riding it really far, say, most of the night too?"

The boy flashed the fingers of one hand twice.

"Ten? You're supposed arrive somewhere at ten?

The boy smiled this time and nodded "yes."

"I wonder where we are supposed to be at ten in the p.m. Let me look at my map."

Wesley unfolded a roadmap of the eastern Midwest, the kind that used to be available free at service stations. He had bought it on-line because he wanted to avoid electronic media during his trip, fearing they might somehow give away his location to his pursuers, if he had any pursuers. He had roughed up the map so it would look normal for an old map, this despite having paid dearly for it due to the seller's claim that it was in pristine condition. When he saw the boy's curiosity, he realized the map would not look normal to him regardless of its condition.

The boy took out a cell phone and called up the bus schedule while Wesley was still getting himself located. The boy leaned forward to show the phone to Wesley, not quite patronizing him but proud, at least, to have the superior technology.

"No, no, no, don't show me that," Wesley complained facetiously, shading his eyes from a view of the screen. "That thing gives you the answer. I get it. But it does not tell the important part of the story, not the part important to me because I like the trip. That thing says you will be someplace at ten o'clock and it tells a few other names of places you will be before that. My map tells me all the places we will see where we do not stop and even all the places we come near but do not see. My map tells me where the rivers we cross are going and where they came from. If you are good enough at reading it, you can see why the cities grew up where they did, and who their neighbors are and lots of stuff I cannot tell because I am not good at reading them.”

The boy turned his phone back toward Wesley to show him a map and he touched the screen to move the map along their route.

“No, no, no, don’t show me that either,” Wesley said again. “You can get the big picture with that thing or the details but not both at the same time. You have to keep adjusting it to study it so you can’t just wander your eyes over it to listen to what it has to say. And it is so small!”

The boy shook his head. “You’re just too cheap to buy a phone,” he said aloud.

“You got that right. Too cheap and too broke. But, truth is, don’t need one. Don’t need much and life is cheaper this-a-way.”

“You really don’t have a phone, Mister?” the boy asked.

“Shhh. We are in danger of having a conversation right out loud.” And then more deliberatively, “Let’s see, that’s sixteen hours from Pittsburgh. It took us about four to get from Baltimore to Midway. I believe we have a long stop in Indianapolis, so you’re going to St Louis. Am I close?”

The boy nodded without enthusiasm. He was not impressed that Wesley could guess his destination, already knowing the time and the route. He knew Wesley was not being serious but did not know how to deal with an adult like this. He began to fear this was exactly the kind of person his mother had in mind when she said to talk to no one not in uniform. Nervously, he focused on his cell phone, checking his mail or his Facebook page or Instagram account or whatever boys his age check to keep from being bored or to avoid interacting with a person beside them.

Without looking away from the small screen in his hand, Rusty said very distinctly "Shoals Valley."

"Shoals Valley?" Wesley repeated with a slight rise at the end barely indicating it as a question.

"I live in Shoals Valley. Ever heard of it?"

"Shoals Valley, Missouri?"

"That's right."

"No I never heard of it. I hardly heard of any place in Missouri. What's the population?"

"How should I know," the boy answered insolently.

"Hey, you live there. I never heard of it. I'm just kind of surprised to hear there are any shoals in Missouri. My map has that a long way from the sea. And if you had some shoals, I would not look for them in a valley."

"What're 'shoals'?"

Wesley watched the boy and did not see him raise his eyes so he let the question hang. Maybe the boy would look it up on his phone. Wesley went back to *Prince of the Clouds,* carefully holding the book so the content could not be seen within the magazine cover. He nearly finished a chapter before dozing again.

He became aware of sunlight on his face. It was bothering his eyes although they had fallen closed and he thought it was affecting his dream although he could not recall anything else of the dream. At least he could say it had wakened him and then he noticed a nudge on his arm. The boy was wakening him.

"What's the matter? Is the internet down?" Wesley asked without opening his eyes.

"You were jumping, like. I thought you were having a nightmare," the boy answered.

"I already forgot what I was dreaming. Doubt it was a nightmare. I never have trouble sleeping."

The boy looked to Wesley with wide eyes as if awaiting some revelation. Wesley guessed the boy was bored. "Nothing interesting on the internet?" he asked.

"My battery's running low. I need to save it in case something comes in."

"Good idea, I'm sure," answered Wesley as if he might adopt the same strategy if he had a phone, which he did have although he was keeping it out of sight.

"What was that thing," the boy asked, "that red thing in your pocket?"

Wesley was tempted to give a long answer. He wanted to tell Rusty of being twelve years old himself and spending the summer with his grandfather in Florida, eating in the drug store and learning all the weird fruits he had growing his yard: carambolas, kumquats, longans, governor's plum, avocado, breadfruit, guava, granadilla, figs, jujube, kapok, key limes, tamarind. A whole song could be sung from their names. But his grandfather did not have pomegranates. They were his mother's special fruit. She served them for the first day of winter in honor of Persephone whose meal of six seeds doomed the earth to winter for half the year. Rusty probably did not know the story and neither would Wesley's current persona.

"Some kind of fruit. I saw it at that fruit wagon back there. The guy said you just eat the seeds. I'll try it later. If it's good, you can have some."

The bus swayed as it turned for another stop. "Columbus, Ohio" the driver announced, stretching out the "Ohio" into a song. "One hour wait for anyone going on to Indianapolis. You get a new driver. Pleasure serving you. Be in the bus on time. Don't take any extra. It's a long walk to Indiana. We are pulling out at 1:15 by the clock on the dash. It says 11:58 right now if you want to set your watches. I'll post the departure time right here on the door." He stretched his back and neck, and then opened the door, going out first to help remove luggage from under the bus. Wesley thought it was a long-winded good-bye.

"I'm getting a sandwich, I think. Looks like they might have some already made up. You want anything?" Wesley asked the boy. He was aware the offer was outside the persona he was playing and hoped it was not especially revealing of his actual self.

"No, I got money," the boy answered.

"I'm sure you do, but how will you order anything if there's no one in a uniform to ask?"

The boy smiled, knowing he was being kidded. He stood up but waited, following the custom in busses and airplanes, for those seated in front of him to exit. When it was his turn, he left, but Wesley did not follow immediately because a large woman who had been seated behind him pushed ahead. Wesley did not care about this small breach of protocol and was pleased when she apologized for it, smiling and saying, "Sorry, but I really got to go." He nodded back at her with a small smile of his own and then thought it was a violation of his character to be too friendly. She was not what anyone would describe as "attractive." She was very large, more wide than tall, and dressed in cheap, loose clothes that unintentionally revealed her corpulence. Her mousey brown hair was straight, not very long and not styled, merely clipped on the sides. Nonetheless, her smile was sweet in the way she offered it although its most conspicuous characteristic was the gap where a front incisor has once stood. To her credit, she was clean with soft clear skin and a firm step that suggested her confidence and independence. *Probably has a loving husband and three kids*, Wesley thought.

He went inside the depot shop. It looked familiar since it was the same sort of shop he saw along the interstate highways that follow the East Coast to Miami, catering to the masses who have time only to urinate and pick up snacks. Obviously those repetitive travel stops on the way to Florida did not embody the full breadth of Southern culture and he had known they did not but they had stuck in his head as what lay between Washington and south Florida, as all he was likely to see of those states when he blew through each summer on the way to visiting his parents in their retirement idyll. It was jarring to see this repulsive branch of civilization in the Midwest, a region he had never seen before, where all his impressions were built on prejudices he learned from others. He avoided the men's room while it was crowded and wandered the snack aisle. He saw a few crispy, oily, and highly artificial looking concoctions that were attractive to him except that he kept seeing them a second time though Mattie's eyes, always conscious of food's healthiness, especially when it was destined for his consumption. He settled on a thin ham-and-cheese on white bread, packaged in clear plastic with a sparse envelope of mustard. It was the healthiest fare he could see. Mattie was not there to oversee so he added a bag of something that looked like toasted trumpets or woven cornucopias which he expected to be salty.

He espied Rusty roaming the snack food aisle. Was Rusty in junior high school or just sixth grade? Wesley could remember being in sixth grade. He was sure he could have managed a long bus ride at that age although it would have been dishonest to believe he had yet become especially mature back then. When had he emerged from boyhood?

He did not feel like an adult until he met Mattie. Many years before that he reached a point where he began to be curious about things beyond himself. That might be a better measure of an important part of maturing. It came with developing an interest in science to replace toys, television, cowboys and baseball, possibly before Rusty's age. Some of those early science lessons remained at the perimeter of his current knowledge of the world. Evaporation, for example, was a lesson learned in third or fourth grade, hard to say which because he dated the memory by the room in which he learned it but those two years of school were on the same side of the building and felt about the same. They did an experiment, the first experiment he ever saw. A large bowl of water was placed on the window sill and everyone observed how full it was in the morning sunlight, and this image is why he associated it with the room. Maybe the central lesson was experimentation, about testing one's expectations, but he was fascinated at the time by the amazing fact that much of the water disappeared all on its own by the end of the school day. This was better than magic, merely the way things are. He tried it at home with a glass of water in his room. It took a long time, past the weekend, but the water completely disappeared. It was disconcerting that this phenomenon was not treated like a trick. Possibly that was because it was too slow to be dramatic. His gray-haired teacher, either Mrs. Brown if it was third grade or Mrs. Straley if it was fourth, went on to mention many ways that evaporation mattered in the world, from drying clothes to making deserts. The examples were numerous. He began to feel foolish for having never noticed it on his own. Some of the kids in class had already known about it although he doubted any knew that scientific word "evaporation."

His formal science education then languished through less talented teachers for some time although he did observe the world around him, hoping to discover things as intriguing as evaporation. For example, he became aware of morning dew and gained some understanding of its origins by listening to the clues around him, like the nightly weather report.

It was definitely in fourth grade that he learned another science fact with wide implications although it lacked the magic of moisture spontaneously appearing or disappearing. In art class, they took turns with a hand lens to look closely at yarn and cloth and thread, determining that they all consisted of fibers. It was again a lesson learned too late, too late to be the first in his class to understand an obvious fact of nature. He looked for fibers elsewhere, finding them in rope for instance, but, surprisingly, not in the new material called fiberglass. He considered asking why it was called that but was afraid the answer would be obvious so he waited for it to appear on its own, which did occur but not until a decade had passed.

The real lesson of discovering fibers was that looking more closely might reveal unanticipated truth behind appearance. He borrowed the magnifying glass from his father's desk and made a point to his parents that he was not playing at being a detective but that he was looking for fibers. They got him a microscope. It stood seven inches tall and could rotate among three lenses to see more or less magnification traded off with more or less clarity in the images. The pamphlet that came with the microscope promised more than he could tease out of the instrument but it did drive home the lesson that there was a world of the tiny that was not consistent with his intuition.

As he matured, the lessons of elementary school were replaced with more sophisticated models of the way things are. He was not aware of how much the foundations laid by Mrs. Brown and/or Mrs. Straley eased his later understanding but he remained aware of how much he learned from Mr. Wilt in seventh grade, his first teacher dedicated to the subject of science. Twenty years into a career that began after law school, nearly all Wesley knew of how an electric motor works had come from Mr. Wilt. In that class, they made one, spinning its tiny axel rapidly, beautifully and purposelessly when connected to a flashlight battery (whose source of magic he never did learn). Apart from the battery's mystery, Wesley understood how the motor worked. He envisioned making a motor that could power a go-cart or forge some other exciting improvement in his life. He never did make a motor on his own or adapt a motor to any use but since seventh grade, he felt he could have if he had wanted to enough.

§§§

Wesley was ten minutes early going back to the bus and drifted slowly while finishing his sandwich yet he nearly missed seeing Rusty turn down a row of semis. He just caught a glimpse of a boy and nearly dismissed the thought of it but realized after a few more steps that it probably was Rusty he

117

had seen and that the boy was not headed toward the bus and might not be careful about the time, so Wesley went back and called out his name. He heard no answer but saw the large woman from the seat behind him running, jogging as well as she could, after the boy. Wesley did not like the look of her hurry so he followed too, although he kept an easy pace. She disappeared between two rigs parked close together. By the time he got close enough to look into the space, she was already into a confrontation with a seedy looking bunch. Three skinny men, old enough to have some grey under their ballcaps and on their unshaven cheeks, sat on stools at a small table, playing cards. A large man, not as soft as the fat woman but carrying a substantial percent of his mass in excess flesh, had a friendly hand on Rusty and an unfriendly sneer toward the woman who was talking fast and loud, rotating quickly among Rusty, the big man, and the card players.

The big man spoke over her in calm loud phrases, telling her to mind her own business and encouraging the boy to stand up for himself. A lanky fellow wearing filthy tan pants and a t-shirt too light for the weather, stood up from his stool and pushed between the woman and the boy, fanning out a handful of green bills to show her he did not "need" money. Meanwhile the large one focused on the boy, saying something about the boy staking him for a quick win and showing him, confidentially, his cards.

The scene was such a parody of petty grifting, Wesley could hardly take it seriously. He hesitated, not to give himself time to decide what to do, he was hardly concerned about that, but to take in the caricature as entertainment. If middle America was this absurd in reality, the conspiracy that drove him out of Washington might be real as well and he was not living inside an insane dream, unless, of course, the sleazy truckers were part of the same unlikely hallucination.

Finally Wesley's internal clock reminded him the bus was about to depart, so he acted. He stepped around the truck and into the aisle, walking directly into the middle of the group, neatly side-stepping, like a dance move, the late shoulder-block from the skinny guy who was now leaning against the heavy woman. They had become more aggressive but that had not bothered Wesley as he knew it was inevitable if the woman kept at them.

"Come on, lad," Wesley said with a large smile, trying to be charming rather than threatening. "This just ain't your lucky day. The bus is pulling out right now. You haven't got two seconds to make a million dollars."

He grabbed the boy by his sleeve and jerked hard. The card players could not dismiss the suddenly active and articulate Wesley as easily as a ranting, working-class woman. Her brashness was a familiar motherly model, but an aggressive posture from a male raised the cost of furthering the venture. The game was up. The only way to get whatever money the boy had would be to revert to a direct mugging and there were now two noisy adults in the mix. Wesley hoped his light attitude to the situation would salvage the pride of the grifters long enough to move fifteen feet and into the view of the bus driver. He never looked at any of them, as if the boy was the only one in the parking lot and as if the boy were his own. As he accomplished his fifteen-foot maneuver, he looked back to catch the eye of the woman. She nodded and backed off, ranting as if there were still a contest of wills to pursue. In a few seconds, it was all over, and in a few more seconds, they were in the bus again, headed to their seats as if nothing had happened.

Wesley leaned back to sleep. He was not especially tired but he did not want to talk about the incident. Rusty spoke anyway. He was fired up by the strange encounter.

"What did those guys want?" he asked as if it were not obvious.

"Just your money."

"Were they going to cheat me?"

Wesley did not imagine the boy was as naïve as his words and yet he sounded innocent rather than sarcastic. It was a not a time to play a father figure so Wesley followed the boy's lead as if the affair had been unique and mysterious with potential for good or harm.

"I really don't know."

The woman behind him slapped Wesley on the head. He turned slightly toward her and continued. "Maybe they would have just taken it once you pulled it out. They probably wanted to play the game enough that you would feel there was a chance you had lost fair and square. That way you'd go away quiet, you know?"

"How do you know they were bogus? Maybe I coulda won something. He was gonna let me hold the cash."

"Maybe. Too late now. You gotta git to Shoals Valley."

"You shoulda let me alone."

"You shoulda stuck to guys in uniforms."

The woman reached over the back of the seat and slapped the boy on his head.

"Ow" he said without conviction.

"Show some 'preciation," she demanded.

Wesley did not even look up. "He appreciates us. Can't you see it?"

"Oh yeah, I see it," the woman added as she sat back in her seat.

Rusty shook his head and looked out the window. After a minute, he asked Wesley, "Want to change seats now? You're not lookin' out."

Wesley settled into the aisle seat and closed his eyes again. He was not tempted to sleep-- he had a thought that he wanted to pursue. Colonel Terzo, the fictional professor in *Prince of the Clouds*, found life lessons in war strategies. What lesson, Wesley wondered, could the successful extraction of Rusty from his trap offer for the war between Wesley and Raleigh? There were parallels - Raleigh was a con artist; he could be ruthless; he had Wesley trapped in a game Wesley did not understand. Was the lesson that he needed someone from outside the game to pull him away? ...Too simple. Even in *Prince of the Clouds*, the applications of battle strategy were not so direct. Maybe the only thing Wesley could gain from this train of thought was that point about not understanding the nature of the game. It would be good to acknowledge this rather than to imagine he knew how to play. Maybe the point was that he should not play at Raleigh's game at all. What would that imply? It might imply dropping off the grid, as he had done, and making a connection back to a minor character in Raleigh's circle who might have some useful information, as he was hoping to do. What was the game anyway?

"You read a lot?" The highway scenes were not entertaining so the boy was ready for conversation.

"Guess I do when I am taking a long bus ride."

"Did you like school?"

Wesley considered several possible answers since he was supposed to be maintaining a persona other than his own.

Nonetheless, he decided it was safe to give an honest answer this time.

"No way. I hated school. I loved summer and weekends, except Sunday night when I could feel school waiting to drain my energy and waste my time."

"Aren't you supposed to tell me how important it is?"

"You didn't ask me if it was important."

"So is it important?"

"You can survive without it, without putting much into it. It good for some folks, no doubt. I could have got more out of it but maybe it all depends as much on the school you get as on what you're like. My school did not try to teach me much I could use. You know, the problems I carry now that came from my youth were not from school or from my brain. I was smart enough to do something in life. I actually learned a hell of a lot when I was young. It's just that what I learned was a lot of useless stuff."

"You mean like Latin and math?"

"Could be like them someway except that I didn't learn much Latin and math. What I learned, what I used to know, was all the stats on every one of the Yankees. I knew how to play, oh, maybe twenty-five card games, not just the rules, but the strategy. I knew what clothes to wear and how to wear them with variations on who I was trying to impress. Not that I was a big fashion stud. I did not have all the clothes but I knew what worked in our neighborhood. I knew the new words, the ones that showed I was paying attention and willing to be part of the young scene, independent of parents and teachers and their kind. Music? Oh, I knew music. Not to sing or anything like that. I sure didn't know the words except for the main chorus or the title phrase, but I knew the groups and which ones were good. I was not following my friends or the cool kids in my taste—I really liked the songs I liked and hated some of the ones that were hits. I had taste, which is easy enough, but the point is I knew all the popular groups when I was young. You may not really appreciate how it was - everyone my age listened to the same music. We only heard music on the radio and the playlist was the same for all the stations for young people."

"Come on. I know, like, you had records. I know how they work."

"Not me. They cost money and that was for just one song if you were buying 45s. I never had a record player anyway. They cost a lot of money. I could have afforded it, but it would have sucked up all my funds and the radio worked good enough for me.

"Now here I am, grown up, obviously, knowing about the Yankees of twenty years ago but I don't give a damn about them anymore. Every year is about the same thing. And I know the music on the radio of twenty years ago and I don't give a damn about any music today and don't listen to the radio, or find things on the internet. And I don't have any friends who know what to listen to or who care what I wear or how I wear it or how I talk. And I don't play cards or checkers or chess but I know how. And I know a little math and it's all I want to know of it, and I don't know any Latin and that hasn't hurt me. School? I hated it. Wish I learned something useful back when I was learning things. Now I just do with what I know. I try not to learn anything new. At least I try not to put myself in a position where I need to know something new. I'm actually pretty good at it, at getting by with what I already know, however or whenever I may have learned it."

"So you're sayin' you don't even have a phone? You don't look that old."

"OK, so I actually have a phone. I just don't use it much. Maybe I've let the contract expire. And I'm not that old. I'm just lazy. Probably that's why I hated school. Always been lazy. I like to blame it on my parents. They always wanted me to do things I didn't feel like doing. So I resisted and did less and less until I didn't do anything at all. It felt good. You think that makes it their fault?"

Rusty laughed a little, not sure how serious this man was. Adults always said schooling was the best thing for someone his age. Or they said learning was a lifelong thing.

"Mister, did you graduate high school at least?"

"Oh sure. That was not too hard. I showed up. I was lazy but not brave enough to skip out. Besides, high school is where the girls were."

"I hear you."

Wesley was tiring of this game and he closed his eyes before falling into the deepest sleep he had attained on the trip.

Rusty elbowed Wesley as they neared St. Louis. "You oughta see that." He pushed his chin toward the Arch.

"Oh yeah. Thanks for waking me up." Wesley leaned over Rusty, careful not to touch him, to see the Arch better. "Never been here. Heard of it but I didn't know it was this big. Maybe you can go up in it."

"Sure you can. My grandma can get us up there." Rusty turned around to the fat woman although it was hard to see between the high-backed seats. "You seeing it? Want to go up inside it?"

"Don't be crazy," she answered with friendly distain.

He turned to Wesley. "How 'bout you?"

"It's rad for sure. I'd like to see it, but I gotta roll, you know." They did not speak again, both studiously monitoring the view outside, until the bus stopped.

Wesley did not lean forward but he kept his eyes on the Arch whenever it was on their side of the bus. It looked exactly like the pictures he had seen of it, or so he assumed although he had never looked very closely at any of those images. The only one he could recall specifically was the one on the 2003 quarter, commemorating Missouri's promotion to statehood in 1821. The small size of the quarter and the relatively small size of all the other images he had happened to see of it over the years masked a wealth of detail that appeared in the original. Yet the Arch was essentially a simple figure that could be accurately represented with no finer tools than chalk and blackboard, simple like the Washington Monument but not the Lincoln or Jefferson. Simple though it was, the actual Arch did not give the same impression as its images. They were almost entirely forgettable while the actual Arch conveyed a scale that was the entire message. It was an uncomplicated, even elegant, shape, drawn so illogically large, it could not be intuited. Could it really hold up its own bulk, and simultaneously safely accept the additional mass of hundreds tourists of which the vast majority were overweight by half, and on some occasions additionally survive Mid-Western thunderstorms, and concurrently stand up to the oxidation of aging, and if its engineering were capable of all this, is it plausible that its artistic merits were so timeless that it would remain popular among the evolving fashions of the heartland? The last question felt snarky so Wesley withdrew it from his mental query.

There was no denying the realty of the monument. It stood outside the bus window demanding to be appreciated. But why, Wesley wondered, should I admire it? It is a marvel, but what of the resources that went into it. Like a medieval castle or cathedral, it represents a dedication of efforts that might have been applied more prosaically to reduce hunger and save lives. Just as the builders of castles hardly imagined they had any say in how their labor was used, the taxpayers who contributed to the Arch had no idea how it would turn out so their vague permission to build it was ill informed at best. Or was this thought another mean-spirited interpretation contrary to all grand effort? Was there ever any prospect of putting the Arch effort into hunger relief or education or environmental protection? Guns versus butter... Better an arch than a bomb...

The bus pulled into its angled parking space in the depot and hissed its brakes to a smooth halt. Wesley stood up to let Rusty get out and Rusty answered as if Wesley had spoken only a moment before.

"Yeah, okay. I know what you mean," Rusty answered and he reached up into the overhead rack for his pack. "See you," he added. Wesley slowly nodded his head up and down as if it were possible. Rusty looked at the fat woman to show his "see you" applied to her too. She nodded her head slowly side to side to repeat her last comment that he ought not be so crazy as to go up the Arch.

Wesley watched the boy go down the aisle. He was small enough to move along without banging against every seat along the way, receding in size with distance and fading into the mist at the remote front of the bus. He could see why parents were so protective of their offspring and why they held out hope their children would be better than themselves even when there was no objective basis for that hope. He was starting to regret that he and Mattie had never seriously considered having children. It was possible a young adult child would have preserved something of Mattie for him in his remaining years.

13. Dupe

"You're doin' something. I know it."

The heavy woman was talking to Wesley.

"Yeah. I'm doin' something. I'm riding a bus to Oklahoma."

"Oklahoma is it? No, I don't believe anything you say. I heard you tell the Pittsburgh woman you was goin' to St. Louis. What do you think of that?"

"I don't really think anything of it. I don't know what you thought you heard or why you heard it."

"Oh, don't fret. I'm not even that nosey. I just got good ears. But that story you told one or the both of them is not the thing. I see what you're reading. I been sittin' right behind you since you got on. You readin' some kind of history book but you want us to think you're reading *People* magazine. Why you do that? *People* is for people like me. You ain't like me and you don't want to be like me."

"Why don't you sit down beside me and we'll talk a bit. You're not quite what you seem to be either."

"Nobody is if you study on 'em. Except me. I think I am pretty much what you see. That is if you squint a lot and the light's not too good. And I look better when the bus is moving 'cause you can't see right straight when everything's movin'. See, I figure I'm pretty good looking when the lights are off."

"Good thing I didn't say that," Wesley answered, pleased that the conversation had moved from discovering his deceptions to something focused on her. But she had not forgotten this point...

As she settled into the seat beside him, she asked "What is the book you are actually reading? History, right?"

"No, not history. It is a novel. Would you believe I keep it under cover because it is disreputable one?"

"No. That's just the point. You could not convince anyone you are dis-re-pu-ta-ble or strugglin' to make ends meet or can't use a cellphone."

"I think I know why you say that but you would be wrong. I am more distraught than anyone on this bus. Okay, I use words that would not appear in *People* magazine but my life is a spectacular failure. I belong in the lowest rank of American society and like many people in that category, I did not really deserve it, did not act in a way that seemed selfish or stupid, not any more than most folks, but here I am thoroughly trapped by my circumstances. Yes, my book might be acceptable to the literary establishment and, and... The thing is, yes, I am hiding out and I am not very good at that either. ...Else I wouldn't be talking to you like this and you wouldn't already be suspecting me of something."

"Don't worry none about me. Everyone tells me things. Everyone figures I won't say anything 'cause obviously I got nothing to say."

"I don't see that. The reason I feel like trusting you is I saw you stick your neck out for that boy."

"Just like you."

"Yeah, just like me."

"Like I said, I'm not nosey so don't tell me your story if you don't want to."

"I already told you everything that matters."

"You didn't tell me nothin'."

"Exactly. That where I am now. So lift me up and tell who you are."

"Modupe Sodunke."

"Excuse me."

"That's who I am," she said with a little laugh. "You could never spell it, but it is not hard to say: mo-doo'-pwey show-doon'-ke. My parents were Nigerian."

Wesley had not looked closely at the woman and he did not want to stare now either but he had not noticed anything in her that looked Nigerian.

"Did you live in Nigeria?" he asked.

"There, see. If you were from the low parts of society you'd have been more honest and said I don't look Black, you know, 'cause I don't."

"Right, you don't look Nigerian."

"You're lookin' at my skin, white as can be, and you're looking at my hair, straight as can be, and you're looking at my thin lips and my pointy nose, my sort of bad English and you think maybe my mother is White and did something with somebody not my father?"

"I don't calculate that fast. Damn near everything I said to you is a lie so I would guess you're just pulling my chain."

"I don't lie for nobody and especially about family. Both my parents are Black. I was adopted. Really backwards, right? White baby adopted by Black Africans living in Philly. Not too many with a story like that!"

"I wouldn't know for sure but I don't know any other combinations like that."

“Don’t be so polite if’n you want to pass for being like me. Just ignoring what I look like and what’s White and what’s Black ain’t being polite anyway. Of course you never heard of a White Nigerian from Pennsylvania.”

“I don’t know anyone from Pennsylvania, except I’ve heard of William Penn and Benjamin Franklin. Did you ever go to Nigeria? Do your parents tell you about it... tell you stories about their family or whatever place they came from?”

“They never said a whole lot about where they came from. They left because of a war. They were rich as far as the Africans get rich. Had enough to get away but not enough to do anything good once they got here.”

Wesley wanted to ask her if her parents had fled the Biafran War but the question would have shown him to be better informed that his character would be. Suddenly he realized he had wanted to ask just to show off, that it was a normal form of conversation for him to show as soon as possible that he was educated and experienced. At least he could be pleased that he had caught himself this time before he embarrassed himself. Now that he noticed it, maybe he could avoid the habit even when he was no longer playing a common man. Dupe was still talking...

“...Some relatives came to visit and I heard them talking with my parents but when they got into the village gossip they did Yoruba and I never learnt any of that.”

“Except for your name, right? Modupe.”

“Not really sure that’s Yoruba. My father was from the north where they are something else.”

“So you do know more about Nigeria than the rest of us!”

"That' what I mean about you being a nice fellow. Jumped on that little thing like it was special, like I was special."

"I won't say that. Everyone is saying we're all unique and shit, and God loves each of us for who we are and we can be anything we want to be and we are every one of us beautiful. I don't believe any of that sermon. Sorry if I offend you with... with..." He was about to say "cynicism" and felt his brain searching for more lyrical phrases to express a philosophy that was thoughtful and personal and insightful when he was held back by the persona he was supposed to affect. A moment later he was disgusted by the persona of his actual self, not for failing to believe in the essential good within humanity but for his proclivity to display his personal values in far more detail than they deserved or that any listener would appreciate, any listener other than an idealized college sophomore of the sort he seemed to be trying to impress.

"We're just sittin' on a bus. Say whatever you want. It don't offend me none. Or I might be offended if you tried to bullshit me."

"Well, as you know, I'm doing that too. Seems like I do it all the time to everybody on every subject that comes up so don't take it personal."

"Most everybody does, I guess."

"Except you? I heard you never lie."

"Yeah, except me. I don't mind being who I am. Don't mind if people know it. I'm not trying to get anywhere. You think it's because my parents loved me so much I never learned to be attractive?"

"That question is a trap. I don't think you are fishing for compliments. Wish I was smart enough to come up with an answer that makes us better friends."

"I was talking to myself, asking me a question, and now that I asked it, I believe it's a good one. Anyways, you gave as good an answer as I could make up."

"Where is this bus carrying you, Ms. Dupe?"

"Goin' far as Oklahoma City. That's so I can get my nephew outta El Reno and take him to his schooling in San Francisco. Drop him off on the weekend. Might stay a couple days or a week. Maybe see the Golden Bridge before I got to get back home to Bal'mere."

"Your nephew lives in El Reno, Oklahoma (I'll allow for the moment that's a real place) and he's going to school in San Francisco?"

"Pretty crazy, huh? It's not college. He's going to learn about electricity. Some uncle on the other side of the family teaches it out there. He's just sixteen, a bit more age on him than that boy you and me got together in savin' from them trucker rowdies. Quit high school. Never been anywhere much so I thought I'd take him out. Set him up with an apartment. Like to see the bridge anyway."

"Do you already have an apartment picked out or do you have to find one?"

"His uncle got him a place near the electricity school. Can't trust a man to fix it up right. No offense."

"My wife and my mother would agree with you."

"Arlington Arms is the place. And I thought Arlington was in Washington, DC."

Wesley remembered not to correct her. She probably knew Arlington was in Virginia. Maybe she was testing him to see if he knew that.

"The uncle's putting me up at the Hotel Fusion 'cause he says there be no room in my nephew's apartment. Didn't say why I can't stay at his place. Treats me like a stranger. I am a stranger but I'm kin too."

"So, I take it you've not been to San Francisco before. How about Los Angeles or anywhere else on the West Coast?"

Modupe told him about her job at a factory-scale bakery where she was a shift supervisor. She described her house and the little things she had done to make it nice and how content she was with it now, how much it exceeded what she deserved as a poorly educated orphan from the hard side of Baltimore. She told him about her "situation," that she had a man-friend and she had always been careful so she had no children and didn't want any because the world was more than full already. And that they didn't even live together because he was too messy but they saw each other nearly every day except when he went on a binge with his buddies although she was opposed to that and tended to punish him afterwards for a few days and then she missed him and they probably loved each other as much as any married couple, more than most too.

She made no attempt to get any information out of Wesley. He could not decide if she was respecting his privacy or really did not care about why the stranger was hiding or where he would be hiding. Nonetheless, he kept his guard up while they chatted until they saw the Devon Tower rise off the hot mid-day horizon. Oklahoma City has nearly a dozen skyscrapers although anyone from New York would argue the number was closer to none.

Wesley and Dupe got up when the bus stopped.

"Don't suppose you be getting out here," Dupe said without conviction.

"Let me help you with your bag," Wesley answered and then gave her a friendly nod and sincere last words, "I think I learned something from you on this ride, something worthwhile." He really had enjoyed talking with her. She answered with a knowing squint of her eyes before she turned to leave.

14. Robbie

"Damn, damn, damn me and every hair on my skinny, pestulous body!" Wesley worked his way carefully through every curse word he could recall in search of some relief from the painful disappointment he was feeling in himself. It was all going so well, school, for a change. He had finally gotten on top of things as he knew he could and should. He had gone to his classes, done his homework, studied for exams. For the first time he would be getting the grades he needed to reach law school and there was still time to pick up his average more before graduation. He had grown up since that disastrous first term when he had, against all evidence, assumed his natural talent would carry him through. No drugs, alcohol, girls or other extraneous distractions. He deserved to succeed. It was so unfair! Somehow he had missed the second half of chemistry. He had understood everything up to the midterm, had liked the professor, even saw the value of the lab sessions, and was fully capable of doing the rest, but he had just forgotten about that class after midterms. There were so many other classes demanding attention. Suddenly he saw a way out. He could explain it to the professor. She was reasonable. It was not as if he had been failing or slacking off when he was attending. But no, really, it was just like that, like he was slacking off. How much more could he have slacked off than to have entirely ignored the subject for two months? There was no chance of recovery. He could not take the final exam; it would only be an embarrassment. He would have to look for a different career. There was no way to get into law school with another failed term. There were no curses strong enough to express the situation. He pounded his fists into his face and felt nothing at all. Beads of cold sweat bloomed on his brow. He did not mind having to reset his life's ambitions. He minded that it was for so small a reason, for a simple lapse in his youth, not a crime, without harm to anyone.

Suddenly his whole body was shocked, as if an earthquake had run past him. He woke up. He had been dreaming. The stranger beside him had jostled him firmly, probably intentionally. He spoke to Wesley without looking in his direction, a kind man although he looked rough with his dark sideburns; long, slicked back hair; torn black T-shirt; and dark tattoos under dense arm hair.

"You goin' all the way, brother?"

Wesley remembered where he was and why he was there. He longed for the disaster of mere academic failure.

"What?' he asked, not because he had not heard the question but just to give himself time to think in the present.

"You goin' all the way?"

It was an interesting way to ask, with an opening for multiple meaning that was probably not intended, although Wesley heard it instantly.

"All the way? Yes, I *am* goin' all the way, brother. Yes, to San Francisco where this bus will take me and then on to finish the rest of my business."

"Finish? You quittin' your business after this?"

"I am not quittin' my business 'til it's done and it won't be done in San Francisco and it won't be done soon and I'm afraid it won't ever be done but I will stay with it until it is finished, and there is such a thing as finishing it or die trying." He has spoken too close to the unvarnished truth but it sounded so ridiculous, Wesley did not mind.

"I admire your devotion. I haven't got anything like that but I admire it."

"I spoke too boldly," Wesley admitted. "That might not be really the way I am. I been sittin' in this plastic seat so long in dead silence, I'm not sure I could talk exactly right no more."

"Where'd you start out?"

"Chicago." *Time to get back to lying as a general principle*, thought Wesley. "I'm Bernard," and he thrust out his hand for an introductory shake. "You goin' all the way?"

"I ain't dedicated. Not at all. Not the way you are. I'm going to Amarillo and that ain't all the way anywhere, not for me. Bet you can't say why I might be going there."

"Since you say it that ways, I know you're not headed to home."

"No prizes for getting' that far, Mister."

Wesley looked him over. He was a mesomorph, still young, with even features and dark dense hair, including his eyebrows, and regular, perhaps slightly squarish, facial features, making him quite good looking in a Hollywood way. He made an obvious guess. "Something to do with a woman."

"Way off. No woman involved. Wisht there was."

"No woman involved? Then it can't be very important."

"I give you that. Nothing I do or did was ever important. 'Sides, it take a right peculiar woman to get hooked up with me."

"That's good. Near as I know, most women are 'right peculiar'."

"I shoulda give you my name. Robbie, not "Robert" or "Bob" so I don't answer to those. "Robbie" spelt with "ie" not "y" on my birth certificate. Least that's what my second mother said. I never saw it." He was grinning broadly and enjoying this anecdote he had certainly told many times. It made him memorable from the start. "What I'm doing about here is *collecting*. We got some time, I see. Would you mind if I tol' you about it?"

"Talk to me, Robbie. I got nothing with me to do, I'm tired of thinkin' and sleepin', and the scenery out there is no help at all, just more of the same, baked browner mile by mile."

"Don't look like anything out there but hot."

"If it were greener and wetter and a hundred years ago, I could be Huck Finn riding my itchy raft down the Mississippi to I-don't-know-where, just getting away."

"Oh I remember that story. He's friends with Tom Sawyer, right?"

"I think that's right. His own story is sadder than Tom's, but worst yet is Jim who rides the raft with him. Jim, that would be you, but I don't believe you got a sadder story than mine."

In his roundabout way and with a country accent that Wesley could not locate regionally, having had more experience with American argot in writing than in sound, Robbie explained how he came to be a collector and what kind of collector he came to be.

He was encouraged to collect by his Boy Scout troop. They had a contest for the best collection of something. He chose stamps because they were free and they were standard items for collecting. There was even a merit badge for stamp collecting. He had no thought of being an innovator in this or anything else at that age, content to do what was least conspicuous and easiest. It was just an assignment to him, like the ones in school except that he knew he would not be getting a grade, just that he would lose the contest along with most of the other boys, letting him get back to what he wanted to do which was to horse around as if he had no homework, no badges to earn, no responsibilities which is not unusual in a twelve-year old boy whose parents press him to accomplish but do not convince him it matters beyond the momentary relief from guilt when he gets something done before the next thing that is overdue comes to mind or is thrust upon him.

But he was surprised in his seventh-grade class when he was asked by his teacher in front of everybody to read his homework assignment describing what he had done on the weekend and the teacher had said collecting stamps was a wonderful thing, that it could teach the collector about different times and places, about art and science and history, and Robbie felt the kids in his class were looking at him with respect, maybe even jealousy, even though he had not thus far learned anything. So he had a personal identity for the first time in his life, accidental, but real enough that he adopted it as his own.

At first, he only collected recent U.S. stamps since they were all he could find in his parents' desk drawer or in the trash at home. It was not a glamorous hobby but it made him better than being unknown. He began to recognize the more common ones and he looked at a few library books that made him an expert in something, as far as anyone he knew could tell. His classmates at school began to give him envelopes from their homes which surprised him because they had never paid much attention to him before. They seemed to like hearing about the stamps they gave him. He did not like the stamp albums in the store because they showed how many he was missing and had no hope of ever finding so he put them on pages of typing paper, also taken surreptitiously from his father's desk, not stolen exactly, as his father would probably have been happy to give Robbie the paper.

And after one year, he had a complete set of U.S. postal issues for first class mail for one year and this he made into an album that could be said to be finished. Following an idea he saw in the Sunday paper, he wrote a paragraph on each stamp, saying something about whatever it portrayed. He had been surprised to enjoy doing the research and understood it was different to do a task that had not been assigned and would not be judged. It felt good to do something all the way. He had always cut corners in doing chores around the house or homework or scouting badges or promises during Lent, and it always troubled him to know who he was and yet with this apparently meaningless exercise of collecting stamps, he had accomplished something, gained infinitely more respect from his peers, and a modicum of self-respect.

Looking upon the finished album, he hungered for more. Just doing another year of U.S. issues would be an embarrassingly small further accomplishment, certain to diminish his public and private image. He had become known for something and had amused his classmates slightly but they would not care to hear much more about stamps.

He was being told to collect foreign stamps but that required more effort than he was willing to make. A few people even gave him some foreign stamps but he was never interested in taking up something that was doomed to failure- he could not hope to collect all of any sort of foreign stamp without spending money.

He noticed that prepaid envelopes, business reply mail, had code numbers on them and he thought he might become the first ever collector of these. He felt creative for having the idea. The numbers would allow him to put them in some order and, like the used U.S. stamps, they were free. He collected them for a few months until he saw something of the patterns in the numbers but not enough to make them interesting. He told people he was collecting them and he found hundreds of examples. He developed a casual way of claiming he was one of the few experts in the field and therein lay his problem. He could not find any expert information: no library book, merit badge instruction, hobby shop, teacher, or grandparent made any mention of postage-paid envelopes. A number was printed in the upper right corner of the envelope where a stamp would normally be, but the numbers made little sense. They were useful for arranging the envelopes but it was not possible to group them into sets or to get any further idea of how to organize them. He could not devise a goal for the collection. Clearly many numbers were never used in his area, perhaps not used at all and other numbers were used by a wide range of businesses. Understanding them would require research in some unobvious way so he abandoned that collection. He had learned the lesson that not everything is collectable, not in a fun way.

Having analyzed his problem that far, he became creative again, taking up the collection of bottle caps. He soon had all the varieties of soda sold in his town and displayed them on a board with a nail through the middle of each one. It was impressive and complete. No new issue was likely in the next year, especially since the market was shifting to aluminum cans. His next step was a social triumph. He moved over to beer bottle caps. As a junior in high school, his association with alcohol in a public way made him seem almost rebellious, verging on mature, arguably cool, possibly self-confident, and experienced. It was enough to salvage as much self-respect as a person of his modest talents and weak personality could expect from high school.

He went through the next ten years, finishing high school and a technical school for learning refrigeration repair, without turning up a new identity; he remained the guy who collects free and meaningless stuff into complete sets, and who knows more about these everyday things than anyone else: matchbooks from restaurants in Cincinnati, pencils from banks across the mid-west, napkins from fast-food chains, college football ticket stubs, empty cigarette packets... But not tree leaves, rocks, butterflies, beetles, that is, not things which may be free but which had established experts with purposes beyond having something to boast about.

"Sorry, I guess I was nodding off. Been too long on this bus. Hope I wasn't snoring again."

"You was a little jumpy is all. Not snoring, you know."

"Anyway, you said you were collecting something in Oklahoma City?"

"Yes. I guess it sounded like I was sayin' that but it was not too honest a way of sayin' it. I was spending too much of my life with stupid piles of stuff, all organized and studied and doin' nobody no good at all. So one Sunday, I alles go to church on Sunday no matter where I'm at, so this one Sunday, and I doan recall where I was, this Sunday the minister asks us all what it is we regrets, said it makes you feel better to talk it out once. Well, I thought about it 'cause that's what you're supposed to go to church for, right? And I thought I doan have any really big regrets. I didn't do much in my time but that's all right, I think. Most folks doan do that much. We can't all be president and it'd be a terrible thing if we all tried to be the top one of ever'thing."

Robbie was not waiting for feedback from his audience and "Bernard" was content to listen so he made a supportive murmur from time to time without redirecting Robbie's exposition.

"I wasn't regretting who I was, but I did have that itch the minister was talkin' about and then it came to me. Well, you see, I never knew my father, not my real father, but I had a good one that adopted me so I didn't regret having him but I regretted that I never found my real father. No, that's not right either. I regretted that I never even tried to find my father. I knew a little about him. I knew his name and I knew he didn't put me up for adoption. That was my mother. She was only 19; they both was. And they got married afore I was born. But my mother put me up before my Dad ever saw me and she told him I died right away of some kinda lung thing. Seems like he wanted to do right by me but he never got the chance. My mother wanted to finish college and become something like a lawyer. The folks who took me in talked to her once. I doan need to find her. I just ought to tell my father I lived and that it's all right. I turned out good enough. Nothing he should regret about losin' me. I wouldn't a made him real proud with all the things I did and I wouldn't make him feel bad about turning to a life of crime or nothin' like that. No welfare. I pay my taxes, you know. Just a man like most men."

Wesley wondered if Mattie might have had a husband and a child before he met her. And what were the odds that this would be the actual child? That while he was looking for Mattie, her son was looking for her first husband and their paths would cross right down to the exact seat on the bus? Long odds, indeed.

"So he's in Amarillo, then?"

"Pro'bly not. I been collecting men with his name and his age since I figured out what I was regretting. Ever' year I get two weeks vacation - we got a solid union to make sure we get our time- and I go to a city and look up all the men round the place 19 years older than me named Terry or Terrance McMasters. There's not so many in any one city, but I been looking for... this is my fifth year of this. I'm sixty now so he be 79. I gotta find him soon or it'll be too late."

They sat silently for a minute before Wesley answered. "Wish I had a story that good to share with you. But at least you cannot regret that you never tried to find him."

"I know you got your own stories. Ever'body on this bus has 'em. I jus' like to talk more'n most. Helps me pass the time, you know. You doan have to listen to me."

"I'm listening. Talk all you want. Tell me about what you do for a living." Wesley knew as soon as he said it that he had said the wrong thing. That was a question from Washington, a big-city question from a place where the scramble for money was essential and the competition for power and prestige defined who you were. This man did not need a prompt to tell of his life. It was a false representation of his priorities to move on to what Wesley had thought most vital up until recently.

The man did not answer. Wesley had silenced him with an impertinent question more surely than if he had fallen asleep. It was a transparent trick to put down this humble man on the bus, an invitation to boast of his own lofty-seeming job, issued out of habit, out of Washington convention, not at all out of any intent to tell any truth about himself.

The man hummed a little as if warming up to say something. He did not like to be defined by his work, not that he cared what Wesley thought of him. He did not want to think of himself in that way. Work was just what you did so you could do other things. It felt uncomfortable to answer nothing so he said, "I do lots of things. Nothing big. Nothing that gets me ahead. I didn't do much with school. I guess you graduated and ever'thing?"

"Oh I graduated. It was after that I wasted what I knew 'cause I was just too lazy to get ahead. I wasn't a drunk or a druggy. Actually I do not even know what I did with my life so far. Maybe I should put more into it now that I can see what it really takes. It's just that now I'm getting tired. I never had much ambition. Just always figured things would work out and they did in their own way.

"So what work you do?"

"You can be sure I never did anything worth talk' about. Talked about it enough anyway, I guess. I've never been to Amarillo. You?"

"Nope. I go lots of cities just once. Still plenty to go."

"Ever been to Texas before?"

"Oh sure. Plenty of times. Big place. Never near Amarillo though."

"Funny thing. When I was a kid, Texas was the biggest state. They used to say everything was big in Texas. There was a cartoon, Rocky and Bullwinkle, I think, and when they crossed the state line, they got bigger. They jumped back and forth across the line to watch themselves grow and shrink."

"Never saw it."

"I'm going to see if we get bigger when we go into the state. Should be soon now."

This topic was no more productive than talking about their careers. Robbie grunting in a polite way and then slouched down and shut his eyes. Wesley turned toward the flat landscape searching for something to see and was soon hypnotized by the monotony and let his own eyelids fall even without any interest in sleeping again.

Collecting had appealed to Robbie for the authority it gave him on something without demanding any actual skill. Wesley had felt drawn to it more than once but not for the reasons that attracted Robbie. It served no social function for Wesley, in fact it embarrassed him and he kept it secret as if he were taking illicit drugs. The hook was the simplicity of a goal and the possibility of meeting the goal by completing the collection. Normal goals in life were always too hard to reach or simply led to new goals. His father's comment after hearing of any accomplishment by Wesley was "What's next?" It was not even, "Good! What's next?" He collected from circulation all the U.S. coins from his birth year, put them in a small box and silently enjoyed their presence in the back of a drawer. When he went away to college, he did not take his various collections with him and he stopped collecting things altogether. It was a relief to ignore the date of the coins that passed through his fingers and the stamps on his mail and the butterflies in his backyard, and the latest record albums by the Beach Boys, and Tinker-Toy station wagons and so on and on. It was one of the few times he had grown out of a senseless habit without a crisis to motivate him.

Amarillo arranged its streets on a grid as cities do on level planes. The Big Texan restaurant advertised a 72-ounce steak with a sign painted on a giant steer. Wesley poked Robbie in the ribs and gestured to the steer. "See, that's how they grow 'em in Texas."

"I been to Texas before," he answered, refusing to be impressed.

Amarillo had one skyscraper. The architect had given it strong vertical lines. The sun was low and lit the western side with a pink glow like the sky had been washed with a pair of new Christmas stockings.

"Good luck finding your Dad. I bet he'll be excited as hell to have you turn up."

"You got more'n hour here. Wanna stop inside for a beer? I hate to be on my own until I get adjusted to a place."

"Well, I don't need to sit right here any extra," and Wesley went inside the terminal with him. He carried his overhead bag which was everything he had brought with him, not counting the clothes on his back and the money strapped under them. They picked up Robbie's checked bag and walked across the street to a place so modest, it did not have its name on the sign above the door unless its name was "Bar." Two of the four booths were occupied. The one by the door had two middle-aged guys in jeans and Western shirts; cowboy hats hung on wall behind them. They stared silently at Robbie and Wesley as if was extraordinary for strangers to appear from the bus station. Wesley avoided their eyes at first and then looked to them and gave an upward flip of his head as a greeting. It seemed a gesture anyone could understand as a friendly way to say "nothing to see here," but they gaped without according any degree of humanity to the new arrivals. Wesley figured the two "cowboys" were either aggressive or stupid. "That's ungenerous," he told himself. "They might just be drunk and bored. Amarillo could do that to you; Amarillo or any of the other places he had seen since Pittsburg," and then he knew he was himself in an ungenerous mood.

The other occupied table was in the darkest corner where three fellows were leaning forward and conversing or conspiring in low tones. One was wearing a rumpled suit and tie while the other two wore sweatshirts with the sleeves torn off. "If I have to interact with one of these two groups, I'll take the rude one by the window," Wesley's thoughts continued.

"Sit at the bar?" Robbie asked.

"Sure."

The bartender wore a T-shirt with a commercial logo Wesley did not recognize. He looked toward Wesley and Robbie but did not move in their direction or speak.

"Two beers," Wesley suggested, raising his voice and looking at Robbie for his concurrence. Robbie nodded favorably.

"You got something American on tap?" Wesley asked. The barman moved without answering and drew the beers.

"You know where you're staying tonight?"

Robbie took a sip of his beer and thought about Wesley's question for close to a minute.

"Hey," he finally called to the bartender. "You got a cheap hotel near here?"

The bartender took the toothpick out of his mouth slowly as if it was a great effort and held it beside his mouth as if it were a cigarette. "There's 'place up gataway. Not too far. You can walk it." He gestured vaguely in a double motion, once out toward the street and then toward the left.

"Thanks, I get it. They got AC in that place?"

"Don't know. Never been inside." He looked around the room. "Doubt any of them been inside," but he called to the two cowboys who were still watching the tableau at the bar, "You boys ever get a girl to go to that Poke Inn up that way? They got any AC?"

One of them shook his head and turned away from the bar. The other one said "Oh yes, I always take my one-time girls there. Can't say I ever thought much about air conditioning but I usually work up a good sweat, you know." He grinned at his own droll response and reached across the table to slap his companion's arm for some recognition of his brilliance. No corroborating movement or sound was forthcoming, just a snort of indeterminant meaning.

Wesley and Robbie drank their beers slowly and quietly. They were inhibited by the limited time available to bring up a new topic and it made no sense to make small talk about the weather for the upcoming week. The television up by the ceiling replayed highlights of the confirmation hearings for Jeff Sessions to be Attorney General. In the Washington pubs where Wesley might have stopped after work, everyone would have been watching and commenting. Possibly not everywhere in Amarillo but in this particular bar, the unfolding national spectacle went unnoticed. Wesley wondered how such a nominee was possible. What had come of America to have this man heading the Justice Department immediately after the second Obama Administration? Of course, Wesley had not yet heard of William Barr nor imagined what partnership an Attorney General could accept with a President as then reigned. He silently formulated snappy retorts to each Session comment. Anyone in this room would think he was crazy if he spoke any of them aloud. Would they be wrong about this stranger involved in a boring news program like it was Texas A&M football? Was he crazy to care about the hearings while sitting here and chasing his flimsy clues to find Mattie? He had cared less about politics than most in Washington. He kept up closely with a small subset of developments for work and followed the rest of them in the automatic way people of his class in a, say, Pittsburg bar might follow the Steelers, gathering enough facts to talk about them but not actually caring and definitely not doing anything to affect their outcome. He reminded himself not to hate Sessions and his ilk any more than he hated the opposing sports team. Still, it would have felt good to ridicule the man, he was so ripe for it with his caricature accent and unsophisticated conservatism and obsolescent style. How much of it was sincere and how much was for the segment of voters he targeted?

"Guess I could go find that place an' settle in. Sure hope it's got air," Robbie said as if talking to himself.

"Reckon I oughter mosey along too," Wesley answered slowly, wondering if Robbie detected the sarcasm in his inept drawl. Wesley paid. At the curb they parted with a wave.

With only a glance toward his erstwhile drinking buddy, Wesley ignored the bus station and studied his watch. He still had nearly a half-hour break remaining, enough for a walk around the block. It should be enough to ease up the kinks in his legs and back, and enough to moisten his collar and make the bus feel a welcome oasis.

The neighborhood was not laid out in blocks, not in any obvious way. Behind the bus terminal, he could see open land reaching far out to a horizon of low hills, the same horizon he had tried to ignore on the last couple hours coming into Amarillo. He figured he would go out a little way and then look back to see if Amarillo looked any better from that perspective.

It took more than half of his available thirty minutes to get to the edge of town. It felt too good to be moving after all that sitting. He nursed the idea that leaving the bus now, unscheduled, might throw off anyone who had managed to track him this far. It would be hard to pick up his trail again, trying to find him in Amarillo when he actually continued on the next day. Besides, the walk through this piece of Amarillo was dreary and he wanted something interesting in front of his eyes. It was just a thought and became a decision as the distance back to the station grew and soon after that it was a fact.

The first fifty feet of desert past the last rusty warehouse was noteworthy only for its scatter of trash. He doubted it had ever been cleaned up so there were probably artifacts here from the earliest days of the city. Nothing looked worthy of a local museum although much of it might have been old. No rusty spurs, or bullet casings or Bowie knives. No empty oil cans or beer bottles from unfamiliar brands. The cigarette butts were widespread but not likely to date to Amarillo's origins. He wondered if their density had declined in recent years as the rate of decay surpassed the rate of accumulation. Maybe the fashion of smoking had not declined as much in Amarillo as in Washington. His knowledge of Texas culture was all rumor, prejudice and Bonanza.

Past the littoral zone was a sparse growth of low viney plants, nearly brown but having enough green that a visiting East Coast observer might hope for life in them. He kicked at one to see how tenaciously it would adhere to its chosen home. The modest, nameless weed clung with deep fibrous roots to the dusty, stony soil as if that spot were the only place it could survive, which, of course, it was.

He slowly drifted his line of sight along the invariant horizon for a vision of a goal or a plan or a purpose or a rationale for his wasteland wander. The competitiveness of official Washington had wrung the spontaneity from him years ago. A few needled trees formed the upper story of the desert before him, none closer than twenty yards to any other, none much taller than him. If he went far enough from the city, not very far, maybe a quarter mile more, he could turn around and these trees would block his view of Amarillo, except for those tall buildings from a part of the city he had not approached and probably never would. Cross-country buses don't go there and people there take planes to get to Washington or San Francisco. When he thought he was far enough that the lower five stories would be hidden from view, he turned around to look. The city looked smaller than he expected since the skyscrapers were closely packed. At night from this point, the true scope of the densely inhabited area would be apparent from the lights on the clouds and airborne dust. It was a city he had heard of before although he could not say where or why, but a significant place. He decided to see it at night from out here.

His footsteps crunched, not loudly, but enough to be odd in a soft soil. There was some kind of crust on everything, as if the desert had sweated a salty film like the one he was wearing since five minutes after he began his minor trek. Listening to his feet murmur to him was relaxing, a point of focus sufficient to replace the innumerable issues that needed resolution. No litter adorned the trackless path he took; no animal, nor even insect revealed itself; no sound, nor car horn nor siren nor coyote competed with the gentle crackle beneath him.

He eventually recognized his legs were tiring so he turned his head up to take stock of his situation. The mountains looked no closer than when he began. In fact, he could see them less well since the light was fading. They would have served, he thought, to orient him if the sun were not already doing that perfectly well. Walk straight away from the mountains to regain Amarillo.

He would not go to the mountains; not a safe thing to try, did not want to and maybe could not do it all. There was nothing more to see out here yet he had seen something. He had seen the size of the desert, enough to extrapolate to a feel for its full scope, he imagined. He had seen the relief of leaving his mission for a couple hours. He had seen how clever he could be, going beyond his strict lawyerly disciplines, by devising one more trick to remain anonymous although the pride in that cleverness conflicted with another pride; he wanted also to be proud of escaping his lawyerly ways by taking a completely spontaneous and irrational action.

He laid down and rested his head on his pack. The sparse brush was more than enough to obstruct his view of everything but the dim gray sky above. If he never got up again, he might never be found. He might never even be missed. *Don't feel sorry for yourself. Maybe Lucas would notice and care.*

He rested without thinking until the sun was gone and almost immediately his damp clothes brought a chill over him. *Maybe Mattie is still out there, San Francisco or somewhere. She would forgive me even if she believed I had some tacky affair. She loved me, I know it for sure as much as anything I know. Is the law any clearer than this knowledge? Is mathematics any more ensured? God? The desolation of Texas desert? One thing is more certain. How I love her. What foolishness we committed to take each other for granted while we built careers.*

With this admission, he was suddenly wide awake. He felt the cold more starkly. He leapt to his feet, swung his bag over his shoulder and began jogging back to Amarillo, hoping to reach the city lights before darkness rendered the terrain underfoot too hazardous to hurry. He was soon forced by the dark to a slow walk for twenty minutes and then adjusted to a quicker pace for the last twenty minutes, aided by enough urban glow to guide the safe placement of his feet.

I'll sleep on a park bench in case they look for me in a hotel. I'll eat dinner someplace cheap after I buy a cut-rate blanket which I will leave in the park. I will be the person I am pretending to be.

Like the person he was pretending to be, he could not quite accomplish his simple plan. No place was selling blankets at that hour. He managed to buy a cloth raincoat. The night was miserable, cold and noisy. All the park benches were narrow, hard and sloped toward the back. When the sky began to lighten, he gave up trying to sleep and spent a full minute scratching the itches in his back before he realized he was feeling the impression of the park bench slates on his soft skin. He was not hardened to the physical discomfort of homelessness. Spontaneity was not working out well for him.

Having breakfast at the counter in a diner for the second time since he was with his grandfather in Florida, he opted for pancakes, scrambled eggs and sausage, and rued his many meals limited to bagels and coffee on hurried Washington mornings. He asked the guy on the next stool if there was another bus station in Amarillo. If he was using this break in his trip to escape detection, he should not pick it up exactly where he broke it. The guy could not think of one. Interstate buses probably make one stop per city. He could take a cab or hitchhike to another city. Or wait a week. Or stop playing at James Bond and just get a new ticket. As an alternative to starting a new bus line, he bought a shiny new shirt and a cowboy hat. He wrinkled the shirt and rubbed some dirt on the new duds. There was time left over to buy another book to hide inside a new magazine during the rest of the trip.

Knowing his snobbery regarding literature, he did not expect to find anything acceptable in the wire rack of five-by-six inch paperbacks, probably selected because they fit the rack. He did not recognize any titles or authors but could recognize genres through the cover art. And then he was surprised to find underneath Danielle Steel's "Safe Harbour" a book three times thicker than any other. Its cover looked like sci fi except that it bore the name Paul Auster. The title was simply a number, *4321*, slightly more than four times the number of pages. He had seen the book before and ruefully wondered who would read it outside the faculty at some English Department. Would any of them dare assign it to students? Yet there was a sticker on it announcing it had been nominated for the Man-Booker Prize, clearly proving it was a meritorious work even if not readable. Thus, it deserved a moment's further consideration. The back cover said it was the story of one life, Archie Ferguson's, told four times. It did not announce how the tellings differed or if it really was sci fi, but Wesley felt a kinship with Archie since he had recently become a new person scarcely related to his former self and was pretending to be yet another person while on his mission across America. Besides, the book did not look fancy. It would not need to hide in a magazine where it might attract the attention of a future Dupe.

His new bus purred powerfully as it left the station and as it climbed the ramp to US 40. Wesley slouched in his seat and let his hat tip forward like a cowboy in siesta except that he could still see under the brim and watch the city go by. Then the external scenery would return to generic Texas plains. Unfortunately, there was not much to see of Amarillo - the skyscrapers stayed away. His only excitement came from seeing a sign for Route 66, a fragment of cultural history. Someday he might don his ten-gallon hat again and drive Mattie out to the Mother Road to tell her one of the escapades on his way to saving her. His restless night was transporting him like a drug into wakeful dreaming.

The complex, gritty cityscape passed into bleak suburban tracts which passed into a plain of tall sparse grasses and mesquite. Wesley had three items remaining on his agenda: look over the other passengers, start his new book, and catch up on sleep. He moved the third item to the top by tipping his hat an inch or two to shade his eyes from light and distraction. Sleep came easily but it did not last long. He sensed something was wrong and sat up suddenly. The bus was not moving.

"What..." he asked of the young woman beside him. He could not immediately form the rest of the sentence while his brain regained consciousness but, fortunately, she understood his question.

"Bus broke down already. Like I need any extra time is this goddam filthy seat. Sorry, guess I shouldn't talk like that to a stranger."

But she just got on this thing! Westley thought before his brain snapped out of stupor. He was the new passenger.

"Don't bother me how you talk. These seats get uncomfortable pretty fast, don't they?"

"You looked comfortable enough. Hardly moved but once so far... It ain't the comfort that burns my ass, it's all the other folks had their butts sweating and whatever on this fabric since they built the thing. Hung on this little hanky thing to protect us from their greasy hair but no fresh covers for the worst part of it."

Wesley responded with a slow, sympathetic nod. "So the bus broke down? Say what's the matter? Say how long it'll be?"

"Didn't say shit about that. But you can go outside if you want."

"I was sleepin'. How far did we get?"

"Not much for sure. Getting toward Bushville. Them cars stuck up in the desert are out that way." She waved her hand enough to indicate back toward Amarillo.

"Bushville's comin' up? Good name for a big city out here. Can't hardly wait." *I can be as surly as you, girl.*

Despite his mental malaise, the chance to see the Cadillac Ranch drew him outside. He thought it should have been on historic Route 66, two tacky cultural icons in eternal association, not on the generic interstate number 40.

When he stepped out of the bus, he was surprised there were no passengers standing nearby. The bus had looked nearly empty. Then he heard some voices and realized they were all standing on the shady side, some smoking, some just taking in the scenery, such as it was. Wesley looked back to see the famous Caddies with their noses in the sand like industrial age ostriches. He could not see anything as weird or interesting as they ought to be but there was something suspicious not too far away, not beside US 40, but on a parallel road.

"That 66?" he asked a skinny, sun-wrinkled old gentleman who had strayed out of the shade; maybe, as a rural Texan, he thought the crowd was too dense for his taste. His reply was so slow and deliberate, Wesley wondered if he had Maine roots, like the Bush family. Maybe Bushville was named for them. The old cowboy looked at the road and took a deep drag on his cigarette, burning it expertly within a dime's thickness of his fingers. He held the smoke in his lungs so it might do him whatever good he sought from his habit and then exhaled slowly. There was no reason to hurry; they were not going anywhere and they were in the midst of a pleasant conversation.

"That's it yonder," he answered, ending the conversation. If he had said "ayep" first, they would have been in Maine.

Wesley felt it would have discourteous to do anything less than stride off vigorously without a further word so he gave a slight nod to acknowledge the gentleman who, in turn, and displaying his own form of courtesy, did not move in the slightest before Wesley turned away.

Each step raised a puff of dust. Wesley felt like a cartoon of speed across a desert, like Roadrunner (meep, meep). But he was not actually moving fast; too hot for that. Maybe if he were more used to the heat or to discomfort in general, he could have ignored the sensations and thought of something pertinent. Unless, he thought, there could be no pertinent thoughts until he reached San Francisco and looked at the address from Lucas, at his only clue.

He reached Route 66 and walked on the pavement edge for fifty yards or so, no longer kicking up dust and therefore feeling cleaner, before deciding the heat rising from the white asphalt was worse than the heat from the pale soil between the two highways.

He was aware he was walking a metaphor whose purpose was still unclear to him: between two times, between two Western cultures, between two identities... that was it, two identities, neither of which was familiar. Familiar was long gone and unlikely to return. His newly formed, real self was constantly in his head and his travelling self was a constant effort in appearances. He liked the idea of Route 66 better but he was, in fact, more the modern highway. When he returned to his bus, would he be returning in his real self despite his emotional identification with the consciously absurd and peculiar isolation of the unproductive ranch of Cadillacs? It was something to ponder through the next few states. The metaphor might become refined to the point where he understood it as much as he already felt it, a tool for framing his trip west to revive, not his old career, but his marriage anyway.

The Caddies on their noses began to look familiar as he approached them and drew his field of view away from US 40. They were covered in graffiti, as they always are.

Art...   I suppose this counts as such.   Part performance, part vision. I wonder if the original artist had audience participation in mind. Wonder what I would have painted if I had brought a spray can. I'm not creative. I'd do a heart with "Wesley loves Mattie" and pierce it with an arrow. I would hate my feeble attempt for being so trite but it is, in fact, all I can think of, all that I could execute adequately. I'd want to show it to Mattie before someone painted over it.

He could see two buses where he had left one. Wesley jogged back to the bus because he thought a little exercise would feel good and, of course, driven by a twinge of fear that the replacement bus was about to depart. Taking a night in an Amarillo park could be a clever ploy to evade the secret forces that constructed his plight and it might be a break from the stress of his vague plan but getting stranded at the Cadillac ranch on the following day would show how incompetent he could be in this new role he was playing. He was ready to break into a run if he heard the bus honk or, worse, saw it start to move. He wondered inwardly with the superstition of his outward character, if changing his bus again would place him on the one, the only one, he needed to get him on to Mattie.

No one was outside either bus anymore. There had been no honk. Maybe it would have left him behind if he had contemplated the nature of art much longer. He bounded up the stairs as if he had calculated the momentum of his jog to carry exactly for the last few feet. He was not breathing very hard, but he was sweating liberally and felt the sudden cold of the air conditioning on his damp shirt.

As he reached for his ticket, the driver waved him inside with a friendly nod. Wesley wondered what was wrong with himself that he could not recognize the driver's face but the driver could apparently remember all the passengers. Was he a snob who did not pay attention to the working people around him or was he merely handicapped by a weak memory? His memory, as measured by 45 years of life so far, was not extraordinary in either direction, good or bad, so the huge discrepancy between his recall and the driver's could be more easily attributed to class prejudice. ...Unless, he rationalized hopefully, the driver had an extraordinary memory like certain waiters or musicians.

He went back to the driver just to memorize him and used the pretext of asking if he had heard anything about the weather on the way to Tucumcari. Wesley looked the driver in the eye and observed his face, long but not so long as to get creepy. Asking about the weather seemed better than asking when they were leaving because that had to be very soon since everyone was back in the bus. The sky was already dusky though the sun behind the gray was surely not yet reaching the horizon. *A storm could be out there. It rains in the desert sometimes. It only gets mentioned when it turns into flash floods. Is that really the usual thing or just what gets said in fiction?*

He returned to the same seat he had before, as well as he could remember without the woman who had been beside him to prove it was the right row. He slouched down to get back to sleep but he was not tired anymore and he was cold and clammy. He could review the metaphor he had lived back there on the way to the Cadillacs. They deserved some mental review too. He steered his thoughts away from the torture of his remaining miles and, more desperately, away from what he would do when he got to San Francisco. The bus was not the right place for that planning. It would be frustrating to gather ideas on that topic and be unable to write them into his computer to be reorganized and highlighted and otherwise improved as he had learned to do in law school in a technique he had personalized and refined over the years. He managed to ignore what for now what he wanted to ignore but his mind never took instruction well on its way to Nod and this time insisted on going back to Robbie.

Ideas came to him about what he should have said to Robbie over their beers. They were brothers in their respective searches for lost relatives. Were they equally ridiculous to imagine their methods had any prospect of success? They should have shared more sympathies although Wesley might have endangered his mask thereby. His stream of consciousness moved onto a critique of how he behaved toward bus drivers and developed some concepts for being more conscious of people outside the confines of his lawyerly and governmental circle. These thoughts on thinking, meta-thoughts, carried him out of the present and he failed to notice the woman had left the toilet in the back of the bus and reclaimed her seat beside him, the somnolent cowboy.

15. Brenda

At night in a bus crossing Texas, the universe is four seats wide arranged with an aisle leading up to the front where a god sits with hands on the steering wheel. The planet of Wesley could communicate with one nearby planet and see a few more. In the back, as far from the god as possible, is a black hole that stinks.

The ecology of this planet depends on energy inputs from gas stations. It would be too apt if this energy always came from Sunoco stations, that is, Sun Oil Company stations. Wesley wondered if that petro-company were still in business. No food was grown on any of the planets. How long could his species last here? If an apocalypse had instantly destroyed all humanity outside the bus, or all humanity in New Mexico and Arizona, they could still make it to California. They could stop at the Sunocos and live on snacks. And if California were also wiped out, they could drive all over the state and eat snacks. Maybe he could learn to cook although fresh food may not last long enough in this scenario to require anyone have cooking skills. Presumably he and the others could live to a natural age for death. He could have twenty to thirty years left without Mattie, more than he experienced with her. The questions on coping with apocalypse were not inspiring; too hackneyed from exploration in innumerable movies he had seen only through their trailers and paperback books whose covers he had unintentionally absorbed somehow.

Wesley wanted to concentrate on his new book, on the content, the words and ideas therein, but when he tried to shut out the rest of the universe, he was still distracted from the essence of his book by the physical reality surrounding him. He found himself repositioning his hands to hold the book with less conscious effort, tilting it so both visible pages were lit the same, worrying that the font and the margins and the paper were not ideal, although he had been reading them for more than fifty pages without any difficulty.

He looked at his bookmark to estimate what percent remained to be read and he noticed for the first time that the corners of some pages had been bent in. It was not the dog ear of a prior reader marking a place or a passage, but the crumple where the book had been pressed against the corner of something. The damage was slight, but it demanded repair. Wesley turned to the first damaged page and flattened the corner. It was tightly creased and only after several scratches with a fingernail could it be straightened. The next four pages were bent, but were easier to flatten. Just to finish the task, Wesley ran the corner of each of these pages between his thumb and finger so they would not spontaneously give in another time to their mutilation. When he opened the book fully to the first of these pages again, he saw a dull red stain on the page. It had bled through from a smear on the previous page. Obviously it had been wet and yet was not mirrored on the facing page so it had been allowed to dry before closing the book. It could be blood, he thought, appropriate for a murder mystery, and there could be an aspect of that in *4321*. The blot was repulsive, possibly infectious. More likely it was snot, also possibly infectious, less fitting for any genre of novels. He would be very careful when he read those pages.

Suddenly and inevitably, he noticed the seat was not comfortable anymore. It had never really been comfortable but he had been able to ignore it. The fabric was covered in a kind of upright, industrial fiber, a fine-waled corduroy, scratchy and none too clean. The seat would not lean back far enough to shift the weight off his spine, and it was too narrow to fold himself into a sideways configuration. He leaned forward with his face pressed onto one hand, his elbow propped, in turn, on the armrest. At least this position was a change; it would not provide relief for long; he could not fall asleep like this. He rubbed his forehead as if he were thinking in the manner of actors in the early days of film and it felt good. He wondered if he liked the massage he was giving himself or just the image of comfort it projected in his mind.

He peeked out of one slightly opened eye and saw room on the other armrest. With an elbow propped on each side of him, he could hold his head in both his hands without exerting any muscle. He rubbed his fingers into his face in a symmetrical pattern, around and around. It was the massage that felt good. He worked his fingers around his eyes, back to his ears and down to his lips which he stretched by opening his jaw. He was falling asleep and waking at the same time, wrapped into the impression, physical and mental, between his fingers. Suddenly he felt someone was staring at him. Without ceasing the motion of his fingers, he slowly bent his head to the side and looked at the person beside him. She was leaning back with her eyes closed. He looked across the aisle and then at the top of the seats in front of him. Not the slightest attention was directed toward him. He was as alone as if they were addresses on a cellphone rather than people actually near enough to hear and to smell their breathing.

Wesley's eyelids began to droop, which he noticed with irritation. He had slept enough, more than enough, and had a decent book in front of himself. It was all just so boring at the moment, but he could not defend wasting his time by slipping into another mindless torpor. He was pleased, at least, that there was no prospect of turning to a cell phone to entertain himself. He did not want to ever lose the capacity to use his solitude, not necessarily productively, but in some creative or amusing way.

When he was very young, he had no cell phone, obviously. He often had little control over where he was or what he was allowed to do, so he was often bored. A few times he played cat's cradle with his sister and a loop of string. She liked it more than he did but he derived a slight satisfaction from thinking of themselves as children from an earlier, more romantic era. He did not appreciate that he would someday think of his own youth in that image.

He practiced finger movement with a little verse his mother taught him that went "Here is the church; here is the steeple..." Next he laced his fingers together with his left thumb on top as he normally did, followed by lacing them with the right thumb on top to feel the oddity of it. That was all he could remember of solitary finger play, but it brought to mind more than one occasion in elementary school when the teacher had them put their "heads down on the desk." Actually, the class understood this meant they were to fold their arms on the desk and rest their heads on their arms. Why would the teacher ever say this? They were told to do it when the teacher wanted a rest or an individual was sick or as a form of gentle punishment. He had never been punished or sick in school, but he could visualize the boredom of resting his head on the desk from a few times when the teacher wanted a break. His arms constituted a fortress against whatever storybook attackers were outside: medieval knights, Indians, Confederates, pirates. He could hinge his hand at the wrist for opening the gate to send out his troops or to check on the enemy. There was not much more he ever thought to do with the situation. Fighting an enemy was a common childhood fantasy. None of his fantasies lasted into an original plot.

And there were a couple times when something was missing from the classroom and the teacher would have the class "put their heads down" until the person who stole the thing placed it on the teacher's desk. This technique never worked and he knew from the first time it was tried on his class that it would never work. Who would believe no one in the class, including the teacher, was watching? All it took was a slight opening of the fortress gate to identify who might be creeping to the front of the room. He, for one, always kept a lookout for anyone foolish enough to try to silently return whatever was missing. The question came to mind of how long he would have to put his head down to have Mattie returned when he looked up again. She would have been surprised and pleased that the heads-down trick worked. All the stress of Wesley's public humiliation and whatever Mattie had endured since she disappeared would be instantly dismissed. If there had been a desk in front of him, or even a serving tray like the ones in front of airline seats, he would have tried.

Outside the bus, nothing had changed in the last thirty minutes. A flat expanse of plowed fields hurried past in the foreground while the few houses and trees on the horizon seemed to keep pace with Wesley's point of view. Wesley wanted to feel himself hurtling closer to Mattie but the abstract motion was not real to his tired eyes – only a steady state of meaningless blur could be sensed in his daylight dream. He watched a homestead in the middle distance slowly go past to assure himself he was moving and he calculated how many such homes there must still be between San Francisco and himself and multiplied that number by the time he watched this house pass. The result was not an encouraging figure although it did not matter at all – this was the situation and he had to endure until it changed as it was sure to do eventually.

The phrase "familiar as the back of one's hand" had always seemed false to him. The back of his hands never seemed especially familiar although he had often studied them when he was young. He had not heard it for some years and imagined the turn of phrase was completely out of fashion, something his youth did not realize a phrase could become. Yet as unfamiliar as the look of his hands was to Wesley, he did have a close relationship with his hands-- it just was not one based on appearances, more like the way he had come to love Mattie after the first years of discovery and passion -- a matter of who she was. She looked beautiful to him, as much as ever, but he knew that he was seeing her rather than her features, her face and skin and figure and so on. He felt proud for this realization and then immediately felt stupid for claiming virtue for something so obvious.

Back to his hands... He liked them, although they had not always been good at whatever he asked of them. For example they were not beautiful and never had been. He had seen beautiful hands on a man, his environmental law professor for example. He would have liked his own hands' appearance if they had been scarred and calloused from experience but they were not that either. Early in life he had learned to accept he was no beauty in his hands or otherwise. Further, he could not carve with them although he had tried many times to learn. He could not play the piano although he had tried a little of that. He could not paint although he appreciated painting and had made a stab at it when he was in high school and been amazed at his ineptitude to conceive or execute anything worth saving even for the refrigerator. He blamed it on his brain not his hands. They had been large and strong and better at most things than most people's hands. He did not ask they be perfect; it was more than enough that they were good. His feet, on the other hand, so to speak, were both beautiful and flawlessly functional, no matter what he asked of them. They had never failed him. It was his secret that there was something beautiful on his body— it was just a part that was hardly ever seen. He liked to look at them in the bathtub and to handle them when it was time to trim their nails. They were the only flawless part of him.

The person across the aisle was surreptitiously watching Wesley and turned his own hands over and around as if he were looking at them. Suddenly Wesley became aware of the movement and, without turning his head or ceasing his own movements, he looked at the old man's hands. They were well formed though not as large as Wesley's, he was pleased to note. They were not thick and did not appear strong as a craftsman's and neither were Wesley's but the old man's had the delicacy of an artist's and Wesley could envy that. They also had the marks of experience, not scars, or not scars visible from across the aisle. Experience was expressed in the spotted coating of age and the inelasticity of the skin yielding to fine wrinkles and coarse creases, and the transparency of the thin, gaunt, spotted, wrinkled and creased covering that did little to hide the mechanics of his body's blood vessels and ligaments and phalanges. More than these physical signs, experience was expressed in the slow grace of his movements, not motivated by conscious effort; semi-independent partners in his life like a good wife, like the wife Wesley had until a few months ago.

Wesley looked down to his feet, or to his shoes. He thought of removing the latter to be closer to his favorite parts of himself. Now that he had turned his attention to them, his feet felt confined. He had changed his socks once since leaving Washington but it seemed likely they were clammy in their laced and leather shells. It occurred to him that his damp socks (not his wonderful feet) might smell if he removed his shoes but that was not the deciding reason for keeping them on. Rather, there was a silent, lingering fear that he might suddenly need to run. Looking out the window, he saw no place for an escape, like Cary Grant in *North by Northwest.* It would require a very bizarre development to give him cause to try escaping but he had ceased to believe in the probable and decided to trust his instinct for constant paranoia. Al least, he felt confident in his ability to run. His feet had an excellent partnership with his legs.

Next he tried rubbing his hands as if they were cold and he realized that they were indeed cooler than ideal. The air conditioning rendered his thin, seasonal clothes inappropriate. He rubbed his hands slowly in various patterns and thought of the times when his hands were wintry cold, warming them with friction, and maneuvering the tendons and bones as if they needed to be loosened. He thought of photographing his hands with his fingers interlocked in various poses. When he bent his fingers and placed them side by side, little fingers beside each other pointing in opposite directions, etc., it looked like there were ten even without using his thumbs. When he bent them to make them fit closely, the three joints of each finger showed separately so he was looking at 24 soft pink rectangles. That might make a good picture. People might think it was a photographic trick to have so many joints in just two hands.

He crossed his arms and leaned them on the back of the seat in front of himself and then rested his head on his arms. It was a new position and felt better for a few seconds until his back began to complain of being stretched too far for resting. A warm hand touched his shoulder...

"Are you all right, sir?" the woman beside him asked.

He sat upright, surprised to find someone so near. He had drawn himself in so much, he forgot there was nearly always someone right next to him in his solar system of two within the bus universe. "Oh, I'm sorry, sorry, sorry, sorry."

His voice receded on the word while he tried to recall the person he was enacting. He had almost said "I am sorry for disturbing you," and was glad he had not sounded so typical of his actual background. "Getting' antsy, you know. I been on this rig since St. Louis and I guess I ran out of things to think about."

"You lonely, Mister?"

It was a kind question, even if odd coming from a stranger. In another circumstance, said in a different tone, it might be a come-on. Wesley looked at the woman: dark skinned, pretty, no make-up or jewelry but with styled hair, about his own age, soft in the body, almost surely a mother. She was looking back without intimacy, like a nurse perhaps. *Am I lonely?* he repeated the question in his thoughts and let the moment for a quick answer pass. *I could hardly be more alone, down to one friend and the possibility of a wife, possibly estranged, somewhere unknown to me.* This woman was no threat to his identity but neither was she an answer to what company he needed.

"No ma'am. I don't know how to be lonely. I don't have a wife or any kids to miss. No brothers or sisters. My folks are long dead. I've got some friends sometimes but I don't need to be around 'em."

She just nodded back and closed her eyes.

"Thanks for asking though," he added. She opened her eyes and smiled a little. "It feels like sitting next to somebody in church, you know, caring about the neighbor beside you."

"What church you go to?" she asked.

Wesley looked to the front of the bus. The key to a successful lie, for someone out of practice, is to stay as close to the truth as possible. "I don't go anymore, but I remember how it was, how it still is, I guess. It was OK. I just dropped the habit, being too lazy to stick with it. I don't stick with anything really much. Good thing I'm not married, huh?"

"I'm sure your church would be happy if you want to go back sometime. It don't have to be every week neither."

"And I'm sure you're right about that. If I do get lonely, I'll remember that."

Remembering his hands were cold, he stuck them in his pockets. He was wearing jeans and it was awkward to get even his finger in them while sitting, which was obvious to anyone who ever wore jeans. He took out his keys to justify the motion to himself. He could not justify having the keys handy. He had only a house key for a house he was selling and a car key to a car he had parked at the airport as one more false lead in case anyone was tracking him. His office key was gone. The key to his wife's car was gone too, since he had sold that already.

"Why don't you walk up and down the aisle a few passes to get those nerves back together." The woman was still trying to help him or she was just irritated by his fidgeting?

"Yeah, yeah. That's a good idea. I oughta try that."

The woman twisted her legs to the side, suggesting his should squeeze past her. It would be a tight fit. He thought he knew unsophisticated people typically face forward when squeezing past someone in a theater and that it was proper in his world to face the person seated rather than pass one's backside in their face. He decided to go with the "proper" method because he doubted unsophisticated people thought much about these alternatives anyway.

He went first toward the front of the bus so no one would think he was desperate to use the toilet. He stood there for a few moments, looking through the windshield where there was much more view than through the low, side windows. The high, wide vista might be pleasurable for the driver except that it was marred by the ever present pavement through the middle. The rush of minor roadside detail was hypnotic, like a cheap videogame awaiting the insertion of a coin to get the game started. He walked to the back of the bus without grabbing each seat as he passed. It always annoyed him when people shook his seat on a plane, even when he was awake. In the back, near the room with the black hole, he stretched and twisted his torso. Then he touched his toes. The woman had been right; a little walk made him feel better.

He bent halfway so he could look outside again. Rolling plains with scattered bushes and a few blades of grass, it was not exactly the same sight he had seen earlier; the horizon had a different contour, a few hillocks passed slowly by, and hadn't he seen cactus earlier? It was more familiar as scenery from the cowboy movies he had known as a child than as any part of the world he had actually experienced. He was torn between interpreting the bus as the entire universe or as a vehicle to a new galaxy. He kept looking outside to reassure himself he was travelling somewhere, even if the distances he faced were astronomical.

A woman came up the aisle, headed either for him or for the black hole past him. He took a few steps forward before she arrived so she would not have the sense he was near enough to hear her doing whatever she was about to do. She looked at her feet as she passed him although he greeted her with a weak "hullo." He thought of saying "buen' dia'," but that would only have been showing off that he could greet her in Spanish, that he knew one phrase anyway. She might not have wanted him to assume she was more comfortable in

Spanish on the basis of her looks. Most likely, she did not want him to greet her at all. She was not making a social call.

He did not know it, but the truth was she came not from the Mexican background he and most other people in Texas assumed. She was from Guatemala where she spoke fluent Spanish as her second language, her first being an indigenous tongue. She and her husband had saved money through the 1970s, even deferred having children (through abstinence), in order to have enough to afford moving to the United States. When she was 25 and he was 27, they had walked across Mexico and applied for refugee status. They had not been persecuted in their remote Guatemalan village and had no way to present themselves as victims of anything worse than an economy with few opportunities to better the life for the children they would raise someday. So they had used papers that a network of relatives provided to show they were Honduran landowners. In the 1980s, the days of Sandanistas and Contras, such refugees were granted admission to the United States relatively easily. Her husband was fatally sick when they finally entered the United States, having starved himself during the trek to the border in order to give more nourishment to his wife. Years later, after she had become a Christian, she recognized her husband's story as a counterpart to Moses who never made it to the promised land. There were differences between the two stories. Her only child was female, conceived during the northern trek, and that child, that daughter, was his proud legacy. The daughter had recently sent her mother a bus ticket to California to show her a first grandson, a new generation being built on the opportunities the trek had made possible.

Wesley tried not to speculate on the lives of his fellow passengers. He was in this bus exactly to be unknown himself and wanted to hide behind the illusion that no one could tell who anyone was. He saw the Guatemalan woman as a person of a certain gender, size, age and shading. That was already more than he wanted to know.

Like a bacterium, the idea of assessing the others entered his bloodstream and he looked to the side and saw a small, slim, older man of pale complexion, and was troubled that his brain was guessing the man's background. He could not have guessed the man was there simply to ride. He had provided his unskilled labor to numerous small enterprises in and around Kansas City from his high school years until his fifties. He had never worked his way up in any of the businesses, not because he had not done his job, but because he had done precisely his job and no one, including himself, believed he could ever do any more. And because he never stayed anywhere long enough to be placed into some unfilled gap and show his adaptability. They were respectable jobs, requiring effort and discipline, and even paid him enough to support himself and save money for a rainy day although that was possible only because he was extremely frugal too. He made few friends although he felt he was himself friendly. He had strong views on how friends should support each other, and be honest and loyal. If he found a woman who met those simple standards, he would have hoped to marry her regardless of anything else about her. Yet he had not met such a woman and had not married. Instead, he developed a pattern of looking for different work in a different place with different people within a few months of starting a job.

About ten years before Wesley glanced at him on a cross-country bus, he took a job that required him to ride a city bus across Kansas City every morning and evening. He saw the same people almost every day and they smiled to him in recognition sometimes. Even the driver spoke to him with familiarity so he began to see the commute as the best part of the day. Nonetheless, he did not make any real friends on public transportation, a fact he attributed to the shortness of his rides. Sometimes he rode the bus to the end of the line and back, talking to people whenever they seemed willing. And then he tried taking an intercity bus to Chicago. He met a women on that experimental ride. She left him in Chicago, but he saw the potential in the medium. Now he took buses for a round trip of about a week nearly every couple months. Sometimes he had good conversations. He would never demand attention. He had learned to enjoy the travelling for its own sake: seeing new cities, discovering new landscapes, trying new foods, collapsing into the isolation of his temperature-controlled, cushioned, safe, peaceful and reserved spot.

If he had noticed the glance from Wesley, he would have smiled and nodded in his practiced way to communicate his willingness to speak, but he did not see Wesley and the moment passed according to Wesley's design, with very nearly the least possible exchange of information.

Wesley stepped one row closer to his own seat and stretched his back again. A small boy in an aisle seat tapped the seat in front of himself with his scuffed and dusty cowboy boots while watching Wesley. His head was bent forward as if he were looking at his hands in his lap and, indeed, his hands were wriggling as if they had a purpose, but his eyes returned to Wesley again and again. *Fair enough*, Wesley though, *to peek at me. Kids get bored too.* He wondered if he should entertain the boy with a comment or some lesser form of recognition and decided against it. These days adults were not to interact with children without an introduction from their parents. The boy was sharp and noticed Wesley had looked his way and seen the direction of his eyes. He turned his full attention to his fingers and tried to form them into something worth seeing but he did not know the story of the steeple and the people or anything else fingers could do on a bus ride. Wesley heard a sound from him, as if to himself. Then it came again, louder, clearly the same sound, but not understandable: "Wereyafromista." Wesley looked down the aisle and focused on the view past the driver of the road ahead, but a swaying of the bus nearby caused him to involuntarily look down for balance. The boy had turned his head around and said clearly, "Mister, where you from?"

Without speaking, Wesley interviewed the boy. He must be about eight, that would be second grade, maybe a year older but not younger. The woman sleeping beside him would be his grandmother though she was not old yet. A tan line showed on his forehead. He wore a hat a lot, maybe a western hat to match his boots or maybe a baseball cap with a tractor company logo to match his farmer dad's. His t-shirt looked clean enough. Possibly cleaner than Wesley's, but he had not been riding the bus as long as Wesley.

The boy did not ask again but continued to look back. A simple gesture with his hands asked "What's the matter with you, Mister?"

"Missouri." That would not be aggressive enough to be child abuse.

"Canton Park, Kansas," the boy answered as if Wesley had been polite enough to ask. Wesley returned a head shake larger than needed, communicating that he appreciated the information. Grandmother jerked the boy's arm toward herself. The boy pulled himself free and she grabbed him again more firmly but did not speak, not loudly enough that Wesley heard anything anyway. The boy turned his head back to Wesley and smiled which Wesley interpreted as "See, she don't control me."

Not wanting anyone's attention, Wesley headed back up the aisle. As he left the boy he muttered, "Have a nice bus ride."

Back at his seat, he found the woman who had been sitting beside him had slid next to the window.

"You want your place back? I don't need it. I just thought it would be easier for you getting back in."

"Very thoughtful of you," Wesley answered and immediately regretted as it did not sound like the person he was hoping to project. "Don't much care where I sit," he answered and then demonstrated by sitting. He decided to stay still a while to prove he had found comfort in taking her advice.

The woman had been right; the walkabout had calmed him. He opened his first book without attempting to hide it since he was used to leaving out the magazine and read with little comprehension. Suddenly, a line from the Colonel brought him back to himself: Always have a line of reserves in life, boy, always! In peace and in war.[ii] His lies to his seatmate about loneliness reminded him he had no one helping him, no reserves other than Lucas whom he would not involve any further. Was there a way to build up some friends to back him up in whatever he found in California? The idea was absurd except that he had not forgotten the kind woman's mention of church. He could join a church, a modern sect of some sort, show some dedication for a few weeks while he looked into the address Lucas had found, and then call on someone in the church who could be as faithful to him as to the church. The woman sleeping beside him might be such a person. Wouldn't she help after they prayed together a few times? *I am no con man*, Wesley admitted to himself with regret. *I may struggle with the ethics of deceit but the firmest barrier is that I lack the skill to pull it off.*

This he thought, but he did not believe himself. He was arrogant enough to think deep down that he could do it, make a loyal friend though pretending to join a church even without any experience in such deception. He was desperate for a way to raise his odds of finding Mattie. In answer to his insecurity, he recalled earlier advice in his book quoted from Field Marshall von Moltke: "No strategic plan lasts beyond the first skirmish with the enemy. Only the ignorant believe they can discern, in a military campaign, the meticulous execution of an initial idea developed in great detail and ending in victory." [iii] It did not really matter, according to the Field Marshall, that he could not at present work out any details. He only needed to have a next step.

Maybe this woman could introduce him to her church. He looked toward her and saw she was awake, apparently staring at the seat in front of her. "You had good advice. I felt better after walking around a little."

"It is hard to sit still all day, isn't it?"

"I'm Rodger," Wesley said without offering a hand to shake. He almost felt Dupe kick the back of his seat and missed having her sitting nearby. "How far are you going?"

"I'm Brenda. I go as far as Blythe, and my people gonna drive me another 45 minutes to get me home."

"Where's Blythe? That in California?"

"Yes, first stop in the state on this run."

"Summer all year 'round there?"

"We get two seasons: hot summer and too-damn-hot summer." When Wesley did not respond right away, she turned her face to the window as if there was scenery worth seeing. She would not be filling in any more personal details. She would not be his experiment on how to develop an asset for his forthcoming quest. And though Wesley had not as much as looked her way again, she soon politely asked to pass by into the aisle. She said he could move over to the window seat, that she would find a window seat on the other side of the bus because the light was better that way. She did not explain how facing north at 7:45 pm improved the light. Wesley reached behind his head and tapped on the top of his seat to show he had felt the kick from Dupe though he did not know who was sitting there now. So Wesley returned again to Morpheus for companionship.

he was looking at 24 soft pink rectangles

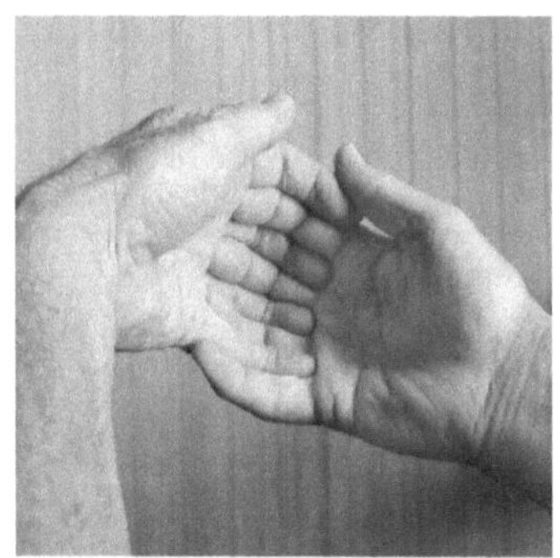

16. Sam

Later, probably not much later, enough to be asleep again, not enough to be dreaming of the past or future universe, Wesley was rudely jarred by a large and hairy man flopping into the seat Brenda had vacated. He did not look at Wesley but maneuvered himself carefully into a position that extended well onto Wesley's side of the armrest. His clothes were rustic, cheap, filthy, and probably smelled although it was nearly impossible to know where any of the body odors in the omnibus air originated. He might have worked in a garage, given the oily stains on his shirt and having his name embroidered above the pocket: Sam Laxness. Wesley had sympathy for the man, fat as he was. Travelling long distance on a bus must be especially difficult for him. It was reasonable to be surly under these conditions.

On the other hand, rude is sometimes crude in any culture and circumstance. Taking up so much extra room without any pretense of caring was irritating no matter how generous the neighboring passenger might be with his sympathies and Wesley's sympathies were nearly worn away at this point in the trip. After all, Wesley was travelling on a long-distance bus trip too, and his circumstance, while not including as much fat, had its distresses too.

The man belched, not loudly, but with enough gaseous volume to be clear as to the immediate origin of the new odors assailing Wesley; liverwurst came to mind but that might be simply because Wesley did not like liverwurst.

"Folks where you come from do that?" the man asked, leaning toward Wesley so close his head was fully past the armrest.

What an aggressive son of a bitch! Wesley thought although he tried to preserve his sympathies for the man. It was proper, in Wesley's mind, to treat public body noises and their accompanying odors as if they had not happened. "Do what?" he answered without looking at the man directly.

"Burb, fart and shit," the hairy fat man answered as he leaned back in his seat although he kept his arm and leg pressed against Wesley as if maintaining a claim to a territory.

He seems satisfied he has established his rank on this planet of two seats. Wesley did not like bullies when they leaned against the weak. Apart from the crisis with Mattie, he did not think of himself as weak, not with all the advantages he had been given, but either accommodation or retreat was inconsistent with his current persona.

"Folks ever'wheres burbs and farts and shits," Wesley answered in a matter-of-fact tone without looking up."

The bully grunted a word Wesley remembered his mother teaching him from a Rudyard Kipling fable about how the camel got its hump: humph. Then Wesley looked to the bully, waiting until their eyes met, and continued in a firmer voice, "Folks out my way don't choose to talk much about those things to strangers."

Silence followed for two or three seconds without either man turning away. Wesley put his left hand, the one away from the bully, into his pocket and slowly withdrew it as if he had taken out something and held his hand with whatever might be hidden in it beside his leg. As he made this maneuver, he stared at the near hand of his seatmate as if waiting for it to move, as if it mattered if it moved.

It was soon too late for an apt riposte from the bully whether clever or aggressive or profane or dismissive, so he lowered his shoulders and leaned back to release the tension that was holding him uncomfortably stiff, turned his face toward the aisle and twisted in a way that moved all of his body onto his side of the armrest, clearly offering no concession to good manners but, it should be assumed, for the simple reason that it was more comfortable to sit that way.

Wesley was surprised at the easy success of his implied threat and felt he was himself now acting the bully. That was a disguise he had not expected to try on nor would he have wanted to act it out. Aside from the negative ethics of it, he would not have thought he could. He also thought it was dangerous to pretend to be quicker to violence than he was. The man was fatter by far than Wesley (who was merely chubby) but not in a comical or effeminate or forgivable way. He had huge forearms and thick fingers that suggested he could make a formidable tussle if he wanted to, especially in the tight space of adjoining bus seats. He had made no effort to hide his balding pate, consistent with his disregard for any other aspect of appearance apart from rolling up his sleeves to display his arms. The remaining hair above his ears had been laid flat with the application of a comb, perhaps having been treated by spit and a press of his wet fingers. He had shaved that morning, leaving several swaths of day-or-two-old whiskers below his jawline, probably out of sight in a casual glace to the bathroom mirror. His clothes were worn thin and far less than clean. If he were a white-collar renegade like Wesley or a suburban man in a gray flannel suit or a store clerk or a librarian or a park ranger or any other respectable thing who might be crossing the country *incognito*, he was wearing a more convincing screen than Wesley's.

A thought passed slowly in and quickly out of his consciousness that he might ease the situation with a "normal" comment, like, "ever been to Tucumcari?" It was not consistent with his current pose. Then the thought bounced back into a different form: "never been to Tucumcari," referring to himself and requiring no answer. A grunt in response would have been a way to agree on peace. *Stupid idea,* his rational mind averred. *Accept your little victory and create no further foolishness.*

Thus, he accepted the truce as it was and even placed his elbow in touch with the back of the armrest. "Never been to Tucumcari" sounded like a song title. Or maybe it could be a short story of his next few hours after which he would never again utter the phrase in truth. What would it mean to have this additional experience in life, seeing the small New Mexico town, remote but for being on the road to California? It was not south enough to be a gateway to Mexico, not dry enough to be a model desert town, not big enough to birth a person or an event Wesley could name, not important enough to retain the youths it produced or to attract new blood since its peak in the 1950s. Yet Wesley knew of it, possibly the only town he recognized marked on his map of the West with a small, empty circle signifying population under 5,000.

It should have been in the Route 66 song (love that song). Isn't it big enough for that? Maybe's it's even bigger than some of the ones that got in. Joplin, Missouri? I never heard of it outside the song.   And where is Winona? Kingman and Barstow don't sound Southwestern so maybe they're in California.   Yeah, of course south of LA in California is still in the Southwest but California has so many towns it must have needed to use more names with distant roots. Funny how the song assumes you're headed west on the road. It goes both ways. Never hear of people moving out of California to the east.

Wesley knew the song well, knew the Nat Cole version and the one by the Manhattan Transfer. He had heard other versions but could not remember who did them. He did not know western cities well, in fact, scarcely at all. Tucumcari is only a quarter the size of any other city in the song. Barstow, San Bernadino and LA are the only California locales in the song.

Wesley was no songwriter but he was vain enough to think he might have a poem in him. A drive through by bus, a delay at the station to watch people he had never met and would never meet get on or off. Would the bully get off? Would he change his seat to press his flesh over the line of someone who would let him?

Wesley might have to make his poem about the inevitable boredom between Tucumcari and California. There would be time enough if he could discover an inspired foundation as the bus passed through. He was a fact-based writer of memoranda and briefing papers. What a grand challenge a poem of any sort would be and ever so much harder without knowing any local history, guessing at cultural attributes, travelling in one dimension, speaking to none of the people he might see, each of whom knew far more than he of the place. Still, Keats had written an ode on a Grecian urn and he was largely uninformed about anything more than the images on the object. His ode was mostly questions to the figures portrayed there. He said aloud, softly, without acknowledgement from anyone, "Sure, I can do as well as Keats, right?"

As it turned out, Tucumcari was still 65 minutes away by the schedule, long enough to get started on a poem. Yet all he did with the time was turn his semi-conscious face to the window to face the flowing moonlit vista and empty his mind as if he knew how to meditate. His focus was on not checking his watch so he could not count down to the arrival in town, thus he could float effortlessly to his destiny, except that it was a significant effort to ignore the progress recorded and the resultant prediction available on his wrist. He had no practice in meditation and soon reasoned that looking at the time would not change anything so he looked at his watch and immediately felt smaller for giving in to a habit from his former life.

Despite his distraction from the passing landscape, Wesley noticed Route 66 was running a few feet south of the bus on its Interstate 40 pathway. He hoped, for no good reason, that the bus would change over to 66 to reach the bus station, but 66 suddenly veered away to the left and just as the bus exited to the right from the interstate, he saw 66 come to a dead end.

They passed a cluster of competing motels, celebrating their connection to the post-war era with unimaginative incandescent signage supplemented by cheap neon declaring "vacancy" and boasting air conditioning, free TV, and pool. Quality Inn displayed a different marketing strategy in its name from Econo Lodge while Super 8 and Motel 6 each seemed to await the day when they would attain a proper name. Then the *Blaze-in-Saddle RV Park* offered a cowboy tie-in to contrast with the Native American appeal of the neighboring *Kiva RV Park* and *Historic Apache Motel.* At this point the road was displaying Route 66 markers, fulfilling his wish to actually ride the Mother Road, and the crossroads started to mark out blocks of mostly single-story homes. The *Blue Swallow Motel* across from *Tee Pee Curios* marked the most legitimate remnants of the Mother Road's local history although the nearby *Kix on 66* diner was trying hard to fit in to the Fifties. None of this deserved poetry though it was a diversion from the sunlight-on-dirt-farm scenes of human legacy he had watched most of the day.

The fluorescent lights of the bus station could be seen from two blocks away as if it were the central attraction of Tucumcari. It was the key institution for Wesley. The driver docked his universe and stood up to stretch without turning off the motor. When he opened the door, he announced "leave in ten minutes." They were close to schedule and should have had twenty minutes. He probably knew the nature of his passengers and was planning to keep on schedule with a white lie.

Sam Laxness was awake and idly watched the departing passengers, showing no interest in joining them and never turning an eye toward Wesley to see if he were leaving. Wesley figured ten minutes was not enough to get a good stretch and he sure wanted to avoid confronting fat ol' Sam. Better to accept sitting still and projecting such was his choice. Sam might have been an asteroid thrown from a planet on the better lit side of the universe and striking another Greyhound planet, embedding itself in the seat next to Wesley. Big as he was, he had not produced the disaster such bulk could have brought. *It is time for a new metaphor*, Wesley noticed. *Sam is too human to be inanimate or alien. I am riding the Pequod, proper home to obsession. I am Ahab and control the path of our ship by the power of the tickets I hold. The driver is no more than the wheel to my rudder. Ishmael is aboard to observe and record and he is but a flea beside my mission. See how I have bullied the bully by force of my new personality? Very Ahabian. To the good, Ahab did find the white whale. Not so fine, he did not survive the reunion. I will have to be careful.*

He would better think of the city coming his way next, Albuquerque, another city with a fine name... Like Tucumcari, also a unique name in North America as far as Wesley knew, but so much bigger he was certain it would be more like the rest of America where cities are not so distinctive as they were before transportation, like the Mother Road, smeared cultural attributes beyond their former borders; television largely, not completely, standardized language; and movies built up a national mythology, widely known but often disbelieved locally.

His resolve to experience and appreciate Albuquerque was quickly proving problematic. Nothing in view of his window deserved to be called "unique." The houses could have been on the outskirts of any city in the region though it was depressing to see a town composed almost entirely of them, supplemented by small retail selling gasoline, auto parts, alcohol, credit, insurance, animal feed, hardware, law suits, quick food and overnight lodging. *What, he wondered, rhymes with "prosaic" (Passaic), with "trivial" (convivial), with "quotidian" (old Gideon), with "banal" (surely nothing has that accent on the first syllable)? Do those sparks of tourist interest in the local achievements of Route 66 lift the small city enough to deserve its exquisite name?*

Wesley's Western Wander

Hot, desert rocks underfoot,
Massive, barren mesas and rugged, red spires rising high,
Clear, vast wasteland vistas from rising moon to setting sun,
Silent, stark, strong and stringent desert biology, too tough to live
      where lesser species drift an easy life,
Share the timeless terrain with an ancient human presence,
But allow no sign of 21st Century souls to reach
      my air-conditioned, cross-country bus,
      purring its rear-engine diesel
      at seventy-five miles an hour
      from Amarillo to Albuquerque,
      Tulsa to Tucumcari to Tucson.

The East and all that I know of America lies behind me.
The Pacific Ocean waits ahead with all I need to know next.
I will find the Ocean (much too big to miss).
For the rest of it,
I will
> apply my shadow of talent,
> grasp at rumors,
> play for luck and
> hope for the assistance of a generous providence,
So my next traverse through gritty Southwest miles,
Possibly years hence,
Will be different from today.
I would it be confident, even triumphant,
As possible only if I be, unlike now,
Accompanied.

Albuquerque was a bright and full-sized pearl on the necklace of stops and starts along Wesley's route. The city lights were conspicuous as a glow in the sky thirty minutes before the bus was due to arrive. For most of that time, the low-lying suburbs were visible though they tended not to hug the noisy highway too closely. A quarter past eleven at night was too early to turn off the city lights, still burning to display familiar brand names in every line of business.

When the bully rose and rummaged in the overhead rack, Wesley ran sarcastic farewell options through his mind. It spoke poorly for his poetry, for his language skills, his creativity, that he could not come up with anything to fit the moment. In the few seconds available he switched his thinking to what gesture he could make to signal he remained a threat. It was not a skill he had learned or tried to learn. It was not even a useful skill in his upbringing or his career. He was both inexperienced and poorly equipped to confront violence. The criminality he had seen in his Washington years as a lawyer was subtle, hidden as mere questionable ethics, usually controllable with threat of exposure or, more dramatically, reprimand; never going any farther than someone losing his job. Even the kidnapping of his wife had left no evidence of violence. He had been lucky to win a space on the armrest by playing his current cover. He was lucky again to discover the best possible response his talents allowed by delaying any comment to the departing bully. His sendoff choice was to not even glance toward the aisle. He moved his head from window to book to the front, as if the noise of so much movement was mildly disturbing and the good fortune of the exit by Sam was not worth an iota of recognition. And then he stared steadily through the window at Sam while he collected the rest of his luggage from under the bus.

Nothin' to see here, Wesley thought. After nothing had held his attention in Tucumcari, after nothing had distracted him from his ill-informed, unplannable, desperate mission, he sought no more in this bigger place but the bus would not leave again for more than an hour so he admitted he ought to get outside and wander about, investing a quantum of energy to the short-run task of building up a little sleep deficit, enough to nap away some of the time remaining in the long night still ahead. He straightened his ten-gallon hat, gripping it with one hand around the front of the brim to bend it a bit more into the well-worn look he wanted, and watched the others exit. Two old men seemed to be asleep while everyone else exited. Wesley stood up, as straight as he could under the luggage rack, and peered through the window down to the driver outside, taking out the bags marked for Albuquerque. Finally, he stepped into the aisle and stretched. Yes, he needed to walk around.

First, while balancing on the last step of the bus, he was hit with the heavy stench of diesel, louder to his senses than the sound of a dozen idling buses purring evenly, harsher to his senses than the severe florescent lighting packed overhead tightly enough to simulate daylight if the sun suddenly forgot to emit all the wavelengths needed for life, more offensive to his senses than the blotchy patina of dust and dirty chewing gum on the parking lot pavement and cracked sidewalk. Every sense already loathed his new environment. His vacation from the now familiar torture of his cramped and filthy enclave inside the Pequod was into a familiar urban corner of the sort he had avoided for a decade of travel by taxi and plane and the Washington Metro.

He took a few steps away from the bus and bent forward to touch his toes although he did not reach all the way. He leaned back and then twisted his neck and his torso to the left and the right. Enough of a physical workout...

There was little reason to be so cranky. The filth was hardly excessive or unhealthy. The decibel level was low by urban standards although relatively high for the hour, assuming distance from a saloon. It was safe (an important point). Most of the crew of his ship had gone inside already. A few were greeting family and organizing their gear, yet it did not seem natural. It ought to have been like the familiar Washington Metro anyway, perhaps at the Reagan Airport station where long and local commercial travel intersected. There were no men in suits and ties accessorized with textured brown shoes and multi-function wristwatches and sleek briefcases. No children either, probably due to the hour. No women dressed to hold his eye, no lonely guitar busking a single song all night long, no rush to get to the next task, no tourists in t-shirts announcing the team or the concert tour that had kept them up so late. He watched the last group of his shipmates happily hugging and kissing two generations of their offspring. Every male in the group wore a straw hat and skin darkened by sun more than genes; every male from six to seventy wore boots and jeans. Wesley knew, in fact hoped desperately, no one was meeting him in Albuquerque, but the scene was depressing for reminding him no one was waiting for him anywhere or would greet him with affection no matter how they met.

Inside the station there was a ticket counter with no one on duty, a souvenir stand behind a locked grate, a panel of lockers, public toilets, and a few vending machines. He felt no hunger but looked through the candy bars and crackers for inspiration. The stuff seemed expensive. He moved over and bought a cola, not a bottled water or a diet drink.

Wesley looked around again closely, surprised to find no pay telephones. He did not want one but it seemed odd. Maybe there was one in the toilet and to resolve that unbidden question in his mind as much as any other reason, he went in the men's room. No phone there either.

He used the facility in the conventional manner and seriously enjoyed washing his hands and face thoroughly. He splashed the cold water into his hair and then remembered he had no comb, so he ran his fingers through a few times and put his hat back on. In the mirror he looked like a fool, Don Quixote without even a Sancho (he would not insult Lucas with that association). He made a face at himself and then another, looking for a way to look more like a wandering Westerner. The growth on his cheeks and chin was helping him get his intended appearance. It seemed helpful to tilt his head down and roll his eyes up without raising his eyebrows. *That's who I am now. Marlboro man. Embrace it! Then get back in the bus, you couldn't ride a horse if your life and Mattie's depended on it.*

17. Esther

"I could just start talking or I could say something little and see what you do, but I'm the kind that puts her cards on the table face up. It a dumb way to play cards, I know, an' I ain't stupid so that's why I don't play cards. I'm saying here, I'm wide awake and can't hardly sleep on these things anyway so if you want to talk or want to listen, I'm in and if you don't, just tell me and I won't."

"What if I'm asleep and don't answer?" Wesley asked, having enjoyed the way the woman introduced herself. He had nearly fallen asleep in the privacy under his hat and did not expect a conversation with a new seatmate at thirty minutes past midnight. Furthermore, he did not peer out from his cover, a gesture he thought was notable since men usually want to see a woman who starts a conversation without any obvious reason. Yet he could understand that the woman was just beginning her trip and might be so wide awake with or even excited by the details of her travel that she had lost sight of the usual meaning of the hour.

"We already done that. This is the third time I gave that speech to you and I took your silence for sleep. Was you asleepin'?"

"Guess I was 'cause I never heard you. Didn't know I was sleepin'."

"Just teasing. I never spoke up before. Looked like you mighta had your eyes shut but then after a few miles, I thought I'd ask or I'd miss the chance to be amused."

"You're not going far then?" Wesley put his hat on his lap but did not sit up straight.

"Not far enough from what I'm leaving behind. Don't ask about that 'cause I ain't talking about it. We can talk about what's ahead if you want."

"Problem. I don't know about what's ahead but it don't look so good for me so I can't talk about it if we're just strangers passing the time."

"An' talking about the present don't work much 'cause it's al'ays movin'. By the time you said somethin' you're taking about the past."

"Hmm," answered Wesley not for lack of words but because it was the right thing to say, to hesitate, a way of crediting her with a clever riposte. He waited a few moments while she relaxed in her victory, then took the initiative. "Let's try talkin' 'bout dreams."

The woman turned toward him, looking down because he was slouched so low. He sat up but did not look right at her. "Generally," he added, "I hate talkin' 'bout them and I hate seein' 'em in TV shows so I reckon I might have stored up a lot to say and a lot to hear."

This woman was a far better companion than the Mr. Laxness going to Albuquerque. Wesley phrased it in his mind, the mind of his guise: *A barking pitbull with a leaky colostomy bag would have been better company than that son of a bitch so this woman would have to go pretty far to lose a congeniality competition against him.*

Conversing with her, who seemed to be a good talker, would use up some time; getting Wesley closer to California where he would more rigorously avoid his natural vocabulary, where he would have to play his few remaining cards smartly. She did not answer right away and sat facing forward and sat upright, giving Wesley the impression she was either considering his proposal or searching for another snappy comeback.

She was somewhere between five years younger than Wesley and twenty years older. He thought at first she was Black of a pale hue but then figured that was his Washington habit – to first assume a person of color was Black. It was a good bet in that town. Out here, she was probably American Indian or Hispanic or a combination of several options. Her skin was fine textured like silk between the hundreds of tiny wrinkles. Her hair was pulled back in a way that disguised its texture, dark with some stray grays that were not necessarily from an age any greater than Wesley's. ...Big boned throughout, especially in the face where her cheek bones pulled the skin taut. *Yes*, he figured, *she looks like a woman who has had a past or, at least, should have had one. Not a past I would have liked to have shared either.* But maybe the strong impression her appearance made was just Wesley's unfamiliarity with Southwestern people.

She agreed to discuss dreams because, she said, she did not believe she could control them and therefore she was not responsible for them and, further, because she did not believe they controlled her in any way either. These ideas were endorsed by Wesley and led to their additional agreement that they tried to control their dreams despite believing they could not.

She continued, "I don't know why I keep trying to make a dream come up when I never could yet in all my life. Just don't seem fair. As long as we gonna dream anyway, why not let us pick something good if we want to?"

"So is there some dream you're always shooting for?"

"Oh I don't know. No, not the same dream really. I might fall asleep in front of the TV and want to do the story on TV over, put me into it and then not make the mistakes in the show."

"Yeah, I can see that."

"Like if it was a murder story, I could catch the murderer faster or if I was the murderer, I could get away with it."

"Did you ever figure out how to do the perfect crime? Maybe something you could use in there. If you did get one but you're too good to use it, tell it to me and maybe I'll give it a try."

"Like I said, I never get to live out the story."

"But you could lie there awake trying to get the whole thing in your head so you can dream about it and before you get to sleep maybe come up with a better way to do the thing."

"Nah, I don't do that. I don't want to do the crime or make the bust. I just want to see the show again with a different ending, you know? Dreams don't make you think while they're playing out."

"Hmm," Wesley answered again. *That's not my way,* he thought. *I'm not _that_ lazy. I'm always building a fantasy of some unlikely success.*

On a bus ride, with too much time for sleep, the daydreams linger. In a semi-conscious state, they feel nearly real. There had been an evolution in the nature of his daydreams since childhood. The fantasy of becoming a sports hero gave way over the years to a fantasy of winning the best girl in school. When practical limitations in relations with girls became too clear to forget, fantasies moved on to job success or fame or riches. At least they tended to begin with these and then to expand in scale beyond any reasonable hope. After more years, these ideas played out as reality imposed itself over his imagination. He consciously shifted his waking dreams to science fiction where impracticality was assumed from the start.

"If you could to go back to a certain age, you choose how old, and relive life, knowing what you knows now, how would it play out differently?" Wesley suggested to keep the ideas flowing.

"That's a dream you had?"

"No, but it could be. Say, if I could pick the dream and then watch it like a movie; like you said."

"And how far back would you go? Where would restart yourself?"

"I don't know. I was askin' you. I thought of the question and I thought of it before but I never had the dream and never speculated much on it." *That's not true*, he admitted to himself. He needed to remind himself of the truth from time to time so he did not actually turn into the guy he was playing. He had relived the last day with Mattie a few times and then realized he needed to relive the month before that day, so he ran that scenario over and over. He could not win that match either. And then he realized he should relive a couple years so he and Mattie did not drift apart, become complacent about the most important part of their lives. That strategy worked except for the critical point that he could not go back in time no matter how far.

Had that been the best time in his life or was it when they had just finished school and gotten good jobs and started to earn some money and saw promotion possibilities so they would have more money and know important people and have some prestige around their colleagues? Back then he sure felt the future was all theirs.

"I wouldn't wanna go too far back." He would not tell any truth. It was easy to lie about dreams. "So, I'm fifty two. I can't start all over when I was young and hafta go through school all over and figuring out how to live and get a job and all that stuff I did really bad and still don't wanna see again and hafta do it all over some better way."

"Me? I'd go back to my biggest mistake and then not make it. Just not go over to (I don't want to even say his name here) to that guy's house when I was 16 and do what I did that day or have done to me what was done to me that day. I know I shouldn'a done my part in it back then. If I got myself away that day, I wouldn't have done it later. Then I could sleep through the rest of the dream and know it woulda come out better."

"That's mighty cool." Wesley was not lying here. He did think she was mighty cool. "You actually had the personality to be better than things was. Don't think I coulda been much different. If I could go back, I'd just look for some way to take advantage of the thing."

"Want to know what I did?"

"I don't need to know. It's your business. But I'm sitting here to LA so if you want, you can tell me."

"You ain't nosey as some I know. Maybe I tell you later. We got time before LA. Right first, you tell me how you take advantage of going back."

"I guess I use my knowledge of the future to do something for myself. Problem is, I don't know anything that would be terribly valuable in the past, say, thirty-five years. Can't go back too far or I'm a kid and got to go through that again. Like, you know, I could see the computer was going to be big but I could not be the one to invent it."

"But you could invest in Apple or one of those guys."

"Yeah, I thought of that. Takes money to invest. I was thinking I could bet on the Superbowls. Start one year with a few bucks. Work it up with the winnings. I can probably remember who won most of 'em as they come along, but that's just turning the fantasy into money. And then getting the car and stuff, a really fine woman, like all the other worn-out dreams. I'm trying to find a way to really do some good before I wake up. Not just get a lot of money."

"You could give it away." She was right, of course, but it was not much of a dream to make money and then give it away.

"Sure that's good, I guess, but, I mean, even that doesn't really take advantage of this huge power I would have to know the future. In a movie, the guy would stop something like a terrorist attack, like 9-11, or maybe defeat the terrorists all the way. I don't know. I never did anything in my life, my 52 years, yet. It wasn't because I didn't know the future... What would you do if you could go back, aside from walking away from that jerk... You might tell me about if you feel like it later?"

"This is like a movie. It's a kind I don't watch but I probably saw something like it anyway. Feels like I did. It's like the kiddy stories where you get three wishes. The game is rigged for failure. It's all right, let me work with it. I like it. There's a way to beat it. We got to, what four o'clock this afternoon or something? I been keeping you up. Put that hat over you face like when I found you and I'll get back to you when I figure out how to use your script."

"I am tired but I'll be all right pretty soon." Wesley tucked himself into a position that had been comfortable before.

He had, of course, been lying about how far back he would take himself if he could. He had more to fix than taking Mattie for granted. He had worked through this fantasy before, not as entertainment, but as torture because every time he tried out a new scenario, it came out better than the actual life he had lived and at yet every moment he knew there was no going back. He had tried out the one that went back the farthest, back to elementary school age. He could be as brilliant a prodigy as he wanted, knowing math and science and literature beyond any explanation. He would know how to attract girls even without using his star power as a genius. He would stay away from sports which had wasted so much of his first youth. He could hide some of his knowledge, revealing it over time to be plausible. But everything would go downhill once he was no longer ahead of his age. When he was in college, presumably the best college in the country, he would be unable to keep up with classes because his talent was only the trick of bringing his memory from the future.

The best strategy would be more modest, more real, if an utter fantasy can be assigned a level of reality. He would take sophomore year of high school and never act the genius for having been there before. He would still know how to attract girls like a more mature person than he had actually been. Given a second chance at life, he would be a much better student and learn what he had never learned. Would he still go to law school? Yes, he would be going to the best, Harvard probably. And he would still be focused on learning what he did not already know rather than living off the head start of the fantasy memories. This was possible. He had huge volumes of unused capacity that could be filled by wasting less. No boring beer parties, no vapid movies, no...

And then I would find Mattie. I would know how. But would she want me if I were this wildly successful guy? Why did she go for me in the first place? Did she want to save me from my underachievement? She did save me— taught me to work at school and in a job, or inspired me to. It doesn't sound like her to need to fix a guy. Would the new me, the one who recognized earlier what he could do in life and how to earn it, be able to land her? Oh, I could just assume that fits inside the fantasy. No, it doesn't. The fantasy is to pick a starting point and figure how it would turn out. She has to be the same person. To get her again, I need to know what wins her. I knew it once and then forgot it or forgot to do it or something. It would be legitimate in the rules of the fantasy to take the best woman I meet in my alternative, high performing existence. Not that I could do better, but it would be less risky than to come back as a different person and aim for the same wife. That makes sense but it's my fantasy and it has to lead back to Mattie and to a safe place for her or I'll just not have the dream. Damn, I can't even have a decent planned dream; always some kind of nightmare.

"Mister, mister, we're pullin' into Gallup. You want to run inside? We're only here 15 minutes he says. You hear the announcement?"

"Wha? Gallup, New Mexico?"

"Of course, it's New Mexico."

"Just a minute." Wesley knew enough to shut his mouth until he cleared his head. He'd just had his deepest sleep in months.

A few people were leaving their seats. Gallup was not a major destination. Fifteen minutes was not long enough for anything.

"I could take a cuppa coffee but I ain't gonna miss my ride outta here."

"They don't have no coffee waiting for you in there at three in the morning! What have you been dreaming?"

"I was really out! Think I was dreaming the perfect crime. Let me run through the plan to see if it is as good as it felt. I've dreamed some stupid stuff sometimes. Come to think of it, I almost always dream stupid stuff."

"Me too. So why do people always talk like dreams are what we want? Like: I dreamed I was living in a beautiful new house, or I dreamed I won first prize in a baking contest and got a thousand dollars out of it?"

"Why do people talk at all? I mean, except for when you're on a bus for hours and hours and just bored? I don't want to insult you, you're very nice and all, but do you ever listen to talk radio? I hate it and I know it ain't doing anybody any good."

"Well, that question's no insult to me. I never listen to it and don't hardly know what's on it. Don't they talk about sports all day long?"

"Yeah, probably. I don't like sports either."

"What do you like then?"

"I listen to music."

"Oh yeah. What kind?"

"I don't know. I like any kind for a while and then I get tired of it so I change to another station and listen to some other kind."

"That's strange! Most folks who say they like music mean some particular kind, like the one they grew up with."

"My family never played the radio. We only watched TV on weekends and they didn't have any music on it. I like thinking of the people playing their instruments with all their skills. I tried strumming a guitar a couple times and I could see how hard it is to make it sound good." *It is so tempting to mention Route 66. Someone in my reality might know I liked it. They say a lie is easier if it's close to the truth, but, no, I got to lie all the time.*

"You never sang in church or school or something like that?"

"I can't sing but just two or three croaky notes. Never did any churching either. Guess you were more respectable than that?" *Damn, all that's true enough. Lying all the time is too hard.*

"Oh Lord, yes. I went to church regular when I was at home. Seems I got out of the habit when I moved out west."

Whoops, she's not from the Southwest. Maybe she *is* *a Black from South Carolina or Washington, DC. Not right for me to ask about that though.* "But you can sing, right?"

"Anybody can sing. I might remember a song when I'm cooking or someways busy like that."

"OK, sing something now."

"I'm sure not going to sing here! Thought you noticed I was a respectable woman."

"If you sing something soft from the church, no one's gonna think poorly of you."

"You crazy, boy," the woman said with a musical lilt and a smile.

The bus backed out of its space and then roared back to its task of finishing the way to California. Wesley turned to look out the window though there was not much to see in the dark, an assortment of shabby commercial establishments with lit signs and some wooden apartment buildings with a few porch lights on."

"Don't think anyone got on in Gallup," the woman said, sensing the conversation topics had worn out. "We were pretty full when I got on. We got a few openings now."

"Sorry, ma'am, I guess I'm losing focus here. How far back is Gallup."

You a mighty fine sleeper, boy. We only left there a couple minutes back. Now we got, what, three hours I think to Flagstaff."

"Do we stay there any time?"

"I got my ticket right here. Says three short stops, 'bout like Gallup, then we get a break in Phoenix. Altogether that's six hours down the road. You need to get out of the seat?"

"Short stops are good. Best to get out of here sooner."

"It's the middle of the night still. Can't remember ever being awake at 3:30 in the morning and not in bed. You go ahead and sleep some. You better at it than me. Don't you hold back if you need to get up though. I don't mind moving."

"Like I said, nice lady. But when I ask to get out, I need to know what to call you."

"'Ma'am' is no good. Call me 'Esther Bower'.

"I'm Willard Goodhue'."   Wesley regretted his choice of name with a woman of indeterminant but non-White color beside him. He was using first names of people he knew and last names of different people he knew. No celebrities.   Nothing unpronounceable or unspellable. Thinking fast and clearly at 3:30 am was very hard. The lesson here, he realized, was to have a new name ready before it was needed. Esther Bower may not have noticed his awkward choice. She did not comment on it and he was sharp enough, even at 3:30 am, to not point it out. "See you later if you're still around."

And then she added, "I'll let you buy me breakfast in Phoenix."

Wesley considered complaining about his finances but then he decided it would be more out of character for an Ahab to lose sight of his whale for the duration of a meal, especially if an indiscrete meal with an attractive woman is what lost him his leg in the first place (his metaphor was already breaking down).

"That'll be the first date I had in years, Esther."

Wesley repeated his new name to himself so he would remember it when he woke up, assuming he got to sleep again. He tipped his hat to Esther and slouched down with the hat over his face. Although there was not much light in the bus, the hat afforded him a further sense of privacy, a place where he could think his thoughts without slipping outside his current flow of personalities and lies.

For two hours, Wesley struggled to sleep and managed a few short periods of unconsciousness. He assumed there was no REM sleep and that he would be a psychological wreck by the time he reached LA. Maybe he could manage some real sleep in the bus terminal there during his five-hour layover. He would have to buy an alarm clock to manage that.

Around 5:30, his bladder insisted it was time to pee. "Esther, ma'am," he whispered, pleased to have remembered to use his default term of address since that would be most natural coming out of sleep. Esther did not respond. He sat up slowly.

"What?" she whispered back. He had changed his position many times since they last spoke and she had never responded.

"I really got to stand up straight for a minute. This is no way to sleep."

"You did pretty good. I got less'n you did."

"Sorry for you then. You oughter stretch your legs out too."

"You probably right, Willard." She stood up and stepped backwards toward the driver. "You go first."

Wesley stretched as soon as he got in the aisle. He started at the top because he had seen that in a health video in high school, turning his head as far it would comfortably turn in every direction. When his neck made a squeaky sound like walking on turkey gizzards, he stopped that and twisted his torso back and forth which neither felt nor sounded significant. He bent his wrists back, one at a time, and swing his arms in a slow arc, careful to avoid the other passengers. Finally he touched his toes, or bent as far as possible toward his toes. The routine may have loosened up some tension in his joints but it was more significant, Wesley believed, for adding to his disguise. No one who knew Wesley would expect him to stretch himself in an organized fashion. Then he went to the toilet, cleaning it as well as possible before he left for the next user, presumably Esther. Perhaps that was distinctly consistent with his true nature but he would take a chance on its being noticed.

Esther had leaned across the armrest onto Wesley's/Willard's side and fallen asleep. He was about to turn around and pace the aisle for a couple minutes so she could get some rest but he realized that was Wesley's thought, not Willard's. He whispered "Miss Esther," and then repeated it with a touch on her shoulder. She sat up suddenly without speaking. "Sorry. I ought to get back in my seat now."

"Whew, I guess I'm tired now. Don't say 'sorry' about wanting your seat back. You paid for it. Let me just step away for a minute then I can get back to forming the dream I wanted."

Now Wesley was thinking of offering her the window seat upon her return because it is easier to relax against the window but then he figured the idea would not be Willard's thought. Wesley tended to imagine people of lower education than himself offered little courtesy.

Wesley had barely closed his eyes when he heard his alter-ego's name whispered from near his ear. Esther had returned too quickly. He turned to answer her but she spoke again right away.

"Didn't you see that man? We gotta do something!"

"What man? What we gotta do?"

"That man in the aisle, you fool. You couldn'a missed him. He's blocking the way back. He ain't breathing!"

The first thing that came to Wesley's mind was that the man could not have anything to do with him or whomever might be pursuing him. There simply was no way they could have caught up with him here. Was this reflex selfish or a practical step in analyzing the problem?

"Lemme see," and Wesley rose from his seat to look back. From that spot, he could not see the aisle more than two seats back and no one was lying there. He worked his way out of the seat and saw half a man hanging over his armrest and into the aisle, with both arms dangling down and his head nearly reaching the floor. The lighting was dim yet strong enough to reveal a small glistening pool of blood. As he stepped closer, staring at the man, Wesley saw more blood drip from his face. No one seated nearby seemed to be awake although any of them might have been trying to avoid the problem or to disassociate him- or herself from the man. Wesley swept his head around, looking for movement from anyone. He knelt beside the body. He did not know how to check a pulse, not with certainty, so he decided to lift the man back into his seat. The man had not been in the aisle for long. He might be revived with artificial respiration; maybe he choked on a gumball. Besides, it was more dignified and the body deserved as much.

The torso was heavy. It was a big man, hairy and soft. Wesley had difficulty in repositioning him. A sound came from somewhere near, either the seat mate or the head that Wesley was holding: que...? The man shook himself free of Wesley. "Qué estás haciendo?," a phrase Wesley did not recognize despite understanding the man's meaning completely and it was not gratitude for saving his life. The man wiped a rivulet of drool from his face with his sleeve. Wesley looked back to the floor and saw the glistening pool was more of the same. The man spoke more firmly in Spanish and felt his arms and wrists and neck as if Wesley had injured him.

I could show you how to stretch that out. I saw a video on it. The notion went unspoken.

"I been told more than once that I got some courage in me but you way more brave than me, Mr. Willard."

"In the dark, he looked pretty bad, Miss Esther. I had to touch him 'cause this lady I know told me we gotta do something."

"That man look bad in any kinda light! Listen to him go on after waking up everybody. He ought be thanking you."

"What's he saying?"

"I don't speak Mexican. You can tell though."

"We can give him a break. I woke him up and you know he's got to be feeling miserable, all bent up like he was. Probably embarrassed too. Want to bet he don't remember any of it in the morning? ...You wan' the window or the aisle?"

"I got my seat and you got yours. Go on in. I'll get in my place when I get back."

The next few fitful hours only made Wesley feel worse and worse. He saw too little of the dark landscape pass by to feel the ship was getting much closer to the whale. He wished he knew how far off was the dawn although it may have rendered the hours more tedious by encouraging a focus on a time he could not effect. What he could do was shift himself into a better position than whatever shape it was currently in. He discovered more positions than tantrix tiles could form. Several felt relaxing for an unmeasured period too short to allow unconsciousness to take over although he was never entirely conscious either. He felt jealous of the man dribbling saliva onto the deck and scaring his shipmates. Wesley retained a senseless hope for sleep and sometimes wondered if he had managed a few minutes of napping.

When the daylight first became evident, he applauded, silently out of respect for the others struggling like him, the apparent resumption of time's passage. It woke him enough to attempt a calculation of the time. The spring equinox was more than two months past so the longest day was less than a month away. The sunrise must be well before six am... unless daylight savings time was in the way. "Spring ahead, fall back" told him how to reset his clocks but it did not show whether the true time came before or after the equinox. It was something he would look up when he got the chance and then he would remember it with some new mnemonic, perhaps one he would invent. He sat up and looked out. The sun had not yet cleared the horizon. The scene was as flat and barren as the sea.

Esther asked if he had slept well and he answered with a prolonged grunt intended to show how exhausting the trip had become for him and to end the conversation so he could continue to try to be unconscious. He could feel her watching him and could not ignore her.

"I think I've got a good dream coming up here. Lemme try to get it under control." He should have pulled his hat over his face after those words but he did not want to move any further and he stared at the open spaces outside. There was more diversity than he had noticed at first. Even in the dim first light, the Sonoran desert has enough colors and shapes to entertain the eye of a first-time visitor. Saguaro cactus rose above the mesquite, adding a vertical dimension in the foreground and cutting across the waves of low mountains on the horizon.

Esther remained still. Wesley envied her repose. He attributed it to her shorter, leaner, looser body and her lesser time on board rather than to any personal deficiency on his part, unless (he revised his thought) his slight extra weight and stiff joints were attributable to poor diet and exercise (which they were).

§§§

"You can wake up now. We're coming into Phoenix."

"I wish I needed to wake up. I wasn't asleep."

"You slept right through the stop at Flagstaff. Hope you didn't mean to get off there."

"We stopped in Flagstaff? I woulda liked to see it. Was it light enough to see anything."

"It was light enough... Lemme think.. No, you didn't miss anything I could see."

"Anyways, it's good to hear I was sleepin'. Maybe I won't feel like... I mean maybe I won't feel so bad today."

"Hey, I know what word you was about to say there, what you felt like. You don't need to be so shy with me. I heard all the words and I used most of 'em sometime along the way."

"Gimme a break, Esther. I'm just waking up. I'm trying to treat you right since we have a date coming up."

"I see that. It's nice. Let's go to breakfast."

Esther stood up in the aisle and reached into the overhead shelf for her handbag. Wesley remained seated while she did that and then she felt the pressure of the line of people behind her waiting to exit and gave him a small smile before walking toward the front of the bus. Wesley now wondered if she had been serious about having breakfast together. It did not matter to him one way or the other. He waited for the aisle to clear and took his only luggage with him

210

outside. Esther was waiting for him and he was surprised to feel a thrill upon seeing her there. Seeing her in full standing profile, she really looked good. He surveyed the area to appear less focused on Esther. The bus was parked at an angle in a row of buses, outdoors but under a roof. Esther asked where he wanted to have breakfast. He answered that he had no idea what was here or what was good but he had faith someplace nearby would be offering a full sit-down breakfast.

"Want to look inside?" Esther asked.

"We could do that," answered Wesley. "Doubt they serve food, maybe they do, but I could wash up first."

Inside he decided to be awed. "Look at this place! It could be an airport! And it looks cleaner than I feel."

They looked for the rest rooms and agreed to meet in five or ten minutes. Wesley knew they had one hour before the bus left and decided he had to be careful about the time. He washed his face and hands and combed his hair with his fingers, finishing his ablutions in four minutes. Back in the terminal, he asked the nearest ticket agent where he could get breakfast and she pointed to a door, adding "There's places on Glendale. Go off to the left when you get outside." So when Esther came out of the ladies room, he was ready with a plan for their date.

He only saw one small restaurant and did not want to waste time looking further. They went inside and found an empty table near the window. He felt awkward and did not know why. The place offered a familiar and relaxed atmosphere. The thrill he had noticed when he saw Esther waiting for him was unfamiliar.

Wesley looked down at the menu and spoke nervously, not because of Esther but because of the time.

Now that they had a place to eat, the remaining fifty minutes or so should be plenty but the waitress or the cook or Esther might be slow. He was already imagining how to pack up the leftovers if they had to leave before they were finished. *Save time to pay*, he reminded himself.

"I don't do dates and can't hardly remember the last time I sat down to eat with a woman. I'm feeling lucky and honored, you know. So you got to show some appreciation, even if it is a regular thing for you. I mean by ordering everything you can possibly eat. There needs to be something left on your plate at the end, you know, to show you ate all you felt like having. And don't worry about looking like you were starving 'cause if you do that you still won't be eatin' as much as me. I don't want to be a pig or nothin' but I do love breakfast the best and I haven't had a good breakfast in a diner for a long time or a decent meal of any kind for a few days now."

Wesley's only consideration when ordering was to avoid what he actually preferred. Mattie might not be the only person who knew he always had two eggs over easy with white toast and pork sausage links whenever he was in a restaurant. They never ever had eggs or white bread at home and rarely sausage.

They said very little during the meal. Esther worried about the time available too. She was still worrying when they got back to bus terminal.

"Oh, did you see which space our bus was in? I didn't realize there were so many."

"And they all look the same!"

"Not that one." Esther pointed to a bus parked along the sidewalk rather than in one of the regular, angled spaces. The side of the bus read "Homeland Security," in big letters and "U.S. Immigration and Customs Enforcement" below. The faces visible through the windows were somber, and solitary, not Department staff, not exuberant immigrants to America.

"I remember enough to know that one ain't ours," said Wesley as they kept walking. "And I remember coming out in front of that door over there so I guess this one's for us.

Inside, settled back in his slot, Wesley took out his newer book, *4321*, and opened it to a random page, then turned back a few pages as if he were finding where he left off, then stared at that page. Breakfast had not proved an occasion to get to know Esther, as Wesley had sub-consciously envisaged it. He felt disappointment at how little had been spoken even though he would have lied and misled if a conversation had developed. He felt his disappointment but he did not want to admit to himself that he felt it. The innocent breakfast with Esther was not the same as the innocent lunch with Samantha since he had never been able to conceive developing or desiring a personal relationship with Samantha. He knew Esther even less than Samantha, but he took her attractiveness more seriously. She was not a colleague or junior to him in any way. Harder to admit, Wesley probably did not even have a wife any more to absorb all his love.

How disloyal it felt to form that thought! He had not given up on Mattie, obviously, yet some doubt of her present existence was merely honest. It did not reduce his commitment to searching for Mattie. He was not feeling any less love for the woman whose attention had moved him from socially insecure to a mature confidence, who had drawn out a sexual nature he had not known existed within himself, who had taught him by her example to achieve professional’ respect and success through careful and strenuous work, who was the only woman he had ever seriously desired.

Wesley looked more closely at Esther to see her humanity rather than as some idealized alternative to the misery of his months of isolation and depression. First, he turned the page of his book, as if he had finished reading it. The movement allowed him to reposition himself slightly in a way that allowed a view to the seat beside him. Esther’s eyes were closed, her head resting on her shoulder and turned toward him slightly. Her skin was taut and smooth; of a color he tried to relate to something familiar, clearly darker than a White person’s tan, not nearly as dark as chocolate though its firm smoothness reminded him of it. There was a rose cast to her shade that might have come from the sun or from a powder; it might have underlain his first impression that she had Indian background and he felt stupid for making that association because he had seen many Indians and never seen a red in their skin tone. She had freckles in a patch at the top of each cheek, making her look like a child when seen from a certain angle. Her eyes were narrow; it was not observable when they were closed. Almond eyes, he thought, another favorable attribute in her face. Her hair was long, pulled back into a ponytail, perhaps a style that was easy when travelling. He looked closely and perceived a possible frizziness close to her scalp, suggesting she might have straightened her hair, but for the most recent growth. Guiltily, he let his view drift downward. Her blouse was thin as it should be in the desert summer, thin enough to show her breasts separately and to reveal the thickness in her shoulders and arms did not extend to her waistline.

Wesley turned the page of his book again and shifted himself toward the window. He smiled at the adventure of his imagination and proclaimed unconvincingly to himself that he was sorry to have disproven the theory that Esther was only attractive in a symbolic way. *I am Peter in Gethsemene. Mattie forgive me for enjoying the nearness of this woman. You are unparalleled in my existence and I know it shall always be so and yet I am a mere man without your certain presence in this world.*

He was not tired any more. He was uncomfortable, aching from sitting in about the same cramped way for hours and hours, disgusted by the scratchy fabric on which he sat in full knowledge that countless others had sat on it during their many unhygienic hours, itchy from the sweat on his clothes seeping, he imagined, into the fabric around him, aware of the odors of his fellow passengers excepting Esther. But not tired, so he read on from the random page he had in front of him, working up to the page number at the first ten percent of his monstrous tome and still not interested in it.

"Tell me something about yourself and I will tell you something, a thing as big or small as what you decide to tell me."

Wesley immediately nodded his agreement to the proposal although he understood it was not the kind of thing Willard would want to do. He liked this woman and he liked her game. *I will protect myself by sticking to a lie, a complete lie that sounds too detailed to be false.* He dogeared the page in his book and closed it, doubting he would ever open it again.

"I was almost married once." He paused to give her the chance to believe that was all he was going to say. He stared at her hard, ready to continue the moment she began to object that he had not played well. She did not flinch. She knew why he had hesitated.

The wait dragged on. To show he knew she knew what he was doing, he admitted a sort of defeat, saying "Okay." Then he continued, "We had been together for a couple months. Maybe that's not so unique. But it was for me anyway. I had said to her one day, 'Don't you think we're going to get married?' and she said back, 'Could be,' so the subject had come up. Not really decided but come up and it come up from me so now it was her turn.

"I was thinking," he continued, "I'd probably go with it if she mentioned it. I didn't push it 'cause I did have some issues. Nothing that she deserved to be criticized for, but things I noticed. I thought everybody got some things like that but then sometimes I wondered if I really loved her wouldn't I not even notice those things? Or is that just Hollywood love or teenage girl romance so I let it go."

"Don't none of us live in Hollywood romances. Wish they had movies with love like people actually get into it. Some issues are too big to let slide, you know."

"One thing, not a big thing, was she was always telling me stuff she thought she knew but really didn't know anything about. Like the day we were going into our place, we lived in a duplex, end of the street, next to the woods, and she told me one of the trees was going to fall on our roof one of these days and I ought to get it cut down. Well, there was a big, ol' tree leaning just a little toward our place so I guess it was possible but what are the odds? We weren't going to stay there for real long. Why would a tree fall during the six months or year when we lived there and none of the trees around there had ever fallen on any of the duplexes? It had plenty of leaves, a big, ol' healthy tree. So I told her she worried too much. You see, she could worry about anything she thought could happen. It's no way to live. She didn't argue with me or nothing. Maybe that's how she hoped to get her way, being nice about it, but that don't work with me. If she wanted it cut down, she needed to fight at least a little to be clear about it. I'd make the arrangement, find somebody to do it, pay for it, maybe try the landlord first."

"You musta been young if you thought the landlord was going to fix something like that."

"Right... And I'm not so young now so I know better about landlords. Anyway, a few weeks later I was walking home from some grocery shopping, just enough for dinner. And feeling good because I found a kind of soup my girlfriend liked but usually wasn't in our store, the one we used, so I would get credit for checking on the soup and getting it for her. And as I was close to the house I saw a big, ol' tree swaying back and forth enough to notice. And then I realized it was pretty windy that day which is something I wouldn't normally pay any attention to. And then I heard the trunk crack and saw that sickly looking oak or whatever slowly tipping and I thought 'Damn that thing is going to smash into our place and wreck it, just like... like that girlfriend of mine said.'"

Wesley had to stop for a breath. He had almost said "Mattie" instead of "that girlfriend of mine." The story had not a word of truth in it but he almost put in one and a big one if someone was trying to find him. The lying had been going so well and he was finding an end for his story and heading toward it and then almost said the story was about Mattie which it was not, not as far as he could tell.

"It wasn't the exact tree she had pointed out and it didn't hit anything at all and it was a dead tree with most of the small branches already gone off it and when it hit the ground, even with going slow, it made a huge thumping whump I could feel all over me and it came up through my feet too. I had to tell myself the damn trees are really heavy and got to be dangerous. That woman was way more right than I could stand, 'cause I don't like to worry even when I should so I don't need a woman who's right about stuff too much."

"And that's why you broke up with her?"

"Yeah, it is. 'Course I never told her why, not the real why of it. I hated to lie to her but I could not tell her about the tree without sounding like I was lying."

"What did you tell her? Or did you push her away so she would think it was her fault?"

"No, I wouldn't do that. I told her I was too used to being alone, I couldn't get married. Needed my space to flake out sometimes, be lazy, live low, not live bad, just low when it's comfortable. It was a simple lie to tell 'cause it was pretty near true except for leaving out the thing with the tree."

Esther was quiet.

Wesley continued. "Could be, and I knew it at the time, could be the tree wasn't any part of it. Could be I was telling the truth. I wasn't trying to. I did not think I was a bum like that, like I was headed to being homeless or something. When that lie slipped out, I felt like I learned something about myself, like maybe I should try out being a bum. I might like it and it wasn't so far off anyway."

"You do drink or drugs?"

"I told you something about myself. Drink or drugs or religion or what tattoo I might have got on my backside wasn't in the story."

"You're right. Not part of the story. None of my business anyway. Sorry. Kinda more of a story than I was looking for."

Wesley grinned and flicked his eyebrows up and down a couple times.

"I had something in mind to tell you and I needed an excuse to tell it but now I need to dig a little deeper."

"No you don't. I'd rather you just told me what you wanted to say."

"Too late. Now you know it's not just something to say about me, it's something I wanted you to know."

"That's a lot of hints. I bet I could guess it now. Should I try?"

"You think you're pretty smart?"

"I know for goddam sure I'm not smart much. Let me guess anyway. I won't get it right, but maybe it'll make easier for you to tell me in the end."

She smiled coquettishly.

"Give me three tries."

"Go ahead then."

"You've got three kids who come first in your life and you're currently single and not looking for company unless it's a man who wants three kids."

Esther shook her head in the negative.

"Okay, same thing except you'll only take company who's a woman who wants three kids."

"That's even farther off."

"All right, all right... I was pretty quick with those. Give me a moment to come up with a better guess. Couldn't be any worse anyway, right? Two quick wrong ones. Just like I would do. Not worried I'm too smart are you now? Good thing for me we didn't bet on whether I could do it. I would have bet against me anyway... Let's see, you were going to say something simple to say, not a story like I told. No one would have thought it should be a long story. I already know some basic facts about you. Seems like all I need to know. This feels like a TV game show and that's an odd thing because I don't think I ever watched one... just a few seconds when I was changing the channel." *Oh god, what if she was going to tell me she's a cop? What would come next? Going to let me go because I am such a good guy or 'here are the handcuffs'?* "Maybe, and here is my third guess, you were planning to say... you wanted to tell me... *What if she was going to say she can see I am faking and I am not the Willard I said I was? No, that's something about me so that can't be it.* ...I don't want to guess something that makes you look better, like I am trying to get on your good side, like maybe I am working toward making a play for you. Okay, first let me say I can't help but notice you are one really fine looking woman and you seem fun and smart and all that, as much as I can tell on a bus ride. I'm not too shy to say that and don't need to sneak it into my guess some way."

Esther listened closely but did not move anything in her face or reveal any thought.

"My last guess on what you might have wanted to say has to be something that I seriously think is possible, not too personal but personal enough you couldn't just come out with it.... You need some cash. You will pay it back but just did not prepare right for the trip or had some kind of crunch on the way and used up your reserve. If that's what it is, we can deal with that, Ms Esther."

"Deal with it? I wonder how..." She waited a moment, paying him back for the way he started his story. "But that's not what I was thinking. I was going to say, I mean what I was going to tell you is how I was a little afraid of you when I first sat down here."

"I never heard of anybody afraid of me. And on top of that, you didn't act any afraid. I can't remember exactly what you said but you spoke right up. A strong woman there, that's what I thought. I remember that part"

"I wouldn't say I was a big worrier most times, like your old girlfriend. Sometimes an old Black lady needs to be careful."

"Don't be old 'cause that would make me old and I don't want be that."

Esther laughed just a little. "I see the way you get rid of trouble is you just say it don't exist. You don't worry about the tree falling just because you don't want to. You're old as me and that's not too old for most things but you're feeling the years for sure just like I am."

"And how is it you were afraid of a chubby old White guy? You could hardly find somebody to sit beside any safer than me unless it's another old Black lady."

"I thought you might be a cowboy, with that beat up hat and beat up duds and sitting there all silent, not even look up when I came by."

"Then you saw my soft hands and soft belly and knew I was no regular working man."

"I don't just mean a cowboy exactly. I just meant the mentality. Oh, some of them's all right. I never knew any real good but some are nice. Still I had a few run-ins with some others and it makes me real careful."

"You sat down anyway. I don't think it was the last seat on the bus."

"I probably sat here because you made me a little uncomfortable and I wanted to be in control instead of afraid so I came in strong."

"Whistling past the graveyard."

"What's that?"

"Something my grandmother woulda said. Anyway, I'm real glad you were strong enough to meet the challenge. You been the best part of the ride. Never thought I be having a date along the way."

Wesley noticed he had not been consistent in how well-spoken Willard had been. This was not surprising since he was no actor. It was surprising that Esther's English had tended to improve. Maybe her initial nervousness had made her try to act tough.

Esther did not know what to say. It felt as if she ought to respond somehow.

"You see how long we've been in LA already?" she asked just to reduce the stress she was feeling.

"Near time to get on with things."

The driver guided the Pequod into its berth where it sat silent for the first time since Esther had boarded back in Albuquerque. The silence was heavy, drowning out the bustle of passengers gathering whatever they had brought on board and filing away. Esther scarcely reacted to the change, denying it was real, waiting for something to say or for Willard to say something. When only the two remained inside, Wesley asked if she wanted some help with her luggage. She answered that the help she would like would be for him to stay in the bus until she got her bags from the storage underneath and was gone away. Wesley thought of some things he might say but they were not Willard's words so he said nothing. He was thinking that if he never found Mattie, he could, he would be able to, find another woman to love. He had never thought that before. But he was not taking reservations. He did not want Esther's phone number although he saw no negative thing in her. He was going after Mattie. He was not taking the rational or smart or safe or legal way. He was all in. But he might someday have a life after Mattie if that's what he had to face.

18. LA to San Francisco

Five hours layover in LA. Wesley had a memory of having decided this layover was where he must begin his concrete plan of action. He needed to sit someplace and write it down. The afternoon of increasing cloudiness had turned to a light drizzle unless it was just a heavy fog. Certainly it was cooler than LA had any right to be. Whatever its exact nature, the weather was wet enough to keep him inside.

The bus station was as good a place as any to lay out a strategy for his first day on the job, assuming Esther was not in the terminal with an interest in further conversation or whatever. He needed pencil, not pen, and paper. He sensed the contradiction that buying this writing paraphernalia constituted his first step but it was a step not in his scheme since he had not written out the scheme yet. There must have been, he surmised, some advice in that *Prince of the Clouds* book about maintaining flexibility but he could not remember any. The brain, being the odd mechanism it is, took him to a quotation he remembered from Mike Tyson: Everyone has a plan until they get punched in the mouth. *I get it, Mike. More true for your background than for a fencer who may be confused when the action starts but not actually cloudy in the*

223

brain. Your background is closer to what I may face. You need an instinctive, automatic response when the serious punch lands. I haven't got that because I haven't trained for this and have no talent for it either. But I'm not really in the ring yet and no one expects me to go in, so I'm going to jump in when I see an opening and then jump back over the ropes and never get punched. I won't score well but I'm not looking for winning on points. That'll be the core of my strategy and I can still have a plan, right?

There was a kiosk specializing in magazines and LA memorabilia (just Hollywood and the sports teams). He got a spiral notebook with a picture of the Dodgers on the cover and a mechanical pencil that encased a tiny plastic woman whose clothes floated away when it was tilted into a writing position.

On the second page (he saved the first page in case he thought of something later that belonged at the start) his list began with item 2 since item one was to buy the paraphernalia.

2. get new clothes
2a. Padres t-shirt (only a local would wear one)
2b. get rid of the cowboy hat (too easily identified)
2c. ditto the unreadable book
2d. what about hair? Let the beard grow, dye, wig?
2e. with new look, stay away from bus station
3. quick eats
4. get a newspaper for local knowledge, esp re: Padres
5. in San Francisco (arrive 5:30 am) get a good breakfast.
6. disappear into the city,
6a. any district with transportation

6b. hotel that doesn't need an ID

6c. one night only

5d. spend rest of day finding next hotel

It was a bad list, leading nowhere. Wesley could not see the boxing strategy emerging, just the anodyne details of hiding before doing any actual investigating for Mattie. His overall purpose was obvious enough. He could put it on top of the first page and try to refine it to clarify his thinking. He tapped the pencil on his chin a few times and then watched the clothes float off the plastic lady, an apt image for Hollywood, especially that she was plastic, although the side was inscribed merely "Los Angeles."

Mattie, it is really exciting to be here, about to start the concrete steps to get you out of wherever those bastards have stashed you. I've got a great starting point with that actress they hired and I know to be careful. I'll be really careful. Really careful.

A thought came unbidden from *Prince of the Clouds*, beginning with Napoleon who was quoted as saying "After so much study, I have no plan in mind." And the novel answered "There is nothing to know about war, except that one must march ten leagues a day, fight and rest."[iv] *I will plan my ten leagues for today and then see where I have reached and plan some more. Right now, item 2, I need some clothes for a different look.*

Unsurprisingly, the bus station was not in the shopping district of Los Angeles. Wesley had time and walked on the largest street for 30 minutes until he found a place that might let him check off an item or two. He passed a guy selling umbrellas and he thought of making his first purchase something not on his list, however, the rain was light and hardly anybody had any form of rain gear and he needed to blend in. In all those blocks he passed in 30 minutes, he never saw a trash can or a dumpster to get rid of his hat and his thick, incomprehensible novel. So he trampled his hat and threw it into a pile of trash in an alley before going in a store. It was trendy and cheap. He looked for the least memorable shirt they had and some cotton slacks, just to get away from the more practical jeans he had been wearing. He could get a Padres t-shirt back at the bus station and wear it under his unbuttoned, new shirt. Subtle, casual, ordinary... He got a baseball-style cap with no logo to keep his head more or less dry on the walk back to the bus station. A wet head might be memorable to somebody. As an indulgence, he bought a pair of socks so he could feel fresher until he settled someplace where he could wash the ones on his feet and the spare pair in his pack.

He espied a chain restaurant and while waiting for his linguini alfredo he decided what to do about his hair. Get a buzz cut. That might make him look different, more so than dying his brown hair into black. He would have it done in San Francisco and he added it to his list.

He lingered in the restaurant until it seemed he might be noticed for his delay. Outside, the rain had stopped and the sun was just completing its last show of the day. He put his cap on with the bill in back. No one who knew him would believe any circumstance could be dire enough to induce him to wear a cap that way.

He found a newspaper box and checked another item off his list. Then he went into a bar to kill some time and see what everybody in LA already knows. It was a well lit place for young people, not a place to get drunk nightly. On a Thursday, it was not busy. He sat in the last table along the wall and nursed a whiskey and soda. No one was seated at the table beside him but at the table past that, three girls in their twenties giggled and pointed, sometimes indicating him. Although he was purposefully nondescript at that moment, he was normally inconspicuous except in the office where his place in the hierarchy made him a player sometimes. Any attention directed his way from girls in a bar was either solicitation or inebriation. He did not look back at them until they approached.   He looked up and said nothing. They were not dressed for solicitation.

One stepped forward. "I took a picture of you. Did you see the camera?"

"No, I've been reading the paper."

"Here, you can have it. I just took it to see how it would come out in light like this. It's a new camera." She waved in front of him a bright plastic box. "Picture comes out right away."

Wesley guessed she was trying to sell him the picture.

"Thanks, but I don't need a picture of me. I know what I look like already."

"No, it's okay. I'm just giving it to you. You looked nice, just so calm and everything."

Wesley took the picture to see why she had taken it. It did not show him in a recognizable way. It was a polaroid photo taken with a bad lens.

"Old tech. Didn't know you could get polaroids." *What do you girls want?* His pack strap was looped around the table leg so they could not grab it and run.

The girl put the picture on the table and laughed a little. Then all three went back to their seats.

"Thanks then," Wesley called when they started to leave. He thought they were too old to be playing with a toy shabby enough to make such a poor quality image. He stared at the newspaper and tried to imagine what they were about. He gave them a couple minutes to do something else, which they did not, and then paid his bill and left. He wore his cap forward now. It might make him harder to follow if the girls or some accomplice wanted to do that. He could not think of a reason he would be targeted. He wondered if the picture might have a chip in it to track him. He took it out, the image had already faded nearly to black. It reminded him of an app allegedly popular among people far younger than himself in which pictures only lasted a few minutes. It seemed to be a way to pressure "friends" into monitoring each other more closely but the logic was not clear to him. He tore it into small pieces and scattered them slowly into the wet street.

He took a circuitous route back to the bus station. The kiosk with the Padres shirt was closed for the night so he would drop the idea of being a fan during the ride to San Francisco where he could try being a Giants fan. The notebook cover promoted the Dodgers anyway. Their logo was ubiquitous so having it did not make him a fan. He waited thirty minutes until his bus was announced for boarding.

The incident with the three girls and the camera was odd but not odder than many things attributed to LA culture. California was part of the United States and almost familiar to him from television and film. The truly strange place was Washington, where he had adapted in ways he could not recognize. The girls were clearly not part of a conspiracy to trap him somehow, either for petty grift or as part of the grand conspiracy that took Mattie away from him. Still, he would be suspicious of everything and everyone until he got Mattie back. He could not ignore the addendum his brain placed on his thought: *or until I give up on ever finding her.*

Wesley carried his bag with him out the door to the line of buses. He waited a half minute and when no one came out behind him, went back inside. No one seemed to be looking out the doorway at him or lingering near the doorway. Nothing suggested he was being followed although he was not sure what to watch for. He felt he was acting in a spy or detective movie. It was silly but cost nothing to play it out. He was near, he presumed, Hollywood.

The bus was not as nice as the ones that carried him across the country, not unclean, but tattered in its fabrics, scratched into its hard surfaces, and one of the rubber ropes that kept the overhead bags from falling into the aisle sagged too much to be functional. LA to San Francisco was more of a milk run. The seat was worn enough to show the sum of thousands of prior users which did not matter at all to Wesley and was exactly the same size as the ones on his Pequod, which was a disappointment. When he first saw that the bus was an older model, he hoped it had been born in an era when seats were better built. He sat on the side with the functioning luggage rope even though he felt selfish for taking up a more secure space with his bag of unbreakable, replaceable, unremarkable and cheap miscellany.

The bus began to fill quickly. Maybe the passengers were regular on this route and did not waste time boarding early. Wesley looked out the window. It was not friendly to avoid his fellow travelers. Being friendly was not among his goals for this trip so he defiantly concentrated on the sidewalk outside. He felt someone sit beside himself and immediately turned to see who he had won. It was a young man, slim, broad shouldered, Black, handsome, so handsome Wesley felt a moment of jealousy until he reasoned that being Black in America was not the key to an easy life even for the handsome. Still, it would have been nice to be so good looking in face and figure. He did not stare, of course, barely saw his seatmate clearly. *He might no be so comely,* Wesley realized. *Maybe I am being generous. I do tend to fill incomplete images with positive details.* Wesley decided to work on his plan until he was tired enough to defeat the discomfort of his seat, but first he laid back to rest his eyes for a few seconds.

"Say, Dude, you going to be sleeping?"

Wesley opened his eyes and turned them toward the voice. *No,* he thought, it's no illusion. *That is one damn good looking "dude."* And his subconscious envied the man's lean face, his smooth skin, his dense hair and the sculpted features of mouth and eyes and nose. He was not as young as Wesley first thought, really about Wesley's age.

"I mean, if you're going to sleep, you could let me have the window."

"Window? Sure. I don't care about it."

They switched seats politely. He was six inches taller than Wesley. *Don't care about the window and don't care how big and beautiful you are. In a couple hours, I'll be in the same city as my clue, my good clue, to Mattie.*

When they had settled in, the guy said "Thanks Dude," leaned against the window and closed his eyes. Ironically, given the deal they just made to change seats, Wesley had no intention of sleeping.

Back to the notebook then. I can check off a couple of early items, the LA plans. I wasn't punched in the nose yet, Mr. Tyson, but I already had to make a revision to my plan since I was too late for a Padres shirt. Glad to be rid of

Thus Wesley worked his way through ideas about what to do to prepare for meeting Samantha, and what to say to her, and what to do afterwards with whatever her reaction might be. Here his planning broke down. There were too many possibilities for what she might say or do, if he even found her at all. But he played out a few scenarios to give himself practice, as he had done when a big meeting was coming up at the office. None of his scenarios ever played out exactly, but sometimes the practice made him more nimble in the actual meeting. The only new idea that he really liked was to learn more about Samantha, assuming he actually found her, so he could find her again if she tried to flee. See where she worked, even if it was another con job, find some of her family, where she went to school, see if she had ever...

"Look at that, Dude! I wanted the window to look out and went right to sleep. Sorry, man."

"Don't matter none," answered Wesley, not sure what personality he should adopt except that it should not be his own.

"I feel better now, I guess. Not tired anyways. Kind of cramped though."

"You bet it is. Must be worse for someone tall as you."

"Yeah. You ride the intercity bus much?"

"Aah, some. See my sister in San Bernadino every couple years. Never been to San Francisco before."

"So you're from LA?"

"Nah. Burbank." Wesley remembered a running joke on a television comedy, maybe Laugh In!, in which Burbank was the most boring place possible, perfect for his present purpose. "You? LA or San Francisco or someplace else?"

"LA, I guess. I'm from San Francisco and still got some family there but I haven't been back in a long time."

"Mm."

"Well, thing is, been in jail the past few years. Nothin' real bad. Don't be scared by it. Passing paper; counterfeit, you know, money."

"How long you been out?"

"Two weeks now. Trying to figure out what's next."

"Your family gonna fix you up with a place or a job?"

"Doubt it. They don't know I'm coming up and don't have a place or a job to offer anyway."

"It's tough, I'm sure. You young, healthy, right? Someone's gonna want you."

"Gotta get back to LA regular to see my parole officer."

"Can't you transfer to one in San Francisco?"

"Not with no job and no place to stay."

"It's tough."

"Wisht I'd stayed with the church. Folks woulda helped me out."

"Wish I had a church behind me too."

"So how long you gonna be in San Francisco?"

"I got a couple days. Mainly to see my daughter. Never saw her yet."

"That'll be great."

"Maybe. Her mama's got a new boyfriend. He won't want me around."

"They gotta let you see her, right?"

"I don't know if there's way for the law to force 'em to do what's right but it won't come to that. I'll see her. She's about four now."

"That's good. Old enough to be getting her own personality, not just a brat."

"Yeah, you got kids?"

"No, never did. Never had a woman long enough to want any either."

"You give me an idea. Might get a church back in Burbank. Might make it easier to get some rights for seeing my girl, if she wants to see me, that is. Besides, I been with a bad crowd some. Not all my friends are like me so I know what being straight means. I can do it if I can just get a start."

"Yeah."

Obviously Wesley had not responded well, humanly, to his fellow passenger who seemed in need of some sympathy if not some actual help. Wesley would have been free with his sympathy in his real persona so he felt justified under the circumstances to withhold it. Advice was out of reach. Wesley knew nothing of such problems and less than nothing of how to mitigate them. His own problems seemed small in comparison but that was only because he was thinking of himself. Adding Mattie's problem would sum to a mess large enough to trump the cards of any stranger outside a hospital. Assuming he could survive the loss of Mattie, he could go on in life and likely outperform the tall stranger by any measure he could imagine. His path forward without Mattie would be painful for the memory of her but not every reasonable path in life would be barricaded. Assuming the bastards who had taken Mattie did not manage to frame him for something (he would not mentally utter the name of the possible crime) that carried a life sentence. Then he would have worse prospects than the man beside him.

That man broke the awkward silence. "Hey, lookit here. I gotta take a piss."

Wesley felt the urge to apologize. At least he could express his frustration with his inability to talk about the man's dilemmas. All he did was stand up to let the tall man into the aisle. He stretched his back out until the guy came back and then took his turn to pee.

Part III: Into a Hornets' Nest

Wesley was disappointed with his hotel room. It was not as flea-bitten as it ought to be for the *noir* role he was playing. It was up to the radically mediocre standard familiar to him from the chain motels alongside I95 where he and Mattie stayed on their annual southern pilgrimage. He expected a South Carolina accent from the clerk at the desk and palmetto palms lining the parking lot. The clerks in his usual motels were well dressed and polite, like the clerk here - no hard-boiled slang, no tattoos. Some artifice showed in the clerk's too dark, too even, hair color and the tiny images painted onto her fingernails, but nothing scary in those details. At least it was a hotel, not a motel. He was on the top floor, only the third, and looked out on brick storefronts of a locality whose paramount attribute was that it lay outside San Francisco, saving its occupants at least thirty bucks a night. He paid cash for a week in advance and did not have to show an ID. Withholding the ID made it *noir* enough for his purpose.

Watching the quiet street through gauzy curtains, he could feel concealed in obscurity for a while but he would keep an eye out for a new place to move in a few days. He had talked to the clerk with enthusiasm for the presumptive business that brought him to San Francisco. Self-employed, he admitted, a useful attribute consistent with paying cash. ...An agent for industrial components in the printing business. ...An engineering background from a small college although he had not finished school, having learned enough to make his own proud business get him through 15 years on his own. And it was getting stronger. He might need to hire some staff next year if the San Francisco meeting went as well as he expected it would.

A small, late model American sedan pulled to the curb a half block away. An Hispanic couple got out, fed the meter, and went into an electronics store, chatting all the while. It had been a long time since he had observed normal people beyond his seat in the bus, maybe a long time since he had cared about them. They had seemed irrelevant to his career just as they seemed irrelevant to his present campaign and yet the people he met in his crossing the continent had each been unique with valid personal concerns despite having no implications for USDA policy.

He wondered if the couple had been speaking Spanish. He had taken French in school but not learned much of it. He envied people who were fluent in two languages. He had become fluent in only one culture, Washington bureaucracy. He knew the language, the heroes, the saints, the history, the current players in his corner of the town. His ego had asserted that his corner of Washington was small geographically but influenced more lives in a week than most people influenced in a lifetime. Now, after being cast out of his corner and looking back, he could no longer see how he had ever taken pride in it. He had done a job, an honorable job, but just a job like the ones most people did. There was no glory in occupying his cubicle even if, as an attorney, he had higher walls than most and an actual door, not a curtain. He had a view through a window from his desk when the door to his cubicle was open but all he saw was sky, nothing as complete as the sight from a generic hotel room outside San Francisco.

He wondered if the couple had children and if they went to family parties to celebrate holidays and birthdays, and whether they sang songs at such gatherings and cooked foods from their childhoods. He suspected normal people had far more diverse experience in their lives than he did and that might make them more resilient than him to crisis in one part of their reality. His focus was so narrow, he would never be going into an electronics store. He was proficient in using his computer, accessing legal and historical information with ease while relying on people like Lucas to update his hardware and software as advances in technology came along. And he wondered whether the crises that threatened the comfort of normal people came from villains as powerful as the ones who had taken Mattie.

A city bus stopped beside a bench Wesley had not noticed. Four people got off and walked away separately. It was not the hour to be starting or ending work or eating a meal. Wesley could not imagine where these people were going. He admitted he could not understand their lives. He knew enough of them, however, not to envy them. Usually he only envied those who were a step or two higher than him in the bureaucracy, people positioned to have more respect and a better view. Who did normal people wish to be, whom did they envy? Professionals like himself, for their presumed salary and power? More likely, if asked, they would think of athletes or famous actors. Or might they be so moral as to envy religious leaders or the public servants who stood in harm's way? Wesley was right to have established his modest and realistic aspirations no more than two steps above his actual station, although he may have been wrong to define his goals in such careerist terms. Normal people probably used a better metric.

The day was already shot, with the search for the hotel in the morning and then sleeping in because he could actually lie flat. The current version of his written assignments for the remainder of the day called for learning the San Francisco bus and cabbie system and setting up a new e-mail account, both of which were accomplished at a neighborhood library.

On his second day, it took Wesley more than an hour to traverse the distance to the address Lucas had given. It lay in a row of small, neat, single-family houses, matching except for the color of their paint, each with just enough lawn to require maintenance in the spring, lining both sides of a street that rose to a near and hazy horizon. When he arrived in the predawn light, it was dead quiet, as if no one lived there. Soon, however, people began coming out, one at a time, making no sound, usually walking off but sometimes driving or meeting a car pool. Wesley had come early to be sure to catch his quarry before she went to wherever she went during working hours.

Samantha did not emerge from her bungalow until 9 o'clock, a late sleeper, possibly indicating she worked late or partied late or both. He followed her onto a bus and for three blocks of walking afterwards. He fell farther behind her with a straight street before them until he realized she might turn down an alley and lose him so he raised his pace, not enough to be running but enough that he could catch up right after she turned or went inside somewhere. He tried not to look at her directly so no one would think he was stalking her although that is exactly what he was doing. From his angle, she looked like a woman to be stalked: tight, short skirt and tight, long legs.

He had not really looked at her back in Washington. He had merely thought of her as a young intern, irrelevant to his work, who he hoped would not ask him for anything, until the day at the conference when she asked him to lunch as if it was her great opportunity to meet him. On that day, he thought she was making a career move and he did not mind letting her think whatever she wanted for the duration of a lunch. Starting an affair with an intern or a fellow was not a possibility, not even a vague interest, hardly a fantasy he could maintain in the forefront of his consciousness, but it was not a bad feeling to let it lie quietly in the back of his mind for an hour with a woman of her obvious, albeit superficial, charm. He could feel no guilt over that moment of innocent relaxation, for it was surely not a sin that caused the eventual calamity, even if it was a step in the course of events.

He was moving like a race walker and felt absurd, which led him to again question whether he was fundamentally sane and whether the paranoia guiding his actions was justified in reality. She turned toward an unmarked door and went up a few steps. She took a key chain out of her pocket and now, he concluded, he knew where she worked. He could monitor her and pick the moment to ask his questions.

"Regina! Is that you?" It was as good a time as any to confront her. He was tired of small measures, of caution that prevented real progress. If he were to find Mattie, he would need to be bold at some point. Wesley did not have his approach planned but he doubted it would be possible to follow a plan very far anyway, like von Moltke said. He had his leverage with her and he knew what he wanted in return for his silence.

She looked back at him from the stairs where she stood and quickly dismissed him. "I don't know you." She sorted out the key to her building from the others on her ring, prepared to enter quickly if this man started up the stairs.

"No, you never did know me but back when you were Samantha, but you did eventually claim some familiarity. We had dinner once at the USDA annual conference. Does that not bring back any memories?"

She put the key in the lock and turned it. With her hand on the knob, she looked back at him. "Who are you?" she asked, genuinely uncertain who was speaking although the name he had called her must have given him some legitimacy.

"I have changed my appearance a bit, but you know who I am. May we speak? Maybe it is best to sit in a public space. Is there a café or a bar around here where we might take a few minutes?"

"No, I'm not talking to you. You look like a creep and no one will believe you, so just forget it. You can't do anything to me. I have big people watching my back."

"Samantha, I am not here to play act. This is your only chance to come out of this quietly and if it gets noisy, it will ruin your life, you know, like you and your pals did to me."

She had stopped looking Wesley in the face, not out of modesty or remorse, but out of fear. "OK, let me drop off my things," came in a quavering voice as her past deed rushed back to mind from the bin where she had hoped it would rot away from inattention.

"No. If you get out of my sight just once before we have our little talk, you won't see me again, Dear, until the trial."

"Oh, come on. I don't know anything. They didn't tell me anything. Why should they?"

"Do you want to do this here?"

She led him on a silent, two-block walk up the hill and over the crest into a wooded area, during which Wesley worried more and more about whether she was taking him someplace to talk or someplace where she could get help, but he figured she was just a minor actress and she was not living near some element of the Washington conspiracy. For all the disaster he had endured, his life was small potatoes by the standards of disasters in Washington. She might have a boyfriend nearby who would get violent for her. Wesley would be ready to disappear if he had to. There would be other ways to work on this although he preferred that Samantha cooperated. She was his best lead -- his only lead really. He might get another one if this one fell through. It was not likely, not certain for sure, but he did not need her to solve everything for him in one day. He could work her another way if she got she the upper hand. Of course, he would not let her get away easily.

She turned suddenly onto a short, informal path that led to a café tucked into the edge of a small woodland. She led across an empty patio area and pushed on the café door ineffectually until Wesley read the sign beside the handle and pulled it open gently with one hand on her elbow to guide her backwards a step. She led the way to a booth in the back while looking all over the room. Wesley looked for an exit other than the door they came through on the way in and saw only an opening to the kitchen that might serve as his escape if needed. He insisted on facing the street. He ordered scrambled eggs without looking at the menu. The waitress accepted his vague order without comment, not even clarifying if he wanted home-fries with it. *Good place*, Wesley thought. Samantha ordered coffee with her first words since they had started toward the café. Wesley thought there was no reason for her to sulk as if he were strong-arming her. She had wronged him and he was being kind to offer her a way out without her going to jail as she deserved. He remembered he was not dealing with someone who used the naive rules of his childhood or the more brutal ones of law school or the smarmy ones of politics which were still logical in a way he could follow.

"I know why you were brought in and I know who is behind the whole thing, but I do not know who dealt with you. Are you going to tell me enough that I can leave you alone?"

"I didn't do anything to you."

"Be real, Samantha. Be real or go to jail. I have given information on you to my lawyer and she will land the matter on you hard unless I tell her I have a better way to go."

"All I did was tell your wife about our affair."

"It's just you and me here. I know we never had anything like an affair just as you know. Have you told yourself this lie so much you believe any part of it? I don't need to prove to you that we never had an affair. My sex life is not the point of any of this. What do you think about why they asked you to do that anyway? You must have wondered about it. I doubt they told you why and if they did, you can be sure they lied about it. You know there are 'big people' behind this. You don't even know what it was all about. I can easily prove you lied to get the job. I can link you to these 'big people' and to the crimes they are committing."

"If you really want to know... Well, I'm more afraid of them than I am of you. Even time in jail for the little I did would be better than what they would do to me."

"It's not that easy. You don't imagine it could end with you and me? Do you think the district attorney or the press would be satisfied with finding out only what you did to me? Anyone could see you were part of something bigger than either of us... something I understand and you do not, something they would love to expose. Get yourself out of this. Talk to me and it will end for you right here. I don't want to go to the press or get the big guys jailed. I want to find my wife."

"Your wife left over one little phone call? She must have been ready to go anyway."

"Like I said, you have no idea why you were asked to make that call."

Wesley was pleased to see her sliding her weight forward on the table. Her elbows were splayed outward with her arms dragging slowly apart. The posture revealed the tension she was feeling but the lean also seemed to show an inclination to open up to him, not a retreat into herself. Her lips did not speak but her body language revealed her change of mind. He did not think it was being faked. She was an actress of sorts, but not a good one. He decided to trust what he thought he was seeing in her and pressed for her to open up at this moment.

"I am not offering this to think about for a week or an hour. Too many things can happen; things you don't know and don't want to know."

Her spine straightened before she spoke and she pursed her lips for a moment in a gesture that might have implied she was about to lie or that she was about to bare her soul. Wesley had not studied people enough to know which but he thought a good con man or detective would know what she was about to do. Wesley did not stare at her in case that might put her off. Instead, he looked at her hands, beautiful hands: soft, unblemished, well-manicured, graceful, gentle, calm.

"All right," she began. "I'll tell you what I know. It's not much. They obviously did not want me to know much. A guy hired me. Don't know how he found me. Paid really well. He said I would not have to do any sex and I guess that was right, but I didn't know what they really wanted from me until I was into it. I only met the one guy. Medium height, mostly bald, about 50, I'd say. Really stocky, muscle more than fat. Always wore a suit -- the same suit, blue with wide pinstripes. I was living out here, looking for work, temping, you know. He flew me to Washington, trained me for two weeks about agriculture policy. I never applied for the job, for the internship -- just reported to work when he said I was ready. I met him once a week to report and to get instructions but he never really gave me any until we had that conference coming up. Even then, when you and I had dinner, I didn't know I was going to call your wife. Sounded like someone really hated you. And then I finished. He paid me off pretty good and made some really scary threats -- not just about me... my family, my future. He beat up a guy right in front of, beat him hard, I don't know who he was, just to prove to me he would do what he promised."

"They didn't hate me. That's not what it was about. I'll save you the truth for now, assuming you find something useful to tell me."

"I was scared right from the start 'cause it was obvious I was doing something illegal. I couldn't get much on the guy; pretty sure I didn't want the details anyway. He drove to Lafayette Park where we met on a bench; near where they play chess. I wrote down his license plate, different cars. I figured it was always a rental car."

"Anybody else see him?"

"He wasn't hidden. We were out in the open, but I don't know who might have seen him. I never brought anybody along 'cause I didn't want anyone to know I had anything to do with him."

"I'm not a cop. I can't do anything with a license number, but give it to me. Did you have more than one rental car number?"

"I followed him back to his car three times and got the numbers just twice. I have 'em on my phone. I'll e-mail them to you right now."

"No, don't take out your phone. E-mail the numbers to me later. I'll write down my address for you."

She's a rat even if she is more scared of him than of me, Wesley thought to himself but it was not his way to insult people aloud, especially those in a position to help him.

"You must have had a way to contact him."

"I had a phone number. It doesn't work anymore but I can give that to you too."

"E-mail it to me but I can't think of any way I can use it. A cop could, and I have a file that will go to the cops if I cannot find my wife otherwise. By the way, it is a thick file."

"That's all I can think of."

Wesley asked some questions to keep her thinking, simple things she could answer like what the guy called himself and what he sounded like, what phrases he used a lot and so on. As he was asking these things he was thinking she probably does have a way to contact them. It would make sense to give her some secure way to call in case something came up, something like this conversation. As they parted, he reminded her he found her and could find her again if she did not give him the numbers she had promised to send.

Back at his hotel afterwards, Wesley lay on the bed. He had not even removed even his shoes, and he let them hang off the side so they would not soil the quilt. He rolled his head from side to side, just to avoid being too still. The energy and discipline that had held him together since he spotted Samantha was giving way to depression. He was not good at this, just as he was not good at anything other than his job. Until the incident, he would have said he was also good at being a husband but events had proven otherwise. The tricks of real or fictional detectives were beyond him. He lacked access to his target's electronic files, to video-surveillance cameras, to phone records, to license plate identities. He lacked the brilliance to outsmart his opponent and the luck to have them outsmart themselves. He did not possess or understand the technology to set up a trap for Samantha or her accomplices. He lacked the means and the will for threat of violence. He did not even feel he was especially obsessed with the task of finding his wife, not that he was unwilling to continue, but he did not have the drive he had seen in fiction, not like Captain Ahab or Nero Wolff or Philip Marlowe or Columbo or Miss Marple.

He could visualize himself living, after all this, a hollow existence without respect of his fellows or the love of his wife or the advantage of talents he had honed through the first half of his life. He flashed back to the moment he got into law school for that was the moment when his life turned around and he felt success even though he had not yet met Mattie. He had just barely been accepted to law school, possibly it was a clerical mistake on their part, but it was then he saw the wasted years of adolescence were over. It was time to be a responsible adult, just as he had been told over and over he should and never before believed really applied to him. Fate had given him one more chance and he knew he could take advantage this time and earn his place going forward. Back then he was not capable of the fixation law school would demand, and might well have drifted back to the habits of his immature self except that Mattie soon arrived in his life to inspire his growth. She did not push him exactly, did not nag him or monitor his attention to work. Her presence was enough to motivate him, to make him want to work, to earn her and their future together because, unlike the relative ease of his life up until then as a healthy, White, bright, American male, keeping her would require his participation, his effort and dedication, and he was ready to provide those.

He stopped rocking his head and closed his eyes. He felt no inclination to sleep although losing consciousness was an attractive image. He wished he knew how to drink himself into oblivion. "And not just for tonight," he said to himself aloud. The sound of his voice woke him from his egotism. It sounded so pitiful. He sat up and spoke the phrase again with more timbre, yet he was unconvinced. *I can be as fanatical as the next guy and this is the moment to be it*, he thought silently. He considered speaking this sentence aloud and then realized his reluctance, even in the privacy of an anonymous hotel room, would challenge his remnant sanity. *In fact, I am crazier than those paragons of infatuation exactly because I can imagine a life beyond this. I choose my obsession willingly. This is who I wish to be, not who I must be.* And still he was not convinced, not about any of it: what he would be doing, why he would be doing it, or whether there was a regular life waiting for him if he gave up this impossible pursuit. He was not convinced he had turned a corner but he had talked himself back into action. Lacking a well-considered strategy, he did what he could imagine and bolted out of his room to begin another stake-out at Samantha's apartment.

The cab got Wesley back on her block about two hours after they had parted ways. He could not dismiss the idea that he was acting in a B-movie or that he did not have a copy of the script, just following the trite conventions of the genre. He lurked in a doorway with a view of the entrance to her building. He did not know which windows were hers or if she even had windows on the street. Nonetheless, over the next ninety minutes he devised a logic for his presence, for his action which had become a boring inaction while he lurked. An hour and a half was not long for a stake-out but he was not in the stake-out business and was getting a sore back. She must, he still felt, have a way to contact his enemies. The enemies would want to limit how many people she met from their side so the big, bald ugly she knew was likely to be the one to turn up and he was likely to turn up because it would be more intimidating for him to get in her face again. As the second hour of standing on the street was beginning, Wesley was losing faith that mere dedication and a theory would get his wife back. He was not prepared to leave before having a new plan and he could not think clearly in the discomfort of standing around. That was when the television show he felt he was playing advanced the plot. A large, bald man in a suit without pinstripes came out of the apartment building. He might be the guy -- Wesley had no way to know and he had no way to follow him even if he were the guy, but he would not let the moment escape. He jogged across the street a half block ahead of the man, not sure what would come next. The jog was good to loosen up his joints after his vigil. The man walked briskly past a couple parked cars and then beeped the lock on a nondescript sedan which Wesley thought might well be a rental car. Although Wesley jogged back toward him, the man was pulling away by the time Wesley was there. He cut into the street and got in the way of the car. He looked inside and thought the man was not ugly but he wore a snarl consistent with a thug. Then the man rolled down his window and swore at Wesley. It was enough to convince Wesley this was the guy and he stepped out of the way quickly to minimize the incident. He was not worried about being recognized but he might become a person of interest if he made any more fuss.

The car bore away and Wesley kept walking without any purpose in the direction it had gone. Like the amateur he was, he had missed his only chance at this play. He could not guess if the big ugly would ever return or what might be a likely time for it. He wished for a café where he could sit in front of a cup of coffee with an attractive waitress, or even just a friendly one, to fuss over him a bit while he thought of whether there was any more he could do. Then he quickly corrected himself and revised his daydream to assume something would be done now that he had given in to an obsession and suddenly, inexplicably, his mind became very clear. In a rush of clarity, he assessed what he had learned and found something useful in it. Samantha was in touch with them, the big ugly did go to her rather than call her, and he must have met her fast and been in with her a long time. The guy was a professional, not actually in a B-movie where the story would mix in some sexual predator behavior to further display the thug's evil nature. Wesley did not see a Biblical evil in the world, but it was an acceptable working model for the characters who had taken Mattie and yet one can be evil in important ways without being evil in every possible way.

And if they were in touch and Wesley could still reach Samantha, he could reach the big ugly. He would set a trap with himself as bait. And once he had sprung the trap, he would abandon all pretenses of personal ethics and get Lucas to help with whatever would come after that.

"Are you all right, sir," someone was asking him, a woman older than himself, well dressed, with gray hair and a furrowed brow. "You don't look like one of the street people."

"Was I acting oddly?" Wesley asked in return. "No, I am not a street person and I am sorry for troubling you. I just had a wonderful idea, or even several wonderful ideas in succession and was hardly paying attention to the world nearby." He reached out to touch her forearm, a gesture calculated to appear appreciative and unthreatening although he thought he sensed the grip on her handbag tighten. The woman was a tourist with a southern or southwestern or otherwise rural accent, Wesley was a poor judge of American accents, but she was to him doubtless from a place of relative innocence, a small community where such a condition is possible.

"You had a strange look in your face," she replied and stared into him. He was not sure if it was the look of a doctor or a lover.

"Say, do you know where there is a cheap furniture store around here?"

"Why, no," she answered to Wesley's amusement. "I'm just a visitor here."

20. The Trap

The new chair was delivered later that day, via the freight elevator. It was the heaviest chair that would fit though the door of his room. It arrived soon after Wesley left the furniture store and was back in his hotel room. It cost an extra hundred to get same-day delivery. He spent money easily as he had cash and had no concern about saving any of it. He had enough to last for a couple months at least and he would either succeed or fail in that time. He attached a large eye-ring to the back of the chair and hid a rope under the chair. He practiced his simple plan a few times, it had to be simple, and then checked into a new hotel under a new name. It was nearly five o'clock when he went back to Samantha's apartment.

She was not home or would not answer the bell so he waited. It began to rain as the sun was setting. Wesley considered temporarily abandoning his post to find a shop to sell him an umbrella or a raincoat, even a blanket or a sheet of plastic but he was afraid of missing her and delaying things even more. He waited under an awning but the breeze blew a mist over him and he was soon damp and cold. He did not mind because he was deep in rehearsal of the conversation he would have when Samantha returned. He was confident she was out and would return. Had not the big ugly assured her he was in control and she should fear only him and not Wesley? His confidence waned by 11:30. He was beginning to visualize the possibility that she had moved out or was not coming back for a long while. After a day like this one, he doubted she would be out on the town. His socks were past being damp and deserved to be termed "wet." He had moved among all the more or less sheltered places in view of her door. Slowly his analysis concluded that standing in the cold all night would only hurt his prospects for accomplishing anything. In fact, he concluded, belatedly, that he should have quit at a specified time so he could be healthy and sharp when he tried next to reach Samantha. And yet by 12:30, he was still at his post and she had not turned up.

Then she was there, accompanied by a large man, walking beside her possessively. Maybe she had been with her boyfriend for comfort after the stressful day Wesley had given her. And why was she coming home so late? Why not stay with him all night? Obviously she had no moral qualms about it. Maybe she wanted to leave for work in the morning from her own place where she could dress and powder herself in the way she preferred. Wesley felt ready for action. He was thinking well. He had been on edge all night but had not worn himself out. He did not want to enjoy doing whatever he was doing on this trip but he could not deny there was a thrill in it.

He ran across the street and waited at her doorstep for them to walk the last few yards. He was not trying to startle her. And he was glad to show he was not afraid to speak in front of her male company.

They stopped before reaching him. Samantha talked to the man with her and then he stepped forward.

"What do you want?" the man asked in a tone more inquiring than threatening.

Wesley had expected something more aggressive and wondered what Samantha had told him. Not the truth, apparently. "I just want to give a phone number to the lady in apartment 12B. She knows me and said she was planning to e-mail some information to me but my computer is acting up."

Wesley reached out with his piece of paper on which he had written the number of the hotel where he left the chair and said to ask for Robert McTreese. This was the name he had used when signing in for that room. He thought the name sounded fake when he first heard it twenty years earlier and then, when he needed yet another alias, it just seemed right. He first heard it when he tried out for his high school swimming team. It was the name of the 400-meter guy, an upperclassman he never actually met because he did not make the team anyway.

"You don't even want to talk to her?" the probably boyfriend asked.

"Well, it's late and I don't know her well and she seems nervous. Just give her the number, OK?"

Back in his original hotel room, Wesley waited for the big ugly to turn up, for surely scared Samantha would side with the more dangerous party and call him with Wesley's contact information. His plan was based on a really stupid maneuver he learned back in high school. It was his way of pushing up his rank in the pecking order when he was around some rougher elements. His school did not have serious thuggery and he had no actual experience with violence, but this trick made him seem dangerous. Oddly, it actually was dangerous but he had not realized it back then.

He had learned a way to render a boy unconscious in a few seconds by cutting off the flow of blood to the brain. He would say something like "Let me show you something" and go behind a bully. Since he looked and sounded unthreatening, they would hesitate, he would keep talking softly and then it would be too late. Wesley would lock his arms around their neck in a way no one had ever been able to break in the first few seconds and then they were unconscious. Wesley would lay them gently on the ground while the other boys, the ones who had not seen the trick before, were in shock. The bully (assuming that was a fair characterization of the victim) would come around in a few seconds, unharmed but always very modest for a few moments.

Wesley knew he could not talk the big ugly into letting him place an arm around his neck and he knew he could not physically confront him, but he thought he might convince the big ugly he was incapable of menace and then step behind the chair to get a beer for him and throw a rope over his head. With the rope running through the eye on the back of the chair, Wesley could control the guy right away without having to face him or touch him. The trick he planned was built on the confidence game of his old approach rather than the way he implemented it. Then he would try to negotiate a trade, the guy for Mattie. That would be complicated too. They would not give her up easily, maybe not at all. Maybe she was not even available for trading. Maybe she was already gone.

He fell asleep in the big chair until 2 am when a burning crick in his neck woke him up. He moved over to the bed and resolved to get enough sleep to be able to function at a high level when the moment came.

The moment did not come before breakfast which he ordered from room service. The next few hours were spent worrying. He kept trying to claim this mental effort was planning but his list of plan elements was only a list of gaps in a plan. He had a start or a next step from where he was, but not a finish, not even a second step. It was a bold thing to believe, but he felt it was a necessary thing to believe that Napoléon was wrong when he said strategy doesn't pay, that "after so much study, I have no plan in mind. There is nothing to know about war, except that one must march ten leagues a day, fight and rest.[vvi]

Wesley preferred to know the end point and work toward it but, despite his boasts to Samantha, he did not know much about his opponent in this. He kept coming back to the idea of calling in Lucas. He did not know how that would help except that it would double or more the brain power on the problem. It would be wrong to ask Lucas. Lucas had his own obligations. If he agreed to help, he would be taking a ridiculous risk and if he decided not to help, he would feel bad even though he was making the right choice. Wesley focused for a while on how he could use Lucas if the moral dilemma of asking him were somehow resolved, say, if he just showed up as he did at the house that day when Wesley was cleaning out the garage.

The telephone rang, the hard-wired one for the room. Wesley had not expected to get a call. He expected they would figure out where he was and just come to get him, but he knew they were very unlikely to do what he expected them to do. It was Samantha. She asked him where he was staying. He said she did not need to know that but he also knew it was not hard to figure out for a group with access like this group had once they had the phone number. Besides, the room did not have a direct line. The hotel desk probably answered with the name of the hotel.

"Samantha, you don't need to know that. What do you really want?"

"They want to know where you are?"

"How do they know I am in San Francisco at all?"

"Wha'? I don't know. They called me and they are asking. What do I tell them?"

"Do you have some numbers for me, like we agreed? If you come up with something, I can move and get you protection."

"I don't want protection. I just want to be out of this."

"Just like me. Probably not even as much as me."

Wesley had stretched the telephone cord as far as it would reach so he could look out the peephole in his door. The cord was not quite long enough but he could look out with the phone in his hand and still hear Samantha from the end of his outstretched arm.

"It's okay now, Samantha. You can hang up. He's here." Wesley could see the big ugly in the corridor. Samantha swore at him, something about how he was going to get what he deserved for dragging her back into this. Her logic was flawed but Wesley just hung up the phone. He regretted showing off to her by saying "he is here" as if it was just what Wesley wanted. It <u>was</u> what he wanted for the moment, but braggadocio was not his way and for good reason. He was counting on their underestimating his smarts and his commitment. He was not sure he was shrewder than them and even if he was, that he was smart enough to get out of this at all well, but he had to assume the smarts was in his favor because without it he had only luck and commitment and that was not much and likely not enough.

There was a knock and Wesley was calm, ready to open the door and take the next step, the only one he had thought through, the bizarre step of attacking this brute with a rope and a trap, as if he had ever done such things.

"What? Who's there?" Wesley asked timidly. He did not stand in front of the door but he placed his hand over the peephole as if he were looking out. If they wanted to shoot him, they might be waiting for the blink in the peephole. He cleared his throat and said more loudly, "What do you want?"

"This is the FBI. Please open the door, sir."

This was a wrinkle Wesley did not anticipate. "Please hold your identification up to the peephole," he answered.

"Just open the fucking door or we'll kick it in."

That took the affair back to familiar territory where the actual FBI was not involved in the nasty side of the caper. Wesley opened the door slowly. He reminded himself to act scared to give his visitor confidence. Of course he was nervous but he had never before found it useful to show his fears. Nonetheless, the shock of seeing two big uglies coming into his room made displaying fear quite easy.

"Put your hands on the wall. I'm gonna pat you down," said the one Wesley had seen before. He faced the wall and placed his hands above his head against the wall. The guy did what he said he would do and then told Wesley to sit down. Wesley had put pillows on the desk chair so the visitor would sit in the trap chair. With two guys through the door, someone would be sitting on the bed but now there was no way to spring the trap anyway. Wesley had given himself to them after his extravagant effort to get to Samantha secretly had reaped no benefit at all. Wesley pushed the pillows onto the floor and sat where he had planned, as if the plan were still in place. He had thought he could control the situation if he were lucky. He never should have thought that. He had no experience with situations like this. In his normal life, the life that had ended a couple months before, he was often in control of the situation, situations where he understood all the variables because he had gone through them many times, like reviewing the annual budget proposal or recommending a response to a lawsuit or teasing out the implications of new legislation as it affected USDA policy or farmers or ag chemical companies or grain shippers.

"Okay, Marcus. I think I can handle him from here. Go ahead and take the car. I'll call a cab once this client decides to cooperate fully."

Wesley heard the arrogance in the remarks but was more impressed by the attempt at sarcastic humor. It suggested he was relaxed and possibly possessed more than the minimum of intelligence, although Wesley had already been willing to concede he was mentally competent. This assessment was Wesley's attempt to hold his euphoria out of sight. Luck had been with him all along. It just had not been obvious. When Marcus was gone, he would be back to the familiar problem of getting a rope around the neck of a man more violent than himself.

Marcus did not walk out immediately. He stood in front of the closed door and looked at Wesley silently, no expression on his face, revealing nothing of his thoughts. Then with no word, he turned around and stared at the door for a second, stepped backwards as if performing a dance, opened the door, and left. Just two were in the room as planned. Wesley fought his inclination to speak, to take control. He waited and held his head down in a posture his father would have said was unacceptable for a man.

"What's the matter with you?" the man asked, proving Wesley's posture was making his point.

"I just want to see my wife. I don't care about anything else," Wesley answered. The man stood in front of him and then started pacing.

"Want to see your wife? Sure. Go see her when we're through here. First, you gotta tell what you want from

Miss Pressman. You're bothering her and I can't let that go on. What do you want from her?"

Wesley was not interested in negotiating with this guy any more than he did with Ms Pressman. All he wanted in life at the moment was for this guy to sit in that chair. Wesley acted confused, incoherent, irresolute, cowardly. He knew he had no talent for acting, for projecting emotions that were not genuine. It had been a weakness in his work, sometimes accidentally offending people or making a weaker case than he intended. All he was accomplishing now was exasperating his adversary. The frustration agitated him, making it less likely he would sit in the trap. Wesley did not think delay was doing him any good so he tried a ploy that came to him on the spot: he pissed. He did not have a lot of urine in his bladder so it was not especially conspicuous except to Wesley himself. He wanted the guy to notice it so its strategic value would not be suspected. He stretched his legs out, showing the wetness in his crotch. A trickle ran down the back of his leg and onto the floor. He rubbed his shoe in it to attract attention toward the small puddle.

"What the fuck? You piss your pants! What a pig! You going to cry now? I am about through with you."

"Sorry, sorry. You have to know this whole thing is too much for me. Let me clean up. I'll tell you what I know."

Wesley jumped up and headed toward the bathroom with his legs staggered apart as if it was painful to feel his own urine.

"Leave the door open," the guy said as he sat down, obviously not on the pillows Wesley had vacated.

Wesley went to the bathroom and turned on the water, hoping the sound would mask his footsteps to the back of the now occupied trap chair. He pulled a loop of the rope through the eye he had installed, flipped it over the big ugly's head, and pulled it tight. The maneuver took one full second. Wesley had already realized he could not direct the pressure to cut off the blood supply to the brain as he did with the arm hold. He would have to count on the slower process of suffocation with the attendant risk of seriously damaging the man. He wrapped the rope around the chair leg with a couple quick clove hitches. The man flipped himself over the back of the chair, trying to get the pressure off his neck. With the rope knotted now, there was already no way to release the pressure. If Wesley left, the man would die, however, the flip placed them on the same side of the chair and the man got a grasp on Wesley with his legs. Wesley saw him reaching inside his jacket, maybe for a gun or a knife, and calculated the man might not need air for as much as a minute. Their hands grappled -- Wesley only hoping to keep any weapon out of play for a few more seconds and his foe confused about why his neck was in this tight grip and how he could get to his weapon and how he would stop from blacking out and whether the noise he was making would bring help or further harm. And then it was too late for the humbled ugly and confusion overtook all his stratagems until he was left only with a concern about how to breathe. His hands went to the rope at his throat. He thought he must have the pocketknife his uncle gave him on Christmas when he was ten and that he must have kept it sharp as he had promised to do. He remembered to take care that the sharp side did not face his throat when he slid it under the rope but there was no danger because the knife had been lost long ago except in his unconscious.

Wesley felt the heavy, wriggling animal wrapped around him go limp slowly, if ten seconds is slow when there is so much at risk. The room was silent for one more second before Wesley jumped up and loosened the rope a couple inches and retied it. The man was not breathing, his neck was torn in the struggle but not bleeding much, just some skin scraped off. Wesley dragged the man's feet around so he was more or less sitting in the chair, although the chair was on its back and began administering mouth-to-mouth resuscitation. *If he needs cardiac pumping too*, Wesley thought, *he's a goner. I don't know enough about it to even try.*

The luck that Wesley did not accept as his due held for him again and the man sputtered back to life like a lawnmower after a long winter although, obviously, a man's life is more significant than a gas-powered tool. The man puked on himself and started to look around. Wesley quickly ran over to the desk where he had stashed the duct tape and taped the man's wrists to the chair before any struggle revived. The man was starting to speak coherently when Wesley taped his mouth shut and then he worked on controlling the legs. The fight had gone out of Wesley's victim and he was soon immobilized. Wesley lifted the chair into its proper position and looked into the eyes of his prey to be sure he was conscious.

"I'm really sorry to tie you up like this. It must be really uncomfortable -- torturous. I think I read about actual torture sometimes based on restricting movement. Something like that was done, or someone claimed it was done, in Vietnam and in Algeria, I think. I'm not sure at all where it was done or where I read about it, but I am sure it is terrible. Now I'm not the sort of person who likes to hurt anyone, not for revenge or ego, not in the least, so I will try to get you out of this as soon as I have gotten what advantage I can out of it.

"I'm not a talkative person either, even if I am a lawyer. I'm the paperwork kind of lawyer, you know. Or do you think this conversation is my way of torture? No, I am dead sincere with you. It's just that this is not exactly a normal time for me. I am way out of my comfort zone and I am trying on so many new personae I am not sure how to act like myself. Ironic, isn't it, that I am entirely incapable of acting, of projecting myself onto an alternative personality with credible gestures and language, yet here I am searching for the actual self inside here after a few days absorbed into this alternate existence you and your people have imposed on me. Or maybe I am just feeling a disorientation from the past month, but I don't think so. I hung onto my original self for most of that time. I thought as I always thought, with relative objectivity, maybe more intensively since your guys blew me up, and it did not get me anywhere. Yes, obviously, it got me to San Francisco and Samantha, whom you know as Miss Pressman, but that hardly did any good for anyone. All in. I went all in with you. You see, of course, it hasn't done any good for anyone either, not yet, but you have to admit, this is not what you expected of me. Or, forgive my lawyerly precision, you do not have to admit anything, which is a good thing since my tape won't let you admit or deny anything right now and I am not about to give you any more freedom in the foreseeable future.

"If you can see that this is not my idea of torture, you would be reasonable to conclude this is my idea of entertainment, for myself, not you, obviously. I cannot say what it is because I am not familiar with this stupid behavior from myself. I do not feel entertained. I feel anticipatory, waiting for Godot and fully as foolish as Vladimir and Estragon for doing it since in my case disaster is rushing toward me. I seem to have drawn an ace today but the hand is not won.

"Okay, I can see new inspiration is not coming to me. I will have to do generally what I already had in mind, in which case this conversation serves the purpose of giving you time to assess your own situation, and decide for yourself, without any hysterics on my part, to cooperate with me just a little in order to save your wretched life. If I do not get the passcode to your phone in the next few minutes, I will leave and try something else to locate my wife. You will be very uncomfortable, obviously, and your very survival will soon be in doubt. Do you see I have no incentive to call in any authority to help you after I leave? It would only shorten the time I have to make another move. Do you see that taking away my access to police and such help for myself, you and your colleagues have made me dangerously desperate? So first let me take out your cell phone.

"...Oh, excuse me, I should set aside this pistol too. I'm not sure how to empty the ammunition, but I suppose it is safe enough with you taped up as you are.

"...Is this your wallet? I see it is. I will leave it with you except for the driver's license, so don't drive anywhere until you get a new one, Okay?" He patted his victim thoroughly to be sure there was no knife hidden away. Although Wesley could not see the man escaping, a knife might help him if he could reach it somehow with one of his slightly moveable parts.

"...Fine. Well done on your part. You barely wriggled. Now I will tape your forearm to the chair and release your hand. You will write your code and then I will make a call on your phone to the last number. You understand? Just nod your head as much as you can. ...Good. Oh, which hand do you use to write?”

Wesley adjusted the tape holding his victim to give a little room for one hand to move. He noticed his own hand shaking although he did not feel especially nervous, not as nervous as the situation called for him to be. His unconscious was the more nervous component and it was the smarter one. Wesley put a pencil in the freed hand and held a piece of paper against the arm of the chair next to the hand. The man held the pencil but did not write.

“You have been thinking all this time and not realized your position yet?” Wesley asked. “I am not going to slap you around to make my point. If you will not cooperate, you are on your own here. How do you know I will help you out if you give me your code? You don’t know. There is no room in your life for any certainty at this point. Take what you get. You won’t like waiting for destiny after I leave. Do you imagine I am incapable of letting you die? How could you wonder about that with your blood dripping down your shirt from the rope burn I gave you?”

The man wrote four digits on the paper.

“Just wait a minute while I see if this works. Yes, I am getting a ring. This is your name on the driver’s license, right?

“Hello, I am a lawyer representing Mr. Raymond Cylinger. I believe you spoke to him about an hour ago. You know him, right?” Wesley looked one more time at the man taped to a chair and left the room, locking the door behind himself and hanging a do-not-disturb sign on the knob.

The person on the telephone was quiet for a few moments. Wesley started to walk down the stairs but before he reached the ground floor, the man on the phone spoke up.

"Who do you want? I don't know any Raymond whatever-you-said."

"Excuse me, please, we are about to go into a tunnel. Let me call you back. It is an urgent matter. I will just be a minute." Wesley went to the front desk of the hotel and paid for one more night. The people behind Mattie's disappearance might have a way to locate the phone, so he decided to talk while walking. It might keep them from starting a search in the hotel room.

When he was two blocks away, he called back. It had been five minutes, enough to get the person on the phone thinking but not enough to know what was happening. It made it appear that Wesley was in no hurry. Wesley was not sure why that would help but it seemed a strong impression to make.

"Hello again. Sorry for the delay. And don't worry that I am the driver. I would not talk on the phone and drive at the same time."

"Who are you?"

"If you do not know who I am, I will have to call some more numbers on this phone. You were the last call; at least this number was. And it was called a few other times this morning so someone at your end knows Mr. Cylinger. He said that was his name. I mean, he nodded in the affirmative when I asked him."

"I might know him. What do you want?"

"If you know much of the situation, you already know what I want. I want to have my wife back."

"There is no way you have Ray. All I know is you got his phone."

"And I doubt you have Mattie within reach at the moment but you can find her and you better do it quick because Ray is not going to survive for long in the trunk of this car where he is very uncomfortable. If you do not help me out soon, he may reconsider what he is willing to say about the operation."

"Put him on the phone."

"Sure. Love to. As soon as I speak with Mattie."

"No one here by that name. No women here at all, so that can't happen."

"Tell you what, Mr....., what is your name please?"

"I'm not giving you my name."

"I would not have believed whatever you said so why not make one up to facilitate our conversation?" There was no answer. "I'm going to call you 'Ratso' then. You remember Ratso Rizzo? I expect you will have to consult with someone higher up. Call me back in thirty minutes. If I do not hear from you then, I will interview Mr. Cylinger again. I have several cards to play after that and yet I prefer to bring the game to a close today. First, I need to know what game we are playing. I need to know if I am saving Mattie or getting revenge for losing her."

"Hold on there. We can work out a deal here. Let me give you an address where you can see her if that's what you want."

"No, that's not what I want. I want her on the phone to this number in thirty minutes.   ...Talk to you later." Wesley hung up and turned off the phone in case what he had seen on television about tracking cell phones applied here.

He was worried about the big ugly, whose name was possibly Raymond Cylinger, about whether the life he had spoken of so lightly really was in danger in the short run. He did not want to kill anyone. Desperation had not warped his ethics far enough to be as casual about life as he tried to project. He jogged back to the hotel where he had left his victim, back to his room, back to several forms of danger. Desperation *had* warped his willingness to accept risk to his own existence.

The lobby looked normal, no ambulance driver or cops. He took the elevator up. No one was in the hall. Suddenly he wished he had anticipated coming back and left a matchstick in the door to tell if the door had been opened, something he had seen in a Bond movie. He listened at the door and heard nothing unless the heavy breathing he imagined was real. He still had the key and unlocked the door. It opened a few inches and hit something solid. He stepped back at first and listened. He heard the breathing and a little rhythmic thumping. After a moment he peered into the crack between the door and the jamb. He could not see anything. The sound of Cylinger grunting came through, giving Wesley enough confidence to push against the door. It did not open but the grunting became more enthusiastic. Wesley jammed his foot into the crack and stepped down with enough leverage to move the door a couple more inches. It was not enough to fit his head inside, but he could see a little more, could see the obstruction was the chair. Somehow Cylinger had managed to slide it against the door although it made no sense to Wesley for him to keep people out. Knowing what was blocking the way, Wesley was able to wedge himself effectively and push the door far enough to let himself into the room. He closed the door behind himself.

"What's that you're saying?" he asked factiously. "You have been working hard since I left. You have worked up quite a sweat, I see. And you do not look good, if I may be forgiven for mentioning it aloud." Wesley checked the bindings and decided they were intact. "Guess I should have taped down the chair too. Were you planning to ride it out of here? No? Sorry. It is cruel to make light of your situation. But tell me, how have you been?"

Cylinger had been exhausted when Wesley first returned. The effort of moving the chair forward a millimeter at a time using only the momentum of shoulder shrugs had done him in. He was rallying for one more push and then he hoped to attract attention with rapping on the door whenever anyone came by. Seeing Wesley and hearing his mockery revived him more than his will could have done alone, and he stared with all the hatred he possessed at his tormentor. His look did him no good, of course, especially since Wesley hardly looked into his eyes.

Wesley dragged the chair away from the door and then taped it to the bed. "That will make it more challenging to get out the door, Mr. Cylinger. Let's review your situation." Wesley sat on the bed at an angle where Cylinger could just see him if he twisted his head as far as possible in one direction and rolled his eyes to that side. "Your best move when we last spoke, that is when I last spoke, was to give me your password. You made a good move and it put me in touch with someone who denied knowing you and who did not help me. I think he does know you and, you will be glad to hear this, I think he cares about you. Unfortunately, from your point of view, he had reason to believe you are somewhere else. Nonetheless, he might send someone here so I need to leave again very soon. I won't be coming back this time, so this is your last chance with me. Last chance at what, you may wonder. Everything, Mr. Cylinger. This is your last chance at everything. We already worked out a way for you to write. Let's use that again."

Wesley peeled away the tape on Cylinger's hand. He had stopped his frantic grunting in order to save his energy.

"Take the pen. Let's see if you can give me enough information to inspire me to send your employers to this room. What is the name of the man I called?"

Cylinger slowly wrote: "I need blood in my arm. Losen the tape."

"You need two Os in this word: loosen. Unless you were just shortening the word to make it go faster. Mr. Cylinger, we are not negotiating here. You are writing to save your life. The name is..."

He wrote slowly: "Bobby Coffitt."

"And is there someone else you prefer me to call? Someone who might be in a better position to help you, and by that I mean to help me?"

He wrote: "Baggy 645-????."

"I guess Baggy's number is on your phone?"

Cylinger's grunt communicated an affirmative."

"And Baggy's last name?"

Cylinger wrote another question mark.

"Anything else you want to tell me?" Wesley asked although he was becoming nervous about hanging out in the last known location of his prisoner.

Cylinger did not move or grunt. Wesley looked at him closely to see if he was likely to survive a little longer.

"To prove my good intentions, I am going to tell Baggy where you are and for good measure I will tell Bobby too. Maybe they can get you out of this quickly. Good luck, Mr. Cylinger."

Wesley walked to the door but once in the hallway, he rushed as quickly as he could to get away. He took the stairs just to reduce the odds of meeting some thugs on the way to his former room. Outside he walked swiftly down an alley to get way from the hotel. He checked his watch and saw it had been 35 minutes since he turned off his phone. He hailed a cab and gave an address on the edge of the city. He turned on Cylinger's phone and called Bobby Coffitt.

"Hello, is this Ratso?"

"Where the hell have you been? You said thirty minutes."

"You're right. I did say that. It turns out I am not especially reliable. How did you make out? Is my wife about to speak to me?"

"No, I can't do that. She is not here and I do not know where she is. But maybe there is something I can do for you if you drop off the man you called 'Cylinger'."

"I did not make up his name like I did yours, Ratso. Didn't need to. Just like I didn't need to make up yours, I guess. ...Bobby. ...Coffitt."

"Oh you can figure that out from my telephone number."

"Maybe, but that's not how I did it. And it's not how I got Baggy's name and number. If you can't do anything for me, I'll call him. Nothing you want to tell me first?"

"I can tell you that's a bad idea, a really bad idea. Won't do you a bit of good. Meet me someplace safe and public and I'll give you the path from here. I don't care about your wife—I just want to get Ray Cylinger back from whatever you have done to him."

"Stay close to the phone. Maybe I will call you back after I talk to Baggy." And Wesley hung up. He was thinking his prisoner was doing well enough to survive a little longer. He could not visualize any way this dialogue was going to get him to go back to his room although he did think he sensed some pressure on Bobby Coffitt to go wherever he was sent. He waited a few minutes for Bobby to call back in case he had something better to offer. Then he searched the phone and found the number for Baggy. He was reluctant to call because it felt like his last option. And he could not ignore the possibility he might be killing good ol' Ray. Therefore, he had to act.

Taking this many steps, one immediately after the other toward a single purpose, was contrary to Wesley's normal working method but it is what happens in war. It seemed to be working even if he had not accomplished any of his long-term goals. Maybe he should have been more aggressive in his professional life, operated more like this, although that was a moot point now. Ominous words from Sun Tzu came to mind: "The best strategy is not to win a hundred battles, but to bend the enemy without fighting."[vii] *All right*, he thought, *I won't get cocky, but I will continue. There is no way to stop now.*

He dialed Baggy's number. A woman answered.

"May I speak with Baggy, please."

"Biggy, you said? I don't know any Biggy. Who're you."

"I will take it that you are asking who I am because you do know Baggy. And you can probably see I am using Cylinger's phone, however, I am not Cylinger. I am not Coffitt either. And I am not any form of law enforcement. Now may I speak with Baggy?"

"Still don't know anyone with that name."

"Ray is gonna need his phone back so Baggy needs to call me in the next fifteen minutes or he will not get a chance to negotiate with me. You see the number there?"

"I'll see if anyone here knows a Baggy."

"You do that and do it pretty quick if you please," and Wesley hung up again.

"Damn," he thought and then said it aloud for lack of practice with stronger profanity. He knew strong language, obviously, and had no particular aversion to using it, moral or cultural. It just did not come to him naturally. He embarrassed himself with his own officiousness. The years of lawyerly practice in the government had turned him into a government lawyer at a level deeper than he had cared to notice.

He looked at his watch to measure the time exactly. While he waited, he wrote down the phone numbers in Cylinger's phone files. Fifteen minutes passed without a call back. He waited five more. He had nothing to gain by calling back. He was playing a game with rules he did not know. He just went with the first thought that came to him and it was that he needed to convince them he had more cards than they knew about.

He wanted to write down all the facts he had accumulated and then make a list of options but there was one task he had to admit deserved priority and he dialed Bobby Coffitt again.

"Hello, Bobby. This is not Ray again. Would you..."

"Where is Ray. Put him on."

"Ray may not be quite able to talk at the moment. In fact he is not looking very well."

"You fuckin' bastard. You're dead if anything happens to Ray."

"Good to hear you care..."

"Shut the fuck up you, you..."

"He is in room 305 of the Empire Hotel on Huntington Avenue in San Bruno, you know, south of the city. That's near Belle Air Park. I am worried about him so I will call 911 unless you think you can get here or get someone here really fast."

"Is he breathing?"

"He was last time I looked. Probably still is."

"Don't call 911. I'll be there in ten, fifteen minutes. No more."

"Like I said, I'm glad you care. I will call 911 in twenty minutes 'cause I care about him too. Hurry now."

Wesley checked his watch and then turned off the phone again. He saw his fingers shaking as if they were someone else's but he decided his hands were as reliable as ever, capable of doing what he asked. A little shaking would not bother his writing or dialing. The hands were not the weak part of the operation -- it was his brain that needed assistance. He had just given away one of the last cards in his hand, a bad tactical move he did not regret. If he were responsible for someone dying, even Ray, he would not deserve to be with Mattie afterwards. He walked back toward the Empire Hotel to see who turned up.

Is that what this is about? he asked himself, meaning whether he was merely trying to recover his partner in life for his own amusement. He missed Mattie and was making all kinds of promises to treat her better. He had never mistreated her, but he had failed to care for her as he should have. He should have put more effort into planning vacations and dinners out. He should have listened better when she was telling about her day and been supportive of her concerns rather than wishing she were not standing in front of the TV or talking over the game. He should have appreciated her devotion to her work rather than been jealous of it. He should have told her more of his devotion to her and at the same time he should have burdened her less with his emotional dependence on her and let her stand more on her own. He should have enjoyed her friends more. He should have made himself more interesting and brought new friends into their circle. He should have remembered that their partnership was more than their jobs because they are both human beings first. They could do their jobs better if they helped each other although that was not the prime reason for helping each other. He thought he had placed priority on Mattie, thought he had understood all of this but it had become too easy to assume it instead of nurture it, too easy to ignore the day-to-day pleasures of being her husband for the far more challenging and obvious demands screaming daily from the office for his attention or he would be pushed aside. In Washington, that was the worst-case scenario, not being fired or humiliated, just being irrelevant along with most of the people around him.

After twenty minutes, which felt like an hour, he turned on the phone and called 911. He said he was Ray Cylinger and he heard a fight in the room next to him and someone moaning for help. He gave the address and then he turned off the phone and allowed himself to relax while he looked across the street.

No one suspicious had entered the hotel, certainly not the second ugly, Marcus, he had met when Ray first came. The police arrived before the ambulance by a minute. The EMTs waited by the curb, apparently in touch with the police by radio. They went in after ten minutes. Poor, ol' Ray came out on a stretcher soon after that. Wesley wondered if he was handcuffed to the stretcher although he was essentially a victim from the police viewpoint, albeit a very suspicious one since it was not his own room. He probably had a police record. He should not have needed to be carried out. Maybe he had injured himself in his struggles against the duct tape; maybe he was faking his state of health to gain sympathy or to aid in an escape; maybe the police were just being cautious. At least a policeman rode in the ambulance with him. Wesley wished Ray well since the responsibility for harming a human being was forcing him to question his own humanity.

It would have been best for Wesley if Ray's pals had taken him away so Wesley would not be in legal trouble. Now a whole new set of actors would be looking for him. It was better for his moral standing that Ray was in the ambulance. Nonetheless, there were benefits to Wesley's case from having the police involved. A thug in dramatic circumstances might convince some authorities to address Mattie's case as a kidnapping, possibly abetted by Wesley pointing out the connection at some point. If the police held Ray a while, he might not be able to pass on information on Wesley's appearance to Baggy and Ratso... unless his lawyer would fulfil a communications role.

Maybe, Wesley thought, *the guy who arrived in my room with Ray was Baggy.* Wesley tried to think of anything that looked "baggy" about him. He could try saying something suggestive on the phone using the number for Baggy, pretending Ray had told him it was Baggy, throwing in a few references to his appearance, claiming he was in touch with the police or the FBI about the case but was holding back on tying Baggy in, in case he could help locate Maggie. It was a very long shot but good to have at least one possible path forward.

Was it a mistake to let Ray go without more to show for his big play? Would it have been worth the risks, most of which were to Ray? Had he weakened his position by showing weakness? On that question, he had an answer. They already knew who he was or who he had been. He had shown a capacity for violence they would never have anticipated and he had shown he was more rational than desperate. He must look more capable of playing their game though the game was not moving very fast.

More police came. Four patrol cars and an unmarked car with blinking lights filled the street beside the hotel. A photographer came in a normal car. Wesley figured she was with the police because they let her drive past the taped barrier at the end of the block. A small crowd gathered although there was nothing for them to see. They stayed as long as the police were there, some thinking something interesting might happen and some sufficiently intrigued by simply being near the mystery.

With the frantically blinking lights and the clueless crowd, Wesley could stare toward the hotel without seeming unduly interested. He sat for more than two hours on the sidewalk and drank a large bottle of Coca Cola from a brown paper bag. For his meetings with Ray and Samantha, he had dressed like the out-of-work lawyer Ray's people expected. He had no great disguise, but was trying to complicate attempts to find him. For the next step, he would shave his head and start growing a beard. He could do a temporary tattoo on his neck.

When the police and the crowd and the daylight were gone, he staggered off to find some dinner. He decided to call the day a draw. On the positive side, no one had harmed or captured him despite the risks he had taken. On the negative side, the only remaining steps he had planned were: 1. to cut off his hair, 2. draw on a fake tattoo, and 3. keep moving where he was living/hiding. It might be better to get an actual tattoo; the idea was surprisingly attractive. He had ideas, not yet plans, for more effective actions, all of them bad. But bad ideas can be seeds of good ideas if creative thinking is allowed to flow and then be critiqued. That was not wisdom from a great general; it was what his government leadership training course two years ago had claimed. He felt well equipped with vague notions, uncomfortable facts, and enhanced personal motivation but could not settle his mind to critique this jumble to tease out a rational approach. The course said brainstorming should be followed by group discussion and he had no group.

21. Calls for Help

Wesley's new room was comfortably shabby and as anonymous as a monk's cell. He had grown up in the suburbs in homes with proper furniture and clean linens but he had never acquired much taste for such appropriate trappings or for antiseptic cleanliness. He had gone along with vacuuming the rugs and mowing the lawn and putting the dishes away before bed every night for the sake, at first, of his mother's sensitivities and, secondly, for Mattie's. Over the years, he had come to believe he was the creature he saw in the mirror, clean and stylish, behaving as he did in service of his love in life but, looking at his cheap hotel room, he felt more at home than he would have expected. *It is just a temporary sensation,* he told himself. His surprising attraction to the low cost of this life exposed his natural parsimony and its diminished demand for upkeep appealed strongly to his inherent indolence, like a vacation stripped to its essentials.

He lay back heavily on the bed, feeling the bounce of its noisy springs. A moment after that he also felt the unevenness of their support and doubted he would sleep easily here, having softened himself for years in the consistent comfort of sleep on a firm mattress adjusted to the high standard set by the wife lying always so perfectly beside him.

His body lay awkwardly on top of the gritty wool blanket, shifting positions to find one where he was not conscious of the lumpy pad beneath him while his mind tried to devise another step to take toward finding Mattie. He preferred to plan with paper and pencil handy but he figured changing his approach, going paperless, might help turn up a new idea. He tried to mentally list his assets, what he knew, what he might be able to use, like the names and numbers he had discovered in their organization; and he tried to list his constraints, like not harming anyone beyond a tolerable level. The lists were not helping generate ideas. They were not complete -- they needed to be written out. He was a pencil-and-paper thinker. He needed a bigger leap in approach to generate a new intuition. His blueprint at this point was only the hope of a plan, and it went no further because he fell asleep.

It was nearly dark in the room when he awoke. The feel of the dim light seemed inappropriate — it should have contained the blink of a buzzing advertisement on the side of a nearby building or, at least, the glow of colored neon. He pulled aside the flimsy cotton curtain on his only window and looked at his view. He saw more than an alley and less than an urban bustle. It was the sort of scene that appeared to have nothing noteworthy but which might appear in a movie fifty years hence, fascinating moviegoers with its anachronistic detail. "Ooh, look at that car!" "They were still using dumpsters." "Were the streets so poorly lit back then?" "Remember those little pizza shops? Why don't we still have them?"

Two days later Wesley did not yet have a next step in mind. He had spent day one in a series of libraries using the internet to link any of the names or phone numbers he had to anyone or any place in San Francisco. He came up with nothing and exhausted his ideas on how to look further. The internet had served him well at work in collecting information from obscure sources but he did not know how to extract secrets from it. He saw that he ought to heed advice from the fictional Colonel Terzo. "Always have a line of reserves in life, boy, always! In peace and in war."[viii] Reluctantly, he turned to the reserve assets on his mental list, a volunteer who would back up what was asked of him: Lucas was the only entry. He had discovered the San Francisco connection to Mattie's case. He was far better able to find something more useful than the dead ends Wesley had recorded in a notebook full of failures.

Wesley bought some groceries in a bodega and walked to his new hotel where he could simplify his environment's sights and sounds, and focus his thoughts onto paper. At this point, Wesley knew he had to stop following the absurd formula of doing the first thing that came to mind or believe that strategic planning was doomed to fail. It was time to turn to that bright young man back in Washington so he sat on his bed with his note pad on one side and his food spread out on a towel on the other side to devise a way to get

Lucas to help. Then they would talk it through to get some new ideas flowing.

Wesley would not pressure Lucas in any way. That would not be fair to him, of course, and it would not make him a reliable partner either. First of all, Lucas was a long way off and the telephone was not to be entirely trusted. The brutes knew he, Wesley, was in San Francisco but any legitimate authorities might not know it and they would be the more likely source of a bug on Lucas. He devised a way to make a secure telephone call, a way Lucas could implement. He had seen "burner phones" on TV cop dramas and figured getting one would be easy enough. But using it to contact Lucas would still have risks he could not easily bypass. He bought three "burners" for himself to feel confident he had a practical and secure link.

§§§

"No names, Lucas. You know who I am, I think. Do you, just yes or no, please?"

"Yes," Lucas answered.

"I'd like to see you this afternoon, buddy, but there is a tiny possibility that your phone is bugged so I'll ask you to call me back from a phone not associated with you. I am being overly cautious but I do not want you involved in my troubles with the law."

"Whatever you say, uh, sir."

"Good. You're getting into the spirit of the thing. Get a paper and pencil to write something down."

"OK, wait a sec... Right, I have a pen handy."

You're going to write a little formula. Ready? 527, comma, 339, comma, 990, comma, 532 divided by X. Read that back to me."

"527, comma, 339, comma, 990, comma, 532 divided by X."

"Perfect. The value of X is the street address of the restaurant where you, me and my wife ate that one weekend. You remember the place?"

"Sure, but not the street number."

"Of course. Just look it up. When you do the division, you will not get a whole number. I did not want this little code to be broken too easily. The ten digits on the left of your result are my phone number, not, obviously, the number I am using at the moment.

"Sorry to be asking you to help me with this. I know it does not have anything to do with you but just a quick drink this afternoon and you will be out of it again. Don't say any more unless the formula is unclear." Lucas was a wiz with numbers.

"It's clear."

"Thanks a million. Pretty cool system, right? Call from a phone of someone who is not connected with me in any way, maybe an unused phone at work, maybe a burner phone. Talk to you soon, I hope, but don't rush. There is no crisis of the moment." Wesley touched the "off" button on the phone knowing his last words were a lie.

Lucas' wife asked him who called so late in the day which caused him to blush with guilt. He had not done anything wrong but he had the feeling he was about to. He stammered a reply to her about someone from work who could not sleep because of a calculation he could not get out of his head. He blushed again at choosing and carefully pronouncing the pronoun "he" to reference the caller even though that part was true. To make the lie sound better, he went on about not solving the problem immediately but writing it down for later, talking too much and failing to convince himself he had any sense in his words. It sounded dishonest to Lucas in addition to nonsensical but his wife rolled over to turn off the light on her side of the bed without any further question. It was odd to have a call like that but it never occurred to her that Lucas was hiding anything from her.   Lucas wanted to call back right away, more from curiosity than from any fear Wesley needed it. "No crisis of the moment" he had heard. It was the only good part of the call and he was not sure he believed it. Nonetheless, it gave him license to turn off his light and try to sleep on the curious call without giving his wife further cause to wonder what it was all about.

§§§

"Hey"

"That you Wesley?"

"Lucas! Glad you could call. I'm sorry to do it such a bizarre way. You as much as anyone understand there is an odd circumstance behind this. I really don't want to play like a cheap novel but there is a dangerous conspiracy out there."

"I know. What can I do to help?"

"What a guy, Lucas! I'm not going to get you into this too deep. It was already dangerous and I have stepped over the line of ever getting out clean. I am almost completely paranoid but I am trying to place some tight limits on what you might face. I trust you, for example, so I absolutely cannot risk losing your faith." Wesley stopped to think. He wished he had written out a plan for this conversation.

"Hello? Wesley?"

"I'm here. OK, I'll give some facts. Probably all I want from you is an ear. It is desperately lonely to be doing all this without a friend."

"I'm listening."

"You know where I went and why. I found Samantha. Thanks for helping with that. She is in touch with whoever hired her to screw me, figuratively speaking. I got into a thing with them. I spoke with a few of them, met two of them, nearly killed one of them. At this point the police know there was an assault, my assault, but I doubt they know any truth about the case. The assault is good because it gives me something to tell the police when I get to that point, something they would like to understand, something to prove I am not just paranoid."

"You assaulted someone?"

"Oh yeah. Violently and with risk to life and limb for both of us. I won. Of course, I cheated. It was not a game anyway. I'm not boasting. I am not proud of it but it seemed the way to make some progress. I needed to take the initiative because they would eat me up if I dithered."

"What about Mattie?"

"Yeah, that's the question, isn't it? I don't know anything for sure about her, but these guys do know about her. Here's what it's got to be— Mattie was closing in on some kind of corruption, big stuff, I mean really big, and they snatched her to stop her. And to distract attention from whatever work she was doing, they created a reason for her to disappear. It was a clever plan, if that was the plan."

"Was she doing something about the corruption?"

"Yes! I mean, I think so. That's the model I'm using. She was for sure doing something secret and it was not anything about national security or politics. She doesn't do those. She's never even paid much attention to either of those topics. So anyway, I figure there are two possibilities about Mattie; either they have killed her or they have not. If they have, then I am finished and nothing matters to me. I am committed on this point. If they have not, it must be because they want something from her. After all this delay, they cannot be trying to get her to change what she was reporting or was going to report. She was very serious about whatever she has been working on lately, what she was working on when she disappeared. So I'm thinking she has hidden evidence they want. I even had a message to that effect although I am not sure who sent it."

"So you're saying if she knew they were capable of something like this, she would have protected herself."

"I think she would have protected herself by keeping her boss apprised or, if he is unreliable, someone else. She must have confided in someone. It wasn't me. I would not have been the right one for it anyway."

"Yeah, why not?"

"I would not be able to deal with the rough characters involved. Corruption is out of my league. The enemies I confronted professionally were mere selfishness and ignorance. Besides, I would get emotionally involved. I probably would have tried to get her to quit."

"She wouldn't quit."

"Maybe she was feeling abandoned by me for trying to stop her even though she never gave me the chance, just knew I would. Maybe that is why she accepted Samantha's story, at least for a day."

“What’s next?”

“I’m OK for the moment. They don’t know where I am or what I know. The police probably don’t know I exist. I left my hotel. I’m setting myself up in another city for now... changed my look too. I’ll work the telephone numbers I have for them.”

“You need help. You’ll go crazy like you said without a friend around to point you toward sanity. I can get away.”

“No, you’ll never find me out here. I won’t give you any more hints about me. I don’t want you taking the risk and I worry that they might be watching you. If you came out here, you would be on their list. Damn, you don’t want to be on that list. Besides, now that you mention it, I do have a friend out here.”

“Someone who did not buy the story about Samantha and all that?”

“No hints for you this, Buddy... Tell you what, if I need you for something, I’ll call your home and hang up when you come to the phone. That means to call me back on this number. OK?”

“OK. Talk to you soon.”

Wesley pushed a button to end the call. He felt good although he saw no substantial reason for it. True, Lucas had been solid, just as he always was. The call had restored an iota of Wesley’s faith in humanity. Of less importance but not insignificantly, it had given him a new idea. It was a weak idea, but it had potential to firm up his faith a smidge more. He looked up the Hotel Fusion and called the number listed. He asked the clerk for Ms Sodunke and then spelled the name for her. He felt lucky again when she said she would put his call through. Modupe had given him her actual hotel and was still there!

"Hello?"

"Hi. This is the guy from the bus, Modupe. Are you Modupe? It was hard to catch the sound of your voice in one word."

"Of course it is, Honey! Isn't this something! I never thought I'd be hearing from you again! You got more trouble for me or just more mysteries? Or you looking for a date? And just call me 'Dupe'." She laughed at her own joke.

"Wish I had time for a date, Dear. I was lucky to find you. Are you about to head back east?"

"I just got here two days back. I'll be a while getting that boy's apartment decent. Besides, I got to punish that uncle of his for agreeing to pay for my stay in a hotel."

"Seen the bridge yet?"

"Easy to see it but I haven't been on it yet. You finish that book yet?"

"Finished it and People magazine too. But let me ask, you have some friends and family out here in the San Fran area, people you trust?"

"'Here', you say? You came to California now?"

"You know I am not anything I say I am. But I'm hoping you see past whatever I say to who I am under that."

"Could give you a try, I guess. You know I make friends pretty fast but two days ain't real long. Lot longer than I knew you. Bet you'd do me a favor if you could though."

"Try me, please."

"I'll remember that. For now, there some people here I can trust. They been living here a couple generations worth. Some family I trust and some I don't. At least I know which is which."

"Good answer. Look, I'm calling for help with my trouble. And all I can give you back is an answer to some of those mysteries. I don't guess you've been thinking on this odd guy but maybe now that I remind of it all you might get a little curious."

"I done things for less pay than that."

They set up a meeting in a cheap restaurant near her hotel for that evening. She greeted him warmly and he returned her warmth with sincerity. She did not mention his haircut but he rubbed his hand over the stubble and grinned. His tattoo was hidden by his shirt. Wesley ordered the special, lasagna, and Dupe ordered a pork chop with applesauce and fries.

He explained that he would protect her by altering some details in his story and went on to explain that his daughter lived in northern California and had disappeared a month or so ago. He believed she was being held by a sex trafficking gang in San Francisco. The police, he said, had looked into the case and decided she had simply moved away without telling him, presumably to get away from him. They would not regard a twenty-year-old already living on her own as a run-away. He had found some good suspects but lost track of them so now he was asking if she could get her local contacts to let her know if they recognized any of these characters. He gave her names and descriptions for the two mugs who had come to his room: Ray Cylinger and Marcus, and the name "Bobby Coffitt" (whom he called "Ratso") and even the name "Baggy," Cylinger's apparent friend.

"I don't want to make trouble for your family, of course. I'll pay something if they want it, as much as I can get together, maybe $10,000. You can split the reward with your informant any way you want. I'm happy to keep the police out of it. I don't need any more risks. But if you have people to ask around, they need to be careful, not to push too hard or too often. These are real people and damn dangerous. If anyone wants to know why I'm looking, tell them everything I told you."

"But what do you want to know?"

"How to get in touch with them, like where any of them are. If someone wants to set up a meeting between me and any of them, that's all right too."

"Don't sound like the sort my folks would know. Could be they know someone who knows something more. The kinda money you're talking about would get them trying."

"Of course your people don't know them directly. But they don't need to know 'em, just to hear about them somewhere. You got to understand I don't want any good person taking chances on this. It's not like you and I know how to deal with them. Just see if the names or descriptions ring any bells with the local folks you trust. Don't give out my phone number. I'd rather not be surprised by the ones I'm looking for."

"How much of what you're telling me is true?"

"Almost none of it, Modupe. But I'll tell the whole truth to you if we find any of them. It'll be too good a story to keep to myself... Remember, don't try too hard. Your folks probably don't know any of these characters or their friends. Your folks shouldn't know them and shouldn't want to know them. Just, if they do... you know, tell me about it."

"Hmmm. I'll ask around. Thing is, it sounds like fun. Guess best not to think of it like that."

"You can have fun as long as you are smart and don't look like you might be talking to the police."

"Do you even have a daughter?"

"For now, I have a twenty-year daughter who's missing."

"Yeah. I see that."

"You going to have dessert? I can always go for pie."

§§§

Wesley sat in a city library at 9 am two days later having made no progress on anything, hoping the familiar, quiet, bookish environment would help him discover new approaches. He had a pad of paper on which he attempted to form lists of considerations to subsequently be organized and analyzed. No new ideas were formulating. He felt he was back in his freshman physics final exam and was completely unprepared to answer any of the questions. There was no one nearby whose paper he could copy. His phone rang. He ran with it to the men's room.

"Yo?"

"This is Dupe."

"Great. No trouble, I hope?"

"No trouble. I got a hit though. I was complaining to my hairdresser about a guy who bumped my car and drove off. Described him, you know. She said she knew of a guy like that, the kind that would drive off unless he felt like backing up and hitting you again first. She said if it was him, I'd better just forget all about it. She said he was called 'Ray Sky'. Sounds like short for 'Ray Cylinger' maybe. Pretty good, huh?"

"Sounds real good. Maybe I could talk to the hairdresser."

"Don't need to. After she told me to stay away from him, she told where to stay away from. It seemed pretty

290

stupid. Who knows what she was thinking? Maybe she was just showing off that she knew something. I wouldn't have listened to her except she came up with 'Ray Sky'."

"So where are you supposed to stay away from?"

"A bluish, good-looking place on the bayside of Park Street between 23rd and 24th."

"First of all, thank you my darling. Second, stay away from there. And I'll call you back to give you your pay if it turns out right."

"You better call. I don't do this shit for free."

"It'd be good to tell anyone you got working on this to stop until I check it out. Don't take chances if you don't need to. Well, I guess they didn't need to in the first place. Just call 'em off the hunt in case this works, OK?"

Wesley sent the address to Lucas in a coded message based on the name of Lucas' first pet. Lucas never had a pet but over lunch a couple years ago he had complained about security systems that asked him for its name. So Wesley had suggested a name to use for security questions and in case he decided to become a porno actor (everyone knows they adopt a screen name based on their first pet and the street where they lived in elementary school.)

That evening, Lucas sent photos of a dozen men. He sent them from a burner phone he bought to be more available to Wesley. When he Googled the owners on the specified block of Park Street, Google listed Cylinger at number 2337 and helpfully suggested other people who might be of interest, other people who had been looked up along with Raymond Cylinger. They all had sketchy backgrounds. Lucas thought the people who Googled these folks most often might be police. Google was hinting at the gang members. More information followed on each of them, just like a police investigation but just using public access on the internet.

Wesley texted back "Possibly brilliant. I'll try to learn the images in case I encounter any of these guys."

He pulled aside the flimsy cotton curtain

22. 2337 Park Street

The street with the address Dupe and Lucas jointly gave Wesley for Cylinger's house had been tree-lined in its heyday. A few of the original trees remained and a couple young replacements had gone into the holes in the sidewalk but most of the gaps were unfilled. The sidewalk was crumbling too much for roller-skating. Wesley watched the people walking past 2337 Park Street. It was a nice looking place, expensive for sure. Two old men sat on lawn chairs two doors away, playing chess or checkers on a small table.

He did not know what he was hoping to find. Cylinger or someone else he recognized might be among them. He might come out today; he might be recognizable; he might go to Mattie on foot; he might go slow enough to be followed. It was another very long shot, the only kind of shot Wesley had left. Enough long shots add up to a likely thing in cards and cyclotrons, but in this world of the street rather than the more familiar ones of games and news magazines, they might add up to nothing at all.

No one passed by for several minutes and Wesley worried his attention would wander. He did not trust himself in this role he recognized from fiction and not from the reality of experience or training or even from talking with someone who have ever "tailed" someone secretly. The neighborhood did not have many pedestrians but among those who went by was a full share of good-looking women. Wesley developed a ploy to pretend to watch them while his eyes were actually watching the door of Cylinger's building. While he did this, he worried he would actually look at the women going by. He had countless times watched the ladies. Ironically, he normally tried to appear to be ignoring them. He was a modern man who knew women were not mere objects for his entertainment but he never felt very guilty for watching them. He enjoyed the scenery of nature; women were part of that. So were men. Some parts of nature were more interesting than others. While waiting for his bus in Washington, he would imagine little scenarios of meeting one of the attractive women. The scenarios lasted no longer than the gap between an attractive women going by and when the next one appeared. In the area of his bus stop, they were rarely far apart, partly because he had a habit of finding something desirable in almost all of them, a habit abetted by his poor distance vision and generous disposition.

Weak vision was not helping his present task. He could see people clearly, at least they were clear by the standards he knew these days as normal, but he had to assess anyone coming out of 2337 and he knew so little about his targets' appearances that he really needed to catch some of the details in his view. His memory of Cylinger and Marcus was dominated by his thoughts at the time: the rapid flow of strategic adjustment, calculations of risk versus reward, repressed terror, acting his role in the play he had written without a script. The pictures of Cylinger from Lucas ranged so widely they could have represented a half dozen different men. His memory of their confrontation was filled with emotions rather than mages. The build would have been hard to describe exactly and none of the photographs showed it any detail, but it seemed the best starting point. With his weak eyes, he could assess the build better than such definitive signs as the shape of the nose or the color of the eyes or the tattoos. "Heavy" would have been the obvious adjective, not fat, not muscular like an athlete, but heavy as naturally endowed and as one would not want to confront. Maybe Wesley was reading more into the interpretation of the man's physicality because of the ominous look apparent in all of the photos, or because he knew the man would be menacing under any circumstances and much worse if he recognized Wesley.

Wesley studied the other pictures from Lucas. No one would think it odd for him to be standing around aimlessly if he had a phone in his hand. After an hour, however, the images had become flat in his mind, patches of color rather than versions of a human. He moved to a new spot, around a corner where anyone who had noticed him before would not be likely to see him. Someone had abandoned a few plastic buckets and tubs against the wall. Wesley assumed they were a set of street drums. It would have been comfortable to sit on one but the users might return and distract him from his task so he stayed away from them and accepted becoming increasingly uncomfortable. He measured the time it took a person to leave the building and walk out of Wesley's sight, ten seconds, and then vowed to never let ten seconds pass without looking toward the door. He counted to ten whenever he looked away. He counted to ten too many times to know how many times he had done it. Hours passed. He went back to the street with the door and pretended to look at his phone. He thought he would give the new location thirty minutes. The other street was relatively safe from suspicion from the target house, but he ought to move from time to time. He split the thirty minutes into thirty segments of fifty seconds in view of the door and ten seconds facing away.

At his estimated twenty-second minute, a man who might match one the images he had studied, Freddy Silberts, came out of the door. Mr. Maybe Silberts looked at his feet while going down the steps to the house and continued to look down as he turned to follow the street. The chess or checker player facing him called out "Fred the Barber" and waved. The other chess player turned around and echoed "Hey Fred." Fred the Barber lifted his hand familiarly without looking up from his feet and continued on his way.

FtB was proceeding on foot and Wesley kept a block behind him on the opposite side of the street as if they were both characters written by Graham Greene. According to the book jackets, Graham Greene had real connections to the British spy agency so there was reason to believe he knew something of clandestine operations although he did not claim to have been a field operative and his experience was back in World War II. Things had changed with the expansion of electronic snooping so Wesley regretted that he had not read any modern thrillers. He lost his quarry when a group of teenage girls stopped to tease each other about how to wear their hair, tugging at each other and giggling. They blocked his view of FtB and distracted him for a few moments. Then FtB was out of sight. Wesley did not want to be conspicuous so he walked fast rather than ran ahead, going past where he last saw FtB. His view of the street ahead was clear. He decided FtB might have gone in a shop so he tried to guess the most likely among a tiny place called "Athens," advertising "stand-up pizza;" a men's clothing shop, offering suits and shirts in its window; a cell phone store with no display of its wares but showing colorful posters that attempted to explain their financing schemes; a classic barber shop; and a mom-and-pop grocery. The barber shop might be Fred's, but pizza was Wesley's guess so he stood nearby to await the emergence of his current quarry. He looked into the grocery; at least he faced the grocery and used the reflection in the glass to watch the pizza shop, anticipating FtB might not eat his slice standing inside.

Guessing how a stranger would behave in the present hour and location, and then acting like that, was Wesley's new hobby since that is what he was to his various quarries. It was a more appropriate approach than trying to act like a character in a movie or book. He moved his head a little as if he were looking inside the grocery at the people checking out and rolled his eyes to keep focused on the Athens door but he was starting to feel conspicuous standing so long in front of a window displaying little more than the back of a rack of bread. He was about to take up a post somewhere else when he noticed Fred-the-Barber was standing in front of him, putting food on the conveyer belt. A flush passed over him although he had no sign FtB had noticed him. Maybe FtB had seen him and thought nothing of it but would think something if he saw Wesley again. There was no reason Fred would know Wesley's face but the communications within the conspiracy could be sophisticated. Maybe FtB had recognized him and had some plan to lead him into a trap. That is what Wesley would have done.

One random appearance before FtB was enough -- probably once was too many. Even so, Wesley stayed where he was, not wanting to look as guilty as he felt by moving suddenly and illogically. This intense moment borne of bad luck and inattention to what was right in front of him, this moment when he froze to await the hot blood under his collar to dissipate so he could regain some confidence, was the key moment in his search. He was staring at the food FtB was about to buy, daring anyone to sense he was avoiding FtB himself, and he spotted a carton of vanilla soy milk next to a package of those utterly tasteless rice crackers, a jar of almond paste, and a box of loose tea. FtB was shopping for Mattie! No one else would have that exact collection of items on their menu, least of all someone who fit the name Fred-the-Barber. The bag of pork rinds was for Fred himself and illustrated the rest of the items were for someone with a different palette and possible food allergies.

Wesley positioned himself between the grocery and the doorway to 2337 so he could keep in front of FtB and thereby not appear to be following. Or, once he was in position, he might hurry ahead and go inside 2337 first, if it was not locked, and then secretly follow Fred-the-Barber to whatever room was Mattie's prison. As he thought about it, he liked the more daring option, to go ahead and see if the door was locked and if it was not, he could turn back to the street as if he had merely knocked and then return to the grocery to be sure Fred did not go somewhere else, assuming it was not already too late to find him again.

Risk versus reward... If Cylinger was in that house, he would recognize Wesley and nothing good would follow. He was making calculations on a scale beyond his experience, on a scale he knew only remotely from fiction, melodramatic scenes not at all realistic but here it was, a reality he only vaguely suspected ever existed and one he never expected to experience. It was not exciting to him, as it is to novices who stumble upon this form of reality in fiction; it merely scared him. He felt anxiety at a level harkening back to his freshman physics final exam. He was not accustomed to it; he did not recognize himself in it. He was not steady but neither was he at all inclined to give up. This risk, whichever one he next chose, was what he had hoped to face since any of the present choices had some slight prospect of success whereas giving up the opportunity before him took him back to near complete hopelessness.

He could only define his future in terms of how it might lead to recovering Mattie. If there had ever been any doubt of whether the future would be endurable, that doubt ended with Fred's shopping list. Mattie was alive and well enough to be following her diet! Meticulous, alive and well! The phrase replayed in his head wherein he contrived to push it into his subconscious so it would not distract from the contest he had entered. There was a euphoria contributing along with horror to the shaking in his hands.

He looked back as subtly as possible every few steps to see if FtB had returned to the sidewalk. He thought he ought not to let his target entirely out of sight. And so he was lingering within the limit of his visual range when FtB exited the grocery. Fortunately, Wesley recognized his sloppy gray sweatshirt and his slinking posture because FtB's face never turned toward 2337 again. He crossed the street, got into a car parked a half block away, made a U-turn and was gone. Wesley had not even been able to see the license number. He could not identify the car and only vaguely knew its color.

The door was probably locked, just as the grapes were probably sour. He calmly walked on to 2337 and tried the door quietly in case someone was inside. Locked.

He felt unaccountably cold, as if a draft had reached him from the attic in winter. His sudden disorientation kept him from noticing how odd it was to be cold in August. He merely reached to his collar to button it up and wondered why he had no buttons on his t-shirt.

Wesley felt no immediate pressure. His whole strategy had collapsed just when he thought it was working. There was nothing for him to hurry toward, no reaction to make. He had taken the risk or was about to do so but he would reap no reward. At best, he had, at least, not been caught by Cylinger.

His mechanical risk assessment brought insurance to mind, and he felt a peculiar disappointment that he could not take out a policy at Lloyds of London against losing Mattie or even against surviving the night. He shook his head in frustration at his ineffectual thoughts and then he realized he was looking at a friendly woman in business attire with a caption: We insure it all! The ad in which she appeared was affixed to the back of a bench at a bus stop. He stepped closer and gripped the back of the bench to be sure he would not stagger and played the music of the new phrase into the front of his mind: Mattie was alive and well. That was enough for one day, wasn't it?

He searched consciously for a rhyme that would turn it into a poem, if only of the sort used to give cadence to jumping rope. Mattie was alive... "arrive" ought to work nicely. One, two, three, four five... he could use that. "Revive" had a good feel to it. "Wive" looked right but did not sound right unless it was plural but then it would not have the right sense since there was only one wife in this song. "Knives" would seem to rhyme and could fit the macabre style of some of those rhymes.

Ring around the rosy;
Pocket full of posies;
Ashes, ashes;
We all fall down.

Wesley sat on the bench to avoid falling down with his sudden confused depression. What next -- the perpetual question. Would Fred-the-Barber be back at 2337 again or would it be a waste of his remaining lifetime to stake out the house that was almost where he was going to find Mattie?

The woman beside him on the bench gave him a sidelong peek. Wesley knew his brain was coming back to reality when he analyzed her posture and imagined she was about to ask if he needed any help. It was a rational thought and showed an awareness of his time and place. He slowed his breathing although he had to open his mouth to appear calm while he still needed more air than a calm person needs. The woman stood up without speaking to him and stood nearby. She was being rational too, he concluded. He considered apologizing for disturbing her but figured that speaking to her would only add to her discomfort. Applying further rational thought, he assessed his need for the bench as greater than hers at the moment so he silently slouched down to gain as much comfort as it could provide. When the bus came, Wesley did not stir except to roll his eyes enough to watch the woman climb aboard without a look back.

It is typically discouraging to fail but it is not failure to merely miss a step forward even if one had hoped it was the last step to one's objective. After losing sight of FtB, Wesley was shocked that the many dangerous and successful steps already taken were not enough. His privileged life had offered setbacks before but there had always been a point at which he won the game regardless of how well he had played. He played only to shorten the time to victory. After failing freshman physics, he had improved his attendance in other classes, an obvious step not deserving praise. It was enough to get him through his B.A. This habit of minimal effort would have busted him from law school except for the drive to impress Mattie. His Federal job did not demand much of him when he arrived. His law degree carried weight among those without one. He could coast along on routine answers to easy queries. It would have paid the bills for 30 years on a small house in the suburbs and a trip to Florida at Christmas and no more, but he was saved from bureaucratic obscurity by the example within his house of Mattie's industriousness. He developed the habit of long hours in the office, and paid close attention in meetings to personalities of his colleagues. And his colleagues and bosses gained confidence in him, with his proper clothes and grammar and accent and professional degree and professional wife and long hours. Promotions came and the job became more interesting and promotions came again. Life had been more than fair to Wesley, pulling him down when he did not try much, although never very far down, lifting him up when he corrected himself. Never a cause for major discouragement; never a reason to deny there was a benign god, at least for people like him.

Wesley's sputtering mind focused in on Mattie again. She was alive and well and imprisoned unfairly. Getting her out would take more than fate. Another list began to form: *First, stake out the goddamn 2337 or the little grocery store until a better idea comes along; there will be plenty of time to think about one. Second point: be better prepared. Third: have a car ready. Sub-points on three: sit in the car, in the back seat of the car and watch with mirrors; lie down in the back seat of the car and watch with a periscope; bring food and play a radio to stave off boredom; and do it every day until Fred-the-Barber shows up to get fussy foods again for his captive.*

He did not admit it to himself, but he had unconsciously expected to see Fred Silberts, alias FtB, or another face from Lucas' photo album on his next day of the stakeout. 2337 had yielded FtB on the first day. But his overall task was not to be so simple. A sample of one stakeout day does not provide good predictive power on all stakeouts, even at the same location. He imagined dozens of reasons why someone might be going in or out of the house and dozens of possible roles the site might play in the story. It could be Cylinger's home, with his wife and children, visited once by FtB. It could be where Mattie was kept tied to a chair in the basement. Neither was likely. FtB had not taken

Mattie's food back to the house so she must be somewhere else. Besides, they would not torture her and still cater to her food preferences. It was discouraging to accept the house in front of him was not a key asset in his war.

Around 5:00, when he had finished his dinner and therefore had nothing more on his agenda, his mind wandered back to his first book. Su Tzu had advised "Never engage stronger adversaries: maneuver instead, until your own men can strike an isolated part of the enemy's forces."[ix] Well, this was an isolated part of his enemy. He started to make notes on how to break in and, to encourage action, on what he might find there. Getting in would not be hard as long as no one was there. By 6:00, when it was getting too dark to write his notes, he waited for lights to come on. At 11:00 it was still dark inside. It was unlikely anyone was there although someone might turn up at any time. He held back on his attack, not from fear, but, he preferred to believe, from a rational restraint. Since at least two heavies were associated with the house, it was reasonable to assume it was linked to the larger operation which had already proven to be highly sophisticated. There might be an alarm or a camera on the house. And if he were detected but not caught immediately, considerable forensic capabilities could be called in to find him, capabilities far beyond Lucas. He decided to cover himself up into something unidentifiable, wear gloves and shoes in the wrong size, and look in the window with a flashlight. He would not have the car nearby and would not stay at the site more than a minute.

He wanted to stay all night to see if anyone came back but he could not stay awake any longer and retired to his hotel by 11:30.

In the morning he decided not to go back to his stakeout right away. Since no one had been there much before midnight, he doubted there would be any action early in the day. He picked 10:00 for his start time. That gave him time to prepare for his peek through the window, assuming no one turned up before dark again, and it put him in position if anything developed around lunchtime. For a brief moment he considered asking Lucas to join him in watching. He found consolation in rejecting such a farcical option -- he was not yet desperate into absurdity. Neither his burner phone nor his government-issued Blackberry had a camera. The fantasy triggered a thought that he ought to buy a phone with video capacity but he rejected the idea as one complexity too many.

His preparations were completed by 9:30, right on schedule, when he gave in to a new idea. He checked into a new hotel. It took him three tries to find one that did not require an ID, causing him to wonder how one did affaires d'coeur in this town. He carried a small gym bag and wore a tie and jacket when he checked in and went immediately to his room to make a phone call.

His call was answered with a brusk "What," not a question or a greeting, but a command to state one's business immediately.

"Ratso!, how have you been?"

"Who is this?"

"Does anyone but me call you Ratso?"

"No one at all calls me that."

"Ahh, but I recognize *your* voice and I do not think your memory is weak enough to have forgotten mine. And yet I do not mind stating my name or, more significantly, stating I am Mattie's husband, though we seem to be separated at the moment."

"I don't know 'Mattie' either."

"Odd that you have not hung up yet on a stranger with my strange claims. I am calling to tell you I have had good news. I know Mattie is alive and someone is taking care of her with consideration on certain points."

"What a smartass! What do you think you know that has anything to do with me?"

"Of course I am a smartass. Didn't you know I am, like Mattie, a lawyer? At any rate, I understand that you might not appreciate my news since it is not news to you. Probably Mr. Silberts keeps you apprised of her health and welfare."

"I don't know any Mr. Silberts."

"Sure you do. The name doesn't ring a bell? Freddy Silberts? Fred the Barber?"

There was a long pause which Wesley allowed to go on as long as Ratso was silent. He hoped Ratso had a way to locate his phone. Wesley did not know how long that might take but the silence might be because Ratso was getting someone to trace the call. That would probably mean he was connected to some kind of policing agency.

"Look here. You got some problem. You want this Mattie person. And you think I know her. I don't want to break your heart and I don't want to get any more phone calls from you so let's say we meet somewhere and you tell why you want to involve me in your problem." Ratso was changing his strategy.

"Obviously neither one of us is being entirely honest here, but we seem to be communicating through all the bullshit. You don't want to be talking on a phone without knowing for sure who I am and who is listening in. So we need a private, a secure place, a secure way to talk. I'll go for that."

"I'll tell you where to go. I'll make it a public place."

"No, that's not secure enough for me. How about this idea? You put a cell phone into an envelope and include a phone number for me to call. Address the envelope to me, Wesley VanMerton, Esquire, care of general delivery at the Post Office at 1 Embarcadero Center. If you cannot remember my name, just ask Mattie. Use a messenger who has no connection to you, obviously. Then I'll send a messenger who has no connection to me to pick it up. Get the phone there by noon tomorrow and I will call the number before one o'clock."

"Maybe."

"Good enough for now, Ratso. If there is no phone at noon, I'll have to take a different route to Mattie and it will hit you harder than this does. I'd hate to use her files before I see her but that is my nuclear option. Once I turn those over, I lose control over everything. No more quiet resolution. I've got a judge in the Ninth Circuit who is already very intrigued. It has 11 Districts so I doubt you can find him or her very easily."

"You sure got problems."

Wesley hung up. He felt calm and successful but he noticed he could not control the shake in his hands. He had a feeling that Ratso was the right interlocutor with the forces holding Mattie. The top people would never allow direct contact. Ratso seemed open to it even if he constantly denied it. The guy who hangs up first is the one in control. Is that an adage? Sounds like something from "The Art of the Deal."

He changed into a torn and dirty shirt and put on a wrinkled baseball cap and went down to the lobby with his bag to wait in case someone tracked the call and came looking for him. It was not a large lobby but he stayed away from the clerk as much as possible and never made eye contact. He was watching for a pair of men to speak to the clerk, as if to get a room number, or just some uglies to show up. Ratso would know of the trap that caught Cylinger and would send at least two of his boys and would have instructed them to take no risks in his room. Maybe Cylinger himself would show up.

It was a dangerous gambit with a hundred ways to go wrong and Wesley listed them over and over, inventing new ones and mentally ranking them in order of likelihood. He did well to last for two hours without the clerk speaking to him. At noon he decided no one was coming and went out to prepare for his peek in the windows after dark. He could hire a messenger in the morning.

He bought a hoodie because he regarded it as required clothing for domestic clandestine operations. He bought shoes a size and a half too small for himself in case he left footprints, and sandpaper to make them seem worn if the footprints were especially clear. He got a small, three-step stepladder because some of the first story windows were more than six feet from the ground. He bought a cheap camera. He did not know what pictures might be worthwhile but figured it was a good idea to be prepared. He bought gloves and a flashlight, of course. And jeans, so his entire outer layer would have minimal biochemical residue to leave behind and so he could destroy the outer layers afterwards to minimize any remaining chemical connection to the place. Then there was the question of what weapon to carry, if any... something that would not look too suspicious if he were merely suspected of something; something he, without any experience in violence, might use effectively, and something that would not be so frightening as to immediately raise the danger of violence. He decided on a geologist's hammer, the sort with a pick on one side. To make this credible, he spent some time hitting it on rocks in a vacant lot to give it some scratches and he bought a small book on identifying rocks in the San Francisco area. This too, he beat about to give it a used appearance. He knew he was taking excessive precautions but there was no reason to accept any risk he could avoid. He kept his new clothes in plastic bags beside him until his rental car was parked three blocks from 2337, where he tossed them into the back seat.

At six o'clock, he had only one more idea for his preparations. He got a take-out dinner with heavy curry. He liked curry but Mattie did not so he had not eaten any for years. Perhaps having food outside his usual pattern would alter his scent and perhaps that would disguise him in some meaningful way. He ate his dinner while sitting on a park bench, casually smiling as if he were enjoying life. In fact he enjoyed the taste of his dinner, but that was entirely insufficient basis to relax. It was consumed within fifteen minutes.

By 6:45, he was parked two blocks from 2337 and began his first walk past his target. He scarcely looked toward the house until he was well past it. Then he leaned against a familiar brick wall and lit a cigarette, raising his eyes to his architectural quarry. The cigarette was partly a tool of his disguise and partly a way to distract an observer from his actual line of sight There was a light shining from one room on the first floor. According to the weather report Wesley had watched, the sun had not set yet but the heavy overcast justified using the lights inside. Wesley walked back past the house and turned at the first corner, knowing he could linger there and still watch the house. Twenty minutes later, a man came around the side of the house, possibly from a back door. Wesley did not recognize him; certainly not Cylinger or FtB.

To give himself a new look, Wesley put on a baseball cap from his pocket and took off his jacket, placing it a shopping bag which he swung as he proceeded. From across the street he stopped to look at his watch, holding his wrist high enough that he could stare at the man from 2337. No unique or memorable features were visible. Nonetheless, it was a clear view and might match one of the faces Lucas had sent. The man left in a late model Audi whose plate number Wesley read and then repeated over and over in his head until he had turned around the next corner and could write it down. By then, he had forgotten the color of the car and all details of the man's clothing. He had not paid any attention to the clothes, thinking it best to invest the seconds on the face. He was not aware that the face had impressed anything on his brain. He made a note to look for the car next time he did his stakeout and to park near enough to follow it.

A half hour later, the sky was nearly dark. Wesley was impatient to look in the house but did not hurry. He had all night. Another half hour and the night was as dark as it would ever be. He went back to the rental car and changed his clothes, collected his equipment into a tote bag and worked the little stepladder out of the back seat. In his best imitation of a casual saunter, he walked around the block and up to 2337. Without hesitating, he went right to the lit window and set up the ladder. Standing on the top step, he could see inside. He was seeing the kitchen. It had a table with some dishes on it, no napkin. The appliances were dated, utilitarian, as one might expect in a bachelor's house. He could not identify any foods except for a couple cereal boxes beside the sink. Some condiments were on top of the refrigerator whose inside probably held beer and hamburger. A pot sat on the electric stove. There were no dirty dishes visible in the sink. Since no other lights had gone on, Wesley concluded no one was in the house, no one who was free to turn on the lights anyway.

The ladder wobbled as he stepped down; one foot of it sinking into the soft soil. Wesley grabbed at the window sill, missed it and slapped the side of the house loudly. He pushed the ladder back to its original angle and braced against the wall going down the remaining steps. He should test the footing next time he used the ladder. He listened for a sound inside the house. Suddenly he became aware of neighborhood noises he had been ignoring. Cars could be heard constantly even though they were not passing on this street. A major thoroughfare must be nearby. A woman was calling her dog. In the house next door, not ten yards off, someone was watching television. Nothing from 2337. Wesley noticed he had not considered fleeing when he thumped the house. He had too much invested to let a single noisy slip run him off. Before moving the ladder away, he stepped on the marks in the soil. A footprint would cause less suspicion than a pair of rectangular holes below the window. He made notes on the details of the kitchen: layout, colors, brands of cereals. It might be useful to claim he had been inside.

There was one other window on the same side as the one he had looked in, but it was too high to see through even from the ladder. Two window wells, offered a glimpse into the basement. Wesley bent down beside the windows thinking he might be a target if he stood in the middle of the window. He shone his flashlight inside: linoleum floor, brown stuffed couch, two folding chairs set beside it, a table, some shelves filled with cardboard boxes of various sizes and more boxes on the floor. No decoration. A small room in a sad looking bachelor pad. Maybe there was a television out of view below the window. The other cellar window showed the furnace and other electrical and plumbing connections. The stairs going up were visible in the back.

He worked his way across the back of the house, seeing in the kitchen from a different angle through the back door and, beside that, into an unadorned bedroom with an unmade bed. Looking in the other side window, he saw the living room and across the house to the bathroom with the window too high to reach from his ladder. The front door opened directly into this room beside a coat closet. He made some more notes, feeling it was better to write down as much as he could while the memory was fresh. It was not necessary to decide if he was brave or foolish. He had seen everything. If Mattie was here, she was in the attic, in the dark, unguarded, and her food was not apparent in the kitchen.

If she were inside, she would be alone. Wesley took another risk; he tapped on the side of the house with his geologist hammer and then pressed his ear to the siding in case of a response. Three quick taps, three slow ones, and another set of three quick ones. Nothing. He did it again and listened. Nothing again. Just once more time he thought and tapped out his SOS. He was not surprised at the silence, nor was he especially disappointed. It would have been great luck to find her this way and his luck had not been running well.

Nonetheless he held his ear to the siding longer on the third try just in case he had missed something. He placed a finger in the ear to the neighborhood and pressed his head against the wall. There was no point in trying this anymore.

As he pushed his footprint into the places where the ladder's feet had last stood, he heard a distinct sound inside the house, not a tapping, more a clattering. Suddenly, silently, a light shone over his head out of the living room window. He ducked and stood close to the house. Someone was walking around inside. For twenty seconds, Wesley held his breathe without realizing it. His mind was completely filled with preparation for flight, quietly if possible, fast for certain, away from the car, ditching his outer clothes somewhere hidden. No door or window opened. He set up the ladder and leaned in from the side of the window enough for one eye to peer inside. "Oh, I had it wrong," he thought. "He's a whiskey drinker, not a beer man."

The man Wesley had seen leave the house was kicking off his shoes and still adjusting the pillows behind him on the couch. He had just come home and had been quiet about it but for the clatter of unlocking the door. He sat facing away from Wesley's point of view, but Wesley recognized the man who left an hour ago and was pleased to refresh the image. He seemed to be settling in for the night. There were no glasses brought out for late visitors. More importantly, he had not looked in the attic to see if Mattie was still there.

Wesley snapped a couple pictures with the flash disabled, doubting they would show enough to identify the man and wishing he had bought a better camera so he could be sure the images would be in focus and the setting compensated for the low light available. It had been foolish to skimp on the camera. He would have spent more if he had thought about it more. He considered moving to the opposite side of the house to take a photo of the man's face but decided it would be too far away to show anything clearly, given the other problems with the camera. Yet, here was a lesson learned: he would get a good camera and use it in his surveillance next time. After seeing photographs taken in innumerable *noir* movies, he could only be amazed that he had not realized their value earlier.

Wesley obliterated the ladder marks and made his retreat along a roundabout route back to his car. The work for this day was over. He could use some sleep. As he drove back to his room, he held his hand in front of his face to see how much he was shaking from tension. It was steady. He would be able to sleep.

He woke a little after seven am, feeling panicked that he might be late before subtracting 7 from noon and realizing he still had plenty of time to prepare for his call with Ratso. That would not make the call easy or productive, but it had not been ruined by oversleeping.

First, he needed to arrange pick-up of his package with the cell phone, if it was there. Secondly, he needed a plan for the call itself. Somehow, overnight, while sleeping, he had formulated a strategy for the call. He knew how easily dreams dissipate in the daylight so he wrote out an outline of what to say. Before the first thing, however, he felt a powerful urge for a full breakfast: coffee, eggs, sausage, orange juice, maybe even a biscuit instead of toast. The clerk at the hotel desk did not know of a diner nearby, but she told him of a hotel where he could get breakfast.

His got his eggs over easy and ordered toast not biscuits, to sop up the yolk. He asked for grits but the waitress did not know that that was. Sans grits and with link sausage, it was another meal he would not have eaten in front of Mattie. Was he enjoying the adventure of searching for her? Was he enjoying the role he played or was it less a role than his suppressed, deeper self? The steadiness of his hand in the car last night and his productive slumber could imply the latter. These questions needed no answer. He would do everything possible to save Mattie. It was only to the good that he enjoyed eating his breakfast.

He went back to the first item: hiring someone to pick up the package. He might need to evade Ratso's henchmen at the Post Office. Fortunately, he remembered the lesson of the night before, the lesson about not being cheap. It was too early to find a shop selling cameras, but he was able to yet again, buy some new clothes to avoid looking like himself or any recent version of himself. He went to a messenger service and asked for someone to pick up a package and said he wanted to speak to the messenger to be sure he knew the place. It took thirty minutes to get a guy despite the company's conspicuous sign proclaiming speedy service. It would have been faster, they said, if he let them radio one of their staff already out in the city on a bicycle. Wesley knew there was plenty of time and was pleased to show no anxiety. He would play a weirdo who needed face-to-face communication but not someone scared of the package.

Finally the messenger came into the office. Wesley went outside with him and converted into a different weirdo, explaining, "I'll pay you one hundred dollars for this, cash. I'll give you half right now. I won't be talking about this to anyone but if you want to, I don't care. Tell anyone you want... You go to the Embarcadero Post Office... little after twelve o'clock. I mean today, noon, you know? You use my ID to pick up a package addressed to me. Just look at the ID for my name. Here, it's my driver's license. This is completely legal. It's just that my father was a postal clerk... retired now. I had some problems with him so I can't deal with them. Maybe I can but I don't want to... You good with your Dad? That'd be good for you both. Anyways, I'll be at the Post Office too. Just hand me the package. No, don't even hand it to me. Just put it on the counter next to me. I'll have an envelope with the rest of your money. Kinda quiet-like check to be sure the money is right and go on about your business. Don't say anything to me or pay any attention to me. Can you do it? You want a hundred bucks for doing practically nothing? It's all legal."

"What if there's nothin' there for you?"

"Then give me my ID and take the other fifty anyway."

"I get it. Cost you a hundred-fifty. I don't talk about nothin'."

"Fifty now, a hundred when it's done."

"Half now, half later.

"Fifty now and a hundred later. You get to count the hundred before you pass over the package. Try to get any more out of me or steal my goddam package and the shit will fly right there in a Federal building."

"Deal."

"Good. Here's fifty and my ID. See you in 'bout an hour with another hundred."

Wesley's strategy was built on the hope that Ratso would follow the courier although that was not essential. He had devised the strategy for getting his package before he went to sleep, before he had his dream about making his call with

Ratso. His fears about the package probably inspired his strategy for the call. He was ready to call, but decided to use the time before six o'clock, the deadline he had given himself, in case he got lucky with the photos he had taken at 2337.

He went back to the camera shop where he upgraded his equipment and used their computer to check the pictures he had taken. They were terrible pictures but he captured a clear profile of the man in the house. It matched one of the profiles Lucas had sent. This one had a name: Terry Caldwell. The only alias listed in Lucas' data was "Two Shoes," thus Terry Two Shoes. None of Wesley's good luck or clever strategizing was moving him noticeably closer to finding Mattie, but it was enough to keep him from despair. Getting a better camera would pay off and the thought made him realize he had made another mistake out of his habitual parsimony. He should have been recording his telephone calls and he looked for a shop to fill that need.

23. Mattie's Fate

Wesley sat in his car two blocks from the post office and made a call. "Lucas? Good to hear you were near the phone. Can you talk a minute where you are? ...Good, but I don't need much time. I'll skip over the courtesies I should extend to you. I'll take you and your wife to the best restaurant in Washington after this is over, if it is safe then to know me. Your list of suspects turned up two hits so far: Fred Silberts and Terry Caldwell. See what you can find about them. Caldwell seems to be living in 2337 Park. Silberts has been there. You get those names? Want to hear them again?... Alright, if you say you got it, I know you do. I have something cooking this afternoon. ...Don't know where it

might go. I'll call you back tomorrow afternoon. That OK?
...I might have a contact for you out here, just if something
comes up. If she agrees to it, she'll give you a call. Her name
is Dupe. She's a White Nigerian; never been to Nigeria.
...Call you tomorrow then and thanks, Lucas."

      "Hello, is this Dupe? ...Don't worry, all is well on this
end so far. My problems are not over but whose are, right?
...Not far enough along to give up the secrets and I don't have
a new request for you, not really. Just thought I'd call and tell
you your tip was a big help. It got me back on the trail of what
I need to be chasing.   ...I'd like to give you a phone number.
Friend of mine who does not know much more than you but
is completely trustworthy, like you. You don't need to keep
playing this thing with me, but if you take this number, you
never tell anyone about it, right? ...So if you can't reach me
and want to, try Lucas at this number. You can tell him
anything, ask him anything, but he may not know the answers.
...I told him your first name, no more. Well, I said you were
a White Nigerian and never been to Nigeria. That was so he
could recognize you if you call. He doesn't have your phone
number.   ...Got a pencil? The number is 202-375-2289.
...Yes, I want this to be fun for you, especially when it all
comes out good. Serious though, very serious for now, you
know. ...One more thing, Modupe, you know I'd be there if
I could do something for you. ...No, not because I owe you
one, although I do owe you one. I'd love the chance to help
you if I can because you deserve it. Good person and all that.
...Call Lucas if you want. Then he'll have your number. Or
just let the whole matter go until something comes up from
my end. ...Right, right. Hey I really need to go. I have a
follow-up on your lead this afternoon. ...Good. And thanks."

There was plenty of time to walk the last two blocks to the Post Office. He did not want to be early so he would not have to wait around. That might look suspicious. Being a little late might be safest. The courier would not leave right away with his bigger payoff still coming.

At five past noon, Wesley went inside. It was not the cavernous room he hoped, with numerous customers comprising a complex environment in which he could conduct his business inconspicuously. No guard in sight; only one person not in line at a window, the courier, obvious with his helmet still on his head and his spandex clothes. He did not look at Wesley, even when he took a position across from Wesley at the standing desk. Wesley put an envelope down and left his hand on it. The courier put a small package on the table. Wesley took the package and released the envelop. The courier looked inside the envelope for several seconds, and left the post office without a word or a glance toward Wesley. When Wesley left, he walked away from his car and around a figure-eight of streets to get back to it. Once again, he had taken a dangerous step safely, and still he was no closer to Mattie.

Wesley drove to the first parking garage he could find so he could prepare for the next call. He would be driving while talking with Ratso in case his location was being traced, assuming tracing his location was even possible.

Firstly, he noted on his legal pad, if Mattie is on the call, he should see what she wants him to do. She may have a plan of her own. She would not be able to speak freely but she might find a way to signal him. His plan beyond the phone call was so open there was nothing to reveal to her. He would look for signs of stress. After so long in their control, she might be relaxed. The stress she feels might be just due to having Wesley turn up. She must be in pretty good shape if they are catering to her food preferences. And for a moment he wondered if she was part of the scheme from the start but that was not possible for more reasons than he could enumerate. He imagined he would be able to read her mood and her health. No one knew her as well as he. Yet he had to acknowledge he had never been able to read her mind. If he could do that, he would not have needed the telephone.

Secondly, and much more likely, he thought about what to say if Mattie was not on the call. In that scenario, he would ask what Ratso or his boss would recommend to end the impasse. He had a little more information to dribble out to show he knew their operation better than they wanted him to. As long as he was missing, he was a threat to them. He would be sure to leave that impression anyway. More than anything, he would be sure they knew he had an ace in his hand. He would stress the possibility of ending this amicably since he cared nothing about harming them. Maybe he could suggest the thugs, presumably including Ratso, could break away from the corrupt politicians that Mattie was after. Let the ones at the top roast and the meatballs could scurry off to oblivion.

§§§

"You will be pleased to know Terry was not especially helpful. I doubt he bothered to mention our discussion to..." Wesley's tape recorder was near the receiver.

"Who's Terry?" Ratso was not impatient in his tone. Wesley thought they were becoming collaborators.

319

"Caldwell, I think is his last name. 'Two Shoes.' I did not need to make up a name for him as I did for you, Ratso."

"What discussion? I didn't hear of any discussion with you."

"I was about to say, he is unlikely to want to mention it to you. It was a little embarrassing, I imagine. Not as embarrassing as Cylinger's discussion , of course. Anyway, I don't have time to go into that right now. You don't sound like you are about to hand the phone to Mattie so we need to arrange for my talk with her."

"I don't have any way to get you in touch with her."

"I know you're nervous about saying anything when you talk to me. You recall, I am sure, that I have other contacts who might be able to get me in touch with her. I will call back day after tomorrow at this time. You must have her available or have a very good offer of how to arrange it or I will have to use other contacts."

"I have a few questions for you first. What about..."

"So long for now."

Wesley thought he cut off the call too soon. He had not learned anything at all but he had no idea how to get any more out of it and could hardly concentrate while worrying about being traced somehow. Had he been convincing? Did he actually have any leverage? All that preparation and risk to have a phone conversation like that. Next time, he decided, he would ask again if Ratso had any recommendation but he doubted that would lead anywhere. It might really be his last contact with Ratso if it was producing nothing after so many tries.

He rented a different car and kept the first one too. He could park one near the 2337 and then walk to the other and drive nearby and generally mix up things like the way he was changing clothes whenever he thought it might help the confusion. He could not do all the surveillance tricks he saw in films but he could make up his own. Sometimes the moves of an amateur are harder to anticipate, or so he surmised.

At ten PM, no one had come to 2337, no lights, no movement. His phone rang, the one used for Lucas and Dupe.

"Yes," he answered.

"This is your friend from home."

"Oh great. Good to hear from you. Any news?"

"Well, I heard from your local friend. Quite a character. Where do you know her from?"

"So she called, huh? How did she seem to you?"

"Interesting for sure. A lot of talk. Good lookin' I bet with all that self-confidence."

"If she's on this team, she's good lookin'."

"She's on the team. Said she already helped you out. And wants another chance."

"She found Cylinger's address. That was big.

"Sure is. And I found Silbert's address. Still earning my pay."

"Is it nearby?"

"Near Park Street you mean? Nah. Out of the city a little. Westlake, south of San Francisco, near Palisades Park. No lake there I could find and no palisades either but near the coast anyway. I found seven Fred Silberts in or about San Francisco but a little follow-up on them made it clear the kind of sleaze you're running with these days could only be this one. Changed his name from 'Gilbertz' with a 'g' at the beginning and a 'z' at the end when he got out of jail but still does some things with the old name."

"Nice to know you could figure all that out. Guess he won't be joining our team."

"You thinking of turning one of that gang around?"

"No, not really. I don't want to be near any of them again."

"He's a retired cop, too. Wonder if he is helping the police or they are helping him."

"I was not ready to bring in the police here and this further makes me doubt I can trust them. If I have something really solid to go on, I'll try the FBI, but only cautiously until they prove they are not involved in whatever this is."

"But you have a good idea what this is about, right?"

"Pretty good. I have a concept or a theory based on what I knew of Mattie's work, but I could be way off. I need more."

"Can I send you the address and a few other facts on him via e-mail?"

"That would be best. But nothing on Caldwell yet?"

"There are a few of them in the area. None of them looks like our guy. I mean looks like or seems like. I don't have pictures of them all. He may not have a house out there. He may be using a fake name. Maybe I'm just not that good at this business."

"He's staying at Cylinger's place. But you shouldn't want to be good at this. It's not what you do. And don't spend too much time on any of this. I don't want to be worrying about messing up your life. Take the kids to the park. Kiss your wife often as you can."

"I'm careful. I know I've got family."

"Did Dupe tell you how I'm paying her?   ...I promised to tell her the truth someday. She liked that. And I'll give you a little truth too, a bite that can't hurt. Cylinger's boss sent me a phone. Seems to be his boss. Bobby Coffitt, according to your research. ...I've talked to him a few times. He's not helpful and I doubt he's scared of me, but he is curious about what I know and what I'm going to do with it. I have a call tomorrow afternoon again. I tell him a little more about his operation every time, just to keep him worried. ...Not sure what I can get out of him but the point is, I suppose, that I have a few lines of inquiry going here. Something may break open. ...You sit tight. Let me know if an idea comes to you. Don't get yourself identified with this thing. Right?"

Wesley worried that he was getting one of his very few friends to take a risk too far. He considered how to get Lucas to drop the whole issue, to convince him the search was over, but it seemed disrespectful to deceive him. He did not know the call between Lucas and Dupe had ended on a similar note, that they had plotted a way to meet each other and go to 2337 and wait for Wesley to turn up and then coordinate with him, but in the end they figured it was disrespectful to deceive him and agreed to defer the plan to see if anything more turned up.

Something did turn up. Wesley had begun to monitor both houses, two evenings at 2337 and then two evenings in Westlake. ...Took pictures with his new camera although he saw no suspects. He was calling Ratso at six pm every day and spoke only lies linked to 2337, like saying he had eaten cereal with Two Shoes and mentioned the type of cereal he had seen in the kitchen and mentioned a day and time for the alleged snack when Two Shoes had been alone at 2337. And how he had not seen Cylinger lately and missed his old pal at his own house. He never asked for anything except a *pro forma* request to speak to Mattie. It was all routine. He just wanted to hold Ratso's attention and hung up within a couple minutes every time. Ratso listened, said little in return and asked for nothing. He was playing his own game of unknown rules. Wesley never mentioned Fred the Barber, as if he had forgotten the man or knew nothing more about him.   And he is the break that turned up, Fred the Barber, at his own home in Westlake on the fourth night of watching it.

It was a small place, crummy looking, not the kind of place to be holding a hostage, a conclusion Wesley reached in consideration of the level of resources going into the kidnapping. If Wesley had seen "Silence of the Lambs," he would have been both more cautious and more aggressive. He watched until the lights were out in the house. He waited an hour longer and then tied a thread across the driveway and to a small bell in his car. He woke at 6 am with the thread still intact and the bell unrung. He watched FtB drive out a little after noon and followed. They did not go north to the city but east on Route 92 across the bay to Dresser on Canyon Road that really did follow a canyon.

When FtB stopped at a closed gate on a long, paved driveway, Wesley did not slow down although he turned his head to get a look. The house was visible, large and garish. Maybe there were dogs roaming the grounds, maybe men with guns. This place was built on a scale beyond the means of the thugs he had been following. FtB may have other jobs, but if he came here in relation to Mattie, he was seeing someone several tiers higher in the power structure of the outfit. Wesley parked a mile away and left a note on the windshield saying he had gone to get a mechanic. Then he loosened one of the battery cables. He walked back with his camera and binoculars to the house.

FtB was standing near the front door talking to someone, a man not well dressed. They seemed relaxed, even jovial. Eventually they separated and began to walk the perimeter, thus, at this time of day, it was men, not dogs. As for guns, they were not apparent. Clearly this was the only place worth watching. Something was sure to turn up here.

By 6:00, he was back in San Francisco and driving around to have his call with Ratso. It would be a completely normal call within their peculiar pattern. The recordings he made of the calls were understandable, that is, the words could be understood, but there was so little content they did not offer any insights. Wesley kept them especially short since he had nothing new to say.

For three days, Wesley watched and took pictures. He worked his way around the outside of the fence when the guards were not patrolling. He threw hamburger over the fence to see if there were dogs at night and the hamburger was untouched. Apparently there were no raccoons inside either. He looked for cameras or sensors on the fencing and saw nothing except one at the gate but he could not imagine getting inside himself. He was not in a movie where the guards and bosses followed a script. If he were living in a movie, the action hero would not have been one as inexperienced in violence and physically inept as himself. He collected the license numbers of everyone who went through the gate.

Lucas was excited to be asked about the property although he could not get much information about it. It was owned by a corporation, a very private one with a few names registered as officers but very little on who they were or what they did. Lucas felt the lack of data was the most suspicious thing about it.

At six o'clock in the evening of the fourth day of watching Canyon Road, Ratso did not answer the telephone. A new voice on the line introduced himself as "legal council for the man you have been harassing" and called for Wesley "to cease and desist."

"Wonderful!" Wesley replied. "Bobby and I have not been getting anywhere anyway. I am glad to have someone who might be better able to help."

"I am not here to help you. I am just telling you to stop calling if you have nothing more to say than demanding to talk to someone my client knows nothing about."

"You will be pleased to know that Mr. Coffitt, whom I prefer to call "Ratso," has indeed said nothing new since I first talked to him, a very cautious man, but it is unfair, or inaccurate to say I added nothing beyond asking to speak to Mattie. I have demonstrated intimate knowledge of certain parts of your operation. And I have explained that I can activate the process Mattie set up to protect herself."

"Go ahead, do whatever you want. But tell me please, if you activate the alleged process this Mattie person set up, wouldn't she lose her protection?"

"I'd love to explain all my options to you and then you could choose among them for me, but I prefer to accept your implied ultimatum."

"What are you..."

"I mean, of course, that you and Ratso will no longer take my six o'clock calls. It is his phone in the first place so he is paying the bill. Would you like to give me the name of your firm so I may return the telephone?"

"Well, yes, that's right. We will not take your calls."

"Ratso always had that option anyway. He did not need you to complain of 'harassment'." But, not hearing you give any name of a firm, real or fake, I will hang up. Please give my regards to Ratso. Unless you can get me a call with Mattie?"

"That is never going to happen. She is doing fine and does not want you calling her."

With that final line which Wesley imagined playing for a jury someday, he hung up and turned the car around to get back to Canyon Road. After a restless and unproductive hour of nosing around the fence, he went to the city. He found a new bar where he bought something for dinner and sat there silently eating the food that was good enough for sots in the poor side of town and more than good enough for him who felt no hunger and ate only to survive to another day. His mind began to race and he suddenly jumped up, leaving a beer and half his potatoes behind. Halfway to the door, he remembered he had left no tip.

That was dumb. Now he'll remember me and may even want to harm me if he is asked about me or someone like me. I'll go back and leave a normal tip. That should be less memorable. Two bucks under the plate should be normal in a place like this.

After placing his tip, he drove two or three blocks in the wrong direction, forgetting he had moved to a new hotel.

That was dumb too but not dangerous as far as I figure it. Get it down on paper before you forget it. I can feel it's going to run out of my brain like rain off a red metal roof. I ought to be slowing down mentally after a meal but there is adrenaline in my veins. A couple stupid moves must have scared me as if I wasn't scared enough. This feels like the critical moment. How can that be with nothing happening except some sudden sense of clarity? I'll take it if it's real. It could be an illusion. Get out the pencil and see what's what.

First, finish the business at hand. Don't want that distracting me.

Friday the sixteenth: Usual call with Ratso diverted to man claiming to be his lawyer...

Analysis: no smoking gun on tape, but a few moments at the end sounded suspicious enough to intrigue a real investigator. He stopped writing. *If I add this call to the other facts and photos I've accumulated, I must be able to interest someone in the FBI, assuming they're not tainted. The whole FBI in on this? No way. Have to assume that whatever Mattie had been examining could not have aroused the whole Federal government. Paranoia has been useful during the investigation but at some point I have to give it up as a way of life if I am ever to resolve anything. Resolve? That might be too bold a target. I will never get back to a niche in the government or any other form of striving for respect, promotion, influence, legacy.*

Wesley imagined an interview with an agent, trying to convince him to take over the kidnapping case. He could not see any way the agent would make him a partner. He would be lucky if he were not arrested for leaving Washington and suddenly disappearing. That would look either guilty or insane. His collection of facts did not point to a motive for kidnapping – the motive was merely what Mattie had told him and was very short on detail or hard evidence.

But he had found so much. He had a roster of suspicious characters, known felons, acting oddly. He had photos of cars that might link to other suspicious characters. He had some odd conversations on tape. He knew some key persons Mattie was investigating. Her office must have some more on that work. He had Samantha. He might have a lawyer retained by Mattie who held incriminating documents.

He had... He had nothing; nothing that proved anything; nothing that separated him from a guilty, deluded, paranoid husband. And he had a hunch that the mansion on Canyon Road held the key.

His life had broken out of its patterns of thirty years of adulthood (beginning with Mattie's influences) in most ways but the most important was that his problem was not resolving itself, was not giving in to his first effort, was not defeated by his inborn entitlements, was not impressed by his actually taking risks, was not even giving in to his unprecedented level of effort.

He went through the assets listed in his notebook. They seemed fully utilized. He could be no smarter, no more committed, than he had been, however, there on the page was the essence of his next step. He had been cautious. Some caution had been necessary, but it had constrained him. He needed to take a bigger risk. There were many possibilities.

Going to the FBI was the right option. He could be held on suspicion of something. For what? He had never been charged with anything. Ratso and the rest might have framed him further in ways he had not heard yet. Maybe that was why they took his calls – maybe it was helping them set him up. But that was giving in to baseless fears. It was not even so bad to be held for a while if it came with a decent agent following up on what Wesley had compiled.

No, goddam no. I am no more the lawyer with the lawyer wife at my side living in the DC suburbs on two GS-15 salaries, secure in the Federal machinery. I am Esther Bower, Modupe Sodunke, Robbie whose last name I forgot or never knew, Brenda Peelers, Sam Laxness, and, yes, even that good looking guy who didn't feel like talking coming into San Francisco, scrapping for a place in the brutal underclass... lost the privileges they never had. A fallen White male, almost a Trump voter. The machinery is not there to support and protect me in my hour of need. I have to wrap it all up myself with my last two friends... No, got to leave them out as much as I can. Got to wrap it all up myself or burn out trying. Not like a revenge movie or a hero movie. Not like any movie. Deal with reality however much it looks like cheap fiction.

Wesley decided to go inside the wire of the Canyon Street place. He drafted a plan by ten o'clock and went to bed and slept well. The plan did not solve anything. He did not pretend he would get in the mansion, but he would take another, a bigger, risk and then find a new bigger risk after that.

He already knew where he would cut the wire. He went inside wearing his black hoodie and too-small shoes. It was only a five second sprint to reach the side of the building. Most of the windows were too high to see inside and, as he already knew, most were blocked with curtains or shades, but he peered into a couple dark rooms, seeing nothing. Maybe, he thought, he could look in them with a flashlight and pick one as a point of entry on some future night when he was accepting yet a higher risk level. Working his way around the building, he came to a place where the walls enclosed a small garden. The space was not easily visible from the outside of the fence so he looked especially closely. On the third floor, facing a blank wall fifteen feet in front of it, was a window with horizontal and vertical bars, a perfect place to imprison a princess. The princess behind the bars had hung two pairs of socks to dry on the bars. Mattie would wash her underwear in the sink when they stayed more than a few days on vacation. She hung the intimate things in the shower and the socks on the open window. This discovery was enough for one night and Wesley, shivering with tension, retraced his route back to the opening in the fence. He repaired it as he had planned and went back to consider how much risk to invest in the window.

I can't get impatient. I should sit on the ideas at least one day before acting, as I always did at work unless there was a scheduled hearing coming soon. Get the ideas out. Work them. Devise some variants. Compare them. Merge the best of them. Bounce them off Lucas. He'll have rational feedback. Am I looking for a way to boast to him of a breakthrough before I go down and never speak again? Impatient? After all this time? Hell, I'm going to attack that window somehow and right away.

He could not find an extendible pole long enough to reach to the third story, so he bought three aluminum poles and some short sections of pipe just large to serve as sleeves connecting the poles. He put a hook on one pole and fashioned a cardboard sign he could hang on the window bars. The sign read "Whom did Bootie hate? Crumple a paper with the answer and toss it below. Leave a fingerprint on the tape." He taped to his sign the paper for her response and a pencil to write it. He thought of requesting the print come from the ring finger of her left hand. It seemed romantic. It also seemed like unnecessary, possibly confusing, detail.

The next night was windy. Wesley did not trust his message to hang safely so he did not put it up, but he went back to Canyon Street to see if anything seemed changed. He saw nothing scary. He took some time exposures of the window nook, using a tripod and telephoto. In one place while standing pressed against an old, bent oak tree, he could see the window with its bars.

He had time to reconsider, improve or abandon his plan, but he only changed his starting time. He woke at 5am and drove out to Canyon Road to post his sign. It was getting light but was too early for reasonable people to be awake. He waited a few minutes for the guard to go by on his rounds. They were not as regular as clockwork and usually took about twenty minutes to go around the perimeter and usually went once an hour. He worried about waiting until one went by; waiting would bring more light. So he went through the wire and posted his sign on what might, if he was lucky, be Mattie's window where she might, if he were very lucky, be the first to find it. Then he waited outside the fence where he was hidden from sight but where he could see the window.

Wesley checked the window every fifteen minutes. It was torture to do nothing but wait and watch. At seven fifteen, the sign was gone. He watched for fifteen minutes, until a guard walked by. Flat on the ground and away from the fence, Wesley could not discern any unusual caution by the guard. Once he was past, Wesley made a dash to the window. He saw no paper on the ground. He bent to his knees to see more clearly. His mind filled with flaws in his program: *I should have had a signal to show the message was ready to pick up. I should have made it easy somehow to find in the garden below the window, not sure how to do that... I should have... Shoulda, coulda, woulda... Next time I'll do it better, right? Is there any breeze that might have taken it one way or the other? No? Have I been calling this a garden? It might have been a garden once. It just a mess now. What's that? Something coming? Can I lie low or break for the fence. Running would be the worse if anyone is around. It's nothing... She just hasn't dropped it yet. If it was her that got it. No! Goddam it! There it is!*

§§§

"Bootie was the cat she brought to my apartment when she moved in with me back when we were about to get married. Bootie hated the corn snake I was keeping in a terrarium." Wesley decided he had enough to make his case to the FBI. He made copies of all his notes and photos, and gave the originals to the agent assigned to him by the San Francisco FBI office. The agent was an older man, nearly bald and portly, not a frightening figure, surprisingly reassuring for Wesley.

"Yeah, I can't prove that her answer is right, but it convinces <u>me</u> she gave the answer willingly. She could have lied and they wouldn't have known. It's not your proof. That's in the fingerprint."

Mattie's note back read: "Bootie hated the snake. I am all right, healthy and alert. They want something from me and I will never give it to them. My lawyer will give it to the press and the Justice Department if I do not call him/her every week or if anything happens to him/her. I am negotiating for more information from them. Please give my love and deepest regrets to Wesley for the mess I left him. Madeline Fremont"

"I should have given her a larger piece of paper. I have a feeling she wanted to get it written quickly any way."

"What is she negotiating?"

"I really don't know what she is doing, but I have a guess she wants incriminating information on the highest possible person in the corruption case she was developing."

333

"And who would that be?"

"I know the highest level person she ever mentioned as being part of this, but I don't want to distract you from the kidnapping. I will tell you all I know about the corruption thing, which I do not know a whole lot about, after you make an effort to get Mattie released from her captors. And if you get her back, you will have no use for me anymore as she will know far more about it."

"What do you think we should do to get her out?"

"I don't know your procedures but it seems you need a search warrant and have plenty of evidence for that. Then take your full team out to the Canyon Road and see if Mattie is still there. Please stop grilling me! I have shown you enough to save my wife."

"I have to agree. You may have. I got the warrant last night and the SWAT team is preparing to go. I'm looking for anything more you know that could help us. We don't want a hostage situation. We have to be ready for..."

"If talking to me is holding things up, I'll stop talking."

§§§

Wesley almost knocked before going into her room but he reasoned, this was his wife and he did not need permission to enter her room. She was sitting on the bed, wearing a hospital gown and staring at the window with such apparent concentration, Wesley looked at it himself and was surprised to see nothing but gray sky.

"Oh Mattie. You are back and you look absolutely fine!" His words were not objectively true. She did not look "fine." She was wan and thin, her long hair combed straight

334

without any style although Wesley had believed his own words, seeing beyond what his eyes saw. He kissed her on the forehead and kneeled beside the bed because he could not bear to let go of her hand once he had grasped it and the chair was too far off to reach.

"Oh my god, Wesley," Mattie responded with a surprisingly strong voice. "How did you get out to the West Coast so fast?"

"Fast? I've been here more than a month already. It took some time to find you."

"What do you mean, 'find' me? When did they bring you here"

"They didn't tell you I found you? It was me who sent the FBI into the manor. It's a long story but that's a key point in it. I guess they have been, and I am glad they are, focused on getting you safe and healthy."

"Manor? What are you talking about?"

"Sorry, that just what I called the place where you were being held. Late in the game, I thought of it as a castle with a princess on the third floor."

"So you found me there? Did they contact you to find something for them. You're saying it wasn't the FBI? Who put that note on my bars? Did Raleigh's people contact you to find something for them. Did you give them anything?"

"It wasn't the FBI. I had to beg them to go get you. The note you wrote was the final piece to entice them. Raleigh's people never contacted me but I contacted some thugs I imagine were connected to him. I sent in the FBI. It's a long story that doesn't matter anymore."

"Oh well, I wasn't quite finished with them but I guess I should be glad this part is over."

"Finished?" Wesley could not understand Mattie's cold objectivity. She was never one to get lost in her emotions but this was an extraordinary moment by any measure. She should have been ecstatic.

"I was building a case, you know. When they interrogated me about what I knew and whom I told, I was always watching for information from them. I kept you out of it."

Wesley had a thousand objections to that assertion but this was no time to argue. He said no more and struggled to quiet the list his brain insisted on drawing up of the ways he had been affected by whatever she had begun. He leaned his face against her breast and held her hand while she quietly squeezed his with more strength than her skinny arms seemed capable of generating and slowly her breathing calmed to a pace that did not frighten Wesley anymore.

Mattie stayed in the hospital that night although Wesley could not see anything that required medical treatment. A police guard stayed at the door. Wesley considered staying in the waiting room but accepted a safe house provided by the FBI. No one was guarding him so he walked a few blocks away and called Lucas.

"It's over, Lucas! Mattie is fine. She is in the hospital right now, just for observation. Don't do anything more. Just sit tight until the FBI contacts you. But save this phone. I'll call you if anything goes wrong. I did not give them your name or your role. I won't until I am sure it is safe. ...Yeah, I guess it is not exactly over. I am unemployed, near broke and notorious. I gotta thank you for hours and hours but right now I need to call Dupe too. Maybe the team can get together soon and get their pay with the truth of the thing. ...It is damn near unbelievable but I am believing it for now. Gonna sleep well tonight, I bet...."

He called Dupe. She had stayed in her San Francisco hotel in case Wesley needed her. He made an appointment for lunch the next day, agreeing to meet her at the hotel. Mattie would be interrogated from shortly after breakfast until late in the afternoon. He went early so he could pay Dupe's bill before she came down. Dupe accepted the hotel receipt graciously but wanted the rest of her pay immediately which took two hours, including all her questions.

"You really gotta write all this out. You spell my name right, won't you? A book on it'll make you rich!"

"As soon as I pay Lucas, I am going to forget the whole story so I guess there won't be any book. You'll just need to remember our lunch today."

Yet there was a book. After the trials, Mattie wrote the book and hit the political talk shows and the book did sell well. She did not become rich but she became famous and got the best job she could imagine in the Justice Department. Offers came in from private law firms, apparently intending to attract clients through her fame, but Mattie preferred public service.

Mattie's book did not give much detail on Wesley's role. Her publisher offered a bonus if Wesley would cooperate even if he did not want to write anything, but he was not enticed. Even if he had not actually forgotten the events, as he had told Dupe he would, he admitted no memory of it to anyone. The questions came to Mattie who was out in public talking about the case.

She and Wesley never discussed her book much. Neither knew what to say to the other about it. Mattie briefly defended her portrayal of the FBI as the key to finding her because it would be good for their reputation, an argument that made no sense to Wesley. She also said she knew he did not want to be glorified and he agreed that was so but did not constitute a reason for leaving the impression he had swallowed the bait from Samantha like a starving trout rather than merely sniffed it from curiosity. Mattie hinted it was better for the book if she were not seen to have jumped too quickly at the first move against her from Raleigh. The book was to be about him and Washington corruption.

After a couple years, Lucas and Wesley talked about taking a bus out to see Dupe. Lucas was thinking of bringing his wife and kids along to see a glimpse of America outside the Washington beltway. Dupe wanted to see the house she had identified in San Francisco and the mansion where Mattie was found. The COVID pandemic got in the way and they never tried again to make the trip. Wesley hoped an additional year of delay would fade the experience enough that Dupe and Lucas would drop the idea of a tour. The subject did not come up although the three continued to send each other a card at Christmas.

Part IV: The Cabinet Maker

24. Wesley's Fate

The cabinetmaker rubbed his hands, working his thumbs between the bones of his palm and stretching his fingers backwards, one at a time, to ease their stiffness and pain. Stretching actually added to the pain, at least momentarily. Maybe the eventual sense of ease was no more than feeling the contrast between the usual background pain and the more intense pain his stretching brought. He was doing it unconsciously, something he often did, but at this moment he suddenly noticed himself. He smiled to think of his hands, his old, reliable friends. Their pain was not a betrayal. Aging was fine with him; it had come with ever more intense familiarity. They had aged along with the rest of him and could be trusted, not to never fail, but to always do his bidding to the extent they were capable and with a capability generally ample and predictable.

At the moment, one hand was sore from holding a table leg and the other from holding sandpaper for smoothing out the cherry wood's simple and sleek taper. He felt the surface with his fingertips. They were rougher than the wood, a fact that pleased him on both sides of the contact. Twenty-three years of satisfying work that had nourished him daily with its clarity of purpose and the satisfaction of finding an object closer to its final state of useful beauty by the end of each day. He worked slowly, thoughtfully, appreciatively, knowing he was an inefficient producer by choice. It was less stressful to anticipate and avoid mistakes than to repair them. He made enough income from his inefficient furniture business to have lunch with dessert at the diner once a week and still save enough to cover the medical expenses that were probably coming someday.

The leg was more intricate at the top where it would be hidden by the sides of the table. The shape of that portion was designed for strength in the joint rather than appearance. Without any visible bracing, the table would easily hold the weight of a man once pinned and glued; it would withstand any clumsy or rude visitor who decided to sit on it or use it as a ladder to change a ceiling light. The design was well considered, original in some minor aspects, with priority first to function and secondly to the illusion of minimalism. The merit of the table in the end, however, would be in the beauty of the wood itself rather than in the shapes it was being given. Thus, the sanding and finishing was the trait most people would notice, if the table ever gained any notice.

A rap at the window announced someone was about to come through the door. People often knocked at the window first because they approached the shop from the side opposite the door. The window could be opened to admit large boards. The door was just for people. It faced the house. A man came in tentatively, waving his hands as if he were not already conspicuous or as if there were some distracting noise from the machinery in the shop even though there was no sound but his own cautious footsteps. He was middle-aged, slim and healthy, dressed in corduroy pants and a handsome shirt with rolled-up sleeves, just shy of "smart casual" attire. He was careful to avoid getting sawdust on his clothes and kept in mind that he would have to brush his shoes after leaving the shop.

"Perry! Good to see you. Come on in!"

"Haven't seen you in a while. Thought I'd see why you're hiding."

"If I were hiding, this would be a poor place for it since I live here. I'd say you were just nosey and, frankly, I'm glad you are. I don't mean to be a hermit. I lose track of time when I've got a good project going."

"Yeah, what's this red gourd doing in here?"

"That's a pomegranate. I'll eat the seeds when I finish for the day. I sit it out here to remind me of the reward to come."

"So that's what a pomegranate looks like. I should have known that."

"That's right. You shoulda. "

"I can recognize a table when I see one, even when it's in little pieces. That your current commission?"

"Well, it's just a small table. We were inspired by the customer's leftover scrap of soapstone from where a contractor cut out a hole for the kitchen sink."

"I can see it will be beautiful!"

"Come on. It's not headed for 'beauty', not observed from a normal distance. It will feel good when it is finished, smooth and solid. I feel decent about it because it's something I can do, easy enough to be done well with my skills and limited patience but requiring some subtlety. Probably I like that it is based on salvage. I am terribly cheap, you know."

"I know you think you are cheap, but I see you getting dessert when you feel like it."

"I enjoy an intimate relationship with certain forms of pie. One has his priorities, you know."

"So let me feel the smoothness and the weight of your table."

"Can't. Haven't even put on one coat of varnish yet. I can show you what it will become." He placed the legs into the position they would take in the frame. Their shapes interlocked enough to stand together before being glued. He held the soapstone top in place, not letting its weight rest fully on the loosely assembled frame. "Something like that."

"Nice design!"

"It's a small table. It might feel like a match to the kitchen which would be nice, but it won't be used in the kitchen obviously."

"Isn't it a bit short?"

"No. It might look that way 'cause you're not used to seeing a table sitting on a workbench. Standard height. Sixteen inches."

"Hmm. How much are you charging for it?"

"Embarrassing question for a businessman as poor as me. I cannot change more than a hundred dollars. You could get one this size perfectly made by skilled workers in South Carolina for that much. The wood costs me $70 and that's with a professionals' discount. My time comes out to pennies an hour. Good hours. Guess I am actually retired. The cherry looks terrific though, doesn't it? I love how the grain flows. It will come out much better when it's stained. The whole design is really just to stay out of the way of the natural cherry figures and the stone texture."

Perry stroked the table leg gently. It seemed the appropriate thing to do. "It is amazing that you can convert a blank piece of wood into something like this."

"I don't want to be argumentative, Perry, but the wood was not 'blank.' It was imbued with splendor waiting polish for it to be seen. A table like this hardly does the medium justice."

"Yeah, sure. An artist speaks. You love your wood, right?

"I do, in a way. Not like loving a woman, of course."

"Yes, women..."

"Woman..."

"I guess that's what I meant. A controversial topic. You see, you are fundamentally argumentative. Maybe a legacy of your past life as a lawyer."

"I wasn't an argumentative lawyer."

"He says in argument."

"*Touché!*"

"How did you, a lawyer, ever get to be an expert furniture maker? Did you take some classes, maybe some kind of adult apprenticeship?"

"Seriously, it is an insult to the artisans out there to call me an expert. I am content with what I do and I know it is not unusual."

"I sure couldn't do it."

"To avoid any more contention, let me answer your question: how did I learn to make stuff like this. Firstly, I realized I wanted to do this. I got that yearning from my Dad, but did not realize I had it until many years later. He did not make furniture, more of a deck-and-barn sort of builder. But he saw the emotional power of working with his hands and I admired that in sympathy. Secondly, I read a little about furniture. That got me excited for sure. It taught me about five percent of what I know about it. I worked out some things on my own. Logic is a natural talent with me. That accounts for another five percent. And then lastly, I made a whole lot of mistakes. They taught me the remaining ninety percent. It's a slow and painful way to learn but once you get used to it, the pain isn't so bad. Cuts into the profit margin, you know. As long as that's not too important, it's okay.

"There is a strength in learning from mistakes. The pain makes the lessons memorable. Learning from reading was fun for me, but not very productive. I abhor taking notes.

Barely made it through school for the struggle with that mental indolence.

"The logic side of my skills was neither enhanced nor diminished by memory. It did not need memory. I could just apply the same logic or a related one if the problem came up again. It is a slow way to function, obviously, and it is my way."

"You say logic is only five percent though?"

"It is the five percent that gives me pride. Though I am pretty good at making mistakes, 'good' because I usually manage to soldier on, it is not a foundation for admiration. So look at this table. You see the joint here with two flat surfaces at right angles? It needs to be strong and it is although it relies mainly on glue. The problem is that a strong glue joint needs ample glue and that is basically revealed, in my way of doing things, by having glue leak along all sides once it is clamped."

"I can see you do not mind making a mess."

"I live like the bachelor I am. I serve my inborn lethargy whenever I can without driving myself to starvation. Anyway, my point in this case is that ensuring the squeeze-out conflicts with the principle of keeping glue away from the raw faces of any wood that will be seen. Stain brings out any history of contact with glue in an objectionable way. So how did I serve both masters in this case? I invented a technique! Yes, yes, I know I am not the first to invent it, at least I am pretty sure I am not the first. But I never read of it or heard of it. It was my own logic and it is the moment I most enjoyed in this piece. Apart, I suppose, from the moment when I show it to my client who then tells me it is so wonderful and I am so wonderful and I remind him, truthfully, neither is true but I will enjoy that argument because I will like the table and believe there is something good in it that I put there. This conversation, by the way is confidential between you and me, right?

"My invented technique is to cut a channel behind the exposed edge. The excess glue can accumulate there and not squeeze into view. I lose a quarter inch of glued surface which is acceptable in this case, based on my experience with failed glue joints. I had to rely on my experience with glue to spread an amount that would not overflow the channel but would fully fill the joint. That was a little stressful when I put on the clamps. So maybe I have become an expert in glue-spreading. I may be better than you in that."

"You enjoy something invisible like that?"

"That's almost what I asked my Dad when I was ten years old and helping him work around the house on weekends. He had me sweep the dust from the space that we were about to enclose inside the thickness of a wall. I said 'why do you care if no one sees it.' His answer was dissatisfying to me: a simple 'I will know it's there.' I would have argued he did not make sense, but I nodded as if it was convincing because to do other would have been disrespectful. Of course I do not take it that way from you. Things are different when you're ten. Long afterwards, but while he was still alive, I discovered his meaning although, unfortunately, I never mentioned it to him. How do you know your pride is in the work itself if it is on display for purchase or praise?"

The table would be finished in a few more days, not because it required very much more work but because the staining and varnishing required overnight drying for each coat before resanding and recoating. Then he would send off his project proudly to its new owner. His pride was not something to be nurtured by his customer, it was the personal and essential reward of a craftsman. Sending off his projects was like sending children off to their adult lives, inevitable, desirable and bittersweet nonetheless. But he had neither children nor much experience with them since having been one long ago. That personal experience might be out-of-date anyway.

He once had a wife. Something about his hands brought her to mind. He wondered why. Objectively speaking, she was long gone from his life. Almost as many years had passed without her presence as with her. He looked toward his hands but he had stopped seeing them. He was just thinking. It was not really she who had come to his mind, not directly. It was the old man's hands he had seen on a bus, on the only intercity bus ride he has ever taken. He was proud to recall he had respected that man's hands despite their unstylish spots and wrinkles, indistinguishable from his own now.

"What's that? Are you muttering to me or yourself? Did you say something about your wife? Were you married? I never heard you say anything about a wife."

Wesley did not answer unless the roll of his eyes toward his visitor was an answer. After that gesture, his eyes briefly turned to a slender book, covered in sawdust, sitting flat on an upper shelf: *Prince of the Clouds*. The answer was obvious. Of course he had a wife. She did not need to be mentioned to be present. Her withdrawal from their marriage had not been unfair. Looking back upon it while wringing his hands as he had done on a long bus trip across America, he pictured Mattie as she had looked to him on the day he rescued her. She was hard, firm in body and resolve; not the helpless, grateful creature he had expected to find.

Sometime before the kidnapping, she had joined and belonged to a larger world than he would or could inhabit. The bizarre escapade around her was not an anomaly, not her destiny; it was her due, she had earned it.

Her value to the world reached far beyond Wesley's house and workshop and the small Vermont town where he plied his trade. Her interviews after the kidnapping had given her the fame she wanted only for the power it brought to her trade, her exposés of corruption and courage inside the Washington beltway. Her books sold well and had substantial effects, anyone would admit, on the public view of Washington, on the profession of politics, on public service, and, possibly, on reforms that improved matters. They never mentioned Wesley although he might have fit into the first one. Wesley had told his story only to the FBI and to Lucas and Dupe. He figured some of Raleigh's team, his gang or mob, knew some critical parts of it. Wesley considered, not seriously, meeting a couple of them in jail to see what they had pieced together. He was especially interested in meeting Cylinger with iron bars between them but it was obviously best if he and his collaborators forgot about Wesley like the journalists who had briefly sought fuller explanations.

his eyes briefly turned to a slender book

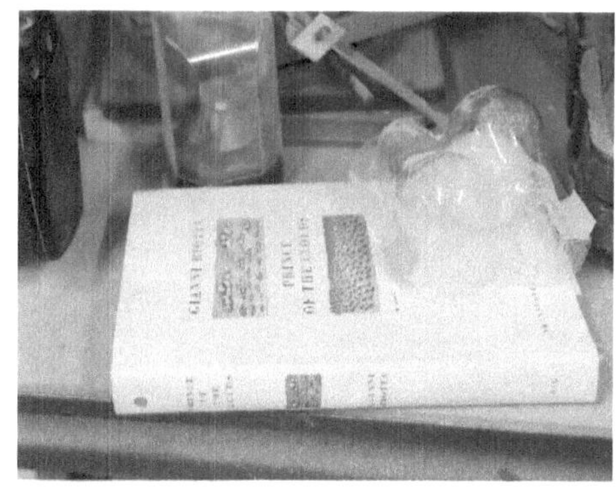

He sent her a handmade card every Christmas which she acknowledged sometime each January with warmth but little news. She assumed he would not have understood her life just as she did not understand his. Wesley, however, felt he understood her and admired her choices more than his own. Their exchange last year illustrates how it had become.

December 15, 2044

Dear Mattie,

Did you notice it will be 25 years in July since the FBI broke into the castle and ended your negotiations with Raleigh's crew of thieves and worse?

Congratulations on the Senate Ethics Committee vote. We even heard of it up here ten miles from the nation's northern border. It recognizes a precedent that will endure. I wonder how many people in your circle appreciate it as the outcome of your efforts even if I know you actively abjure recognition. Doubtless you have other efforts simmering but they are hard to see from my cabin in the woods. I continue to watch the papers for news of you.

If, or more likely, when you want a respite from the pressures of your career, please consider a few days in my remote nook, away from the daily news, continuous responsibilities and elevated excitements of your life. Bring a guest if you like.

Have a merry Christmas!

With unending love,

Wes

8 January 2045

Dear Wesley,

25 years already? We are aging so fast but I am well and expect to continue with this work at least through the current Administration. I don't want to go through another transition regardless of who wins.

You know I hate to get out of DC. When a break comes in a case, things can move very fast and I need to be here so no one (with good or bad intentions) steps in where I ought to be.

It's not the place where you live that is so odd and romantic – it is the times in which you are living. No one else writes Christmas cards or any other kind of letters. You were never like that when we were together so I wonder how you found out it would be so attractive for you.

It is wonderful that you are fulfilled by your work up there on the fringe of modernity. I sincerely hope you can put it aside for a few minutes one day and give me a video call. Just send a message to Sarah to get it on my calendar. Wish we would talk more, Dear. Please keep in touch.

Acknowledgement:

Thank you, Ronnie, for editorial assistance. All errors, remain with the author since I did not accept all your corrections.

Wesley's phone number used with Lucas:

Restaurant street number – 127

Code given on phone call - 527,339,990,502

Calculation –

$$527{,}339{,}990{,}502 \div 127 = 4{,}152{,}283{,}390.015708$$

Wesley's number - (415) 228-3390

By the way, area code 415 is San Francisco, 228 was the telephone exchange at my last home before retiring, and 3390 was my first phone number, a party line with only four digits. We answered if we heard a long and a short ring.

Endnotes:

[1] Gianni Riotta, *Prince of the Clouds*; Farrar, Straus and Giroux; New York; 2000; p. 79.

[1] Page 94.

[1] Page 231.

[1] Page 230.

[1] Page 230.

[1] Page 231.

[1] Page 184.

[1] Page 94.

[1] Page 109.

Other novels by Carl Mabbs-Zeno

Birch Bark and Blackberry Thorn

Neige Noir

A Pale Shade of Honor

A Witness Too Silent